Endée Quaï Press

BILLY'S TREE

Nicholas Kyriacos lives and works in Sydney

Billy's Tree

NICHOLAS KYRIACOS

First published in 2006 by Scribe Publications

Published in Australia in 2023 by Endée Quaï Press
ABN: 2157 8447153
endeequai@gmail.com
nicholaskyriacos.com.au

A catalogue record for this work is available from the
National Library of Australia

ISBN: 978-0-6456665-7-1 (Paperback)
ISBN: 978-0-6456665-8-8 (Ebook)

Edited by Aviva Tuffield
Typeset in 12/16pt Granjon by J & M Typesetters
Text designed by Katie Mitchell
Printed by IngramSpark Australia

This book is dedicated to the memories of
my father, Dimitri, and mother Maria

And to my wife, Krystall
And to my children, Dimitri, Maria and Yanni

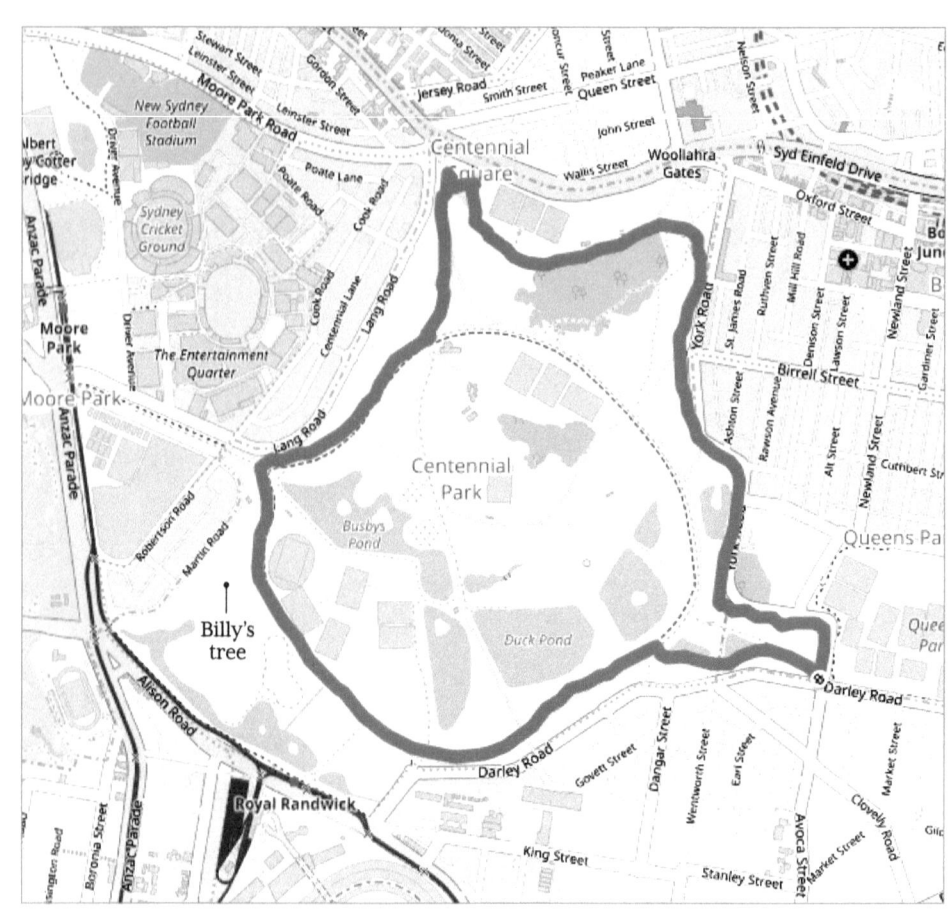

The past is not the past. The past, present and the future are, as they always are, part of each other, bound together.

When people tell their stories, they usually enjoy feeling proud, and delight in being named and in claiming their own history. Not so the stolen children ... Listen to me, we say, let me tell you what has happened to me, let me tell you my story. If I can make you understand me, I may better understand myself.

Carmel Bird

ONE

And he sure as hell wasn't telling

It's not all that bad, is it, Johnnie, since your world closed in on itself. There's enough of you present now and again for you to know that. There are those times you sort of drift to the surface of things. You float through layers of forgetfulness and the shapes of things you don't understand and take a good long look at the world before you retreat into that shadowy land where no one can reach you.

Sometimes you discover yourself on Old Tom's bullnosed verandah, like you do now, sitting straight as an upright ironing board on one of those two wooden paint-flaked benches. You stare over the road at Moore Park. The darkness of your world lightens and some things take shape, like all those others on the verandah, and the faraway vague roar of the traffic. You take a look to your left and right, at those codgers sitting in a line. You see their mouths working away — they remind you of the dummies at the Royal Easter Show with those wide-open mouths you'd once popped ping-pong balls into — but more often than not you can barely hear their talk, just like you can hardly make out the thumping rush of cars, motorbikes and lorries beating the stuffing out of South Dowling Street.

And that's when you hear the sighing again. It's like a great murmur down the far end of a long tunnel. It's a vague deep longing sound that gives you the creeps. You see it as a sort of cloud, or the final deep and sudden intake of air of a dying man. Or the sound some bloke'd make when he's being strangled in a dark lane. Maybe your Uncle Jimmy's right: maybe it is the whole bloody world exhaling its sadness.

You look again at these blokes and the old Greek sheila on Tom's verandah. They're there, alright, like silence, or an idea. You know that if you're to reach out and touch them your hand'd go right through them, their distant voices'd dissolve and then they'd fade away, right before your eyes.

At home that morning you stood on your tippie-toes and looked at your face in the bathroom mirror. Beyond your reflection you saw your misty existence receding endlessly into a place of your own making. Yeah, by golly, it's a good feeling imagining you've no part to play in this bugger of a life but, fair dinkum, it's an insistent bastard of a world — the steam and fog of your shower got sucked out of the window and you saw yourself being stared at by your own big sad eyes, as dark as shadows. You saw the reality of what you'd become, a little black kiddie lost in the middle of his own never-never, your frizzy hair glistening like a bush pig's arse. You heard your Uncle Jimmy's voice, a distant echo down the hallway. He led you to Tom O'Flaherty's terrace where this ancient bloke, his mates and the Greek lady were often to be found, meeting for a cuppa.

Major Bob Ryan's sitting next to you on Mista Tom's verandah, smelling of Johnson's baby soap and Old Spice. His hair, dyed black, is as tight as a second skin. He doesn't look into your face. If he did he'd see the flickering and knowing look in your eyes. You're preoccupied with the park over South Dowling Street. It's heavy with dew. The sun's low over the Moreton Bay fig trees which stand like cardboard cut-outs against a blue spring sky. From where you sit you can hear the birds going at it, hammer and tong, your Uncle Jimmy says as he rocks back onto the bench and slaps a thigh. Kookaburra Kon shakes his head and rolls his eyes at your uncle's joke, which you've all heard before. You watch kids from the local selective boys high school practise before their Saturday morning cricket game. You'd like to join these boys but you know you could never summon the courage to cross the road, leaving the security and safety of Redfern. Redfern's a good place. You're okay here. With these blokes and the Greek woman. But out there it's a nasty world, bad stuff happens. Like what happened to your brother Billy, what he told you before he done himself in, eh.

Your mug of tea is warm in your hands. You detect the smell of mouldy old things spilling out of Mista Tom's terrace. His chooks in the backyard are having a domestic. Major Bob's hat is in its usual position on one of the spears on the iron lace fronting the footpath. He wraps both your hands around the mug you're to drink out of. You see, smell and hear, are conscious of your own presence. The words of those doing the talking take on a clearer shape. You visualise the sounds rolling effortlessly from their mouths, some of them floating before your eyes, assuming a pattern you begin to understand. You try to connect the disconnected. Major Bob turns, stares hard at you. He knows. You're here. You've returned.

You make the effort. Your head motions like a deranged pigeon, swallowing air, your mouth opening and closing like you're about to throw up. The rest of those blokes and the Greek woman catch on. They stop their talking, lean forward to stare at you, cups of tea held halfway between saucer and mouth. Old Tom resting on his walking frame. Major Bob's glass eye at odds with his good one. Your Uncle Jimmy's grin fit to burst his face in two. The Greek woman's knitting abandoned in her lap, nodding her toothless head in encouragement, like a pecking chook. Kooka Kon's ciggie's hanging out of the corner of his mouth.

It'd once been so easy for you. To speak, that is. But your tongue's lost the gift. Your thoughts get all clogged up. Your words, if that's what they are, become entangled in some dark place while making that journey from mind to mouth. The gruff noises and gurgles that fall out of your mouth are as foreign to your ears as to theirs.

You withdraw, your grunts and gasps turning backwards into your own self. The others on the verandah fall back. They know you're gone, again.

Your own world, thick with silence. You travel back down the gloomy tunnel, hearing the sounds of the morning trailing off. A pleasant drifting into forgetfulness through a mute distance of nothingness. It's like you're under water, deep below the light that flickers on the corrugated surface of things. You drift. It's quiet, quiet. Your own existence is a blur to yourself. Yeah, you're safe there, alright. No one can hurt you.

Some people reckoned that Johnnie Butler's world shut down because the South Sydney rugby league team was given the bum's rush, getting booted out of the National Rugby League. Others carried on like a pork chop in one of Redfern's many pubs about the kid's crazy-as-a-two-bob-watch mother, who'd gone on a drunken rampage the very same day before racking off, leaving the kid to fend for himself.

But Major Bob Ryan knew better. And he sure as hell wasn't telling.

And why tell, anyway? Everything's working out just grand, isn't it, Bob, now that Johnnie's living with his uncle? A man just had to watch himself, that's all, and not let anything slip out because, after all, it was a matter of some shame. And if a bloke did keep his mouth firmly shut about Johnnie and his family, well, by golly, a man would go to his grave knowing what he knew, isn't that right, mate?

Late that night Major Bob Ryan drew all the curtains in his terrace. He switched off the religious programme on Radio National. He unlocked his secret room, went down on his knees and prayed before a congregation of icons. He placed the phone off the hook, then took out from under his mattress all those newspaper cuttings of the suicide of that man whose identity only he and Johnnie knew — Billy Butler. He cut them into tiny pieces then flushed them down the loo. Only when he'd finished did he realise he was bathed in sweat.

What the hell's got into Major Bob?

It was a couple of weeks before that Johnnie'd gone missing, on Friday, 15 October 1999, the day Souths got the flick. It was also the day when Ned 'the Neck' Rivers, Johnnie's neighbour, was ready to take up arms over the kangaroo-court job done on his footy team. At one of Redfern's pubs he led the talk on organising all sorts of protests, of marching to the NRL's headquarters and beating down doors and occupying the boardroom until Souths were readmitted to the comp. He got all righteous and misty-eyed, too. This was the working-man's footy team, for Christ's sakes. Well, he'd show the bastards.

Some took the opportunity to get as drunk as skunks. Others — professionals and tradesmen, pollies and media blokes — got all worked up about what the big end of town'd done to the Mighty Rabbitohs. Their anger was fearsome. The airwaves were filled with their indignation. Letters to the editors of all the daily papers went flooding in. Long-lapsed Souths fans returned to the red and green fold. The NRL could go to buggery. Taking on the supporters of the oldest league club in Australia? These melonheads, it was clear, didn't know Pitt Street from Christmas.

But in all the fuss over Souths, no one'd noticed that Johnnie'd given school a miss that day.

While the pubs in Redfern did their mighty trade, Bob Ryan, his posse of mates and the Greek woman joined a small team from the black community in scouring the streets and lanes for Johnnie Butler. The big bloke was all chockers with his old man's blubbery anxiety. He still managed to organise those that came forward to help, though. He wasn't called the Major for nothing. He gave out enlarged photocopies of a page in the street directory, Redfern divided, by a red highlighter, into clearly defined grids, sending off members of his search party with instructions to report back to him at a prearranged time and place. He fixed people with the no-nonsense glare of his good right eye and the crazy cockeyed stare of the other, barking his instructions with no please or thanks-for-coming-mate. But it was all a waste of time. The Major'd been wrong. The kid hadn't stayed in Redfern at all. But who'd've thought he'd go all the way to Centennial Park?

After four days and nights the coppers (by this time fed up with the Major's critical hectoring) got a call from some early morning runner who'd come across the boy in an isolated part of the park. They alerted Aboriginal welfare, reluctantly picked up Major Bob and his Greek mate Kooka Kon, then met up with the jogger, who directed them to where Johnnie lay. Bob Ryan got out of their car and ran — ran, for God's sake, at his age — in his old man's fashion, feet scraping the ground, arms flopping by his sides, his wheezing heard by those who trailed him, his reddening face threatening to burst a blood vessel. The cops shook their heads and rolled their eyes, waiting for this old cove to come a cropper.

Centennial Park's circular paths and trails were already alive with the sounds of mothers briskly pushing strollers, the whoosh of cyclists, the chatter of the walkers, the heavy panting of the runners. And it was on such a ripper of a day that Bob Ryan's thoughts often returned to that Jap prisoner-of-war camp he'd been interned in during the war. He knew it was at such glorious times of the day, with the sky streaked with the colours of a fiery dawn, that life could suddenly turn on you and give you a mighty kick in the bloody teeth.

Johnnie looked like a dog's breakfast. Bob Ryan went down on his knees, drew the kid towards him from the Moreton Bay fig tree he was slumped up against. Johnnie Butler reeked of piss and shit. His clothes, hair and face were full of grass, leaves and dirt. Bob Ryan loosened his embrace to search the boy's face. Johnnie stared past him, eyes fixed on a clearing beyond the man's left shoulder, close to the nearby pond with its embankment of flattened wild grass which, the Major reckoned, the boy'd slept in. The kid looked vague and wide-eyed and unseeing; and when he didn't respond to Major Bob's insistent breathless questions; when the wild look in his eyes became cloudy and dull; when he fell like a bag of spuds after Major Bob and others'd helped him to his feet, Bob Ryan knew the boy was in real deep shit. But the coppers'd seen it all before. It wouldn't be long before this kid'd rack off again and they'd be back here, in this park, looking for him. Major Bob glanced up, his face tightened, his front-row forward's arms blotched an angry red, and gave them a bloody-well-do-something look that demanded action. The blacks protested when Bob Ryan said he'd take the boy home, threatening to call Nanna Dora. Bob Ryan knew Theodora'd left for Darwin to help a girl who'd been jailed for some minor offence. He was safe from her for the present, would deal with her fearsome anger when she returned. During the heated exchange between the big man and the blacks, Johnnie threw his arms around the gut of the Major. There, he thought, giving them an eyebrow-raised look that enraged them further. The kid's mine, so give me a hand or push off. Bob, the boy and Kooka Kon were driven home.

Bob Ryan stood on the footpath outside his terrace, beckoning Johnnie Butler into his home. He looked at the boy, the kid standing there practically at attention. Johnnie stared down the road like he could float away at any moment, fading into whatever world it was that'd claimed him. You're pushing me, God, Bob thought. You've been giving it to me my whole damn life. When are you going to back off?

Some neighbours stared from behind curtains. What the hell had got into Bob Ryan now, bringing that useless kid and the boy's no-hoper black friends into his home?

'Come on, Johnnie. You need a shower and something to eat. Then we'll go and see the doctor, eh, laddie?'

And then, what to do? Major Bob couldn't very well let the boy get on with his own life, not after that mother of his'd gone on that demented spree, destroying, in her fury, much of the light furniture in her home, smashing windows and pictures, emptying the fridge and pantry of all manner of food stuff, and throwing it here and there before walking out on the kid.

But why Bob? It surely wasn't his responsibility? Not when the local blacks were kicking up such a stink, saying he'd be better off with one of their own.

Well, that's what everyone who knew the Major wondered (except the old Greek woman, who fiercely defended him in her bodgie English). But hell, the bloke was close to eighty, had no connection with the boy prior to the day earlier that year some time after he and his mum had moved into Redfern. So what was going on? There was a story, here; something's up, people reckoned — but there weren't too many willing to confront him, not when they all knew he was the sort of bloke who'd fix you with that scary don't-you-even-think-of-asking straight-faced scowl that told you to mind your own friggin' business when they stopped him in the street to yarn. He'd see their glances shifting to the boy, whose hand he held; they'd stand there too long whinging about Souths, or the weather, all polite and friendly as they tried to find the words to ask what he knew was on their minds.

They could all go and get lost as far as he was concerned. Bob Ryan knew that if the authorities found out what'd happened to the boy they'd institutionalise him, and then the kid'd really go off the deep end. The man knew what such places did to kids. So the Major took him in, and if people didn't like it, well, tough.

But someone dobbed him in. It was touch and go for a while with that welfare lot of do-gooders. They were making all sorts of threats to take Johnnie off his hands. He wondered if they knew who he, the Major, was, how far he was prepared to go. One exasperated welfare worker said, before slamming the phone down on Bob Ryan, that he couldn't give a shit about his standing in the community. The law was the law, and no General-Corporal-Captain-or-whatever was going to use standover tactics on him. A bloke his age taking care of a black kid with Johnnie's problems? Had he gone off his rocker?

Major Bob shows Johnnie how to make his bed
WEDNESDAY, 20 OCTOBER 1999

It's been a week since you'd clammed up and Souths'd been given the once-over. You're seeing doctors. They ask questions, show you pictures, get you to draw and colour in. You don't know how to explain to yourself, let alone to them, that you feel like you're caught in some faraway place. Or how it is that there's sometimes more of you here, in this world, than anyone'd ever guess. So you go along with the lot of them, to the meeting at the hospital's adolescent centre, on your daily walks with Major, cups of tea at Mista Tom's. You hold people's hands. You sit and stare at nothing. Everyone's waiting for the day when you come back.

That morning, after your daily dawn walk with Bob Ryan, he dropped you off at Zoe Poulos' for the huge breakfast she often made for you. She reckons if anything's going to make you well it's food, so she stuffs you silly. Everyone's telling her to lay off. She ignores them all.

She walked you back to Major's terrace down the road where you're staying (Nanna Dora's rung from Darwin, threatening a donnybrook) and left when Bob Ryan answered the door. He had you sit in the lounge room while he got ready so you could walk to Tom's together. You don't like Major's house. It's not that you don't like him. But he's got you wondering why he fusses over you so much. Nah, he's a bit of alright, really, even if he comes on too strong. But that house of his, so clean and neat — if you didn't know better you'd reckon he had nothing better to do with his life than dust and mop and sweep all day long. A good bloke and all, but golly, who'd wanna live with someone who instructs you on how much water you should pour into the bath by sticking a piece of masking tape on the side of the tub? Who stands there looking at you like he's about to deliver another lecture? Who has you leaving your shoes outside, there, to the left of the doormat, *nice and straight*? You'd go dizzy, too, sitting so still and having to look him in the eye while he told you another of his stories that went on forever. And what of the food: a kid can only cop so much of pie and mashed potatoes each Monday and Wednesday, fish and chips on Friday, and so on.

You walked from room to room as the man showered. He took ages. As you wandered about the dark house (lights switched off to save on electricity, fine curtains drawn), you run a finger along the framed pictures of some stone village in another country. Not a speck of dust. It amazed you. You checked out the kitchen. No plates or cutlery to be washed. No grease marks on the stove. And everything so old. You stood outside the shut third bedroom, the one he'd told you never to enter. You put your hand on the doorknob then changed your mind. It was fear that prevented you. Of him, should he've discovered you there, of what might be inside. You returned to the lounge room and sat on the fat old couch that smells of another time and place, and played with the doilies on the arms. You got up, wandered aimlessly, looked at the cut-glass and brass vases on the mantelpiece, the dark-stained piano in the corner, the pictures of unsmiling bearded men and frilly-laced women on the wall, taken thousands of years ago. The place gives you the willies.

You went to the bookcase, picked up a bookend shaped like a rearing unicorn. Where it stood was a piece of blu-tack, indicating its position. You looked under every metal-framed photo, behind the broken-down cuckoo clock, a picture of Jesus pointing to a heart shaped like a blood-red tomato — blu-tack everywhere.

The man took his time shaving. You heard him pissing against the side of the toilet bowl, like he'd told you a dozen times was what any decent fellow should do, to minimise the offending noise.

Bob Ryan was ready. On cue, he said: 'Prim and proper. Whatever you do, lad, do it quickly and do it well.'

He was holding his hat. The creases on the legs of his daks were sharp enough to cut your finger on. His black leather lace-up shoes shone like a mirror. His white, long-sleeved shirt smelled of something that had you thinking of rotting flowers. He checked the stove (twice), then every window and door to ensure they were secure, took one last walk around the house, seeing every light was switched off (waste not, want not, son), showed you (three times) how to make your bed then, satisfied, took you by the hand. He led you out onto the verandah, put on his hat, checked the zipper on his fly, straightened his tie and braces, consulted the time on his Waltham fob watch and locked the door.

You squinted in the sunlight, relieved to be out of his musty terrace. It was a bonzer day, you saw, all glittering sunshine, the street full of jacarandas and wisterias in bloom, which the man pointed out to you. He stroked the trunk of a blossoming tree in his front yard which, he'd once told you, he'd brought back as a seed from that Jap camp. You walked, holding Major's hand, saw the blue sky as flat as a sheet. The world was a dreamy place.

You arrived at Tom's. You're not that far gone not to know there's some design in where people sit. Kooka Kon looked up from his paper and saw you approach. You felt good, walking with Major; built like a brick shithouse, he moved like he was going somewhere important, to a meeting or something, his back straight like he's marching, still in the army. From a distance you saw Old Tom, smiling. Kooka Kon taking a drag on his cigarette. You arrived, counted the three stubs at the Greek's feet.

Major Bob took his position, placed his hat on its customary spear, straightened his tie again then made a comment about the loveliness of the day. 'Well,' he then said, 'whose turn is it to make a cuppa?'

A prang at the lights on the corner of Cleveland and South Dowling Streets had the traffic banked past Tom's terrace. A bull-necked man driving a delivery van into the city was stopped outside where they'd all gathered. He reached across the cabin and wound down the window, leaned across the compartment, stuck a gap-toothed grin out the window and shouted for the entire world to hear: 'Who's keepin' minutes, Bobby-boy!'

Bobby-boy? Tom and Kooka Kon exchanged a malicious smile. Old Tom stroked the side of his face, taking a sidelong look at his smouldering mate.

It was Ned 'the Neck' Rivers. He'd seen these three blokes of late as he went about his delivery business, sitting in a row on the verandah like a bunch of branch-bound cockatoos. Ned was reminded of a game he had as a kid, popping corks out of a gun at a row of magpies lined up on metal rods.

'Havin' another committee meetin', eh Bobby?'

Bob Ryan held his cup and saucer in one hand. He licked his lips several times. The Rivers had always been fools. Major remembered this man's grandfather, who had his family live a destitute life while he persisted with a system he reckoned was bound to make a bundle at the track. Major Bob sipped his tea, glaring at Ned the Neck over the rim of his cup until the man edged his van forward.

It was Major Bob who, after a period of time had elapsed, took up the idea of creating a committee to watch over the boy. Long enough, Old Tom knew, to make it seem as if it was Bob Ryan's idea. They met regularly enough, after all. They had their rules of engagement. The formality of the title appealed to the Major. *The Committee* — yes, why not.

Johnnie meets his uncle
FRIDAY, 22 OCTOBER 1999

Who was to say that the boy's uncle'd agree to take on the boy? And if Jimmy Butler did, but was still that smiling, whistling dill that Bob recalled, would welfare give him the nod? Uncle or no uncle, the guy'd been a bloody dunderhead. But three days after Johnnie'd been found in Centennial Park, the Major finally gave in to Old Tom. And besides, Nanna Dora'd rung several times a day from the Northern Territory, where she'd stayed to organise the funeral of that girl who'd died in custody, giving him a belting over the mobile. There was no choice. It was contacting Jimmy or that furious welfare mob, led by Theodora, would take the boy away.

Bob Ryan hadn't seen Jimmy Butler since the man'd disappeared right after Souths' last grand final win in 1971. But you couldn't ever forget that beanpole of a bloke, that loping walk, the arms swinging like he was on some sort of a parade and his huge clownish grin — if, that is, he wasn't wearing that dog-eared expression when things were going crook that irritated the Major no end. There was no halfway look with Jimmy: he was either cackling with laughter as if life was one big joke, or so morose you didn't want him hanging around.

The Major scowled. Jimmy-bloody-Butler, he'd rarely had two bob to rub together. And he loved the grog. What chance that this was going to work?

Well, Bob Ryan'd keep an eye on him. No thin streak of pelican shit was going to be responsible for Johnnie Butler being sent to some Home, no bloody way.

As luck would have it the man'd moved to La Perouse earlier in 1999. Nanna Dora insisted she accompany Bob Ryan and Tom O'Flaherty. They took a cab out to La Pa, finding him out at the cemetery near the graves of his wife and mother.

A sister? And a nephew? Jimmy Butler had a sister and a nephew? The man needed no convincing. He returned to Redfern out of a past completely unknown to Johnnie, not half the silly bugger the Major recalled.

Wilting under Nanna Dora and Major Bob's campaign of persuasion and intimidation, the authorities agreed to let this Mr James Butler look after his nephew for a given period. They'd review the situation in the near future, do what was best for the boy. Bob Ryan regularly dropped by to make his military-style checks to ensure the boy was being properly fed and clothed. He'd walk into the single-storey terrace through the back door, without knocking, go from room to room wearing that eyebrow-raised look that Jimmy would've liked to punch in, going into the loo, for God's sake, and lifting the lid to ensure it'd been jiffed, checking the pantry and fridge to see that the place was well stocked with food. He was, Jimmy Butler saw, the same smart-arsed prick who couldn't help telling you how you should live your bloody life. Old Tom, on being told by Jimmy of the Major's inspections, shook his head and wondered what everyone in Redfern was thinking: what the hell had got into Bob Ryan?

The Hill Run Man

DECEMBER 1999

Several weeks after Souths got kicked in the teeth, and all of them but the Greek woman and Nan Dora had planned to meet at Tom's. Jimmy Butler was already there, sitting with Old Tom on the verandah. Kon Tsakiris arrived with that Saturday's *Herald* under his arm and a preoccupied look on his face. As he opened Tom's gate he glanced over South Dowling Street to some bloke getting out of a red sports car parked on Cleveland Street opposite the selective boys school.

'Nice auto,' he said. 'Soft top, fucking beauty.' He whistled a half-curved appreciation.

Jimmy saw the longing on the Greek's face and winked at Old Tom. 'You gunna buy one of them flash cars, Kooka? Show off like a big tycoon, eh?'

The Greek grunted. Jimmy Butler let out a choking laugh. He was sitting to the far side of the first of the two benches closest to the gate, hands on hips, elbows turned outwards, his gangly legs stretched to the iron lacework, hooting his delight. Kookaburra Kon stood waiting impatiently for him to draw in his legs so he could take his customary position on the far side of the other bench.

'You got enough room?' he asked.

In Old Tom's backyard the chooks and rooster were having another blue. Flapping wings scuffled the morning, the hen's screeches all awry as the rooster went on his rampage.

Jimmy did not hear the Greek. 'Oi, Tom, how them chooks goin'? Where're them eggs you said you was gunna give me?'

Kooka Kon stood, breathing heavily.

'You know what they say 'bout bein' an egg, don'cha?' said Jimmy Butler. 'It's real crook, ya see, 'cause y'only get laid once.' Jimmy Butler gave a long *hee-hee-hee* that had his whole body flapping like a beached fish. Kon sighed hearing this joke for the third time, two days running.

When Jimmy Butler recovered he made room for the flustered Greek who, forgetting himself, sat in the centre of the two benches, right next to Tom. Jimmy looked at the man, raising his eyebrows. He curled his lips downwards and pouted, nodding slowly several times. 'You sure is a brave man this mornin', Kon.'

'Eh?'

'Yer sittin' in Bob's possie.'

'Oops!' Kon Tsakiris moved too quickly. He felt like a reprimanded schoolkid. It sure was a day for little humiliations. He took out his packet of smokes.

Kooka Kon lit a cigarette and opened the paper. He went straight to the Business section. There was bound to be a bargain sooner or later, a pub in some little town, a sandwich shop some bloke was flogging off 'cause he was strapped for cash. Just keep looking, it was bound to come. He tried to ignore the fellow with the sports car but couldn't. The bloke was pushing buttons on his remote control to close the soft roof. You could hate a man you didn't know for having such a vehicle. Especially when you had to get rid of that clapped-out Holden you couldn't afford to repair so's it'd pass the rego test. The old clanger was a disgrace, anyway, better off without the old rust bucket. He fixed a stare at the car, his blood throbbing. A vertical vein appeared on his forehead, right deadset between his eyes.

'Eggs are on the kitchen table, Jimmy.'

'Arrr, yer a good fella, Tom.'

'An' by the way. Yer wrong about the egg, y'know. Worst thing is, it comes in a carton with eleven others, all eggheads like you.'

Jimmy could barely control himself. His cackling laughter rent the early morning. Kon thought the black man was one of the biggest dills he'd ever met in his life.

In the yard the rooster was going on like a car doing a wheelie. Sydney was turning on a ripper of a morning. There were the warm scents of summer, the lazy stillness of an early Saturday morning, the sun's light glistening on that great stretch of green grass leading to the terraced slopes at the southern end of Moore Park. But all Kon Tsakiris could see was the man with the poncy car doing his stretches — and that man's watch, sparkling in the sun. Probably a fucken Rolex, Kon thought. He drew on his cigarette, exhaled, then spat on the ground.

The Great Wait. That's what Major Bob called it. It was a shocker of a time, hanging on until November of 2000 when the judge hearing the appeal for South Sydney's reinstatement was to hand down his judgement. They got so preoccupied arguing over Souths' fate (not so with Kooka Kon, who couldn't give a hoot about the Rabbitohs) that they sometimes forgot Johnnie was even there. For as long as it took them to finish off a pot of tea the boy could, and often did, stare over the road at the park, usually with that fixed unseeing look in his eyes. But then there were those occasions when the world'd take on a shape he understood. He'd blink, turn his head to discover himself sitting between the Major and Old Tom, and it was nearly always Bob Ryan who'd notice first.

'Johnnie? Are you there? Can you hear me? Look at me, lad.'

But the kid's eyes'd cloud over. He might lean his head to one side and stare at his hands, at the ground or, on one particular December day, at some mad bugger who, after getting out of his red sports car, ran up and down the hills of Moore Park.

But Bob doesn't always notice, does he, Johnnie? Sometimes you emerge from the world you've drifted into and hear them jabbering on, giving each other the bum's rush as they tell of their exploits, some experienced, some observed, many exaggerated and a few downright imagined. Crikey, they sure could tell stories, that lot. The old Greek bird and Nan, too. It was a real gift when they got going. But you've got a gift, too. Their words wash over and through you. They're like rivers of sound, carrying you to places you can see and feel. Yeah, too right you've got a gift, 'cause you know how to damn well listen.

It was a couple of weeks before Christmas, a lazy wet Sunday afternoon, getting on towards evening. Rain fell lightly, playing a mournful and intermittent dirge on the corrugated iron roof of Tom's verandah. Old Tom sat, mouth open, leaning forward on his walking frame. He watched the departing figure of the Greek woman, dropping his guts now and then, but the others made out like they hadn't heard. His head was bent so low he looked like he was about to pack down in a scrum. Major Bob was playing solitaire on the small table they placed the tea things on, a thoughtful look on his face. He looked across at Old Tom. He could see his old mate's gums. Tom O'Flaherty sat so dry and still, if it hadn't been for that lizard of a tongue occasionally moistening his lips and the mouth that opened and closed now and then, you'd have thought the old fella'd carked it. Mates for over seventy years. The Major sighed, went back to his cards. But his concentration was gone. All the talk of Souths' prospects of getting back into the comp were crook. The kid was showing no signs of coming back from wherever it was he'd racked off to. Kooka Kon was turning the pages of the *Trading Post*'s 'Businesses for Sale', grumbling nonstop about his prospects of winning the climbing Jackpot Lottery (useless, he reckoned; only those already rolling in it won lotteries). Time to go soon, Bob Ryan thought. Finish this hand, call it a day. Get back home, fix a quick meal for himself, have an early night.

Johnnie Butler was drinking sweetened tea from a mug, listening to the whoosh of the vehicles as they barrelled past Tom's terrace. Major Bob cast a sidelong glance at the kid. The boy looked like some horror was shuffling behind those eyes that stared at the long stretch of glistening turf at the base of the hills of Moore Park.

'Johnnie? Are you alright? Do you want me to take you home, lad?'

The boy responded, turning to focus on the man. Johnnie knew it'd be dark soon. He'd felt the oncoming shadows shuddering. He was scared of the night.

Major Bob looked up at the grey wet sky, a great drift of cloud cover against which the trees on the far side of Moore Park were etched, dark shapes in the deepening late afternoon. He watched as Zoe Poulos walked to her home on foot. She clomp-clomped her way to the first turn-off, the black umbrella low over her head, her slight figure, all in black, a determined magpie. She'd delivered a small tray of baklava to Tom, collected her money then left.

'You should have walked her home, Kon,' said Bob Ryan. 'It could bucket down any moment now.'

'Ah, she'll be alright. It's not too far.' He'd put aside the paper and was checking the dates on his lottery tickets. The Jackpot was up to several million but he wasn't getting excited. The Gods'd always been against him making it big-time. He had Buckley's. Waste of money buying those loser's dreams every week, but he couldn't help himself.

Failure had aged Kon Tsakiris. He would, he now knew, never return to the ancestral village on the island rich and successful. The bust, done in marble and standing on a waist-high plinth would never be seen in the village square, honouring his generosity in restoring the church and schoolhouse. All those dreams weren't worth a pinch of goat turd. He often told himself he couldn't give a stuff about his failures; everyone had to die sooner or later, after all, and who'd give a shit anyway, in years to come? But it didn't work. He'd come a buster, made a mess of things, was as bitter as a lemon.

Zoe Poulos' arrival earlier that afternoon'd brought an abrupt end to his whining. She wouldn't stand for it, threatening once to give him a mighty whack across the back of the head if he didn't shut up. Others might've thought her a good old cheese but she was a terror to him, and he was glad she hadn't stayed for a cuppa.

'Ah well, what do you do?' he said. 'That's life. Ay-ya-ya-ya-ya-ya-yaaahhh.'

Bob Ryan leaned forward. 'Come on, Johnnie. Your uncle'll be waiting for you. It's about time we pushed off.'

But the boy, as still as a piece of furniture, was staring at the park.

'Our mate's here,' said Old Tom. 'Johnnie's seen our mate.'

Middle-aged if not older — it was difficult to tell from that distance — the Hill Run Man was sprinting up the slopes of the park. Those on the verandah watched him now as he forced his legs up the long steep incline. Reaching the summit he stood, dog-tired, hands on hips, gasping for breath. Johnnie couldn't make out the man's face but saw the full head of curly grey hair and the dark skin.

After a brief rest the man made his way back down the hill then ran again to the top where, after one sustained effort, he stopped, almost bent double, straining to breathe. On another occasion he fell to his hands and knees, gasping violently.

'He's overdoing it,' said the Major.

'Been out here ev'ry second day or so,' said Tom O'Flaherty. 'Tryin' to prove a point, I reckon.'

Major Bob turned to Kooka Kon. 'The boy,' he said, 'needs to get out as much as possible. Now that you've got rid of your café why don't you take him for a walk now and then, try to get him to kick a ball around Redfern Park with you? Would you like that, Johnnie?'

But the boy was sitting tight on the bench, his knees pressed together, his hands a tight ball in his lap. Watching the bloke in the park going for it again, then collapsing, well and truly rooted, halfway up. The bloke was stuffed, even Johnnie could see that.

'We'll have you playing for Souths' juniors one day, won't we, Johnnie?' said Bob Ryan.

'I'm not interested in your football,' said Kon Tsakiris. 'You people go crazy for this rugby league. Anyway, Souths, they're finished.'

The Hill Run Man got up. His runs completed, the fellow walked to the footy field then, after a pause, began to jog, stepping off either foot. Johnnie saw the imaginary tacklers the Hill Run Man was evading. The boy saw him break through an unseen line of defenders.

The man walked to a bench where he'd left a large sports bag. He returned to the field with a ball which he kicked high into the air. Johnnie Butler imagined himself collecting it then exploding into a short sprint. He swerved this way and that, doing the occasional goosestep.

Bob Ryan intruded on the boy's imaginings. He nodded his head and said, 'Not bad for a bloke his age.' He turned his attention to Kooka Kon. 'You'll take Johnnie for walks then, Kon?'

'Maybe.'

'Good. Thank you.'

'Ay-ya-ya! You always do this to me.'

But you're no longer there on the verandah. You're punting the football high into the sky. You eye it steadily, positioning yourself underneath its fall. You catch it cleanly then immediately leap to one side avoiding the marauding opposition. You chip the ball over the heads of those who are swarming to bring you down, run through their confused ranks to where you instinctively know the ball will land, collect it as it bounces awkwardly on the wet ground, hold it hard to your chest, swivel, swerve, score a try.

'Not bad,' repeated the Major. 'Not bad at all. He must've been quite a player in his day.' Bob Ryan broke into applause.

The Hill Run Man, on hearing the clapping, looked here and there until he spied Major Bob, whose hands were above his head, applauding. He paused, to ensure, perhaps, he was not being mocked, then waved. He collected his bag from the park bench then walked to his car, parked on Cleveland Street.

'Expensive car,' said Kooka Kon. 'I bet he didn't work all his bloody life in a café and corner shop.'

When the car turned into South Dowling Street, the driver turned to look at those gathered on Tom's verandah. He slowed down, stared, his eyes off the road. He looked for so long and so hard at them, when he should've been watching the road, that he veered out of his lane. He hit the cement median strip, lost control of his vehicle, the driver behind him almost running into the rear of the sports car. There was a squeal of tyres. Gears were crunched. Brakes were applied. Abusive language was directed at the Hill Run Man. He regained control, drove back into his lane then accelerated, belting headlong into the darkening evening.

The boy'd stood. Tom and Kooka Kon exchanged a quizzical look. The Major's head followed the car's departure.

'Now whatd'ya reckon that was all about, Bob?' said Tom.

But the Major did not reply.

'Bob?'

Bob Ryan did not hear. Old Tom saw him shift uneasily on the bench.

'What? What is it, Bob?'

'I don't know. I'm not sure. Did you recognise him?'

'Nope, but he sure as hell recognised one of us.'

Tom O'Flaherty saw Major Bob adjust the hat that needed no adjusting and, after the car was out of sight, flick the specks off his trousers that were not there.

'For a moment, then,' Bob Ryan said, 'I thought …'

'Thought what?'

'No. Sorry. I must have been imagining things. Come on, Johnnie, let's go to Jimmy's.'

Tell us a story, Bob

It was a shithouse of an off-season. For the first time in Tom's memory, Souths weren't going to be fielding a side on the paddock. He could, after all, recall the first game of rugby league played in Australia, way back in 1908, which featured, of course, the Mighty Rabbitohs. And here they bloody well were, the club side which'd won more grand finals than any other, the oldest league team in the country, for God's sake, on the sideline, waiting for the lawyers to slug it out and for some Justice, one bloke, just the one, to decide, after the completion of the 2000 season, the fate of the Bunnies.

The yarning turned more and more to the past.

'Well,' the Major said, this being a sign that their attention was expected. 'Well,' he repeated, 'it's one of the greatest games I've ever seen. It was 1955 and the Rabbits were playing Manly. We had to win to have any chance of getting into the finals, you see, and there we were, down 7–4 with one minute of the game left on the clock. Clive Churchill refused to leave the field even though he had a broken arm. He —'

'Wrist,' said Tom. 'He'd broken his wrist.'

'Yes, you're right. I stand corrected. Well, he took the ball in his good arm, like this — are you looking Jimmy? Kon? — and the Manly players thought that Clive, being in so much pain, was going to pass the ball. The opposing players hung back, you see, to go for the bloke Clive was going to give it to. Churchill saw the gap. He cut through the defensive line and sent Ian Moir over for a try. The crowd went absolutely —'

'It was Les Cowie,' said Tom.

'Tom, I was standing behind the try line. Clive Churchill kicked the ball, regathered, stepped off his right foot, accelerated, sliced through the defence, passed it to Moir who scored.'

'Okay, okay, if it means that much to you, Moir scored. Just remember one thing, though. You're gettin' on. Memory ain't what it used to be.'

'In case you'd forgotten, Tom, you're twenty years older than me. Now, can I continue with my story?'

'Yeah, go ahead, young fella.'

Jimmy was grinning like an imbecile. Old Tom winked at Kooka Kon, who was enjoying Bob Ryan's irritation.

'Thank you, Mr O'Flaherty. Well, we were drawn seven-all. The game was over, but a draw was no good to us. We had to win to stay in the running for the finals. Clive Churchill was taking the kick for goal from the sideline. His arm was hanging limply by his side. The rain started to —'

'Rain? Wasn't rainin'.'

'Tom, do you want to finish the story?'

'Yeah, reckon I'd better. Here's how it *really* happened …'

Bob Ryan stormed into Tom's house to make another pot. Jimmy Butler and Kon Tsakiris were doubled over, rocking on the benches, laughing their heads off without making a single sound. Johnnie Butler looked like he'd understood nothing.

But Bob Ryan had his good days. Even Old Tom had to admit that the big bloke knew, like no one else, how to capture the moment. He might take his time in a way that made some people restless, squinting his good eye and nodding to himself as he paused to gather his recollections. He might speak in fully rounded sentences that went on forever. Fact was, Bob Ryan had a natural flair with the spoken word. Old Tom told him so once. The Major grunted, as if being told nothing new, and continued with his story.

'Those were the days when we were allowed to run onto the field. Tom and I would sit on the Hill and as soon as the ref signalled the end of the game, we'd leap over the fence and belt across the paddock to be the first to pat our heroes on the back. Well, there was that Saturday afternoon in June 1930. Sydney'd had a month of on-and-off wet weather, you see, then a week of solid rain leading up to the game. The Sydney Cricket Ground was a quagmire. Halfway through the game and our boys looked like some species from another era, covered head to foot in mud — cavemen, they were, practically indistinguishable from each other. Just before full time the wind picked up and blew some of the clouds away. The sun broke through, a huge beam of light like you see in those illustrated kids' bibles, shining on the field. It was the sun, you see, another gorgeous Sydney sun.'

How come your mother'd dragged you from state to state, town to town, settlement to settlement, so that there was nothing you could cling to that you could call your own? You're not like the Greek woman who can say, *I from Kastellorizo. Is islan'. In Greece.* You're not like any of them, really, 'cause you never stopped anywhere long enough to call a place home. You can't even remember more than a couple of the names of the places you've stayed at.

And how come, after you'd settled in Redfern and'd begun to feel some attachment to the place, your mother did her block and, full as a boot, practically destroyed your home before pissing off, leaving you in the lurch. Wasn't easy being you, was it, Johnnie Butler? Easier, less painful sometimes, to imagine yourself being someone else.

You might be sitting there at Old Tom's while Major's telling one of his stories, pulling at your shorts, your knees working away like you're busting to go to the loo. You might have that thick-as-a-brick look, staring blandly at that mad bugger who comes every second day now to do his hill runs, a cap pushed low over his face and wearing darkies, like he's hiding something. You might have that skew-whiff expression, your head slanted to one side, but you're there, taking hold of Major's footy past and making it your own.

So that it's you charging across the dreamy paddock in 1930. It's you, standing awestruck as the Bunnies' player turns, looks down from his great height and smiles, ruffling your hair and winking his acknowledgement. You see that Bob-Ryan-life of yours in black and white, like those old Pommie war movies you watch in the dead of night on the telly when you're too afraid to sleep. There you are, walking the streets of Redfern all those years ago, your little boy's eyes lighting upon a Rabbitoh dressed in civvies, in a queue at the tram stop Mista Tom and Major'd told you about, or at the local butcher's (now gone), buying some chops and bangers for mum, or leaving the factory down the road, the day's work done: and the great man himself nods, seeing your adulation, so's your little boy's heart swells with pride and you run, searching for a mate to tell. All fine men, they are, like those smiling pink-skinned (not like your ugly dark skin), square-jawed blokes on pub posters, hair parted in the middle and slicked down, broad-shouldered and handsome, like old Hollywood film stars.

It's safe, becoming another person in a time you can manipulate. It's you, young Bobby, in knickerbockers and a cloth cap, smiling broadly at the world.

Jimmy tells Johnnie-boy a thing or two

Well, what'dya know, a bloody uncle, your mum's brother and you knowing sweet bugger-all about him. And what's more, him having a past with Major and Mista Tom, all those years ago. It sure is a crazy small world, by golly.

But Uncle Jim — he's a ripper. A couple of weeks after they found you in the park, you both moved into a terrace up the road from Major and Yaya Zoe. Bit weird, just you and this scrawny bloke who loped around the house like a black version of the Pink Panther. But you took to the funny bugger. Legs like matchsticks, mismatched clothes from St Vinnies lighting him up like a Chrissie tree, a grin wide enough for you to stick a melon into, and him laying on all his bullshit stories. You wondered, not long after you'd moved in with him, whether he talked even when he was by himself. Too right, you soon found out.

You wake up in the middle of the night from a fitful sleep and hear him, his yacketing and foot-stamping beat down the hall sending vibrations into your bedroom. You know he's going nuts because he's busting for a drink. And you going all funny because you're too afraid if you sleep the nightmares about your brother Billy'll come back. You're two of a kind, you and Jimmy, and you know it. You can see the day coming when you might even love the silly bloke. He's the only one who can make you smile. He's your mum's brother.

You open the door of your bedroom, look down the hallway and see him at the kitchen table, both feet stomping a tune, the fingers of one hand drumming the top of the table, the other, fag between thumb and finger, making a half-circle in the air.

"T'sall I can do, Johnnie-boy, to keep off the grog. Ain't easy to stop, yer know, when you've been drinkin' since you was a little fella. You wanna cuppa tea, sport? Keep yer uncle comp'ny?'

He throws himself into a tale, you not knowing half the time what he's talking about. But you don't mind. Better'n lying in bed, you crawling under the cover, curling up into a ball, crying for what you did to your brother. Much better to sit here and watch his rubbery face tell its own story.

'Ooooh, yeah, I seen the dust, y'know, come up quick, them willy-nillies comin' atcha outta nowhere. Damn groun' hot as a fag end. Bloody dry leaves an' twigs an' spinifex goin' fer yer eyes.'

You enjoy the walks he takes you on most evenings after dinner. The aimless strolling and the smoking, he tells you, keep him off the piss. Tea, walking, smoking, talking — his saviours, he says. You follow him through the narrow lanes of Redfern (he soon learns nothing can get you to cross its boundaries, which you know well), past stubby terraces whose front doors and domestic affairs open directly onto the footpath. He seems unable to walk and talk at the same time. He stops, sits on someone's brick fence. You watch, fascinated, as he takes out his tobacco pouch and, with one hand, rolls a cigarette. Despite the trembling, the finished product's a perfect white cylinder.

'You like that, eh, Johnnie-oh? Pretty good, eh, sport.'

He smokes in silence for a while and then tells you of the time when all that was left of a dying waterhole was liquid mud.

'Things got real crook, y'know. It was real hot, an' me an' Rosie we was that thirsty. Light shinin' off the road. Them roads go blue when they're real far off, y'know.'

His legs are tucked under him. His hand shakes so badly you wonder if he's going to be able to locate his mouth to take another drag.

'Me an' Rosie we done it tough, y'know. But I tell ya, Johnnie-boy, we seen them shootin' stars. The whole fucken sky full o' stars. Jeez it was unreal. Yeah, me an' Rosie — she's the one what got me off the piss, y'know. She was a good woman, that Rosie.'

Sometimes he takes you into the backyard when the need for a drink has him going bonkers, and he wanders up and down, around and around the perimeter of the yard, through the long grass and knee-high weeds, the ground littered with used teabags and the chewed and twisted ends of his fags.

And when the demon urge eases he tells you of his Rosie, who'd passed on not that long before Major, Nanna and Mista Tom turned up in a cab at the cemetery out at La Pa looking for him. Once, he touched on the subject of his failures as a footy player, when even the great Clive Churchill told him he had the talent to be the Little Master's heir.

'Us Aboriginal people, I seen 'em come to Sydney outta the bush. I knew many of 'em. All me people, an' yours, too, eh. You re'mber that. Our people we play for them Rabbitohs. I played too, y'know, back in them early '70s ...'

He stops mid-sentence. You see his eyes cloud over. He throws the unfinished cigarette hard to the ground, grinds it with the toe of his shoe long after he's put it out. You've not seen him angry before.

'I ever tellya, Johnnie, of the time I seen a town outback? Fucken heat shimmerin' and blindin' ya? An' that town, oooh, say 'bout five mile away, floatin' 'bove the horizon? I tellya that one?'

Nah, you're not fooled. You know he keeps rattling on because it fills the silence. But he isn't fooled either. He's told you himself he's full of hooey. He makes you forget stuff. Once, you came close to laughing at one of his jokes.

And you don't mind that much if it's repeated (you hear the same stories over and over), or even if it's rehearsed. You came upon a joke book one day, under his bed, and recognised a couple of the jokes he'd ticked off that'd been part of some story he'd told at Mista Tom's.

You're at the kitchen table. It's late afternoon. You're thinking that sometimes, behind the stories he and Major tell, there's another. And it's the untold tales, or the ones begun but not completed that you want to hear the most. You know all about untold stories, don't you, Johnnie. One of these days you might even tell them about Billy.

'C'mon, sport, let's eat. I'm as hungry as a black dog. Better feed ya in case Major Bob comes round like a fucken inspector, lordin' it over me.'

He takes some things out of the pantry and fridge. He sits, makes you a sandwich. 'I ever tellya 'bout the time I heard the fucken ground sigh, mate?'

Onya, Nanna

Nanna Dora drops by in that people-mover she's used that night to pick up under-the-weather blacks after closing time. She's wearing one of those rainbow-coloured shifts she throws together herself that has you thinking of a potato sack. Her humungous boobs swing like chandeliers. She's wearing sneakers. You wonder what she looks like under that great big Akubra she always wears. Maybe she sleeps with it on, like the queen and her crown. She looks as weary as hell.

She barks at your Uncle Jimmy for the unwashed things on the kitchen bench. He's on his best behaviour. He's scared of her. He's gone all silent, grinning like a kid who's been caught doing something naughty.

She knows you've got problems sleeping at night, so after giving Uncle Jimmy a lashing for this and that, and telling him she wants the kitchen stuff cleaned now, right now, she takes you into the yard.

She sits you down on a bench. At your feet are the shelled pumpkin seeds Yaya Zoe'd dropped while sitting with you that day, after delivering a baking tray of food.

Shadows shift. There's the sighing of a breeze, the weight of a low blue sky. A plane tunnels through the orange sky. Moonlight enlarges her breasts. You'd like to rest your head between them and feel the comfort of her stubby body. She's talking beautiful words that mean nothing to you, but they make you feel good and calm. You feel a smile straining your lips.

You're fascinated by the fluttering movements of her hands as she talks. Her dreamy voice lulls you. You're getting tired. She puts an arm around you, draws you to her. You snuggle into her. And then you realise she's reciting a poem about a little black kid on a beach. You think of the lullabies your mother sang to you. A fist of longing beats somewhere inside of you. Nanna's voice is as fragile as a flower. The poem is about you. The poem is you. Onya, Nan.

You look up to see your uncle standing in the doorway, listening. His eyes are full of sadness.

Yaya Zoe ain't a bad old thing

Johnnie Butler learned, then, from a young age, though not in words he could, at the time, enunciate, that storytelling involved particular rituals. For the Greek woman, known to some as Grandma Zoe, to most as Yaya Zoe, it was an activity she associated with her kitchen table. It might've been while they drank a cup of tea (real tea leaves, not that rubbish in tea bags), or over breakfast.

She looks at you face on, with an open gaze, speaks to you with that direct and imperial manner that'd once scared other kids, but not you. You knew all along she was a softie. And she tells you stuff. Her life, as much of it as you can make out, lies there on the kitchen table in all its honest detail. You sit after breakfast at that old dark-stained wobbly thing. It's a smallish kitchen, with one window facing south. Jars of olives line the kitchen bench. There's the smell of cinnamon, crushed nuts, flour and butter in the air. The old water heater fascinates you. You watch the tiny pilot light, waiting for it to suddenly flare and roar into life. The walls haven't been painted for yonks. They're as blotched as slabs of marble but clean and cold to touch. As clean as a nun's bum, your uncle says. The light is switched on. Unsmiling sombre-faced saints stare down at you from every wall. Yaya Zoe talks to them. She reckons they talk to her, too. She's nutty like that, but you sort of understand. After all, you hear Billy's voice too, at night, when you can't sleep.

'You finish?' she says.

You push the plate towards her.

'You want more?'

You push the plate further away.

She gives you more.

You eat, even when you're about to bust a gut. But what can you do when she stands there, adjusting those steel-framed glasses, smiling her toothless smile, nodding and sighing, happy to see you stuffing yourself silly? Then she makes a pot of tea, sits, and begins.

It isn't all Greek to you. She throws in the occasional word in English. Her hands make all sorts of patterns in the air. She jabs at the tabletop. Her face has you thinking of plasticine. And anyway, you don't mind if you don't catch on to everything. You're happy to fashion your own story out of all those gestures and foreign sounds.

She'd taken a fancy to the boy early on, like she'd done to many other kids in the street. There were times she'd cross the road just to pass a mum pushing a stroller or a pram, sometimes stopping to chat, her face a mass of wrinkles when she smiled, fit to burst. Some afternoons, her cooking done and the trays of baklava delivered to the local shops, cafés, restaurants and selected private customers, she'd walk to Redfern Park and, nibbling on pumpkin seeds, making a mess of the grass under the bench she sat on, she'd watch the schoolkids mucking about on the play equipment.

A few months before Souths got the boot she watched as the boy and his mum arrived in her street with a couple of battered suitcases and a mixture of bewilderment and hope. The old woman stood at the front gate as the cabbie carried that single cardboard box of grocery items. Her eyes met the boy's. She smiled. He stopped, blinked, smiled back, waved a hand, and her old heart was his. It was that simple.

Later that day Johnnie Butler responded to a knocking at the front door. It was the woman, holding a tray of baklava, there to welcome them to the street. He knew she was a good old thing.

She'd walked the streets of Redfern each morning for three consecutive days after the fifteenth of October of that year. She'd covered several times the area Bob Ryan had allotted to her, trying to find the kid. And when at last the Major rang to tell her that Johnnie'd been found in Centennial Park and was now in his home, she immediately left the half-made pastry on her kitchen table. She rushed to Bob's in a plastic Uncle Toby's Oats apron tied over her black shift, sleeves rolled up way past her chook-skinned elbows, arms covered in flour. Yaya Zoe pushed past all the local blacks and embraced the boy like he was her own. Major Bob sat on his lounge, grim-faced, his lips a tight line. And when the boy stood, arms by his sides, his eyes wide open but seeing nothing, she knew he was crook. Both her hands flew to her face. That single choking sound had no effect on the boy. She walked home slowly, tears smudging the flour dust on her cheeks.

Yaya Zoe'd taken one look at that uncle of his and knew the man could, any day, return home off his face. She knew the signs. She remembered her own father, back on the island. And besides, anyone grinning as often and as broadly as Jimmy Butler made her suspicious. His ridiculous walk annoyed her. She bought him razors and frowned if she ever saw him unshaven. His uncombed hair, she reckoned, made him look like a black rooster. She and the Major had their unstated pact — they'd keep a close eye on the silly fellow.

Yaya Zoe was happy, then, to take her turn. She'd intended scaling back anyway on the number of trays of baklava she made. So she created the time to do her bit. Major Bob had drawn up a timetable. On specified days the boy'd be taken to her home for brekkie, or for a cuppa. She'd talk to him. Sometimes she'd see the flicker in his eyes and she knew, oh yeah, others might not believe her, but she knew he was listening.

Major Bob once started to tell the boy of the Jap camp he'd spent years in. He stopped halfway through his tale. Johnnie saw his eyes go all misty and dark and restless, just like Jimmy whenever he spoke of his days as a footy player. Not so with Yaya Zoe. No half-finished sentences or untold stories with her. No clouding of eyes with this old bird. There was no pause, no weighty silence in which the woman considered what should or should not be said. Whatever she thought of saying, out it came.

He'd seen her himself standing on the second-highest rung of a ladder, whacking the branches of an olive tree (planted by Bob Ryan in 1948) with an old cricket bat to dislodge the fruit. He'd heard she'd once kicked a snarling dog in the snout. She changed her own light bulbs. She stuffed him full of food. His uncle said that, even if she did give him a hard time, she was a bit of alright.

Greek Easter

April 2000

Johnnie Butler watched while Zoe Poulos filled a teaspoon with sugar and held the laden spoon halfway between the bowl and his mug. He liked sitting around the table with all those other Greek women, assembled in Yaya Zoe's home to make crosses from palm leaves for the coming Palm Sunday. One of them smelled of naphthalene. Another brought with her the odours of her husband's fish and chip shop. Half of them were in black. They often talked at the same time. But not when Yaya Zoe had something to say. He liked seeing her holding court, her story unfolding with an emphatic gesture of her head and the movements of her animated mouth and eyebrows. As she spoke the other women looked at each other in agreement and nodded, their mouths turned emphatically downward in indignation. Johnnie Butler watched their hands, a flurry of activity, making perfect crosses.

Having poured the sugar into his mug and stirred his tea, the boy saw the spoon Yaya Zoe held then become another voice. She was thrusting accusations at the source of some insult. The other women scowled in support, as animated as a box of crows. She described in the air some undulation that accompanied her tale. The women sighed, shaking their heads in disbelief.

It's getting dark so you leave. You know Yaya Zoe's standing at the gate watching you as you walk home. There are palm crosses in both your hands, in the buttonholes of your shirt and in your hair. You feel like a walking tree. When you get to your gate you wave at her. You hear a voice, wonder whether it's your own.

Old Tom's sanctuary

Tom O'Flaherty has his own way of telling stories. Whereas the others tell theirs with words, Old Tom communicates his with those relics he's collected over several decades.

The man's lounge room has such a stale smell that you crinkle your nose each time you enter. Lumpy dust-covered couches'd been pushed long ago away from the walls which are chockers with photos. The room is heavy with the rows of cheerless faces, of blokes dressed in their footy gear, arms folded, hair parted in the middle. Coaches stand to one side, under boaters or Stetsons. In one photo a moustachioed official's coat is drawn to one side, revealing an impressive fob watch and chain.

It took your breath away when you'd first entered and seen all those black-and-white faces, as serious as an angry teacher's. Golly, what a bowerbird Mista Tom is. You stood still, flattened as a magpie, wanting to back out of the throbbing room.

You make repeated visits to this *sanctuary*, as the old man refers to it. Old Tom isn't to know that, in time, it's his brass bell, rung to signal the first league game played in Australia, that you embrace as your own. You come to love those countless photos, too, the guernseys that've been worn by the legends themselves, the darkening silver trophies, the letters, contracts and, most nerve-tingling of all, the crackling faraway voices preserved on reel-to-reel tapes. It makes you dizzy just leaning your head to one side trying to count the number of tape covers, all classified (by Major Bob) according to year.

In your dreams Mista Tom always appears as a young man. You see him holding that bell he's taken out of its glass-and-wooden display box. His posture's erect, the walk's decisive, his mouth's full of teeth, the eyes are no longer rheumy. He holds it by its wooden handle and lifts it high over his head and rings that old thing until its sound reverberates out of the lounge room and terrace, up and down South Dowling Street and over to Moore Park, where the Hill Run Man stops, halfway up the slope, to listen.

'I don't reckon,' you hear Mista Tom say to Major one day, well after Greek Easter, 'that we're gunna win the appeal. Reckon we're done like a doornail. But if I'm wrong an' I ain't around to see it happen, then this bell's gotta be rung after we're reinstated. Just as the boys come runnin' outta the tunnel and onto the field. Now that's a moment worth stickin' round for.'

Yeah, that lot could tell stories, alright. A lot of what was said was all piss and wind, of course — well, that's what Johnnie heard Tom say one day. And if anyone was going to stop one of those blokes getting too far up himself, it was the old man. It still made Johnnie dizzy, though, the racket they made, the competition between them — like a bunch of kids, they were. There were times when Old Tom, knackered by all the noise, would tell them all to rack off. All that yackety-yak; it taught Johnnie Butler that each life needed its stage and audience. He understood that in telling him their stories he was reaching out to them, too. His silence was a form of communication.

But it can be so confusing. You take Major's and Old Tom's pasts and try to make them your own. And yet, you're terrified of what's come before, like the death of your brother and the disappearance of your mamma. And isn't that what Mista Tom's lounge room is: a memorial to the past? And these old codgers going on and on about *the glory days* — you become as agitated as a fart in a bottle just thinking about those few recent events in your own life you can sometimes recall.

And what about your Uncle Jimmy? Where the hell did he come from? How come your mamma never told you anything about him? Her own brother? What's his story — his *real* story? You reckon there are things *out there* that're festering in dark corners, to do with your mamma, Uncle Jimmy or other rels you know nothing about. And these blokes, talking like they don't have a care in the world. But you'd seen the mood change. It happens so sudden-like. Major shifting his big arse on Tom's bench and staring at the ground. Or your uncle, stopping mid-sentence, his eyes turning so sad you want to put your arm around his shoulder; then he grins like a boofhead, trying to cover it all up, but you'd seen it all, that passing moment.

And what about you, eh: on the same day as the judgement to do with Souths' appeal, on Friday, 3 November 2000 — just over a year since your world's closed in — your own past collides, there on Tom's verandah. The day your voice returns. You were right. You were always right. Squirrel away the past? What a joke.

The Appeal — Courtroom 21A, Law Court building
Friday, 3 November 2000

By the time Justice Finn was ready to hand down his judgement, Victor Batrouney's hill runs were well and truly over. He'd become reacquainted with Bob Ryan and Redfern. Coming back wasn't as painful as he'd thought it would be, either. Perhaps it was because all those old relatives of his that'd once given him such a hard time had either died or cleared out.

He was in the city, standing outside the Law Court building to hear Justice Finn's decision. There were kids truanting, oldies decked out, from head to foot, in red and green. Perhaps he shouldn't have come alone. Maybe he should've gone to the club with Bob. Maybe it would've been best if he'd stayed at home. He'd pretty much forgotten about the Rabbitohs and got on with his life out in the Hills district. There were his thriving business with all those cabs, his wife and adult kids, the six-acre block he'd bought years ago before prices went silly. He'd thought he was safe out there from the memories of what he'd done to his mother, his old family photos hidden from view in a heavily masking-taped cardboard box in the three-car garage, his son and daughter following his wife's Anglican rather than his own Maronite traditions.

So why did he go to the court? Was it really to do with the Rabbitohs, the team his father'd once followed with a passion as strong as that of his footy mate, Bob Ryan? Or with his mother's accusation that his betrayal in marrying Susan and giving up uni was a blow against his own father who'd died in that Jap camp? Victor couldn't separate them. They were all locked together in some terrible embrace that no amount of reasoning could untangle. That was the problem, he knew. Couldn't think about Souths without feeling some connection with his old man. But you couldn't pick up the *Tele* or the *Herald* without some reference to those Souths supporters going on about the injustice of it all. A man could try to ignore all that indignation and anger, but unresolved issues have a way of taking on a life of their own. And so he began his hill runs, turning up at Old Tom's one day, knowing Bob Ryan was there.

And now he was at the court, getting all choked up. He told himself it was because it was a cause — for the Aussie battler. It wasn't too romantic a thought, was it? After all, most who followed the Bunnies were your working-class Aussies while those who would have Souths out of the comp were suited boardroom bastards out to make a quid. It was a line pushed by some in the media, too, who rallied to Souths' case — and there were plenty of them, too. The whole shebang had become a class thing, ridiculous, Victor thought, in the year 2000, and yet here he was, getting all gulpy and moved by the sorts of things some of your high-flyer supporters were saying to all those media people on the steps of the building.

Ned 'the Neck' Rivers'd had a crook night. He'd got up late that morning feeling real knackered after a heavy night at the club. Head all woozy, mouth tasting like the bottom of a budgie cage. But he had to play his part, do his bit. Show those smart-arsed business types that knew fuck-all about footy that he wasn't going to put up with their malarky.

First thing he did on getting out of bed was to go out to his tiny front lawn. Hair like a punk rocker, pyjama fly gaping open, he raised the Aussie and Souths flags on the two twenty-foot poles standing between the wheelie bins and that mongrel of a frangipani that was too big a fucker to cut down. He threw down an improvised breakfast then bolted for the city in his delivery van. No work today. No way was he going to miss this historic day. This was David (who was David, anyway?) against those bastard Gorgons. He wound down the window of his car and shouted out to a group of blokes pacing up and down the footpath, smoking nervously: 'Jack! Joey! Over 'ere!'

The men saw Ned's grinning face leaning out of the window.

'Bunnies! Bunnies! Bunnies!' he shouted.

'Oi! Oi! Oi!' they responded.

Victor Batrouney walked past the many media people from the telly and radio stations who'd already set up their equipment on the footpath. They were there to relay Justice Paul Finn's decision to the homes, factories, warehouses and offices up and down the east coast of Australia. There were newspaper reporters, too, taking down all sorts of statements. When Souths' legal team arrived, accompanied by the club's president and well-known media blokes, Victor Batrouney pushed forward to hear the various statements made. All this talk of a fair go for the Aussie battler, people power and injustice. It made for dramatic news items. It got a lot of the supporters all worked up. Victor Batrouney found himself being drawn into the emotionally charged moment. He followed a path opened up by a man with a crazy-eyed feral look about him, who charged through the crowd like a half-back sidestepping for the line. Victor pushed his way through the crowd into the foyer of the building. He squeezed into the lift with the bull-necked man.

'Goin' our way,' the man said to Victor Batrouney, breathless with excitement. 'Name's Ned. You a Bunnies supporter?'

Victor Batrouney nodded.

And because Ned the Neck liked what he'd said, he repeated it. 'It's our day, y'know Vic. I'm tellin' ya. Can feel it in me bones. It's goin' our way.'

They managed to grab two of the few spaces left in the gallery of Courtroom 21A. Victor Batrouney looked across at Ned. The man sat back, eyes wide, brows uplifted, breathing through his mouth, his fists on his restless knees like a kid posing for a class photo at school.

You ducked out of school yesterday during little lunch and no one's cottoned on. Least of all your Uncle Jimmy, who's gone all wild and woolly as he wears out that rectangular trail in the grass of his backyard and fills the house with sad used teabags, the smell of Drum roll-your-owns and his animated monologues in a frontal assault on the urge to get back on the piss. As for Major, he's been preoccupied with today's appeal. Tom's holed up in his terrace, as usual. Kooka Kon's become unbearable to everyone, obsessed with the injustices of a world that'd let a wealthy Vaucluse Jew win the ten-million-dollar Jackpot Lottery.

A few kilometres from Sydney's CBD and the whole of Redfern's as fidgety as hell. You can sense it. You watch through the fence palings as Mista Tom's chooks do their block, declaring war on the cowering rooster. The dogs you see as you wander the streets have a helpless look, their lolloping tongues too long, their eyes too startled. When people discover you've been missing since yesterday some'll say that it was because of the Bunnies and your nervousness about the outcome of the appeal. But there's such a shitload of other stuff no one knows anything about — except Major Bob. Yeah, you've heard him mumbling to himself in his secret room, going off at someone in your defence when he thought you were off in your vague world.

You'd like to get up the courage to leave Redfern even if you know it's a bad world out there, like Billy and Major'd told you. One day you'll do it. There'll come that moment when you'll cross South Dowling Street, taking one step at a time, walk through Moore Park and head into that isolated section of Centennial Park, right where Major Bob found you just over a year ago. So bloody simple. Then you'll walk to that Moreton Bay fig tree where you slept those three nights after Billy'd done himself in. You gotta do it, eh.

But your legs turn to jelly each time you try. So you wander the streets having done nothing about making good that promise you'd made to yourself. And your brother. Ah, Billy, letcha down, mate.

You stand in the middle of a narrow lane. Standing, breathing, looking at nothing. The longer you're there the more you feel your world turning into a blur, something outside of yourself, so you shake yourself into consciousness and set out to return to South Dowling Street. I'm comin', Billy, you'll see, you'll see.

In the streets surrounding Souths' clubhouse you notice the trucks and vans, the cabs and motorbikes parked wherever there's space — on the footpath and in the park, all the legal spots having been taken.

You stop on the way, seeing people from every direction making their way to the club. Some oldies are wearing a red and green guernsey (thrown over their shoulders) that's so old and tattered they might, you reckon, have played in it themselves years ago. They wear scarves, caps and T-shirts, trail banners and flags, hold onto huge bunnies.

You walk along roads normally flat chat this time of day. Now they're eerily still. You look into the barbers and the pubs, the Leb sweet shops and the Greek cafes, into the second-hand clothing stores and the lounge rooms of terraces, seen through the front windows. Everywhere you look people are gathered around their tellies to hear what that Justice Finn has to say.

You get closer to South Dowling Street and your heart goes *ka-thump, ka-thump*. You turn to look at your own shadow as if it's some bogeyman ready to pounce. And then you feel the earth heave. There it is. You sense its breath on the back of your neck. You stop and succumb to its embrace. You feel that deep sigh that's suspended somewhere between sky and ground. It fills every pore of your body and gets deep into your bones, wrapping itself around you and making you sad, so sad that you're rooted to the spot wanting your mamma. It ain't fair. It just ain't fair. Ah, Billy, what did I do to ya?

You shake yourself free of its heady melancholy presence, arrive at South Dowling Street just down from Mista Tom's verandah. You see yourself in the hazy distances of Centennial Park's flat stretches of lawn at sunrise, in the densely wooded groves where you'd once searched for the ball with that brother of yours who'd appeared suddenly, only to disappear from your life forever within a week. You see yourself with Billy Butler searching amongst the pine needles and shadows for the ball, laughing as some of the park's many rabbits scamper here and there; see the inclining willows on the banks of the pond that you've both climbed, hanging upside down to retrieve the ball, proud and disdainful swans keeping a safe distance.

Zoe knocks the stuffing out of all of them

Major Bob sat quietly in the club with Kooka Kon, the Greek wondering about all this heat being generated over a footy team —

some people never grew up. Kon wanted to go home. But to what? The sight of his wife leaning on the kitchen bench, wondering out loud (again) how they were going to make ends meet?

As for the Major, he didn't like what he saw. There was the anger on the faces of some who expected the worst. One bloke, as full as a bull's bum, was talking about riots in the street. Eyes had become hardened. Mouths snarled. Strewth, thought Bob Ryan, taking in the whole auditorium that was filled to explosive capacity, you sure could see a donnybrook flaring up if things didn't go Souths' way. From a distance he saw Jimmy Butler arrive. He hadn't seen the man for a couple of days. Jimmy made a dash for the loo on the other side of the room. All that damn tea.

Bob Ryan saw the bar attendant, too, and the look of irritation on the man's face well before he arrived. The attendant had better things to do than deliver phone messages. But you didn't want to get on Major Bob's bad side. He'd give a bloke a verbal biff in the ear, in front of your mates, too, no sweat. Nah, just deliver it and get back to the bar where those pulling beers were raking in the tips.

'Need to find Jimmy Butler,' the man shouted. 'Can I give you the message?'

The Major gestured towards the toilets. 'He's in the john. What's up?'

'It's the school. 'Bout Jimmy's nephew. Sounds urgent.'

Bob Ryan took the call, filling his free ear with a finger. 'Eh? Pardon? Missing? He's missing? He might be in the club. There are kids all over the place truanting from school.'

The woman told Major Bob that the boy'd left school unexpectedly the previous morning, that he hadn't returned that day. 'We've been trying to contact his uncle for two days. Even dropped by his home yesterday afternoon myself. Left a note when no one answered the door.'

Major Bob, red-faced, heaved his way towards Jimmy as the man came out of the toilet. Jimmy Butler saw the Major coming at him, wearing that scary determined look that he knew well. Jimmy's mouth went as dry as sand. His stomach became a tightened ball. He imagined himself poking the Major in the eye, Three Stooges fashion, then skedaddling out of there forever. He racked his brain, trying to think what it was he'd done wrong.

'Why did Johnnie leave school early yesterday?'

'He left school?'

'What? You didn't know?'

'Oooh, I was goin' down real bad yes'day. Had no sleep, just a little, walkin' room t'room, drinkin' tea like it's comin' outta me ears, drivin' me —'

'I'm talking about Johnnie! How long? How long since you've seen him?' The Major would've liked to have given him a good kick up the arse. Twenty years ago he might've grabbed Jimmy Butler by the collar of his shirt. Thirty years might've seen him biff the man. Useless as a glass door on a dunny.

'Ooh, let's see. Since brekkie yes'day ... nah, brekkie two days ... oi! Whereya goin'?'

The Major had Kon Tsakiris and Jimmy Butler gather on the footpath outside the clubhouse. He gave his instructions as to where they should search for the boy.

'Bob's your uncle!' said Kooka Kon, pleased at his joke.

Major Bob scowled. Kon backed off.

'I'll do the east,' Bob Ryan said. 'We'll meet at Tom's in ... what? Thirty minutes?'

Bob Ryan passed by the terrace Johnnie Butler had once lived in with his mother. Perhaps, the man thought, the boy was pining for her and was, that very moment, sitting at the front door, or in the backyard, waiting for her to return. It was a long shot, he knew, but worth the digression. He shuddered as he recalled finding, with Yaya Zoe, the boy's bunnies ripped in pieces, their blood smeared over those lovely murals Johnnie'd spent weeks creating on his bedroom walls.

Not finding him there, he walked as quickly as he could to Tom's. He saw them from a distance, Kon standing to one side, smoking, leaning on a telegraph pole, while Jimmy was bent over, talking to the boy who stared over the road. The Major, wheezing loudly, went down on one knee in front of the boy.

'You left the school, Johnnie. Are you okay?'

'You gunna be the death of me,' said Jimmy. He took the boy in his arms and held him hard. 'Sorry, Johnnie,' Jimmy Butler said, the boy's chin resting on the man's shoulder. 'Never noticed you was missin'. Tryin' to be a good dad to ya, yer know? Sorry, sport.'

'Where have you been Johnnie?' said the Major to the back of the boy's head. 'Where did you go?'

The boy pointed to Centennial Park.

Jimmy Butler let go of his nephew to see the extended arm pointing emphatically over the road. He and the Major exchanged a frown just as Old Tom, seeing them from his lounge room, appeared at his front door.

'What's the story, boys? Switched the telly off. Can't bear to watch. Say, what're you lot doin' here anyway? Why aren't you at the club? Decision's gunna be announced soon.'

'Tom, there's no time to talk,' said Major Bob. 'I'll explain when we get back. Now, lad, you stay with us. Give me your hand.'

They farewelled Tom, then set off. At the first turnoff, however, they were stopped short when they saw Yaya Zoe's slight figure clearly distinguished from a distance.

Jimmy knew that his mismatched St Vinnies cast-offs were no great shake, but this? What'd got into the old girl? And people reckoned *he* made a proper goat of himself every time he stepped out onto the footpath. Because here was Zoe, without her glasses, dressed to the nines. When he'd never seen her in anything other than her black clothes, what'd possessed her to get all dolled up in such a blaze of colour? He looked her up and down as she made her way closer to them, letting go of the boy's hand, trying to take it all in. That long scarf draped over her head, trailing the ground, the thick jacket, with fur stuck here and there, and those squiggly gold lines patterned all over the place. Pointy slippers, brightly coloured vest, a wide sheet of silk that had him thinking of a rainbow gone mad wrapped round and round her waist. And, fair dinkum, all that jewellery. He'd always known the old girl was as good as gold, but this was ridiculous. She was a bloody walking jewellery shop! There were gold rings on most of her fingers, bracelets on both wrists, a heavy chain and cross around her neck, long earrings dancing on the padded shoulders of her fur-lined coat. Bob Ryan let go of the boy's other hand. Jimmy Butler was delighted to see the man was lost for words.

'Zoe — what — why all this? Where — what's going on?'

But Kookaburra Kon knew. These were your traditional clothes, handed down from mother to daughter and worn by women on the day of their wedding. Yaya Zoe — a bride?

Some bloke driving a truck full of fruit and vegies slowed down to take a closer look at the Greek woman. A couple of truanting kids, making a backstreet secretive beeline for the club, came to an abrupt halt. Faces appeared in windows. Some people came out onto their verandahs.

To you she looks like something out of that illustrated book your teacher reads to you during the odd lunch, something about the Arabian Nights. Or about that boy who knows the magic words that roll back the rock that hides the cave full of treasures. She's grinning her toothless grin. She's beautiful, you reckon, and you suddenly remember Major telling you what a good looker she'd been when he'd first met her, not long after some war. It was always hard to imagine her young, and pretty, but now you look at her like she's some sort of fairy godmother. Your uncle's smiling, as happy as a dog with two tails, you reckon. You look at Kooka Kon, who's staring at Zoe, his jaw gaping. And Major, not knowing what to do or say.

And then you know. It all comes so suddenly to you, just as she takes your uncle's hand and shakes it, farewelling him. You wonder, as she kisses Kon on both cheeks before playfully slapping him across the back of the head, and tells him she hopes he wins the lottery one day, how it is that no one else realises what's going on. You become all wooden as you feel a great shadow sweep across your world. Your head throbs. You know she's leaving her farewell to you for last, but what are you going to do when she rests her eyes on yours and you know that that's the last time you'll ever look into her face? Something is laying its heaviness upon you. You feel a shapeless sadness embrace you. And, just as you'd expected, there it is, that long and deep exhalation, that heavy sigh of grieving.

And the others don't have a clue, do they. You wonder if death is going to hang around you all your life, like a rotten smell. You watch as she farewells Major, the muscles in your face tightening. You don't want to see this, you don't want to be here. You'd like to step outside of yourself and pretend it's not happening.

But it's the woman's love that drives the sighing away and keeps you there, seeing, understanding. She wishes Major a happy eightieth birthday. She's holding his hand in both of hers and you hear her say: 'You help me always. You good man.'

He protests, concerned that Yaya Zoe is not wearing her glasses, that's she's in danger, wearing all that gold.

She reaches up to kiss him. You've never seen Major like this. He's like a big boy, all vulnerable and lost. You see him silenced by her gesture. He bends down as the woman places her hands on his shoulders. Her eyes are closed for a long time, her lips on his cheek too long. You're only a little boy but this, you know, means something.

Kooka Kon stares at nothing. Your uncle's gone all serious. Everyone's standing there like statues. You feel the blood drain from your face when she turns to you. You want to retreat from what you're afraid she might say to you, but there's too much of the woman and right there in your face, too, all that glittering metal and colour and her shrivelled-up face softening into a huge gummy smile. She runs her hand over your head and it's then that you finally get it. How is it you'd never realised that for her you're the son she'd never had?

She strokes the side of your face, over and over, bends down and kisses you repeatedly on both cheeks and on your eyes, then tells you what you can barely contain yourself to hear: 'You love your mamma. Always you love her. She sad. Very sad. I know, I know. One day she come back. You listen. Yaya Zoe know. Okay?'

You watch her shuffle off. You stand at the street corner with the others as she walks past Old Tom's terrace. She pauses to shake his hand before resuming her walk towards Cleveland Street. You hear Major's faraway voice, barking instructions. Kooka Kon rushes after her. Your uncle goes into Tom's to ring the Greek priest.

And you, you wonder how it is you don't cry. You know what it means to have the stuffing knocked out of you. You think of Billy. Just one more death, one more departure in a life full of farewells. You stare at the lengthening space between yourself and the woman. You watch as she waves at passers-by, shakes hands with some who've come out to stand at their gates. She slows down the traffic.

And there it is: she stops, turns, and though she's too far away for you to see, you know she's smiling at you. You can imagine the many kind lines around her mouth and at the corners of her eyes.

You look up at Major. He blinks. His bottom lip has a life of its own.

TWO

Zoe Poulos (nee Zantakis) shows off her hair

Was it a process Zoe Poulos was immediately conscious of, this shaking off of the years as she walked? Did she knowingly discard them so that they dissolved there on the footpath, while Major Bob's, Kon's and Jimmy's cries for her to *come back, come back,* went unheard? Was she aware that she was allowing herself to tumble back in time as she turned left into Cleveland Street, conjuring up those events that marked the years?

She is on a boat. She is a young woman, sent out to Australia to marry that man Yorgos Papadopoulos, known widely as George Poulos. She shakes her head of his intrusiveness to find herself even further back in time, as a bride on the Greek island of Kastellorizo, the future unfolding before her in a blaze of sunshine, blue waters and bright expectations.

She walked past the Vietnamese baker and the Turkish butcher on Clevo and into a world of the imagination, as some fact in a story to be told and retold by all who saw her on this memorable spring morning. The footpath on which she walked became narrowed, cobbled with marble flagstones, reflecting the dazzle of a Kastellorizian sun.

And as long as people knew how to tell a tale, Zoe Poulos would remain a small part of that great book of stories and myths that spill out onto, or emerge from, the streets of Redfern; that on the day a great stillness and silence descended on that inner-city suburb of Sydney, Yaya Zoe walked in and out of shops and memory, pursued by Kookaburra Kon and, later, the Greek priest, holding down his distressed stovepipe hat. People walked away from their tellies in the snooker rooms and pubs to stand on the footpath and watch. Others looked down from the balconies attached to second-storey cafes, having abandoned the game of backgammon and the Turkish coffee to follow the woman's progress. She wandered in and out of the factories and warehouses which stood, shoulder to shoulder, with derelict terraces, recently opened restaurants, art galleries and second-hand goods stores, enriching the ongoing tale of *Reth-fen*, as she called it, with its thugs and footy heroes, its gangs and Quakers, its Irish working class, its blacks, Asians, Serbs and Croats, Greeks and Lebs, and its more recent influx of young professionals with their restored terrace, fancy car and fashionable dog: all emerging to gape at yet another unfolding chapter in the life of this suburb.

Yannis Zantakis' caique had once butted the coasts of the Middle East where his gold-capped teeth, raucous laugh and love of alcohol distinguished him. He'd return to Kastellorizo with the sole intention, it seemed to his wife, of more futile attempts at impregnating her with a son.

The 1920s and 1930s saw the quick demise of an already stumbling economy. There was an exodus to that larger island — *Afstralia* — on the other side of the world. Yannis Zantakis was forced to sell his boat to pay off debts. He began stalking the narrow paths of the town. He fell out of one café and into another, supported by a bottle of raki, diminishing wads of drachmas or whoever happened to be there. By the time war broke out the money and gold had been largely consumed; except for the leather pouch of gold coins his wife had, over many years, secretly saved and hidden. Yannis Zantakis marched off one day, to the great relief of his wife and distress of his daughter, Zoe, to get at those *Ghermanous*, and was never seen again.

One day, well after mainland Greece had been overrun, the German planes flew over the island itself, destroying most of the town. Zoe Zantakis' mother died under the weight of a collapsing wall. Zoe found the leather pouch in the gaping hole of the floorboards.

She moved in with her Aunt Eudokia who had many daughters of her own. Without her mother's strict guidance, Zoe Zantakis had the audacity to linger around the cafes, playing with her fair hair. Her teeth dazzled. Her aunt feared a scandal. She consulted her sisters.

How were they to marry off someone as old as Zoe Zantakis, who was well into her twenties and who had no dowry to offer a prospective husband? On an island already depleted of young eligible men? One of them wrote of the family's problem to an old Kastellorizian in Sydney.

The arrival of a letter (via a marriage broker) from a Yorgos Papadopoulos, who'd been born in Athens of Kastellorizian parents, asking for her hand in marriage, could only have occurred owing to the intercession of the Mother of God. Did Zoe Zantakis have any choice? If no other offer came, what would become of her? Where would she live? Who would support her? Her Aunt Eudokia strongly advised her to accept.

A week after the letter's arrival, Zoe and the oldest woman on the island saw, while praying in Saint Constantine's Church, the Mother of God smile and nod her head. Final confirmation came when Zoe saw God's will clearly evident in the favourable pattern in the gritty residue of an upturned cup of Turkish coffee.

After an exchange of black-and-white prints the engagement was confirmed. Most on the island were overjoyed for Zoe. The aunt with whom she lived was relieved.

Zoe Zantakis had her worries, though, which she kept to herself. Yes, she would marry this Greek-Australian. But there was that round full chin and those thin lips, and that silly crooked smile. He stood in a three-piece white suit, his left leg raised onto the side of a buhl footstool. Black wavy hair, heavily oiled and receding, was swept back from his forehead. As for his eyes: well, they were, the young woman thought, like those of a startled goat.

She went from house to house to bid her farewells. She laughed generously and shook her hair to and fro, impatiently accepting their advice and gifts when she was thinking of other things: that man Yorgos Papadopoulos' large two-storey home, for instance, and his thriving meatworks business, which he had described in his second letter. Zoe Zantakis saw herself sitting crossed-legged in the lounge rooms of the finest families in Greek-Australian society, wearing those gowns she'd seen in English magazines. And with her husband she'd be noticed here and there, hanging onto his arm, attending this ball and that dance. And the sons she'd give him would go to the universities other Kastellorizians now living in Australia had written to their own families about. Her boys would become lawyers or doctors, join church committees so that people would nudge each other and say, *Look, look, there are Zoe Papadopoulos' sons. What fine young men they are!*

Zoe Zantakis packed her trunk for that long voyage, taking great care when folding those traditional Kastellorizian clothes that had been handed down over many more generations than anyone could remember. In a secret compartment in the lid of the trunk she hid the pouch of gold coins. The jewellery was sewn into the fur lining of her jacket.

Zoe stood on the caique with three other proxy brides. As it sailed out of the harbour her Aunt Eudokia wondered when she could take possession of, and restore, Zoe's family home, to use as a dowry for her own eldest daughter.

George's do-drop-in hot-dog stand

George Poulos alighted from the cab. He'd come to the wharf early, dressed in his finest suit (even if it was over twelve years old), to give himself time to calm his nerves, to practise the look he'd give his bride and to rehearse, in some corner, the little speech he'd prepared.

On this, our first meeting, let me say how honoured I am ...

He shrugged his shoulders, tugged at the lapels of his jacket and passed his hand backwards and forwards over his balding head. The collar of his shirt was sweat-stained. He gnawed at a fingernail. He took out his worry beads and threw them about with some fury.

It is not in my nature to give long and lengthy speeches ...

He arrived in Sydney shortly after the end of the Great War as a youthful sixteen-year-old, his passage paid by relatives in Athens. He was to work, save, help put up others who would follow him, perhaps even assist them in finding work. George Poulos was glad to be rid of the lot of them.

It was while he was working at the Pyrmont waterfront that he discovered beer. His fellow workers, freckled men who spoke out of the corner of their mouths, forced him to get rid of that string of worry beads he sometimes played with, like he was some sheila, and change his name, too.

He tried to be liked. He knew he tried too hard. George Poulos couldn't help but smile more broadly than he would have preferred, never quite becoming the distant bloke he aspired to be. He tried making up for his shortcomings by shouting them all at the pub.

The letters kept arriving from the rels in Athens. He threw them away without opening them.

George Poulos' body became languid, his stomach overflowed. It was all that beer, he knew, and Tony Bragg's hot-dogs that he got stuck into before, during and after Souths' home games. Sometimes, when Bragg was busy with some other scheme to make a quid or two, George Poulos took over the running of the hot-dog stand. He enjoyed the activity. People noticed him. And the money wasn't bad, either.

It was a few years before the war when the Greek thought it was time to settle down and go into business, maybe even make a quid himself. He'd save the deposit, buy the hot-dog stand Tony Bragg'd been trying to flog for months, pay it off week by week. Yeah, why not. And being located right outside the grounds where Souths played and trained would give him the opportunity to consolidate his role in the Rabbitohs family. George's do-drop-in hot-dog stand. Sounded like a goer. Yeah, the future was bloody rosy. *Bhhh-uuurp.*

Mayte, yer a-goner

George Poulos stood on the wharf watching the approaching liner. The glare off the water made his eyes weep. He was glistening with sweat. He felt like a cooked goose.

He passed his hand backwards and forwards over the top of his head again then took out that photo of his fiancée. Three younger Greek men gathered to one side, waiting for their own brides. They stood amongst their parents, sisters and brothers, aunts, uncles, cousins and friends, making such a Greek racket that George Poulos was embarrassed. He could tell the expectant grooms from the others: they stood in their dark suits and hats, white shirts and polished shoes, no doubt purchased for the occasion, so that George Poulos looked at the shabbiness of his white suit and wondered whether he looked like some reffo.

He closed his eyes to the sun and the pleasant slight breeze, and thought of other things. George Poulos smiled as he imagined his bride serving his customers. Old Bragg and others thought he wasn't up to running his own show, but he'd shown them, too right, even seeing his way through the difficult war years (he got out of doing military service by turning up at the enlistment centre wearing borrowed thick glasses and limping on a walking stick). He saw her enquiring of the customers — pickles? tomato sauce? — then taking the sausage out of the hot water and slapping it into the pre-sliced bun. She'd look up and they'd be startled to see her beauty, because she was such a good-looking sheila.

He took his mind further into the future, too, where he saw the sons his wife would give him sitting at his feet as he sliced the rolls, asking questions about the good old days. Perhaps after they'd left school they could join him in the business. He could live the life of Riley (who was Riley, anyway?), lobbing into The Bat and Ball to shout beers like a millionaire. He was grinning his lopsided grin.

George Poulos wiped the sweat off his brow, plastered down the few strands of grey hair on his head then searched anxiously through his pockets. He found his small bottle of cheap pomade which he proceeded to spread liberally over his scalp and, when he thought no one was looking, under the armpits of his jacket.

He could visualise the eyes of the woman whom he was only minutes away from meeting. He stood breathing through his open mouth. He shuddered at the thought of her young body and his sagging gut; this, yes, and that photograph of himself he'd sent her, taken all those years ago.

George Poulos lifted the collar of his coat in a vain attempt to hide the wrinkles on his neck. He passed, once again, his hand back and forth over his hair, in the process pushing the isolated strands of hair forward so that they stood at a conspicuous angle to his glistening scalp.

The liner was ploughing its way through the morning and his lies.

Mayte, he thought, yer a-goner.

Zoe meets her husband

The city, Zoe Zantakis saw, overflowed with a greyness of blunt buildings and shops, of churches whose steeples scraped the low sky. The inhibitions and anxieties of three of the four women were cast aside as, recognising their men, they squeezed the arms of the women on either side of them, letting out little shrieks. Only Zoe Zantakis stood quietly by, unable to associate the older George Poulos on the wharf with the Yorgos Papadopoulos in her photo. The other women were now making little hopping movements on their toes and hammering the rails with their clenched fists. Cries of *There's mine! There's mine!* were heard from both the boat and the wharf.

And still Zoe Zantakis stood, clutching the gold crucifix hanging loosely around her neck, scanning the faces in the group. And then she looked again at that older man standing to one side on his own. There he was, Yorgos Papadopoulos, looking up at her. He was grinning broadly. The hair on his scalp moved with the breeze.

Zoe Zantakis walked down the gangplank to meet her husband. She looked into his eyes.

In them, she saw the years and years and years.

THREE

Ghhhaaarn the Rabbitohs!

FRIDAY, 3 NOVEMBER 2000

The real matter of contention between the parties was whether commercial interests should be permitted to commodify something that Souths considers is valued in a section of the community. Souths' view as put in correspondence with the National Rugby League was that Rugby League is an icon to be preserved for the people who love and support it, not a product to be carved up to the media for their own financial gratification. It is usually only fortuitous that some legal principle can be found that could provide such preservation as is sought. This is not one of the fortuitous cases. The order of the court will be that the application be dismissed.

Justice Paul Finn

It's as if you and your uncle are watching one of those pre-dawn movies with the sound turned down. It might be the biggest crowd you've ever seen, the Souths' auditorium might be groaning and heaving and thumping like some monstrous engine, yet it makes no difference — you still feel yourself fading away. The place can't hold you. You give in, willing yourself to drift, like the receding footsteps of someone walking out of your life. You're alone, listening to your own shallow breathing, feeling yourself on a knife-edge separating two worlds. Train stations pass in a blur. Indistinct rooms with yellow-stained mattresses on the floor throb in time with the weeping in an adjoining room of a lonely old man. Your legs ache from the effort of arriving and departing. Weeks and months and years of finding refuge in glass-shattered bus shelters, under newspapers on park benches, on the exposed coils of knife-slashed back seats of dumped cars. Your soiled undies stick to your arse. You lick the inside of an empty milk container that's been torn apart. Someone's weeping closes in on you, breath brushes your ear. You're not alone after all. It's your mamma, her comforting arms reaching for you out of a layered past, her voice, with that of Billy's, gnawing at the edges of your silent world. You feel your own voice gurgling in the depths of your guts. You whimper like a stricken animal. You're floating now, and hands on either side of you grab hold of yours to hold you down in case you drift right away. Your head pounds. *I'm comin', Billy, I'll cross that road. I gotta, mate. Didn't mean what I said.*

You pull away from the edge. You look, see yourself sitting between Major, who looks old and bushed, and your bewildered uncle, whose legs are as restless as a rattlesnake. You know you're safe; that these blokes'll always be there for you. It's a good thing that they're looking at the biggest telly screen you've ever seen at the front of the auditorium, otherwise they'd've seen your eyes fill with tears.

Old Tom sat alone on his verandah, open-mouthed, waiting for his mates' return from the club, wondering what the hell had got into Zoe getting all dolled up in that Greekie gear. He'd get up if he could be bothered, go into the house and come back from his bathroom with a piece of tissue paper and a comb, which he preferred to the harmonica, and play a mournful tune. It might be a bonzer day, all sunshine and blue sky and lovely spring warmth, but he felt as crook as a mangy dog. Zoe was off her rocker. Souths, he knew, were dead meat and they were gunna be given the arse, you could bet your boots on it. He backfired a series of farts and felt the better for it.

Kooka Kon and the Greek priest led Yaya Zoe to her home. She insisted she was okay, that she be left to herself. No, she would not go walking the streets dressed in those clothes and jewellery. Yes, she promised to stay indoors until Kon returned in an hour or so to check up on her.

She went to the icon box in her bedroom and slid open the glass door. She smiled as she lit the wick floating in a bowl of olive oil, sighing as she murmured a prayer, her eyes wide as the wick flared, illuminating the unsmiling faces of ancient expressionless saints and a melancholy Jesus in the recesses of that wooden box on her wall. She knelt before this iconostasio. The old woman, this bride of Christ, heard Saint George reply to her supplication. She heard his horse neigh. She was ready to be taken to her Lord. She was ready to die.

Kon Tsakiris sat in the chair the Major'd kept for him. The men looked towards him, their faces asking about Yaya Zoe. He gave them the thumbs-up and smiled, nodding his head several times.

Kon felt happy. Decisions had been made on this day, problems confronted and resolved. He'd been moved by what he'd seen. Embarrassed, yes, but who could not feel sympathy for someone like Zoe Poulos? She might give him a hard time because he was such a whinger. She had little time for him whenever he went on about his dreams of becoming a big shot but sat around, doing fuck-all. But she was right, wasn't she, to be so dismissive of such dreams? He'd botched up, hadn't he? The whole idea of coming out to Australia in the first place was to make it big and return to the respect and envy of all those rels and friends in the village. It was never really the money. Now he spent much of his time hanging around, like he was waiting for a cab that would never come. Truth be told, he enjoyed her playful harassing and scolding. Major Bob reckoned she'd been a stunner in her youth. You'd never guess it, looking at her now. And here she was, losing her marbles. Who knew what was going to happen to any of them? It was time to ditch all that dreaming (he would spend hours planning what he'd do with his winnings from all those long shots). He'd failed, after all, at every attempt he'd ever made to make a quid, with the solid reliability of a confirmed no-hoper. Seeing Zoe all done up with those bridal clothes was more than a jolt. The man realised it was time for him to wake up. Time to quit wasting his money on lottery tickets and the gee-gees and the occasional all-night game of poker with his Greek mates. Time to accept he'd only ever be able to put food on the table and pay the essential bills. Well, so be it! He'd do it — invest what he'd squirrelled away into some blue-chip company, perhaps HIH, go to the Holy Trinity Church at Surry Hills and light a couple of candles for good luck and get himself a part-time job. It was sensible.

Kon Tsakiris felt good and clean inside, relieved, too. He looked across at the Major, the little kid and the boy's gangly uncle. His wife and children, a few Greek blokes from the old days and the Committee — it was all he had, really.

Victor Batrouney's lie

Victor Batrouney observed the old and young sitting uneasily in the gallery. A handful of women to his left knitted scarves with some fury. Probably hoped to wear them for Souths' first game after being reinstated into the comp. He saw them exchange intense knowing looks, their lips tightly contracted. He overheard them debating how Justice Finn'd enter the courtroom. One reckoned he'd come in with a deliberate slow walk, emphasising the importance of the occasion, led, she said, by a couple of blokes in robes holding something in brass. The women caught him looking at them. They smiled, giving him encouraging nods of the head. One of these women did not recognise Victor Batrouney, but he remembered her — she'd lived down the road from where he'd been brought up, had a wooden fence painted red and green. He remembered as a terrified kid taking refuge in a shop after her dog had chased him halfway around the block.

Ned the Neck interrupted Victor Batrouney's reminiscences by digging an elbow into his ribs. He was smirking at a fellow who was making repeated visits to the loo who, Victor was impressed to see, bowed towards the empty chair Justice Finn would soon fill.

When the man returned and sat two rows in front, Ned said, sniggering, 'Oi! Mate! Yeah, you. Yer bowed to the chair.'

'Yeah, what of it?'

'To that big chair, that fucker over there behind that bloody wooden bench thing.'

'Yeah, so?'

'It's empty.'

'Out of respect. You bow out of respect.'

'To an empty chair?' Ned laughed. The man glared.

Victor Batrouney'd followed the regular reports of the five-week trial in the papers. Some writers'd focused on the supporters. He knew that for many of these diehards it'd been a long haul. He'd read how some of these oldies'd come practically every day with provisions of devon and tomato and corn beef sandwiches, a thermos of sweet black tea and some Cadbury's dark chocolate to see them through the long day. Some brought a blanket — a red and green blanket — to throw over the legs when it got a wee bit cold. Victor Batrouney imagined them listening to the evidence and statements, trying to make sense of that which made no sense to them at all. They must've wondered, he thought, about the law and the little bloke it was meant to protect. And yet they came, day after day, remaining loyal to their roots in a way that shamed him. He thought of his father, dying in that Jap camp. He thought of his mother who'd died so young, and with so much bitterness towards him.

One tall old fellow sitting behind Victor Batrouney took out a postcard which he'd brought along to show. 'It's from me father. Wrote it when he was eighteen, fightin' at Pozieres, in the Great War. It's a family heirloom. You can read it, but don't touch.'

Victor Batrouney stood, turned and took his turn to read the card, which the old man held with a piece of tissue paper. Victor shook his head and clicked his tongue in wonder that a young man in the trenches could write home, in those beautiful loops and skating figures (they reminded him of the letter his own father had written to the child he knew he'd never see, not long before he died) asking about the health of Father and Mother, before writing: *And how are Souths going?*

The tall man held the card for Ned to read, casting sideways glances at Victor Batrouney. 'Say,' he said, 'do I know you?'

'Sorry?'

'You live in Redfern?'

'Me? No.'

'Ever live in Redfern?'

And before he knew what he'd done, Victor Batrouney found himself saying no.

Others, younger than Victor Batrouney, discussed the great games played years, if not decades, before.

'Clive Churchill wouldn't come off the field, even though he broke his wrist early in the game,' one young man said.

'It was,' Victor Batrouney leaned forward to say, avoiding the postcard man's considered frown, 'in a tackle five minutes after kick-off.'

'Is that right?'

'First time he was tackled in the game.'

'Yeah, that's right,' replied another fellow. 'I've read about it, too.'

'I was lucky enough to be there,' Victor Batrouney said.

'You were there? On the day?'

'Yes I was.'

'Tell us, tell us.'

Justice Paul Finn's sudden entrance into Courtroom 21A brought an abrupt end to his story. And like everyone else who was watching, he was taken aback by the Justice's entry. He wasn't expecting a blast of trumpets, but even he'd seen himself rising with all the other supporters in the sudden fearful silence, bowing as one (deeply, like he'd once bowed to the priest during a Maronite liturgy), then settling for a long delivery. He was unprepared for the man's unheralded hasty appearance, the slight bob of his head to the room and that briefest of judgements, before shooting through. The Justice was in and out before you could say we was robbed.

The memory of what happened to Billy returns in a rush, just as Finn enters. The jostling, the to-and-froing ceases. The bars are quiet. A thick pall of cigarette smoke hangs over people's heads and to you it looks like a bad sign. You look around the room. Everyone's staring hard at the screen as a bloke in robes starts to mumble in his papers.

Maybe it's the sudden end to all the noise that has it all coming back. Something had to fill that great big hole and for you it's not so much a rush of moving sequential images as a series of disconnected snapshots, frozen still. Only this time you won't give yourself a bum steer, playing funny buggers with what you've been avoiding these last thirteen months. If you're going to summon the guts to do what Billy and Major've told you never to do and walk out of Redfern; if you're going to go to that Moreton Bay fig tree in Centennial Park and make your peace with your brother, then you sure as hell aren't going to do it by turning whacko whenever the memories get too prickly.

You're licking your lips to make ready the easy passage of those words that are taking a firmer shape in the back of your throat. Anyone looking at you'd reckon you're staring at nothing, but you, you hear the wind whistling and sighing in the leaves and branches of Billy's Tree. The floor beneath your feet grinds, tilts towards the park.

There was no cry of despair or outburst of anger in Courtroom 21A, as some had expected. There was, however, that lengthy stunned silence that people would long talk about. They knew Souths'd come a buster, but there was no making out all that that galoot of a judge'd said before he bolted. And Victor Batrouney, who did understand, wondered how there did not exist that one law, amongst those thousands of laws that could be found in those trolley-loads of folders and books these lawyers dragged in each day, to save a footy team.

'It just don't make sense,' said the man with the postcard from Pozieres.

'It just isn't right,' said the man who wanted to hear Victor's story of Clive Churchill.

'An' I thought we was a deadset cert, y'know? Thought it was goin' our way,' said Ned the Neck.

Victor Batrouney shook hands with them all. Ned was close to tears.

As they were getting up to leave, the postcard man approached

Victor. 'Batrouney. You're Leo Batrouney's boy. I remember your father around the corner from ...'

Victor Batrouney gave a tight-lipped smile then fled from the gallery with Ned Rivers.

The supporters from the courtroom made a wearisome walk down the long corridor to the lifts. To Victor Batrouney it felt like they were at a funeral. The only sounds he could hear were the shuffling of feet, someone's muffled crying and soft murmurs of incomprehension. He looked behind him, as much to ensure that the postcard man was not close by as to survey that stunned and mournful body of men and women and kids, ludicrous in their red and green banners and flags and clothes and posters, like it was some sort of circus procession that'd taken a wrong turn and lost its way. But the faces — Victor Batrouney saw the ferocity and tenaciousness growing by the moment; and then he knew why he'd come: sure, it had to do with his old man, and his youth, too, which he could never quite let go of. But it wasn't just personal. It *did* have something to do with Souths. There *was* the bullshit and the straight-in-your-face lies he couldn't stomach, and those articulate corporate men who thought of this game as a commodity and'd turned dingo on the Rabbitohs.

On the footpath outside the Law Court building Victor Batrouney saw the women who'd been knitting the scarves, sobbing in each other's arms. The postcard man, red-eyed, was gazing thoughtfully from a distance at Victor, who lowered his head to stare at the ground, his lips a hard thin line. On looking up he was surprised to see Ned the Neck at the top of the steps, making a statement to one of the telly reporters.

'Rugby league,' he said, 'is dyin' in the bush 'cause those mongrels who run this great game of ours are treatin' it like a business. Well, it ain't. I'm just a supporter, y'know, but I know one thing, this club'll never sacrifice its name or its colours to those bastards down at head office. We'll never play in a substandard competition. We'll never merge with another club. We got rissoled today in this court. Let's go to the court of public opinion. Let's fight on.'

Johnnie Butler finds his voice

'What's that silly wombat sayin', Bob?' said one old woman.

'We're gone,' he replied.

What the Major could not understand was why there'd been no words of comfort from the Justice for the supporters. If Finn had to deliver such a blow, thought Bob Ryan, could he not have taken the time, once the official proceedings were over, to offer words of comfort? To place the arm of the law over the collective shoulder, to look them in the eye, to throw off the indecipherable legal bullshit and show, if nothing else, that the loss and pain were felt and understood?

''Ardly missed a game for fifty-three years, Bob,' said the woman. 'That silly ol' gaffer's put us in the doghouse,' she said, sobbing in little convulsions. The Major put his arm around the woman then bent down to speak to her. And when he'd finished she smiled up at him, her eyes glistening, and hugged him hard. There was, Major Bob knew, no avoiding what he had to do.

He made his way to the front of the auditorium with that fierce look Kon Tsakiris knew well. The Greek watched as Major Bob nodded here and there, shaking hands with practically everyone within easy reach. He might be a pain in the arse sometimes, Kon thought, a wowser who'd work you over until you gave him the answer he wanted to hear, but, you had to hand it to the old coot, he wasn't someone who'd sit back and let things happen. He was as sturdy and as dependable as that copper boiler in his laundry he refused to get rid of, which is how Kon often saw the Major: Bob Ryan, that ancient, dependable copper tub. Many of the oldies, Kooka Kon saw, were turning to the Major for some direction, with the faces of children lost in the dark.

Jimmy watched too as the Major got to the front and demanded the microphone. He saw him in profile. Jimmy Butler thought of Alfred Hitchcock, boiled mutton, Brylcreem and starched collars; and a younger Bob Ryan who, years before, came looking for and found him in far-western New South Wales, offering him a possie with the Bunnies. And how, after Bob'd given him the chance of a lifetime, he'd blown it. And here was the Major, still taking charge of things like he was the sheriff of Redfern. Jimmy envied, admired, looked up to and was often infuriated by the man. One thing a bloke could say about the big man, though, was that he was true blue. Yeah, there was no bullshit about Major Bob Ryan alright.

The Major thought about all the money that'd been spent fighting the good fight. Going in tooth and nail hadn't been enough to win. The club could well be on its knees, he thought. All this, all this, to keep a bloody footy team on the paddock. A man could understand fighting the Japs to keep his country safe and free. A man could comprehend fighting a suffocating guilt to make up for the sins of the past. But this? All this just so's a footy club can stay alive?

'Well,' he began, 'there was that game against Newtown in '31, when we had three men injured off the park, and we were down 12–3 ...'

You know you love the man. He might insist you drop in after brekkie with Yaya Zoe and show him your milk moustache. He might grind his teeth whenever there's a mention of your uncle being on welfare. He might be as mean as cat shit and have you standing outside the grocery store for ages while he checks the addition of the receipt and every cent in the change. He might tell you and everyone else in the world how to live their life, like a door-knocking Christian. But there was also something about the man that had you thinking of Uluru. And it wasn't just that big arse and pillowed gut of his. There was something immovable and permanent about the bloke.

You see yourself in years to come telling your own grandkids of the events leading up to you facing your past; the day you'd watched as Major Bob Ryan told a huge gathering of the fight-backs he'd witnessed, how he told them what they wanted and needed to hear. And your silent world opening up, revealing its secrets, and you regaining your voice.

The Major knew the trick of pausing after this word, that phrase, of the long silent sweep of his eyes to make some personal contact with his audience. It was what he'd learnt to do at that Jap hellhole in Burma to give comfort to those who were hanging in. And when the stories were done he stood there, on the stage, sweating in the heat of memories that were burning a hole on the inside of his skull. His legs were turning piss-weak. The back of his shirt was drenched. But there was more that was needed to be done.

There was a time when Bobby Ryan led the concerts in the Redfern Town Hall. People'd drop by the Ryan home of an arvo, too, in the hope of hearing him sing, accompanied by his mother on piano (when Father was out bush, on work; he thought singalongs were frivolous). And Mrs Ryan and her son would often oblige, just one song if young Bobby was in too much of a hurry for footy training.

But Bob Ryan hadn't sung for yonks. He was relieved that it didn't take him more than a couple of bars to find a passable voice, so that some of the older women suddenly remembered why they had, in their pre-war youth, fallen in love with Bobby Ryan. And it didn't take them long, either, the Major was pleased to see, to join him in singing the Rabbitohs' anthem. It was a horrible racket, with blokes he knew who'd never dare join in a song now belting out that hymn, singing out of tune and barely in time, the shrill sounds of the grannies rediscovering their own voices. But he couldn't give a stuff. It was a great din that shook the building and stirred the blood. That's what counted. It was an act of defiance and solidarity. No one needed to be told.

The thunderous applause that shakes the building has goose bumps running up and down your arms and on the back of your neck. You feel your lips forming the silent words *hip-hip-hooray* when someone calls for three cheers for Major Bob, three cheers for the Mighty Bunnies and three cheers for the struggle ahead. You look around the room and the sad faces of moments ago are all gone. They're fighting mad. There's resolve in their eyes and hard grins on the faces. People are slapping Major on the back, others are pumping his arm, some old women, their eyes shining, are kissing him. Kooka Kon and your Uncle Jimmy are standing on chairs, soaking it all in and you, you're feeling like there's so much goodness in people, you dream of a better world. There you are, in Centennial Park near the tree where you found Billy, only now you're on a picnic blanket. It's a corker of a day. There's an abundance of food on throwaway plates. Nanna Dora's sitting regally on a wicker chair, smiling, her face a mass of kindly wrinkles. Old Tom, smelling of mothballs and wearing his ug boots is in a wheelchair, a glass of black and tan on a little table to his side, ripping out a tune on his harmonica that's got everyone either clapping, clicking their fingers or moving their heads and feet in time. Yaya Zoe stops her darning to snap at Kooka Kon about something-or-other and everyone, even Kon himself, laughs. Mista Tom stops his playing, grins his gums at the world then drops his guts before resuming his song. Jimmy gets up and, like the day itself that's so gloriously warm and kind, kicks his heels and prances around like a wilful puppet on a string, all uncoordinated arms and legs dangerous to get too close to. And you, you're off with the fairies, knowing that all those who've told you it's a dog-eat-dog world are wrong because there, across the great sweep of grass, beyond the kids shrilling on the cricket pitch you see your mamma walking towards you, her arms outstretched for you to run into, and from Billy's tree comes your brother's voice, telling you of his forgiveness.

The Major fell to his chair. 'Glass of water, please, Kon, if you don't mind.'

'You okay, Bob?' asked Jimmy Butler. He'd seen the Major's lips making lizardy little movements, like he was rattling off a rapid-fire run of Hail Marys or making all sorts of promises to God. Jimmy saw the man's stomach heave.

Major Bob nodded to Jimmy, drank the water Kon brought to him then looked into the boy's ashen face.

'I'm fine, Johnnie, I'm okay now.' He put an arm over Johnnie Butler's shoulder and patted him on the back.

But his breathing, Jimmy saw, remained erratic.

'Bob?' said Jimmy Butler. 'We got a little surprise for ya.'

The Major sat, eyes shut, weary and deaf to the man's voice.

'Bob?'

'Surprise?' He opened his eyes. 'What surprise?'

'C'mon mate. All them people waitin' for ya.'

Major Bob stood with his arm still around the boy's shoulders to steady himself. He followed Jimmy Butler and Kon Tsakiris to the club's boardroom, whose double doors were closed.

'You wait 'ere, matey,' said Jimmy. 'Don'cha move, okay?'

Jimmy and Kooka Kon opened one of the two doors just enough to let themselves in, then quickly shut it.

Moments later both doors were suddenly and dramatically

flung open. Major Bob saw a table laden with food. In the centre was a huge birthday cake. Behind the table stood his many friends. At the signal of Victor Batrouney, who'd arrived just in time from the city, they threw streamers over the table and out the double doors, some curling over Bob Ryan's shoulders.

'Happy birthday, Major Bob!'

You look up and watch the man stare, unblinking, into the beaming faces of those behind the table. You feel Major Bob's weight as he slowly brushes aside those streamers on his shoulders with his free hand. He begins to tremble. His mouth falls open. He inhales deeply, quickly and noisily, a great wheezing sound that has the others leaping towards him. You feel the convulsions grip his body and he falls to the floor. He kneels, one hand on the floor for support, the other still on your shoulder, now sobbing. You let go of his grip and, at the same time as you throw your arms around his neck, your voice is finally released.

'No! No! Na-ooohhh!'

FOUR

God'll see us through, Leo

SHINO SONKURAI, 1941

Deliver me from my frailties, dear Lord Jesus Christ. Behold in what corrupt flesh You have placed me. Does it not suffice that I have such a terrible enemy within to conquer but that You strike down Leo Batrouney, one so sweet in nature?

The convulsions returned, the sweat glistening on Leo Batrouney's near-naked body, the bamboo stretcher he lay on squeaking and squealing. Bob Ryan was grateful to be able to keep himself busy by taking the rag out of the bucket of water next to the stretcher and bathing the man's emaciated body once again, feeling his mate's racing heart. He rested his hand on Leo's forehead, took comfort in inhaling his mate's breath, saw the marbled eyelids, as fragile and as beautiful as a flower, felt cleansed by his act of love.

'Bob?' Leo'd opened his eyes. 'They've gotta operate, eh?'

Bob Ryan looked at the ground, nodded his head.

'You'll be here when they do it? Promise?'

'I'll be here, Leo.'

Leo Batrouney paused, gathered his strength, continued. 'Remember how my father wanted me to study Law? It's Shamla

… before we left Sydney for Singapore … her pregnancy.' He stopped, coughed, brought up blood.

Bob Ryan wiped the man's mouth clean. 'We can talk about this tomorrow, Leo, when —'

'Listen, Bob. Dad'd be proud, me too, if my kid went to uni. I've got a letter. You'll take it to Shamla … when you get back? You know, in case I don't pull through.'

A voice from one of the dark corners of the tent suddenly tore into the night. 'When are you two gunna fucken shut up! Jesus Christ, can a bloke get some sleep!'

Bob Ryan'd been enthusiastic about enlisting, encouraging his mate to do likewise, much to the rage of the Batrouney clan. And it wasn't just because of his keen sense of duty. Truth was, Bobby Ryan was glad to get as far away as he could from his old man and the memory of those sweet-smelling priestly hands that could suddenly turn nasty. There'd been all that suffocating talk of My Father's House, and how a thing done must be done quickly and well — and there was only ever one way of doing things, whether it was sitting straight-backed in a chair and eating (food to the mouth, Robert, not mouth to the food), or praying, the hands knotted (higher lad, there, on your navel, away from your naughty parts).

On the day they departed from Sydney, Senior Constable Francis Ryan stood to attention, all laired up in his copper's uniform and, in response to his son's extended hand, which he chose to ignore, stiffly saluted. His mother embraced her only child, embarrassing her husband with her woman's weeping.

The Batrouney family was there in great numbers, standing on the wharf some distance from the Ryans. Shamla refused to return Bob Ryan's wave.

After the fall of Singapore, the Japs loaded the prisoners onto the rice trucks at the Singapore Railway Station. They arrived at Shino Sonkurai on the Thai–Burma border hungry and dehydrated, the guards driving them bonkers with their barking and headcounts. They began work on their arrival, joining those other prisoners in clearing the forests and making those roads that would be used to bring in supplies for the building of the railway line.

At the end of each day Bob Ryan'd wander down to the river alone to bathe in a spot he knew he could strip off, unseen. He'd sit in the shallows watching the darkness fall, keeping an eye on those prisoners through the shrubs who, unashamed, bathed naked in groups. Once cleansed of the mud and filth, he'd pray. He knew God'd sent him to this place for a purpose, prayed that he would be worthy of the task given to him.

Men judge me worthy but You see the confusion which wracks my soul (and body) and how I suffer. I beseech You for strength that my endeavours to cleanse my spirit (and body) please You.

Bob Ryan turning into his old man

He knew discipline was the key to surviving. Hanging on, mentally and physically. The Japs were bastards. That was a constant. There was a strange comfort in knowing that. But what about a man's mates?

On some days, with the stomach full of wild yams, say, or after they'd got stuck into the bats they'd caught, skinned, gutted then boiled in onion water, he'd see the blokes getting on like a string of penny bungers. It was like God'd answered his prayers, or some inroads'd been made by the sermons he'd been giving, timing them (ten minutes after dinner each night) with that silver Waltham fob watch he'd manage to save, and which was permanently wound.

They'd share whatever food they had, putting up with the fact that they lived in each other's pockets (Curley Johnson's joke) or, more likely, he then added, in each other's shit, looking forward to the day when the whole shebang of a war was over; they'd give the Japs and Koreans a good hiding then piss off out of there, go home and be mates with each other forever.

Some of the men were happy to go along now and then to hear that junior officer-bloke that Curley laughingly called 'the Major', who, he reckoned, had more arse than an elephant, conducting his layman's version of a Mass, going on and on in his sermons about all that seek-and-ye-shall-find bullshit and the glories of heaven to come. But that bloke sure could string words together; he could, Curley reckoned, sell ham sandwiches in a synagogue, but even if Curley and some of the others didn't believe a word of what Bob Ryan had to say, it wasn't a bad way to kill time.

But then there'd be those occasions when a man'd burst into tears, just like that, when there'd been nothing you could see that'd provoked his bawling; or the day when two men, with murder in their eyes went gammy-brained and had each other by the throat because one of them'd snored like a foghorn the previous night. But it didn't surprise the young officer some began to call, in all seriousness, the Major. Maybe it was because he had the gall to throw himself into a lecture at any moment that suited him, harassing grown men (some older than himself) on the necessity of keeping clean, of combating the flies that bred in the filth and shit, in their nostrils and up their arses; he was a cocky bastard, who would tick off those who took more than their fair share of tucker from the pot; who had the audacity to appoint himself as the man who'd round them up (or try to, at least; most told him to fuck off) and give them a talk to lift their spirits. Men wondered what he'd dare to do next. Confessions? Him charging into the bushes when a bloke was as horny as a rhino, grabbing them by the prick when they'd gone hiding in search of some relief? The Major to some, a major fuckwit to others, blokes had their choice: most chose the latter.

I need you, mate

'Can't it wait, Bob?'

'No, Leo. If the leg stays … well, you know what'll happen.'

'Sure you can get off work? I need you here, mate.'

Bob Ryan would've liked to lie on the stretcher and hold his mate, to feel the beat of his heart. Leo's head was tilted back. Bob Ryan imagined himself placing the tips of his fingers on his lips, then transferring the kiss onto Leo's cheek.

'I'll be here, Leo.'

Why, Leo, why, mate?

Within the hour Bobby Ryan was lined up with all the other prisoners. Something was up. Tokyo, they soon found out, was unimpressed with their progress. Work had fallen behind schedule. The new order was given: all men able to work were now required to labour each day from five in the morning until ten each night. Bob Ryan's request to stay behind and assist in the amputation was met with a fist to the face that sent him reeling, his left eye streaming blood. He was marched to where he would spend the next seventeen hours moving rocks and fallen trees, guilt-ridden for the promise made that could not be kept.

They returned to the campsite after midnight. They would be awoken at 4.30 a.m. to resume work.

Leo lay asleep, a huge wad of material wrapped tightly around the end of what was left of his leg. The material was full of blood. Bob Ryan felt dizzy. His head swooned. He slumped to the earth, whispering Leo's name in a hoarse voice not his own, holding his head in his hands. He hadn't been there to comfort when he knew

Leo would've looked up at him with those helpless eyes full of terror for what awaited him. Leo knew, as they all did, of the cutthroat razor, the short carpenter's saw, the needle and thread and the small amount of ether that'd keep him unconscious, if he was lucky, for the twelve minutes needed to perform the operation.

Weary beyond imagining Bob Ryan stood up, looked at what was left of Leo's leg. Was he imagining things?

Perhaps it was the stump itself throbbing, a twitching muscle, the last gasp of some piece of tendon or loose shred of flesh as the leg began the slow process of hardening. Under the thick dressing the movement was unmistakeable. He struggled to his feet, stood standing for some time as he steadied himself, then went out to get a couple of blokes. As they slowly unwrapped the bandages Bob Ryan leaned on the centre pole of the tent.

He saw the maggots fall out of the dressing well before it'd been completely removed. He saw a great heaving body of those grubs tumbling over each other, burrowing into the open wound. The three men reeled at the horror. Bob Ryan stumbled out of the tent to vomit violently in the night.

At 4.30 the next morning, despite the fever and the infected eye, the Japs insisted that he, and all the others in the hospital tent except for Leo, go out to work. Bob Ryan's mate was left alone. On his return he discovered Leo Batrouney missing.

The Japs were besides themselves, thrashing about with their bamboo canes and their fearful shouting. Flares were lit. Beds were upturned. Tables were kicked over. Everyone was ordered to join the search.

Bob Ryan stumbled alone down to the river, to that spot where he would bathe and pray. Leo Batrouney's body floated, face-up, in the river's shallows.

The Japs dragged Bob Ryan off his dead mate, kicking him repeatedly. One of the guards, his face contorted with rage, aimed his rifle butt at Bob's swollen eye.

My strength is exhausted. I renounce this hateful world and my vows, made in Your presence; feel my heart turned to stone. I weep. I pine. Death now would bring a most exquisite joy, freeing me from a grief I cannot bear.

Happy Birthday, Bobby Ryan!

Everyone knew Bob'd come down with something crook. The signs were there: the beriberi and pellagra flared violently, the dysentery was bad, real bad. Blokes came to visit him, and he saw in their faces their thoughts of his forthcoming death. Maybe it was best if he just gave in. After all, he'd have to face Leo's wife and family. What was he going to say to Shamla, Leo's parents, that huge Batrouney family? And how could he possibly avoid her, if he was to return, since Leo'd given him that letter to take to her?

Major Bob Ryan was down to half his normal weight when two regulars at the sermons he once gave came into the hospital tent. It was the third of November, 1943, his twenty-third birthday.

They took him to a clearing, holding him upright before two tall long screens made of bamboo and leaves and blankets, joined in the centre like swinging doors. From behind that clumsily made screen he heard the whispering of voices. He stood, his right arm slung over the shoulder of a fellow prisoner, a stick in his left. In one swift dramatic movement the screens were parted, revealing a makeshift table, behind which stood many of the men.

On the table a feast had been prepared. He saw the remains of a prize fish someone had somehow procured, cleaned of maggots. There were tiny mounds of precious rice, gathered in a decorative display in the middle of huge leaves, shaped like soup tureens. There were boiled roots, an apple core and a yak's bone.

'Happy birthday, Major Bob!'

They threw streamers of leaf-entwined vines at him, some of which curled over his shoulder.

'Happy birthday, Bobby!'

He saw the food so painstakingly gathered and prepared. He brushed the streamers off his shoulders, a great heaving sob welling in his gut. His breathing quickened. He fell to the ground, his love for and gratitude to these men, the guilt and sorrow he felt for Leo Batrouney, the pain racking his body and everything else, everything else transforming him into a blubbering kid.

Bob Ryan sailed for Australia from Singapore at 10 a.m. on 23 September 1945 aboard the *Esperance Bay*. A number of seeds from a tree close to where he'd found Leo's body were in his trouser pocket.

The *Esperance* sailed down the east coast of Australia. Bob Ryan saw the Byron Bay lighthouse and recalled summer holidays spent up the coast with his mother.

The boat arrived in Sydney at night. It anchored off Clifton Gardens. A great collection of launches and small boats came out the next morning waving placards of welcome, some with signs on which were written the names of the returning soldiers.

Welcome Home, Bobby Ryan, one of them read, the letters painted red and green.

He'd lost the sight of one eye. The malaria would come and go for years, the pains in his neck and lower back would remain for the rest of his life. He'd never play footy again but, by crikey, he'd survived.

FIVE

Zoe Poulos and Bob Ryan taking a while to settle in
1945–2000

On the day Souths lost their appeal for reinstatement Zoe Poulos awoke well before dawn and, hearing a noise, switched on her bedside lamp. It was Saint George. She saw him turn his composed features in her direction. He struck such a dramatic pose. Clothed in the military uniform of his day, his lithe body forever fixed in the saddle, the saint's stallion reared above a dragon that writhed, vanquished, at the flaying hoofs. He was looking with some detached curiosity into her face. She rose up onto her knees on the mattress, made the sign of the cross and kissed the icon. When he returned her smile and nodded his beautifully curled head, she knew her life was coming to an end. Now the waiting was over. She would soon join her God. It was a happy day.

She put on her glasses then, with a lightness of heart, set about performing her daily rituals. Zoe Poulos lit the censor. She went from room to room chanting her hymns, pausing in front of each icon for a special supplication. She offered her favourite blessing before the large pile of Christmas presents she'd collected over many years in memory of the child she'd lost. Zoe Poulos had been giving them, one at a time, to Johnnie Butler, since not long after the boy's arrival in Redfern

But an event of such significance could not be hurried. The Greek woman would leave this world of dreams for the real world to come, dressed in her finest clothes, her body cleansed of all its impurities. She ran the water then stepped into the cracked porcelain tub. The water's warmth soothed her. She lay back, closed her eyes and smiled, recalling her husband's mad schemes to make a fortune in those chaotic postwar years. Had he really wanted to use her gold to purchase, then export, bags of sugar to Japan where he'd said there was a shortage? To buy, too, a whole apartment block in the ruins of Dresden which, he'd claimed, was *going for a song?* Zoe Poulos raised the sponge and squeezed the water onto her face, remembering she'd once been that young bride Zoe Zantakis, with the flowing golden hair and the rouged lips, laughing in nervous anticipation of the good life to come.

Not long after their marriage at the Holy Trinity Greek Orthodox Church in Bourke Street, Surry Hills, George Poulos informed his bride that, to pay off certain debts he would not discuss with her, he'd had to sell his hot-dog stand. Some weeks after they'd moved into his single-storey terrace, she found out he'd fallen behind in rent, when she'd been led to believe he owned their home. But one — just one — of those gold sovereigns of hers would keep the landlord at bay for a few weeks. Would she mind? Its sale would also give him time to scout around, during the day, for a suitable business opportunity.

But nothing came of those ventures he said he spent much of his time enquiring into. He'd go out with a posse of Aussie blokes, all ponced up, returning at all hours smelling of the night. She began attending church on a regular basis, finding comfort mixing with women from the old country. Despite being pregnant with their first child, Zoe, to prevent selling off yet another of her coins, took up the cleaning job at Souths' new footy clubhouse which some neighbour with an eye-patch, who lived up the road, had found for her.

Zoe Poulos became resigned to being married to a fellow who was more boy than man, who walked about the house when he could have been out working. One night he ran through the house then hid in the outdoor loo. They'd both seen the shapes of three burly blokes through the window of the front bedroom. These men shouted for George Poulos and, when he would not respond to their summons, beat angrily on the front door. Before leaving they hurled a brick through one of the glass panels in the door. It landed in the hallway at the feet of his wife. George Poulos cowered in the dunny, venturing out long after they'd left. He fled the house just before sunrise, his eyes wide with fear. He would go into the country, he said, find a job then send for her. He stared down both sides of the street then bolted, in his white suit, one hand holding down his hat, the other a battered suitcase.

Bob Ryan wakes up suddenly, cries out, discovers himself in a sitting position on the floor. Sweat runs down the back of his neck and face, into his eyes. His hair is plastered to his head. His torso gleams in the grey light, his tongue's a piece of sandpaper, his skull's throbbing like he's been drinking kero, or else he's been bashing his head against a wall. Shapes loom in the half-light. The silence is terrible. He feels hands reach out for him before realising they're shaggy vines wrapping themselves around his neck. A wall of trees closes in on him. A prayer sticks to the roof of his mouth. He looks up, sees a man hanging naked from a rope tied to the ceiling, toes twitching, shit oozing down his thighs. It's Leo Batrouney, his death mask of a face contorted in a sneering grin.

He rushes out of his bedroom, down the hall and into the front yard. Heaves his guts out on his lawn.

Bob Ryan stands, breathing wildly. The street is still, there's not a breath of wind. Looks up, sees George Poulos making a dash towards Clevo. The Greek woman's bedroom light is on. He creeps to her house, sees the woman through the curtains kneeling in prayer before the lighted icon box on a chest of drawers, then walks back to his terrace. Bob hoses the vomit into the lawn, returns to his own bedroom. Hearing his mother coughing in the bathroom, Bob Ryan prays to the God he no longer believes in.

After her prayers Zoe Poulos dragged out from under her bed the chest she'd brought out from Greece. The leather pouch and all her sovereigns were gone.

Several weeks after George Poulos' flit, and with Father gone bush again on work, Bob Ryan broke his self-imposed isolation to pay the woman a visit with his mother. He'd often smelt the incense from the street when he walked past her home in the hours before sunrise. Seen her relighting the wick that floated in a bowl of olive oil, flickering before that congregation of saints that stood impassively in her iconostasio. He'd noticed her on two successive Sundays heading off to church. Intrigued by her attendance at such an early hour he'd followed her once, seen her from the street cleaning the pews and sweeping the floor with a handful of other women, in preparation for that day's liturgy. Her faith attracted him.

She spoke to him and his mother at the front door, which she held half-open, declining what she came to understand was an invitation to join them for Christmas lunch, only two weeks away. But how could she, a woman living alone, afford to be seen by other Greeks socialising with this young fellow? Tongues would wag. It would be a scandal. And besides, his lanky pastiness and that eye-patch gave the man a fearsome look, and she'd heard, too, from other Greeks in the area, of this fellow's strange behaviour, particularly at night. He'd returned from the war, they said, a different person from the one who'd left. He was a single man, an Australian not of her faith — how could she have even considered going?

While Zoe was walking to her cleaning job one day, he rose suddenly from his gardening work at the front of his terrace, doffed his hat and made to talk. He stood there, hat in hand, she staring at the ground waiting for the right time to scurry off.

To avoid meeting him Zoe Poulos took to taking the long way to work, sometimes joining up with Athena Voutsakakis, another cleaner at the clubhouse.

This woman arrived unexpectedly at Zoe Poulos' home two days after she'd been told, in confidence, of Zoe's pregnancy. What was she going to do, Athena Voutsakakis wondered, after the birth of her child? How would she support herself when she could no longer work, when there was no mother or mother-in-law to take care of her child? Where would the money come from to pay the rent and buy the food? And far, far more seriously than these short-term concerns: had Zoe Poulos given any thought to remarrying, should George Poulos never return? Who, Athena Voutsakakis said, would marry a woman of Zoe Poulos' age — she was, after all, in her mid twenties — who'd been touched by another man? Who had no dowry? Did she really think that a woman with another man's child had any hope of becoming betrothed to one of those many young Greek men pouring into the country? If she were childless she might have a slim chance of marrying someone not from her own island, from whom her previous marriage might be kept secret, but as for that unborn child — well, if she didn't act, a lonely and poor life was what awaited her. No, she had no choice. The pregnancy had to be aborted, and soon.

Zoe Poulos lived alone. Her father's relatives were on Kastellorizo, her mother's in Brazil where they'd emigrated. Who was there whom she knew, whom she could go to for advice? The woman prayed herself to sleep each night, and woke every morning begging for advice. She lit candles at her church every day after work. She looked for signs in the bottom of her cup, in the grains of the Turkish coffee she took to drinking. The ancient icon of Saint George, left to her by her maternal grandmother, stood aloof. She backed away at the last moment, out of shame, from confessing her heartache to her priest.

The man with the eye-patch dropped by late one morning with his ailing mother upon Zoe Poulos' return from work. She saw them coming and retreated to the kitchen so that she would not be seen through the window in her front door. She ignored their knock. Long after they'd gone she opened the door to find two Christmas presents on her doorstep. She unwrapped the cardboard box on her kitchen table. Inside was a small potted olive tree, from him. In the smaller parcel were two handmade doilies, from the man's mother.

Francis Ryan returned unexpectedly early from his country work. He was sitting in the lounge one morning waiting for his son to come back from his walk.

'Is she awake, lad?'

Bob Ryan was startled to find his father up. 'Who?'

'That Greek woman.'

'I don't know.'

'Ah.'

Bob Ryan made to go to the kitchen to make himself a cuppa. The *Herald* was under one arm, the milko's delivery in his free hand.

'I hear you've gone to see her a couple of times.'

Bob Ryan halted his progress in the doorway. 'She's on her own, Father. She needs help.'

'People notice things around here, you know. You and that woman aren't the only early risers. Tell me, what are your plans for today?'

By the time Bob Ryan had done his walk, had breakfast and pottered about in the garden, he was that tired he had to lie down, hoping to be able to take a snooze. Receiving a war pension ate away at him. He would have liked to go out and earn a crust, but knew he wouldn't be able to see out a single day at Eveleigh. It got on his goat, too, that he was made to feel dependent on his old man. It brought out the father in Father, and the boy in himself.

'I'm … going to rest. Maybe see Tom this afternoon.'

'O'Flaherty tells me you're intending to return to the railway.'

'Yes.'

'You'd do me proud, son, to go back to the seminary.'

Bob Ryan stood, holding tightly onto the handle of the container of milk, unable to reply.

'You're not going back, are you?'

Bob Ryan was facing the kitchen, his back turned to his father. He shook his head, waited for the man to bowl him another yorker.

'I see. About that woman. Why did you go to see her?'

'I thought she might want to join us for Christmas lunch.'

'Ah, lunch. She's not coming, of course.'

'No.'

'She's got her own kind, Robert. She's not one of us. I'm very disappointed in you. And your mother.'

'I thought that —'

'You and Mother thought wrong. It will be Father O'Grady who will be honouring us with his presence for Christmas lunch. He'll be talking to you about going back to your studies. Pass me the *Herald*, please.'

Bob Ryan was brewing a pot in the kitchen when he heard his father's voice from the lounge room: 'By the way, why are you telling people your nickname in the camp was *the Major*?'

Two days later his father went bush. The days felt lighter. Mother and son sat out in the backyard Bob Ryan was developing into a garden retreat. One day the shrubs he'd planted around the entire perimeter of the fence would obscure them from all eyes. They'd drink their tea, talk and, now and again, even laugh.

He'd successfully germinated one of the seeds he'd brought back from the camp.

Zoe Poulos would often watch Bob Ryan when her presence at her front gate had not been noticed, the man on his hands and knees searching meticulously and methodically for the weeds which he'd remove from the small patches of lawn in the front garden and on the nature strip. One late afternoon, on the day her Christmas holidays had begun, she walked past his home when she thought he was not about, to take a closer look at the highly ordered garden: the flowering shrubs in ceramic pots, the hedges that bordered the short straight path that led to the house, the ferns that grew in baskets he'd hung from hooks on the verandah. Zoe marvelled that a man whose home had, on one side, the disorderly and ugly mess of tyres and spare parts of a car repair workshop, on the other a small timber yard, would bother creating a thing of such beauty.

Bob surprised the Greek woman when he suddenly emerged from his terrace, having seen her through the flyscreen. Zoe Poulos couldn't very well walk away, as she'd've liked. His smile and desire to talk held her, and she liked, after all, the sound of his voice. She looked up and down the street to ensure no Greek eyes were observing her, then stayed on the footpath, while he stood on his side of the gate. They communicated with facial gestures and hand signs and the few words the woman knew in English. She thanked him for the Christmas gifts. He lifted his hat to excuse himself when his mother's voice called him in for dinner.

That night Athena Voutsakakis arrived with a delegation of other Greek women. They had Zoe Poulos undress then sit in her bath, which they filled slowly with hot water. They gave her small glasses of ouzo to drink, which sent her mind in a whirl and had her vomiting in a bucket they'd placed by the side of the bath. They forced her to stay in the water that scalded when she clambered to get out, slipping and knocking her cheek on the side of the tub. When she shook her head at yet another glass of ouzo, two of the women held her while Athena Voutsakakis poured what was left in the bottle into her mouth. A fourth woman, holding an icon in one hand and swinging a smoking censor in another, prayed that God forgive the woman for what she was doing to her unborn child.

Zoe Poulos had two weeks to recover before returning to work. The Greek women organised a roster amongst themselves, sitting with her the whole of that first night and the next day, and in briefer shifts for the week that followed. They rubbed olive oil into the bruise on her cheek, helped her get up to clean herself of the blood she was discharging. They helped her bathe, changed the sheets several times each day, brought around a mattress when her own had to be washed and dried in the sun, did her shopping, cooked her meals.

When she finally emerged to return to work, accompanied by Athena Voutsakakis, her face pale, her eyes bloodshot, her walk unsteady, she tried to avoid the look of concern on the face of Bob Ryan who was returning from his walk. She hurried past him as best she could, her eyes averted.

That afternoon, as she sat at the kitchen table weeping for the child she'd killed, there was a soft hesitant knocking on her front door. She did not answer when she saw it was him.

On Christmas day Zoe Poulos attended church. After lunch, which she ate alone (she politely turned down Athena Voutsakakis' invitation to eat with her family), she unwrapped the large gift she'd purchased for the child she would never give birth to. She left the pedal-driven car in the lounge room until twelve days after Christmas when, as was the custom in this new country, she took down the tree. She rewrapped the first of those gifts she would purchase each December from that year onwards, then stored it in the second bedroom.

And over fifty years later, before your world closed in upon itself, and watched by the old Greek woman, you fly up and down the footpath in this little car. You sit on the floor of her lounge room, dressed in a sailor's suit that'd been all the rage in the 1950s, playing with a forty-year-old meccano set.

In the Ryan household after Christmas Mass, Father O'Grady rose from the head of the table to say grace before getting stuck into the lamb roast. Bob Ryan, his mind wandering, looked up during the prayer to see his father's steady gaze upon him, the older man knitting his brows at his son's restlessness. After the meal Father O'Grady promised Francis Ryan he'd keep mum about what he'd witnessed: to his father's humiliation, Bob Ryan tipped the entire contents of a large salt shaker on the meat, saying, 'Mother's a good cook, but she's miserable with the salt.' The issue of Bob Ryan returning to the seminary was not raised. His father told Father O'Grady that his son was taking a while to settle in.

Several weeks after Zoe Poulos' first Christmas in Australia, she awoke to a loud commotion of voices down the road. She ventured out to her front yard to see, on the footpath, a small gathering of concerned neighbours outside the home of the Ryan family. The Greek woman hesitantly approached, nodding to those residents she knew. Bob Ryan was sitting on the step of his verandah, his face in his hands. From the safe distance of the nature strip, some people were offering words of comfort to the man. Most stood there bewildered, at a loss as to what to do.

They made a path for the Greek woman, whose initiative surprised even herself. She made her way to the gate. Zoe Poulos had never seen a man cry before, and approached with some caution. She'd never previously set eyes on the man's father at such close proximity, either, and now understood what people meant when they referred to the similarity between the two men. Francis Ryan stood in the hallway, ashamed and embarrassed. The front door and flyscreen were open. He was encouraging his son back into their home, his wife to their bedroom. Margaret Ryan leaned on the wall of the hallway in her nightie, her head inclined to one side, coughing into an open hand.

'You'll come inside, lad,' said Francis Ryan, whose dressing gown was wrapped tightly around his neck. 'You'll come inside and we'll pray together, as a family.'

He squinted at this Greek woman who had, unlike the other neighbours, dared to open his gate and enter his property. He lifted his head, looked sharply down at this foreign woman who made to place her hand on his distressed son's shoulder. She hesitated, seeing Francis Ryan thrust both fists into the pockets of his gown. She smiled at his son.

Bob Ryan stood, returned her smile, walked past his father, whose open palm gestured towards the hallway of their home.

The next morning Francis Ryan left once again for the bush, partly because of his work, mostly because of the humiliation his son had brought upon the Ryan name. He was gone several weeks.

Two days after he'd left, Zoe Poulos gave Bob Ryan an icon of a saint who, she knew, healed the ill and broken-hearted. The following day she gave him a tray of baklava.

Bob Ryan returned the baking tray one week later. The woman

made light of her gift and smiled when the man gestured to his stomach, indicating the weight he'd begun to put on. So the woman baked another tray.

One day she was walking past his home and, looking down the side passage, saw him working in his back garden in his singlet, the ribs beginning to recede in his burgeoning flesh. Bob Ryan looked up and saw her observing him. Embarrassed, he rushed into his home, emerging later in a long-sleeved shirt.

While he spoke to Zoe Poulos, Margaret Ryan, strong enough to do some housework, came across the food — canned and fresh — that'd gone missing. Her son'd hidden it in his wardrobe, under his bed, stuffed it in his shoes and socks and the pockets of his jackets. She returned the food to the fridge and the pantry. She kept it secret from her husband. She didn't mention the find to her son.

Talk to me, mate

It'd be good to have the old Bobby Ryan back, Tom O'Flaherty thought. Sure the man was going through a rough trot, but how could you help him when he wouldn't breathe a word of what'd happened in that bloody camp? Fair's fair, Tom'd been like a big brother to him, hadn't he? They were mates, weren't they?

It was close to five in the arvo. He knew Bob Ryan would arrive on the dot, and so he did. The tray with all the tea things was there, waiting.

'Could set the time of day by you,' Tom said, smiling mischievously.

Bob Ryan took out the silver Waltham fob watch that was connected to a chain looped onto a trouser button, considered the time, wound it and returned it to his pocket. 'Well, someone has to keep the world in order, Tom. How are things?'

'I reckon we'll be getting out of our slump, Bob. We've signed this little wizard of a bloke — Clive Churchill. Reckon we're in for some wins. Finally.'

Bob Ryan stirred his tea (three times in a clockwise direction, Tom O'Flaherty once again noticed).

'When are you gunna come back, mate? It'd be good to go and see Souths play together. Let's get them pre-war days back, eh?'

Bob Ryan paused before answering. 'Well, Tom,' he replied, nodding his head slowly, his head tilted to one side, his mouth curved at the sides. 'Well ...' he repeated.

Crikey, thought Tom, I'm not askin' him about the meaning of life.

'You heard the joke about the three wells, Bob?'

'No.'

'Well! Well! Well! Now, d'ya reckon we might shift gears and speed things up a bit when we're talkin'?'

Bob Ryan looked askance at his mate. 'It's that bad, is it?'

'Bad? You make me wanna reach out and grab yer by the bloody braces and shake yer.'

'Sorry, Tom. I'm crank-starting myself. I'm hanging in, if you know what I mean.'

'No, I don't know what you mean. C'mon, Bob. "Crank-starting"? What the hell does that mean? Talk to me, mate.'

Bob Ryan sat heavily, breathing audibly.

'You're not gunna go all quiet on me now, are ya?'

Silence.

'Sorry, Bob. Just tryin' to be honest, okay?'

Bob Ryan nodded solemnly. Tom O'Flaherty knew he'd feel as guilty as hell when his mate finally got up to go (at exactly five-thirty).

'Been to see Shamla yet?'

'No, Tom.'

'How's your mum?'

'As crook as Rookwood. But you know what Mother's like —

she'll soldier on.'

'Listen, Bob. The job's there for yer, at Eveleigh. Reckon it might be the best thing for yer to come back. What'd'ya reckon?'

'Maybe. Look, are Souths playing a home game this week?'

'Bloody oath!'

'Well, then.'

'Three bloody wells, then! Meet me here at two. We'll go together.'

If it can't be Father Robert, then …

Towards the end of 1948, Joey's, the Sydney Catholic high school Francis Ryan'd insisted his son attend, despite his wife's opposition to her son boarding, contacted Bob Ryan. They were putting on a do for all their old boys that'd served in the war. They enquired about his rank and details of his service for the school's archives, asked whether he would attend. He filled out the acceptance form and sent it off.

When the day arrived Bob Ryan decided, at the last moment, not to go. His furious father came across the invitation. He held it in front of his son's face, pointing an accusing finger at the word *Major* then, without having said a word, let it fall at his son's feet.

Major Bob visits Shamla

It took almost three years for Bob Ryan to summon the courage to visit Shamla Batrouney. Her son, Victor, was at the local primary school. The woman sat on the edge of her lounge, her hands in her lap, listening as he spoke haltingly about her husband's courage. But the bitter woman, knowing she could not bring dishonour upon her family name by remarrying, had grown silent. When Bob Ryan finished the account he'd spent years rehearsing, the woman shifted slightly, looked at the ornate rug on the floor but did not speak. She hadn't offered him a coffee, something to eat, even a glass of water. When he got up to go she did not reach out her hand to accept the letter her husband had written. Bob Ryan placed the envelope on a dresser, bade the woman farewell, then made to leave.

'You left something out,' he heard her say as he stood at the door, looking out onto the street. 'You didn't tell me how he died.'

Bob did not turn to face her. And for the rest of his life he wondered what it was he'd mumbled to her as he fled the house.

Towards the end of the 1949 footy season, with Bob Ryan much recovered, he made contact by phone. Shamla Batrouney passed him on to her brother who, after a long pause, refused the family's permission for Bob Ryan to take Victor to see the resurgent Souths team, and that wonderman Clive Churchill play. Further contact was discouraged. By 1953, when the boy gained entry into Sydney Boys High, the selective school opposite Tom O'Flaherty's home, any contact between Leo's boy and Bob Ryan was accidental. They would exchange a brief greeting. It came to nothing more.

Bob Ryan, Sheriff of Redfern

By the late 1950s Bob Ryan had been working at Eveleigh with Tom for some years. His punctuality had become well known. People arrived for the meetings of the Workers Union and the local branch of Legacy to find him seated, going over the minutes and the agenda. His fob watch would be open, an accusing finger pointing to the time, an eyebrow cocked and a hard glare directed at the latecomers. Some people called him the Major, which he clearly liked. Behind his back others referred to him as *the Sheriff* or *That Big Shit*. He ran meetings with an intimidating efficiency.

And unless he was working in his garden he was never seen out of doors without his hat, braces and tie. He stood on the tram for women much younger than himself, continued doffing his hat at passers-by he knew long after many men had discarded headwear. He and his father stood like statues at the front pew for Margaret Ryan's funeral. Some people commented on their lack of emotion, others on the fact that the remarkable similarities between them had them looking more like brothers than father and son.

And like his father, Bob Ryan went bush too, only his purpose was as a talent scout for the Rabbitohs. It was clear he had a preference for recruiting black players.

Bob Ryan spent as much time out of the house as possible. His father's work continued to take him regularly out of Sydney. The times spent apart suited both men.

No, there was no mistaking the ordered life Major Bob Ryan imposed upon himself. People saw it in the luxuriant plant life in his garden, which often won the annual award the local Council began at his urging; there were the same number of ferns planted down both sides of his home, each separated from the other by a palm tree; there were the straight lines of hedgerow flowers, the two identical ceramic pots on either side of the front door with their shaped blossoming bougainvillea shrubs, the rows of alternately hung staghorns and elkhorns on the wall of his verandah, the path that led from the front door to the gate with its twin borders of dahlias and roses. Then there was that manicured lawn in which no weed was allowed to grow. Bob drew comfort from the plants that flowered at particular times of the year and the sturdy growth and brilliant blossoming of that tree he'd brought back as a seed from the camp. Their regularity, the ordered world which gathered round all sides of his home were things a man could rely on, and control.

He watched with pleasure, too, the olive tree grow tall that he'd planted for Zoe Poulos years before in her front garden. It bore fruit every two years, which she pickled and bottled herself.

When the great migration of the 1960s saw many Greeks settle in Redfern, Zoe Poulos' sweet-making business prospered. Her kitchen became a boiler room, churning out trays of baklava which she sold to the local delis and coffee shops. Greek women helped out for a bit of pocket money. Locals shook their heads at the foreign-lingoed gossiping they heard from the footpath.

When the hour came to slide the trays into the oven all her helpers had to leave the kitchen while she held an icon over the stove (she would not disclose the name of the saint) and recited that secret prayer that guaranteed her cooking's success. One woman, who poked her head into the kitchen when she was supposed to be in Zoe Poulos' lounge room, was banished from her home for several weeks.

The money she made from her sweets went into kero cans and used olive oil and yoghurt containers that were dug (at night) into her backyard. When her home was released from rent control, eventually coming onto the market, she put down a hefty deposit and took out a small bank loan, for which the local Greek priest went guarantor.

Zoe took to saying her baklava *it go like hotcake*, made trays for the Holy Trinity Church's fundraising efforts, joined its Ladies' Auxiliary. She left Souths and took up a cleaning position at the Kastellorizian Club in Darlinghurst.

By the time Konstantine and Maria Tsakiris arrived in Australia with their two children at the tail end of the great migration, Francis Ryan was dead. The Major returned to the family home; earlier a bitter blue (which Bob Ryan never spoke about, not even to Tom O'Flaherty) had seen him take up residence at a nearby boarding house. Leo's son enraged his family and scandalised the Lebanese community by moving out of Redfern to shack up with an Australian girl he'd met at uni. Old Tom — which was the name some people now knew him by — retired from Eveleigh. Bob Ryan continued working at the railway workshop and as a talent scout for the Bunnies, returning, during Souths' great period in the early 1970s with a fellow from Ginlambone, outside Nyngan, named Jimmy Butler. This bloke caused a minor sensation in the brief time he was with the Rabbitohs; but the black man took to the grog with a vengeance and, several months after his arrival, disappeared without a trace.

Zoe Poulos lived frugally as she struggled to meet the ever-increasing demands for her baklava. She paid off her housing loan. By then, the lines around her eyes, mouth and neck, the grey hair tied permanently in a bun and the black she always wore in mourning for the child she'd lost, had given her the appearance of what, she knew, she'd become — safely ensconced in her single status, Zoe Poulos became a feature of Redfern, known as *the cleaning lady* or *the little Greek woman* by some, *the baklava maker* by others. She'd long grown accustomed to living alone.

And then there was that Greek world into which she immersed herself. There was her church in Bourke Street, of course, within walking distance of her home. Her attendance, begun as a way of lessening her feelings of guilt regarding her lost child, became more and more regular until the time came when she felt some emptiness if she did not attend the weekly liturgy. The woman lived a life which moved to the rhythm of her church, fasting each Wednesday and Friday, receiving communion most Sundays. She attended the midweek liturgies of important feast days, too, before or after her morning cleaning job. The Major found her a handyman who built her a larger wooden iconostasio with sliding glass doors which he bolted to the wall in her bedroom, and which she filled with her most precious icons. Each morning upon awakening she would light her brass incensory, say her prayers then proceed to every room in her home, blessing each in turn. She grew to love her saints, some of whom occasionally spoke to her. She celebrated their presence in her life with a passion she might otherwise have directed at a brood of children and grandchildren. She looked forward each year to Easter and the Great Fast, going without all animal products for forty days, suffering for her Lord in anticipation of His crucifixion, rejoicing in His resurrection. On Easter Sunday, after her friends had celebrated lunch with their own families, many of them, including Kon and Maria Tsakiris and the Major, would descend on her home for dinner. She taught religion to the Greek kiddies at the local primary school. She shopped mostly at businesses owned by Greeks. At no stage did she contemplate returning to Greece. Redfern was home.

Konstantine Tsakiris purchases the Kookaburra Café

Konstantine and Maria Tsakiris worked two jobs apiece. At night they cleaned offices. During the day he worked at the Holden assembly plant out at Pagewood while she sat hunched over a Singer sewing machine. Initially things went according to plan: within two years they'd saved enough to purchase outright the Kookaburra Café — both the business and the property — from its Lebanese owners. Kon could see the day when they would return rich to the old country. He learnt the local lingo quickly, reckoning he had *a nose for a bargain*. He began playing the stock market, despite Maria's urgings to invest in property, putting money on mining shares which, he reckoned, were a sure thing. It was *London to a brick*, he took to saying. Everyone was into it. Soon they'd return in glory to their village and he'd be the big shot he longed to be, driving the latest Merc, his pockets stuffed with the American dollars he'd donate to pay for the restoration of the village church and schoolhouse.

'Your shop's getting a bit rundown, Kon,' said the Major, who bought his milk and bread each day from the café.

Bob Ryan was helping the Greek man slide three old pub posters behind the bookshelves used for storing grocery items. The huge paintings, done by hand on six-foot sheets of thick glass had been found, wrapped for protection in innumerable sheets of the *Herald*, in the cupboard under the stairs.

'Ach, it costs too much money,' Kon said, 'to fix up.'

'I don't know, Kon. That new shopping centre they're building is going to eat into your business.' He surveyed the shop, saw the art-deco light fittings with their missing panels, the cracked black-and-white marble tiles on the floor, the tarnished manual silver cash register and scales, the tattered posters of the Parthenon, the Greek islands, the cedars of Lebanon, the wobbly high-backed dark-stained timber seats and tables.

'What's the point?' added Kon. 'Anyway, we won't stay long. We'll sell the shop soon, go back to Greece. I tell you, Bob, we'll make a killing soon. I bought shares that will go through the roof.'

But Kon and Maria, like so many others, never recovered from the mining boom that had people go silly. He'd invested all their savings, taken out a loan, urged, too, his relatives from the village to send him money which he invested in companies he knew little about. The overnight crash left them heavily in debt.

They began operating the business on a Sunday but that new shopping centre in nearby Surry Hills, and the modern brasseries opening here and there, took away much of their previous clientele, just as Major Bob'd said. When there were no customers in the shop Kon began switching off the lights to save on the electricity bill. He stored the used teabags in an old canister to make that second pot of tea. Maria pulled their children out of the private schools. The few grocery items on the bookshelves, behind which he'd slid those pub posters, gathered dust. The sloping wooden boxes on one of the walls were stocked with sad-looking vegies and fruit. The large glass lolly jars on the counter were full of jelly beans, milk bottles, cobbers and liquorice sticks that few kids rushed after school to buy.

The sleeping years

In the mid 1980s Zoe Poulos resigned from her job at the relocated Kastellorizian Club in Kingsford but continued mass-producing what had, by then, become her claim to fame: *Yaya Zoe's Baklava* was featured one day on *The Bert Newton Show*. She refused to reveal to Bert that special prayer that guaranteed her cooking's success. Her *fucktory,* as she informed a national audience, had expanded from the kitchen to the lounge.

A path was worn in the protesting floorboards as teams of women, their black clothes smudged with flour dust, nattered their way from one room to the other, Greek music blaring out onto the street.

Bob Ryan retired from Eveleigh about the same time.

The Major was to say later that, at least for him, those years before the time bomb he'd been sitting on finally exploded were *the sleeping years*. Kon and Maria hung on to the shop when they should have walked away. The grown-up Victor Batrouney dropped out of the law course he was studying at uni to drive cabs, returning to Redfern for his mother's funeral, which Bob Ryan did not attend. And the Rabbitohs, after the glory days of the 1960s and 1970s, struggled year after year to make it to the finals, experiencing the longest drought in their history.

And one day, in March of 1999, a black woman with her little boy moved into a terrace on the same side of the road as Yaya Zoe and

Major Bob. Jimmy Butler relocated into nearby La Perouse in the same year. Victor Batrouney began his hill runs opposite Old Tom's terrace.

Souths' Judgement Day
FRIDAY, 3 NOVEMBER 2000

Zoe Poulos stepped out of the bath, dried herself then wrapped the towel around herself. Her wet hair, tied in a bun, felt heavy on her exposed neck. She put on her rimless glasses, which gave her face a childlike look, walked into her bedroom, dragged out the wooden chest from under her bed, opened the lid then smiled at the warmth and colour and beauty of what was presented to her. She placed the open palms of both hands over her mouth. She said a brief prayer of blessing in memory of those ancestors who had bequeathed her these treasures. It was all there in the methodical order in which she'd packed them, the day before she'd left Kastellorizo.

Yaya Zoe removed the bath towel, stepped into the white silk undies, the edges of which were sewn with strips of fine gold cotton, then into the first of the two sets of stockings, the one light blue, the second, the external pair, a pale brown. The long white silk of the *pokamiso* was soothing to the skin; the second dress, made of unboiled yellow silk, had been made for her when she was a child by her maternal grandmother. Zoe removed her glasses then slipped over her head the thin felt *kavathi*, its red and gold weaving decorated with a bright floral design, and the satin *zepoumi*, which the woman tied several times around her waist. Over the velvet vest, decorated with fur around the neck and open front, and heavily embroidered with patterns of gold thread, was thrown a large burgundy fur-lined coat. On her head she placed a tasselled velvet hat over which she attached, with a silver brooch, a multicoloured shawl which reached down to the ground. She removed the false bottom of the trunk and took out a flat, long jewellery box. Yaya Zoe threaded a heavy gold cross through a long thick chain then fastened it behind her neck. Beneath the jacket she pinned a vertical row of large silver buckles. She placed rings on each finger of both hands, clipped antique bracelets, on which were attached numerous Turkish and Austrian and British gold coins, onto her wrists.

Zoe was now ready to step out into the street to bid her adieus. She closed the front door but left it unlocked for the boy who might come for breakfast. She forgot to put on her glasses.

Some time after Yaya Zoe has left, you arrive for brekkie. You won't attend school that day, having decided to attempt overcoming your fears of the world outside Redfern by crossing South Dowling Street and walking to Centennial Park. While you eat the cereal the woman has left for you, watching cartoons on the old black-and-white television in the dining room, the courtrooms in the Law Building and the auditorium in Souths' clubhouse fill up with supporters. You depart after eating, leave the telly on in the middle of a western, walk to Mista Tom's house and stand there, looking in the direction of the park.

The Greek priest, contacted by Jimmy Butler, found both Zoe and Kooka Kon on Cleveland Street. The two men led Yaya Zoe home, the shawl billowing behind her.

Zoe was exhausted. She stood at her front door until Kon and the priest were out of sight. She would lie on her bed in her traditional bridal clothes, become betrothed, in her sleep, to her God. When she awoke she would be in His kingdom.

She opened the front door and heard a voice coming from inside her home. She recognised the neighing of a horse. She prayed, facing the iconostasio in her bedroom, then walked down the hall and into the dining room. The woman immediately fell onto her knees and, making repeatedly the sign of the cross, approached Saint George. His horse was rearing. Her eyes filled with tears.

After Major Bob recovered from his collapse in the club he realised he could run away from his past for only so long. There were stories that needed to be told. There were people like Jimmy and Johnnie who deserved to know the truth. Once the doctor'd left, the Major turned to the boy.

'Johnnie,' he said. 'You've got your voice back, lad.'

The boy nodded his head and smiled.

'Say something, Johnnie. I want to hear your voice.'

'Billy's dead.'

Major Bob stiffened visibly in his chair. He looked away from the boy. Too late, too late. Jimmy had seen his response.

'Billy?' Jimmy Butler said. 'Who's Billy?'

'Billy's me brother.'

'Brother?' said the boy's uncle. 'You ain't got no brother.'

'Billy's me brother. He's dead. He took me voice.'

Jimmy looked to Kon and Victor Batrouney, who shrugged their shoulders in confusion, then to Bob Ryan. Yeah, thought the Major, the past is crowding in on me alright.

'What?' Jimmy said to him. 'You know somethin', Bob?'

It took some time for the older man to respond, knowing that once the words were spoken there was no going back.

'Can we meet at Tom's? Kon, get Zoe. Jimmy, ring Nan. I've got something I need to tell all of you.'

SIX

Johnnie Butler meets Bob Ryan

<small>July 1999</small>

It was a mystery to all who knew Major Bob why he took such a sudden interest in the black kid and his mother. It wasn't as if he was on the Butlers' doorstep the day of their arrival. Nah, his abrupt involvement occurred several weeks later, towards the end of the 1999 footy season. But crikey, when it did happen you didn't want to rub him up the wrong way by querying what he was up to: he'd fob you off with a waspish glare like he was going to grab you in a full nelson or something. And there were, after all, so many other concerns: would this be Souths' final season? Would the NRL make good its threats and, come October, throw the Rabbitohs out of the comp if they didn't merge with another club? What was the man doing, then, in getting himself involved with that family that would only cause him trouble? Why would any white fellow go out of his way for that woman whose eyes burned with that fierce hostility, who wouldn't even return a person's greeting when some comment might've been made about the loveliness of the day; when she'd walk straight into you on the footpath, some people reckoned, if you didn't make way for her on the rare occasion you might come across her during the day? They'd seen Nanna Dora, her foster kids and her team of helpers delivering pieces of second-hand furniture on her arrival to help her settle in. Good. As it should be. The blacks could take care of the blacks.

Why, then, did the Major perform such a backflip so long after their arrival?

The big fella felt sorry for her kid. Okay, but who didn't? How could any decent person not look at that little boy and, knowing the drunkard he'd one day become, not feel sorry for the little bugger? They could already see him, a lanky useless young man staggering home pissed to the eyeballs, bitter and angry at the world. Most didn't expect him and his mother to stay long, anyway. Others would've liked to tell them to rack off to the Block, that part of western Redfern that was like another world, a black world, then they wouldn't have to watch their street invaded each arvo by Johnnie Butler's black mates from school and Nan Dora's foster kids, treating the street like it was their playground. But one day the shit'd hit the fan and they'd find the woman and her kid mysteriously gone. Their street'd be all white again and they'd wonder, now and again, whatever happened to that little black boy that'd once lived down the road.

There grew another point of contact, too. The child's mother, for reasons no one could fathom, made an exception of the old Greek woman who was sometimes seen entering their home, ludicrous in her black clothes and those oversized red and green oven mittens someone'd given her, shaped like bunnies. People would stop to observe her as she waddled down the street carrying a steaming pot or an entire baking tray of baklava. The Major would watch, too, astounded, as the old woman entered the boy's home, sometimes without even knocking. She'd emerge after half an hour or so (what was she doing in there all that time?), carrying empty and unwashed kitchen things she'd delivered, laden with food, on some previous occasion.

Yaya Zoe began to dispense those Christmas presents she'd once purchased every year in memory of the child she'd lost. Bob Ryan would see Johnnie come out of her home, all spruced up and decent-looking in the clothes that might have been forty or fifty years old, but which'd never been taken out of their wrapping.

Major Bob occasionally saw the boy in Yaya Zoe's home. The man'd drop by to drink one of those heavily sweetened cups of Turkish coffee which he had, after some persistence on both their parts, taken a liking to while she, in turn, drank the tea she'd become accustomed to. He would eat a piece of her baklava. They would turn the pages of her photograph album, or the one he'd bring along, sitting shoulder to shoulder at the kitchen table, telling stories. When Johnnie Butler learnt of the regularity of these Saturday morning meetings, he'd turn up, right on 10.35 a.m., five minutes after Bob Ryan's arrival. The Greek woman'd run her hands through his hair, check his ears, examine his fingernails and, if satisfied, give him a piece of her baklava and something to drink and, now and then, another of those Christmas presents.

And so the boy would sit on the floor playing with the gift purchased, in memory, all those years ago for another; and the two old folk, after a great deal of smiling at the child's joy, would resume their ritual, she with the tea, he with his coffee and the Greek sweet, both with their tales, Johnnie with the cowboy suit and holstered guns or the pick-up-sticks, or constructing something out of Meccano pieces, listening in to those stories of lives that seemed to stretch so far back in time.

How do they do that? You wonder how they can recall so many events in such detail, experienced so long ago, or told to them by their own parents or even their grandparents, when you don't even know who your grandparents are. How can Yaya Zoe describe the lanes and paths, people and events of that island she'd migrated from all those years ago, and Major recreate the days of his youth in Redfern when there'd been horses and buggies, and milk and bread'd been delivered to people's doorsteps by a horse-drawn dray, when you don't even know where you were born? It's a strange sort of comfort you feel sitting there and listening to these two oldies jabber on. Sometimes you wander around her home and stare, fascinated, at the oil-lit flame in her iconostasio and the sombre-faced saints in every room, or the rows of pickled olive jars, the sundried fish roe, the large tubs of yoghurt she'd made and stood in the laundry, under a heavy blanket. But one ear's always cocked to their talking. One day you leave with that inexplicable sadness and return home, go into your bedroom, shut the door, crawl under the covers of your bed and imagine yourself looking at the family photo album that does not exist.

One Saturday morning after Major's had his coffee and sweet with Yaya Zoe, he watches as you fly up and down the footpath in that forty-year-old kiddies car that the Greek woman has given you that day. You stop outside her gate, make a sound deep in your throat, of a car accelerating, play with the steering wheel and gearstick.

'Everything alright, lad?' Major asks you. He's put his hat on. He's holding a bag of Yaya Zoe's vegie and fruit scraps for his compost heap.

You nod your head, turn the stationary wheels to the left and right.

Nanna Dora's kids arrive, hearing of her latest gift to you. They stand around the car waiting their turn to have a go.

Yaya Zoe goes inside. You know she's going to fetch something for them to eat. She's a good old bird, this Zoe.

'And your mum? How's your mum, Johnnie?'

The Greek woman returns with an armful of fruit which she

distributes to your mates.

'Good, Major. She's sleepin'. Bin sleepin' all mornin'. Come home late from work.'

'And you're eating the food that Yaya is bringing to you?'

You nod your head, get out of the car for one of your eager friends.

'By the way, what's your name, Johnnie?' the man asks you.

'Johnnie.'

'Yes, yes,' he says, smiling. 'I know. What's your second name? What's your surname?'

'Butler.'

Yaya Zoe saw the man flinch. She saw his face crease into a frown. He was staring hard and unflinching at the boy.

'Butler. You're a Butler.'

'Yeah. Mum's a Butler too. Both Butlers, eh.'

The Major immediately thought of Jimmy Butler, whom he hadn't seen since the day he'd mysteriously and abruptly left Redfern almost thirty years previously. 'Your father's name's not Jimmy, is it lad?'

'Dunno who me dad is.'

'Maybe he's your uncle?'

'Dunno. Dunno no uncle.'

Bob then reached down, pulled back the sleeves of the jumper the Greek woman had given the child on some other occasion and ran his fingers up and down the boy's right arm, between the elbow and the shoulder. He was breathing heavily, arse up, head down, the braces straining on the buttons on his trousers.

The woman watched, made a questioning sound but the man did not hear, or chose to ignore her.

'No markings, lad.'

'Eh?'

'Tribal marks. No tribal marks?'

'Try … try what, Major?'

'It's alright, son.'

The woman concealed her curiosity behind the palm of her hand.

My God, my God, it's him
EARLY AUGUST 1999

So, you've come back, Mary Butler. You've ballsed things up, haven'tcha?

But like Nanna Dora keeps telling her, and she keeps repeating to herself so she can hang in when things get real crook and she doesn't hit the piss again, she owes it to her little kid. She's gotta make it up to him, eh. Maybe when she gets a job that keeps decent day hours she'll be able to do the stuff normal mums do with their kids. And that'll test her, eh, seeing in the clear light of day all those streets and buildings that've ground in her head at night while she was on the run from those shithouse memories. 'Cause it's hard enough for her as it is, coming home in the dark hours stinking of cleaning stuff.

Fair dinkum, you'd have thought all them years away from Redfern would've had her forget. But it ain't the way. She might think she's through with the past, but the past sure ain't through with you, Mary Butler, rushing down that tunnel of night, a migraine thumping like someone's in her head, belting the inside of her skull with an iron bar. She's stalked by a fistful of recollections of what was said and done to her, and Jimmy, and little Billy, the night's thick with the buggers, they're crackling underfoot, shifting and surging in the shadows, pressing against her. She arrives, breathless, hot with sweat, fumbles with the key at the door, stands breathing in the hallway. Now she's safe.

And then all a mamma has to do is go and sit on the edge of her boy's bed, smooth down his blanket and stroke his pillow over and over when the kid's fast asleep and comfy and needs no attention. Then she reckons all's hunky-dory with the world. Yer doin alright, Mary Butler. Be proud.

Go on, make yerself a mug of hot chocolate, have a slice of Yaya Zoe's baklava. And when she's done she might even let her hoarse voice once again fill the silence of the house, repeating like an old wind-up gramophone whose needle's got stuck in the groove of a wax 78: *I've got a steady job cleanin' offices at night (thanks, Nanna). There's cooked food in the house (yer a beauty, Zoe). I'm off the grog. I've got through 'nother day an' I'm doin' good. I'm half the decent mamma I've always wanted to be.*

She might even touch that icon that Yaya gave her, which the Greek woman reckons'll give Mary Butler strength and might even have a chat with her someday. Hit the sack, Mary. Smile and say goodnight to those two old sheilas that emerged from the streets to give unconditional love. It's Redfern talkin', Mary Butler, that's its way of sayin' sorry, sorry, sorry.

G'night Nan. G'night Yaya.

But she could be a bloody terror. Jesus, Nan, calm down.

Mary Butler saw the woman's stumpy figure through the frosted glass of the front door, that oversized Akubra like a cloud hovering. She was standing there, arms crossed, like a mean-as-shit teacher, ready to head-butt her way through Mary's piss-weak excuses if the house wasn't clean and tidy, grinding her teeth if there was no milk in the fridge for Johnnie. When she did finally come in she was at it straight off, pummelling Mary Butler like she was a punching bag. And when it was all over, there were hugs and scoldings (at the same time). She's the mamma what you was taken away from.

One of these days Mary Butler thinks she'll look in the mirror and not see that sadness in her eyes that no amount of smiling can give the jack to.

What's happened? What's happened? One night your mamma comes home just before dawn stinking of Windex and Mr Sheen, and makes such a fuss of you that you wake up. Again. But when you open your eyes she turns her head, staring like mad at something she's seen through the flimsy curtain in your front room. Her mouth's open, her eyes're wide with terror. She rushes into the hallway. You see her, standing there breathing like she's been running to save your life.

You rush to the window, look out onto the street. Nothing. Just Major going for a walk.

Nanna arrived within thirty minutes. 'Oh, pur-leez, tell me yer didn't call me round 'cause you've seen a ghost?' She gave Mary Butler her white-knuckled glare when she saw the younger woman licking her lips, her eyes darting about the room. 'You've got the mad thirst, haven't you? Don't you even think about it, Mary Butler. I'm tellinya now, and I'm warninya. Look at me. I said, Look at me. You listenin' to me?'

Mary stood in the kitchen, holding her hands in a tight ball, rocking backwards and forwards. 'They tol' me he was dead. He's s'posed to be dead. I seen 'im, Nan, with me own eyes, I seen 'im.'

Nan took Mary Butler to the lounge room, sat her down.

You hear them from your bedroom. Who the hell is this Billy your mum's talkin' about? Your dad? Your mamma's sure copping a belting from Nan. But things change after you hear your mamma say, 'I'm doin' me best, Nan. I'm doin' good, ain't I?'

Long after the sun's come up you can still hear the drumming voice of the old woman's voice.

Mary Butler felt like such a lark. She could hardly believe what'd caused that roar of memories, coming at her like the whoosh of an out-of-control train. Get a grip, Mary. Ghosts? What next? You turning dipstick and, like Yaya Zoe, having two-sided conversations with her saint?

My God, my God, it's them
MID AUGUST 1999

In late August of 1999 Major Bob had his fears of the boy's identity confirmed.

He was awoken one night by a loud and insistent knocking on his front door. It was well after midnight. He switched on the outside light. Through the glass panels and security door he saw Yaya Zoe, her distress immediately obvious. Incoherent words were pouring out of her. She was gesticulating wildly towards the Butlers' home.

Johnnie, he thought. Something's happened to Johnnie.

She tried to prevent him, once his door was open, from going back inside to put on his dressing-gown. The woman gripped him by the arm as soon as he returned, wrapped tightly in his kimono (no matter what the emergency, a man had to look decent) and led him down their street, her loud and distraught voice waking up some of the neighbours on both sides of the road. Lights were switched on. Front doors were hesitantly opened. People began venturing out to their front gates. Some emerged to follow, bleary-eyed, eventually gathering around those attending the boy's mother who was slumped on Yaya Zoe's verandah.

Major Bob recoiled from the sight of the woman. Mary Butler

had several bruises on her face. Blood was running out of her nose. Her skirt was hitched up around her thighs. She was naked from the waist up. And there was Johnnie, holding his mother fiercely around the neck.

It's a strange thing, he was to say much later, how the chance event can alter the story of your life. What if Mary Butler, for instance, hadn't gone to Yaya Zoe's for assistance? What if the woman's top hadn't been torn off by whoever had assaulted her? What if the thought had not occurred to the Major to take the boy in his arms then pass him to the Greek woman so that he could check Mary Butler for any injury requiring immediate attention?

With the ambulance turning into their street, Major Bob got down on one knee to check the woman's pulse. He turned his head to one side in a futile attempt to avoid breathing in that rank stench of urine; he knelt in the pool of piss that the woman lay in, which stained his pyjama trousers. And as he looked over the woman searching for injuries, just as he was about to place his fingers under her chin to check her pulse, he saw the distinctive markings on her arm.

Major Bob reached out and, trembling, touched the scars, the likes of which he hadn't set eyes on since he'd last seen that man Jimmy Butler. It's the same family, the Major thought. My God, my God, it's them. The woman, roused from her stupor, half-opened her eyes and saw the glazed image of this white man's face. It's no ghost, Mary, it's him, him, him.

'Fuck you,' she murmured. 'You fucker, comin' for me kid, eh?' And then she tried to spit at him.

The saliva dribbled down her chin. She reached out, trying to claw at the man's face, but Bob Ryan retreated and the woman's arms flailed about in the air.

Zoe Poulos saw it all. She saw the hardening features of her old friend. She saw him step back from the boy's mother and stand to the rear of the crowd of onlookers while the ambulancemen did their work, crouching down to do what they could for the broken ribs, cheekbone and nose, the swollen and bleeding eye, and the bruises all over her face, prior to carrying her away on a stretcher. The Greek woman held the child tightly, the boy's face buried in her stomach; but the query in her widened eyes and uplifted brows, directed towards the Major, went unanswered. But she knew there was some story here.

For twenty-five years Major Bob Ryan hadn't looked at that diary he'd stumbled across all those years ago, which he'd placed in a small padlocked metal chest and hidden in the roof of his home. On the night of Mary Butler's hospitalisation, with the child staying at Yaya Zoe's until Aboriginal Welfare was consulted to figure out what to do with him, Major Bob carried a ladder from his garden shed into the hallway of his home; he placed it under the manhole cover, climbed one, two rungs, hesitated, got back down, stood there for some time, climbed again, this time to the top rung, then changed his mind once more.

The Major took the boy in the following day, lying to all who asked when he said he'd contacted Nanna Dora. Anyway, what was wrong with him taking care of the boy for a couple of weeks? Didn't he have a spare bedroom? Didn't he have the time to walk the child to and from school each day? Help him with his homework, give him pocket money, drive him every week to the hospital to visit his mum? (Best you tell your mother you're staying with Yaya Zoe, lad. You know how fond she is of the Greek woman. Set her mind at ease, know what I mean?) And besides, by the time people'd found out, he'd have shown them he could take care of the kid, and by then the mother'd be home.

It was during the days that Mary Butler was in hospital that Bob Ryan drove everyone nuts badgering them for help in doing up her home.

Put yer cards on the table, Bob

'That little one's not your responsibility, Bob,' Tom said.

'I know, I know, but who's going to take care of him if I don't?'

'Come on, Bob, there are all sorts of welfare groups that'd help the kid.' The old man shifted in his chair then, after some consideration, decided against pursuing the subject for the moment.

Over the road they watched the Hill Run Man warming up before attacking the terraced hills. He finally began his ascent, slowing down dramatically the steeper the slope became, those pumping arms of his out of whack with the legs labouring in slow motion. He collapsed onto his hands and knees when he reached the top.

'Been comin' out a couple of times a week or so,' Old Tom said. 'Usually early in the mornin', sometimes late in the arvo, 'bout this time. I dunno, Bob. Man his age'll go for a light run or a walk, like you. Reckon there's some story here.'

And when the Major's hard staring at the fellow was over and he turned to look at his friend, he saw that Old Tom'd been observing him with a measured gaze.

'You've told Dora you're taking care of that boy?'

'Of course.'

'When you gunna bring him round so's I can meet 'im?'

'Oh, any time, really.'

'You're not avoidin' it are you, mate?'

'Avoiding it? Now why would I do that?'

'Dunno, Bob. Just that you didn't tell me 'bout the night you found the woman.'

'What do you mean? Of course I told you, Tom.'

'Not everything. Zoe came round. She told me 'bout the marks on the woman's arm.'

And when the Major shrugged off the query but did not respond, Old Tom, too, knew that there was more than one story here.

'By the way,' the old man said as the Major stood to go. 'Didn't tell you. Read the obituaries in the local rag. Woman called Rosie died last week. Out at La Pa.'

'Rosie?' Bob Ryan said. 'Rosie who?'

'Rosie Butler. 'Parently she an' her hubby'd been out at La Pa for some time. Jim's his name. Y'reckon it might be Jimmy?'

Yeah, the past was crowding in on Major Bob Ryan alright.

When Major Bob visited the old man the next day after he'd dropped the boy off at school, Tom O'Flaherty waited until they'd started drinking their tea before asking the question which had been bothering him.

'You do remember Jimmy, don't you, Bob?'

The question caused the Major to jerk his head and Bob Ryan, everyone knew, was not a man easily startled.

'People come and go eh, Bob. Life's a bloody train station. By the way, how's our mate Kon comin' along?'

'He's in a bad way, Tom. He's barely covering costs these days. Those corner shops are a thing of the past.'

'Poor bugger,' said Tom. 'Has he got any plans?'

'He's not sure himself. He says there are some young fellows interested in converting his place into a modern café, downstairs and upstairs. He might lease out the whole building, move out and live off the rent. At least he doesn't owe anything on the terrace.'

'Invite him round.'

'Here?'

'Yeah. Needs the comp'ny, I reckon.'

'Ah, you're a good man, Tom O'Flaherty.'

'Yeah, well, maybe. Get a bit lonely meself. Besides, I need the points.'

'Points?'

'Yeah, you know, to get through them pearly gates. I'm thinkin'

I'll be leavin' soon, anyway.'

'You'll outlive us all, Tom.'

The old man laughed. 'Not that sort of leavin'. Me daughter Margaret reckons I should go an' live with her down south.'

'Well,' said the Major. 'Well,' he repeated, 'that is news.'

'There'll be one less thing to keep me here after the October announcement. And how's our young fella, Bob?'

'He's fine, Tom.'

'Funny, ain't it, how no one's makin' any stink? 'Bout him stayin' with you, I mean.'

'Uh-huh.'

'When's his mum comin' home from the hospital?'

'She's in for a few weeks. She took a bad beating. I'll be taking Johnnie to see Souths play this —'

'You still goin' ahead and cleanin' up her home?'

'Yes. About the game this week, I —'

'Bob, you remember that night you found her? Outside Zoe's?'

Ah, Tom, let it be, for the love of God.

'You weren't the first whitefella to go to her aid. You know that, don't you?' And when Bob Ryan did not respond he said, 'Zoe told me others tried to help her.'

'Tom, what are you getting at?'

'She didn't react to them like she did to you.'

'Tom, do we have to —'

'She spat at you, mate. You approached her, she opened her eyes, she saw you — and she spat at you. Said something 'bout you stealin' her kid. An' now you've gone and taken the boy in. Don't you think —'

'She hates whites, Tom. She —'

'The others who tried to help her were white too. She wasn't spittin' at the colour of your skin. Strewth, Bob, she was spittin' at you. At Bob Ryan. I don't think gettin' so involved is a good —'

'I just want to help, Tom,' Major Bob said with some irritation, then added softly, 'I think you're right, though.'

''Bout not gettin' involved?'

'No. About Souths. Come October I think they will kick us out. There's talk of appeals, marches, rallies. The club president says we'll go all the way to the High Court if necessary.'

The old man considered his mate's reply, then said, 'I'll miss me footy. They've buggered our game. Even if they do chuck us out an' we fight an' get back in — it'll never be the same again. I've got me memories, though. They can't take them away from me. I'll live with them.'

'Good memories, too.'

'Great memories, mate, great memories. Tell me, Bob, were there any blackfellas in your camp?'

Bob Ryan blinked unhappily.

'I reckon it's him, Bob.'

'Who?'

'Out at La Pa. This Rosie Butler. Reckon she was Jimmy's wife. Wonder what he's been up to all these years. He letcha down, didn't he.'

There it was again, that tone that turned a question into a statement.

'Well,' Bob Ryan said, 'he had a gift. It was a shame, really.'

''Bout the boy, Bob. And his mother. You've been doin' a lot for them.' He turned to face his mate.

'Why don't you just say what's on your mind, Tom?' Bob Ryan was staring at the passing vehicles barrelling hard into the uneasy morning.

'Been thinkin' 'bout Jimmy this mornin'. How you went outta your way for him. All those chances the club kept givin' him. You know why he was given so many second chances, don'tcha? They did it for you. Gifted, yeah, but a bloody slackarse. An' now there's the boy an' his mother. An' Zoe says you told her Nan's got no problems 'bout you takin' the boy in.'

'That's right.'

'Got news for you, Bob. Nan's out of contact up north, helpin' some blacks in a bit of strife. C'mon, mate, put your bloody cards on the table. You bent over backwards for Jimmy. Just like you're doin' for the boy and his mum. What's the story, sport?'

Tom O'Flaherty saw his mate's eye twitch repeatedly, saw, too, his tongue constantly lick his lips. And an old friend doesn't ignore you for some light reason when you've turned to face him.

Major Bob shook his head without looking at the old man, sighed, stood up. 'I'm going to Kon's,' he said, 'to do some shopping.' He put on his hat, straightened his tie, opened the gate, stepped out onto the footpath.

The Major was about to bid his farewell when the old man said, 'What d'ya reckon heaven's like, Bob?'

'I don't know, Tom. I don't think we're going to have to wait too long to find out, though.'

It was the light moment they needed.

'I'll meetcha there, Bob, in the red and green corner.'

'Even better, Tom, on the Hill, for the view. We'll watch all those great ones who've gone before us, throwing the ball about.'

'One more thing, mate. We've known each other for about seventy years. An' that was the first time.'

'What was?'

'Just now. When you didn't answer me question. You've never avoided me before. An' when you lied 'bout Nan knowin' the boy's stayin' with you.'

Major Bob left without another word being spoken between them. The older man watched him walk until he was out of sight, and it occurred to Tom O'Flaherty that his mate had aged a great deal of late. It also occurred to him that the story that remained a secret to Bob Ryan would, sooner or later, have to be told.

The Major did not visit or phone the old man for two days.

On the following Saturday when they finally saw each other, Kooka Kon was sitting in his lounge, smoking, coughing like a madman, going over the real-estate section of the *Herald*. It ate away at him, seeing the prices Redfern terraces were fetching when he could've bought half a dozen or more for a song all those years ago. Bloody Redfern, that working-class semi-industrial dump, now in demand from all those yuppies who wanted to live near the CBD. Who'd've thought it'd come to this?

He had some money stashed away where Maria would never think to look. One last shot? Just one? Sooner or later a man's luck had to change, surely? He waited until the Holy Trinity opened, lit a candle, prayed, then went to the newsagent and slammed down on the counter eighteen $50 notes.

'Winning number for Lottos Super Saturday, Theo.'

Jimmy Butler was walking on Congwong Bay Beach at La Pa, smoking his rollies, feeling shitscared for reasons he couldn't understand. He was on the blink, alright, pining for Rosie, feeling useless and doomed, finding it hard going keeping that promise he'd made to her to keep off the booze once she'd gone. He sat on the rocks at the northern end of the beach, unaware of the gathering storm that was about to suck him back into the life of Redfern.

When he got up to go he stepped into dog shit, pulled his shoe off and hurled it into the water.

Yaya Zoe had finished making her sheets of pastry for the baklava she'd bake the following week. She'd had a blue with Saint George that morning, who'd told her a woman her age should take things easy. She spent an hour on the jumper she was knitting for Johnnie, filled one bag with bread crumbs she'd feed the birds in Redfern Park later that day, another with the vegie and fruit pieces for Major Bob's compost, then walked to church. She stood on the footpath with all the other Greek women after they'd finished their cleaning for that day's liturgy, squawking their goodbyes at the same time, when she saw Kon approach. She smiled, overjoyed to see this cynic finally coming to his senses, her heart fit to burst at the intense look on his face as he lit a candle and prayed.

Bob Ryan was out exercising with the boy before dawn on the same day. He discovered himself going down South Dowling Street. He hadn't meant to walk to Tom's but, before he knew it, there he was, standing outside his mate's home while over the road the Hill Run Man was doing his sprints. Apart from that long internment at Shino Sonkurai he and Tom O'Flaherty'd never gone for such a long period without seeing or speaking on the phone to each other. The Major had, of course, been busy twisting arms to receive the assistance he needed for the cleaning, painting and redecorating of the boy's home. But there was something else keeping them apart: there was that question of Tom's which still hung in the air, the one Bob Ryan could not or would not answer.

There was a light on in his mate's front bedroom. The Major could hear the radio. Through the curtains he saw Tom moving about. Bob Ryan played with the doorbell, giving his signature tune: the first bar of Souths' anthem, so that the old man knew who was there.

Tom O'Flaherty opened the door and flyscreen, saw his friend and the child, let go of his walking frame and spread his arms. The two men embraced, something they'd never done before.

'I'm sorry, Bob. Shouldn't've pressed the issue.'

'I just can't talk about it, Tom.'

The old man nodded. 'Of course, Bob, of course.'

'It's the shame, you see.'

Ahhh, so there it was, thought Tom. And the old man knew what guilt could do to a fellow. He didn't need to hear any more because it was, after all, *a matter of some shame.*

'If you ever wanna talk about it,' Tom said, 'you know I'll listen. And not judge. But I'll never ask again, Bob.'

'Never?'

'Never,' replied Tom.

'You said never, Tom.'

'That's right.'

'Just how old are you, Mr O'Flaherty?'

'Ninety-nine.'

'And what, pray tell, does *never* mean when you're that old? Just how much longer do you intend hanging around?'

The old man reached across and patted Bob Ryan on the shoulder. 'You always were a mischievous bastard. Now show some respect to those older than yourself and do what you're told. Go inside and make us some brekkie.' He turned to the boy. 'Well, little fella, you must be Johnnie Butler. Pleased to meet you, son.'

Bob returned with a tray on which were placed the steaming mugs of tea and slices of toast. The two men and the boy sat in silence as the sun rose, watching that crazy bloke over the road doing his hill runs.

That night, well after midnight, Major Bob crept into the boy's bedroom. When he was sure Johnnie was in a deep sleep he left the room, closing the door behind him. He went into the backyard, carried his ladder into his home, positioned it under the manhole cover in the hallway, climbed it, holding onto the wall for support, then removed the cover. He felt around until he found the metal chest which he'd placed there decades before. He carried it into the kitchen, removed the dust and dirt and grime off the box with several wet sponges, broke the lock with two screwdrivers, opened the lid then lifted out a large leather-bound dust-covered book. He sat at the table until the early hours of the morning, reading the diary of the Lollipop Man.

SEVEN

The Butler stories

SHIRLEY ARRIVES IN SYDNEY, 1955

Shirley Butler'd been on the move for so long she was numb with weariness. She sat in the compartment of the train with her two children, her back and neck stiff with pain, a wary eye on those whites who gave her more than a look of passing interest, all three watching the landscape change as they got closer and closer to Sydney.

Mary, her feisty five-year-old, had seemed unfazed as the flat, hard-edged plain, which her mother knew well but which, despite its vastness, offered so few places in which one could hide, had begun to fill with trees; her other child, the seven-year-old boy named Jimmy, held his mother's hand and whimpered like a lost puppy, longing for the familiarity of the endless red earth on which one could see, from a great distance, the approaching enemy. With her other hand the woman clung to the duffle bag in which all their possessions had been hurriedly thrown five days previously.

The train finally pulled into Redfern Station. The woman and her boy wore that vulnerable expression common to many blacks arriving in the big smoke for the first time — it was such a giveaway to anyone who might've been observing them; and the man who stood leaning against the stairs, his thumbs tucked into his braces, his keen eyes, under the brim of his hat, taking note of the full-blooded woman with the two half-caste children, reckoned that this woman was arriving in Sydney with no man to support them and with no job to go to; that they had no fixed destination other than to seek some refuge from people unknown to them, strangers in all but the colour of their skin. This woman had, he knew, taking out a notepad from his coat pocket, no plan other than to give hope to their desperate aimlessness, very little certainty other than the fact of their arrival. And, just as he'd envisioned, there was, indeed, no one at the station to greet them, to take hold of that filthy bag the woman held so tenaciously, to lead them to a home where a warm welcome awaited them that would soothe the weary body.

The man took note of the skin colour of the two children, which was so much fairer than that of their mother's. And he stared down at the girl who'd paused, frowning, at the top of the stairs, turning her open gaze away from the interest he'd shown in her family. It made her uneasy, how a fella could follow your movements with his shifting eyes without barely moving his head.

This man made written notes, detailing, in order, the time and date of their arrival, the place from which the train they'd travelled on had begun its journey and, conforming to a grading system he'd long ago devised, the colour of their skin.

Shirley Butler'd heard of the growth in the number of people in the Aboriginal community in Redfern after the end of the white man's war. She'd heard of the great size of this city, too, with its sprawling suburbs and its streets that had no end that you could see. Here, she reckoned, she could lose herself, finding safety in its confusion and anonymity. Surely, the woman thought, looking at this vast and noisy place, its dizzying activity overwhelming her, she and her children would be safe at last.

The fellow followed them from a distance. The woman stopped a black child in the street. He took a mental note of the direction this child pointed in, indicating that part of Redfern he knew well. And then he departed.

Mary Butler, who'd been turning around repeatedly to stare at this man, was relieved to find him gone at last.

What'll we do if the white man he comes?

There was so much Shirley Butler was uncertain about. It was as if she'd become aware of the fact of her own existence once she was no longer a child, as if some fog had lifted one morning, or a flooding river had receded to reveal to herself the reality of her own being so that she could say, *Here I am, me own past like some cloud, like it's been lived by someone else.*

The woman had few answers to give to her son when he asked why it was that she'd lived for a time in an orphanage in northern Queensland, whose dwellings, long corrugated iron buildings in which she'd sweltered in summer, remained a vague memory. She just couldn't remember arriving or how long she'd been there. Shirley Butler had a clearer recollection of the mission in Mulgoa, and the farms at which she'd worked as a domestic servant. She knew that her daughter'd been born in Moonahculla, an Aboriginal reserve near Hay, but was not sure of the date; she knew that her boy had been born three years previously, but did not know which of the two sons of the station manager she worked for was the father. She did know, however, of the ever-present danger to her children.

So the woman took the advice of those mothers who'd returned one evening from their work on the farms to find their children gone forever. She kept on the move, travelling on foot, or hitching rides with other blacks to reserves, staying for a while at Cumeragung and Brungle, the boy walking by her side, the girl, initially, strapped to her back, the small duffle bag held in her hand or slung over her shoulder. She lived in huts or camped in the bush, arriving always at nightfall or after dusk to give her the opportunity to spy out the dangers before the dangers spied her; she would make a bough shed then light a fire which the three of them would lie beside as they slept off their weariness.

The woman worked at fencing, ringbarking or pegging roo skins, living with any blackfella who, she reckoned, might offer her some protection when those white blokes she'd heard about suddenly arrived, searching for half-caste kiddies. She found herself in Box Ridge Station in Coraki on the north coast of New South Wales.

Many of the other kids on the station also had white fathers whom they'd never seen. Their mothers came from all over the state, some even from Queensland and the Northern Territory, arriving with the language of their own tribe which, along with many of their peculiar customs, had to be discarded. There were so many at the mission from so many different tribes, the only language they had in common was a crude form of the white man's tongue.

Shirley Butler took up with a blackfella there, too, shacking up in his shed, joining him for the daily foraging of bush tucker. She'd take her children into the scrub or down to the creek or the swamp and teach them what her blackfella had taught her. It became her primary obsession. You never knew when your kids might be called upon to hunt for turtle, platypus or porcupine on their own. You had to be prepared to live off your skills and wit. Mary and Jimmy'd sit under a tall river gum on a sandy bed, or in isolated pools of still water and watch from a distance as their mum and her fella stalked a roo, eventually joining her, in time, for the hunt.

At night, the cooking and eating done, Shirley's fella would have them sit around the fire bucket outside the shed, teaching them his language or recounting stories of the black man's legends, or the ways of his tribe, whose lands'd been taken for the white man's farms, whose members were spread far and wide.

This was a life that offered some sort of beginning for Shirley Butler; that here there might be some sort of continuity for her and her children; that life on Box Ridge Station had given her a permanency of sorts.

She herself had little to tell, however, could not recall anyone telling her stories. When her own life was such an ill-defined recollection of days and events, seasons merging with place names barely remembered, what could she say? And besides, there were the simple matters of collecting and preparing food, and keeping an eye out for dangers which consumed her life. So she hunted the animals and collected the berries and yams she'd prepare for their meal, keeping a watchful eye on the horizon for the white man. Sitting around the fire at night gave rise to the possibility that one day Jimmy and Mary, with children of their own, might ask her for a tale: then Shirley Butler might be able to look back on the day-to-day events on this mission and tell her children and grandchildren of the abundant life in the creek, the nights that were full of stars and the years of wandering that'd finally come to an end.

Her unease of the white man never left her, however. It was a matter of some humour in the camp how obsessed she was with such fears: if she ever had to leave her children alone for any length of time, she'd mix charcoal with the animal fat she kept in ready supply, smearing their bodies so that, if the white man came, looking from a distance for half-caste kids, he'd see, if his eyes happened to rest on Jimmy and Mary, a couple of full-blooded children. She showed them the gullies and hollows they were to scramble into if the sudden need arose.

But what if the worst happened and, if the white man did arrive, took her children? How would she, in years to come, after a lifetime of searching for them, recognise her children when they'd grown old and she happened by chance to fall upon them?

When they went by the different names the white man gave them and were moved from one side of the country to another, how would she, passing them in the street, know they were her children?

The elders at the mission would not break the custom and take her under-aged children through the rites of initiation; so she took them well away from the camp, lit a great fire, heated a long and sharp piece of metal then burned several lines, similar to those markings of her own tribe, into the arms of Jimmy and Mary, there, between the elbow and the shoulder of their right arms.

The white man comes

Shirley was out of the campsite when the whitefellas came. She and her children were making their way back from the hunt, carrying a dead turtle and armfuls of yams and nuts when they heard a sudden loud and prolonged scream. Shirley Butler saw, from a distance and through the scrub, two men bundling a couple of children into an idling car. She acted out of instinct and with a practice long-rehearsed, pushing her children flat to the ground, pressing their faces into the earth. She lay between the two, her arms around their necks, her lips moving against the ear of one, and then the other.

'Don'tcha move,' she whispered.

She looked up to see several women and men rushing from sheds, from one of the many scattered campfires and from some thickets, pummelling the vehicle with their fists while the mother of the two children desperately tried to open the locked door of the rear of the car.

'Don'tcha move,' she breathed.

The two men were about to drive off when the mother of the two children threw herself to the ground in front of the car. She raised herself to her knees and her kids, seeing their mother's face contorted with horror and hearing her gasping cries, became hysterical.

'Don'tcha look. Don'cha even breathe.'

Shirley Butler watched as the two cops, unable to reverse because of the men and women standing at the rear of the car, conferred in the front compartment. And then one of them got out, approached the mother, bent down and spoke to her. Shirley saw the panic slowly subside in the woman's face as the man helped her to her feet, then held her by the elbow as they walked together to the rear door of the car. The second man, who'd remained inside, unlocked and opened the back door. The woman got in. She was engulfed by her children.

Shirley Butler stood after the car'd driven off and it was, she reckoned, at a safe distance from the camp. She and her children walked to where the men and women and children of the mission stood as one, watching in silent confusion as the car sped off in a cloud of dust. They followed the progress of the swirling cloud. They screwed their eyes to make out that vague form of the car, waiting.

And then their worst fears were realised. They heard the sound of the vehicle's motor subside, then that of the handbrake being applied. Through the settling dust they saw the motionless car, a black mark on the horizon. The front doors were opened and the two men got out. One of them was about to open the rear door when he stopped, looked back at the camp, took out his binoculars then pointed. Shirley Butler saw his outstretched hand and the sunlight glinting on the glasses. She saw the two men pause to look back towards the gathered mob.

The white men sprang into action, opening, from either side of the vehicle, both of the two rear doors. One wrestled with the children as the other grabbed their mother and hurled her out onto the ground. They slammed shut the doors, rushed back into the front of the automobile and sped off.

Shirley Butler immediately threw her few belongings into her duffle bag and left, deciding, on the spur of the moment, to make her way to Sydney where, she thought, she and her kids could lose themselves in a great crowd.

Shirley Butler was overwhelmed by relief and confusion as she stood outside Redfern Station. She and her kids were greeted by a rush of men in overalls who clambered down the stairs to catch the train home after their day's work at the Eveleigh workshop. She'd been told of the vast numbers of foreigners, refugees of the war, who'd made a new home for themselves in Sydney. She'd been told of the languages they spoke which only their kind could understand and the houses in Redfern they were moving into en masse, terraces which fronted narrow streets and lanes. She stood on the footpath catching snippets of their strange tongues, saw passing trams sending sparks across the road, saw, too, huge grey buildings some distance away in the city centre. She sensed the preoccupation people had with getting on with the business of their daily lives, rejoiced in the mad rush and loud clatter of the traffic, the pollution from which she recoiled, the anonymity she felt was, at last, hers to celebrate, the ignorance she had of this vast, crazy place and, most of all, its ignorance of her and her family.

That night the Lollipop Man sat at the desk in his bedroom, still wearing his shirt and tie. One thumb was tucked under one of his braces. As he smoked his pipe he paused in his work to consider the events he'd witnessed at the station that day, filled his fountain pen with ink, sighed, then resumed writing that daily entry into his diary.

One's attention cannot but be drawn to the large number of full-blooded black women drifting to Sydney and the wretched half-caste children trailing in their wake. Many arrive without husbands to support them, compounding the magnitude of the problem facing the Commonwealth. It wrenches one's heart to see such children loafing around the streets, rarely attending church, often not attending school. They know little of The Gospels. Many can barely read or write.

One must be prepared to take whatever steps are necessary to merge these half-caste children into our white society. If not we face an unthinkable danger: that three races will develop in Australia — white, black and the pathetic third race of half-castes, which is neither one nor the other.

The full-blood presents no danger. It is a slow breeder. The sinister half-caste, however, is increasing in number. Action taken now for such a merger will ensure that Australia will one day be entirely free of the Aborigine.

Jimmy Butler is stolen

Shirley Butler was taken in, on the night of her arrival, by one of the many large black groups sharing terraces in Redfern.

She began looking for work the very next day, going from factory to factory, warehouse to warehouse; but who would give employment to a woman dressed in such a mishmash of shabby clothes, whose English, if that's what you could call it, people barely understood; who needed, it was clear to see, a good scrub with solvol in a hot bath.

While the woman trudged the streets her children remained at their new home. Mary went indoors late in the afternoon, tired of the games of marbles, cocky laura and hopscotch. She was standing at the window looking out at her brother who continued with a ball game on the footpath when she saw a black vehicle drive up and down the narrow street. Mary recognised one of the two men in the car as being the one she'd seen at the station the day before. He got out of the car and leaned on the bonnet while the second man herded the light-skinned children together. Mary Butler watched as they were given a lollipop. One of them was her brother. She stood, staring, frozen in terror, as Jimmy and two others were lifted bodily and placed in the back of the car.

Mary pressed her face hard up against the window. She saw the back of her brother's head through the rear window of the vehicle.

The man she recognised was about to get into the driver's side of the automobile when he happened to see Mary Butler. Their eyes met for a long moment. And then he began his unhurried walk towards her. The girl rushed to the front door, locking it from the inside moments before the man made to enter the terrace. He turned the handle a few times, rattling it hard, pushing against the door. He stood there for several seconds, hesitating for some time before deciding to leave.

When Shirley Butler returned, she saw some women kneeling on the footpath and in the middle of the road, tearing at their hair, beating their heads with their fists. She rushed in a mad frenzy to her home, hammering at the door. She cried out for her boy, called out the name of her daughter, but there was no response. She pushed a fist through the panel of glass, opening a large gash in the palm of her hand. Shirley Butler unlocked the door from the inside, opened it, rushed from room to room, the blood trailing behind her. She found her girl huddled in the closet under the stairs.

Shirley Butler held her daughter tightly to her breasts, moaning and cursing and wailing, beating her head repeatedly on the wall.

'We gotta go, mamma,' Mary said. 'That man he gunna come back for me. C'mon mamma, get up, get up.'

The girl tied a handkerchief around her mother's hand, gathered up their belongings then led her out of Redfern. They walked all night, taking side streets when they could, wandering in a haphazard direction towards La Perouse where they knew there was another community of blacks. They arrived in the early hours of the morning. The woman's hand was freshly bandaged. An old vacant tin shed was found for them.

Jimmy Butler was taken to a children's home in Glebe where, on arrival, he was dipped in lye, his clothes removed by Matron with a pair of tongs. The following day, to ensure no contact was made by his mother, the Lollipop Man organised for the boy to be sent to an orphanage in Queensland. He left three days later.

And forty-four years later the brother and sister took up residence in Sydney only a few kilometres from each other, Jimmy in La Perouse, Mary in Redfern.

Where possible the half-caste child should be removed from its family at as young an age as possible, preferably from its mother's breast, thus creating as great a distance as possible from its place of birth, language and customs.

Case Study Number 84 is that of a boy named James Butler. The movements of this half-caste child, his sister and his mother are typical of the nigger. As far as can be ascertained, based on facts given the writer by said boy, he and his sister were born to different fathers, as is often the case. He was born in 1948 or thereabouts, in Moonahculla, a black settlement near Hay in New South Wales. He has distinctive scars on his right arm, between the elbow and the shoulder, as shown in the diagram below. After his birth the mother took her children to Cumeragung, for reasons unknown, then ...

When Mary Butler was taken some years later from La Perouse, Shirley Butler did not react as expected. She saw the Lollipop Man and one other man get out of a car as she made her way up the steps from the beach at Congwong Bay; saw her pregnant daughter gathered up in the arms of the younger man from the street overlooking the bay, where the girl'd been playing with a number of other children. The woman watched as her daughter lashed out at the man as she was thrown in his car, observed in silence as the automobile drove away from La Pa down Anzac Parade.

Shirley Butler ascended the stairs up onto the road. She went down on her knees among the sweets that lay strewn on the tramlines then, after several moments, fell to the ground with a thud. She lay in a foetal position on the lines, holding herself tightly, making no sound or movement. The locals, who looked out from behind their shop counters and their homes, thought the woman'd been knocked down and killed by a passing tram.

The waiting for Shirley Butler was over. The constant state of alertness was no more. There was now nothing to hope for, nothing to fear. There was nothing more these whitefellas could do to hurt her.

La Perouse

1955–65

Days after her appearance in La Perouse, Shirley Butler acquired her nickname: she was *the silent one.* The woman never laughed and rarely smiled. From the time of their arrival she found it difficult to cuddle her daughter. She provided for her girl, though, in that quiet mechanical way she had of doing things, which had some people almost forgetting, at times, that she was there.

Shirley took to doing what the other black women did: she would accompany them to the nearby scrub to gather dry sticks to stoke the fire that boiled the water under the single copper in the communal laundry; she collected the shells of the cowrie, fan conk and pippie, then sat with the others as they cut them into decorative shapes of the Harbour Bridge, hearts and babies' shoes. They'd gather each day on the knoll overlooking the beach and make boomerangs from the bent limbs of trees some of their menfolk brought back from the mangroves at Weeney Bay, near Kurnell.

On the weekends, when the white people descended on La Pa to swim at the beaches or to watch the snake man perform his tricks in the pit, she'd sit in the old Aboriginal cemetery alone, looking out over the water. She'd glance up now and then to watch her daughter diving off the bridge to Bare Island to recover the coins the white people threw into the waters below, and try not to think of her son, who'd been as strong a swimmer as she'd ever seen. She'd turn her eyes away from the games of footy her daughter played with the boys, too, recalling her son's crazy antics with the ball that left his and the opposing team members breathless in wonder, confused and doubled over with laughter. He was, people used to say, a born athlete who would go far.

She'd stay as far away as possible from the white families while still keeping an eye on Mary, waiting until the white people'd packed up their belongings, purchased a boomerang or brooch from Frankie the Boomerang Man, who'd give her a small commission, then boarded the tram or ferry. Shirley Butler did what she could to avoid them, and it wasn't her fear alone of the white man that drove her from them: their smiling faces, the women walking arm-in-arm with their men, the large parties of Greeks and Italians who fussed over their children, grandparents and grandchildren on the picnic blanket were sights too painful to bear.

And when they were gone she'd accompany the other black women back down to the water's edge where they'd collect oysters, dig for pippies, catch crabs and, at low tide, gather muttonfish with a file or strong knife, prising them off the rocks. When the tide was high she'd watch Mary fearlessly dive for octopus with the boys. As they roasted pippies at dusk on the beach on a flat piece of tin over a fire, she'd look up at the road and imagine the black car and the man with the sweets carrying her Mary away.

She was at the school one morning, helping to distribute milk from a big can. It was a task she volunteered for, to ensure her daughter hadn't run off from class again

'She'll be trouble for you, Butler,' the Reserve Manager said. 'You'll see, you'll see.'

Mary Butler left school as soon as she was old enough. She joined her mother from time to time down at the beach, where she helped make fishing nets. Mother and daughter would stretch tight the two coils of rope, seeing the net slowly take shape under their skilful hands which held the needle and twine. They spent little time together, so it was an activity that gave comfort to the woman. They'd sit side by side on the sand, sewing the net onto the cork and lead lines then tanning them so they wouldn't rot in the water.

'Tell us a story, Mamma,' the girl would say.

When the net-making was done, mother and daughter'd sometimes help the men in catching small schools of whiting, bream and blackfish. Once a year they made a quid or two selling the mullet to the Greeks, who had the mad desire for the roe they'd salt and dry in the sun.

'Tell us 'bout your mamma,' the girl'd say.

And the woman, so that she would not disappoint her daughter, would create imaginary stories of the life of that mother she'd never known. But Mary Butler caught her out one day.

'You're bullshittin' me, Mamma. You're tellin' me different things each time I'm askin'. Why ya bullshittin' me?'

Shirley Butler sat on the rock ledge at the beach, looking out for schools of fish so as to alert the men in their boats. And her daughter, grown bored with the mother who would sit, and look, and say little, got up and dived into the sea. She swam out and

clambered aboard one of the smaller wooden boats, joining the men, one of whom, the mother saw, she was overfamiliar with.

The Reserve Manager arrived and stood next to Shirley. 'I'm warnin' you. If I catch her you know what'll happen, right? Hangin' round all day with the men. Girl her age. I'm lookin' to find her home work. For her own good, mind. Okay?'

Shirley Butler returned to her home one week later to find the manager and his wife sitting on two of her fruit boxes. She was not surprised to find them there. They regularly entered people's shacks unannounced, to check on the cleanliness of their belongings or to search for the alcohol that was regularly smuggled into the Reserve.

'I've found your girl a possie out at Camperdown. She's old enough to go out and work. Better for her, don'tcha think? She'll be a house servant to a bloke I know. Good family. They'll take care of her, right?'

From the day that her daughter began work Shirley Butler no longer joined the other women during the afternoon fossicking for food. She'd sit under the Moreton Bay figs, which were known as the Dreaming Trees, waiting to see her daughter return safely by bus from wherever it was that the white man had sent her. She was particularly fond of that tree under which King Billy had died.

She'd do some dreaming of her own sitting up against its massive trunk, every few days going into the bush to collect wild flannel flowers, kangaroo paws, peach blossoms and boronia to lay at King Billy's grave.

When her daughter fell pregnant to the white man of the house where she worked, Shirley Butler knew that it was only a matter of time before her child was taken.

Shirley Butler was carried from the disused tramlines into her shack after the Lollipop Man had driven away. She sat by the open and empty fireplace, day after day, refusing to eat. The other women came by to replenish the kero in her single lamp and, when fuel was unavailable, to light her candles. They brought her the fish they'd cooked, returning the next day to find her sitting where they'd left her, the food untouched.

The black does not pine for her offspring in the same way as the white woman. She will soon forget about her child in the same manner as a dog, losing its litter, soon forgets about its pups.

Of late a great concern has become apparent. The half-caste is multiplying at an alarming rate.

The ultimate purpose, nay, the only solution is to quicken the biological absorption of the half-caste into the European population to breed out the colour.

Case Study Number 172 is of one Mary Butler, whose brother, James, was rescued ten years ago, on 15th September, 1955. It was not possible to glean information from this girl, who displayed behaviour of a singularly recalcitrant nature. The major sources of information come from employees at the home in Glebe, notably Matron Caroline Smithers and Sister Jennifer Nicholls.

The tribal scars, as shown in Diagram 1 below, observed on the Case Study's right arm, are consistent with …

Shirley Butler died several weeks after she'd last seen her daughter. Her emaciated body was laid to rest in the local cemetery. Some of the locals gathered the flowers they knew to be her favourites, laying them on her grave, knowing that the woman had, at last, found peace.

And thirty-four years later Jimmy Butler would spend time each day at the cemetery, in mourning for the mother he could not recall and the wife he had lost.

Mary Butler
1965—99

'You let go! I want me mum! Let go!'

Matron Caroline Smithers emerged from the office of the Glebe orphanage, all crisp and neat and military, pouting her lower lip. Her hair was tied back tight and flawless. She watched under arched brows as the pregnant girl squirmed and twisted to free herself from a young policeman's hold. Mary Butler broke from the man's grip, turned, swore again and spat into his face.

'Officer! The language! Gracious.'

The Matron sighed. Another difficult case. She smoothed down her heavily starched uniform, rang a small bell she kept in her pocket then made her way slowly to the car, the dozen or so keys on the huge ring hanging off her belt singing a discordant tune. At least the older policeman was there, who knew how to handle such cases until some order was imposed.

Faces of kids appeared from behind barred windows, attracted by the noise. They watched with blank impassive faces as Mary Butler ripped into the bewildered young copper. Kitchen workers stood in aprons, leaning on doorways to observe. Someone shut the iron gate the car had driven through. A voice was heard barking at the kids at the window. Their heads disappeared.

Several nurses, summoned by the Matron's bell, came on the scene, flapping about in their stiff whiteness like startled pigeons.

Mary Butler kicked the young policeman in the shins. The other man, surprisingly agile for someone his age, grabbed the girl from behind, wrapping his arms around her in a tight embrace, immobilising her. In one swift movement he picked her up and pressed her against the car. She was suspended off the ground, the man's face pushed against the back of her neck.

'Now,' he said, his lips close to the girl's ear, 'you listen to me, lass. I want to hear you promise me that when I leave you'll follow Matron's rules, then I'll let you go. And then you can get on with your new life and I can get on with mine. What do you think, lassie?'

'You wanna know what I think? I think you're the devil an' you're gunna rot in hell!'

'What if I told you I might come back, then? You wouldn't want that, would you? When your baby's born, I mean. You wouldn't want me to come back and pay your baby a little visit, now, would you?'

The man felt the girl's body stiffen.

'I think we have an understanding.'

After the man's departure Mary Butler was led into the bathroom.

'Remove your clothes!' snapped Matron. The keys were off her belt. She was counting them down, one at a time, like they were prayer beads. 'I have to check for lice and nits. I shan't say it again. Now, be still.'

'Be still your fucken self!'

'Sister, bring the ironing cord. And make sure it's wet.'

The following morning Sister Jennifer Nicholls gave the girl a bar of chocolate. 'Here, thought you might like this.'

'What's the catch? What'd'ya want?'

'Nothing.'

'Bullshit.' But she took the chocolate anyway. 'Matron'll go crook on ya.'

'Only if she finds out. Our secret, okay?' she said, as she was leaving.

'Me name's Mary.'

The Sister stopped, turned to face the girl and said, 'I know. I've always liked that name. You can call me Jenny. When Matron's not around. See ya later.'

On visiting days Mary Butler would play dominoes, pick-up-sticks and cat's cradle with Sister Jennifer, listening to the sounds of greeting and farewell of those women who came to visit their children.

'Why ain't me mum comin' to visit me?' she asked Matron Caroline one day.

'I don't know.'

'Me kid'll be comin' soon. Be good to have me mum visit. She know I'm here?'

'Of course.'

'She ever rang?'

'No.'

'Can she visit?'

'No. But if you continue to be good I'll think about it after your child is born.'

Mary Butler named her son after King Billy. Jenny reckoned Billy was a little beauty.

She approached Matron again.

'Willya tell me mum? Willya write to her?'

'No.'

'Please? I'm tryin' to be good, y'know?'

'No.'

'She don't ask 'bout me?'

Matron looked up from her desk. 'Why don't *you* write to her?'

'Me?'

'Yes, you. You do know how to write, don't you?'

'You'll let me? You'll send 'em? You never let me before.'

'You've been cooperating. From what I can observe. So Sister Jennifer and others tell me. Let's have a trial period, shall we? Just continue following the rules. Everyone playing their part, girl. It's what made the British Empire great.'

As Mary Butler was about to leave the office, Matron added, 'You've been heard speaking your own language to your child. That's not allowed. You know that. Don't let it happen again. Understood?'

Mary Butler sent letters and cards to her mother, simple notes in the simple English she'd been taught at the school in La Perouse, telling of the growth of the fair-skinned boy.

'I thought I told you not to speak to your child in your native tongue. I won't tell you again. This is your last warning.'

'Has me mum never rung? After gettin' me letters? Not one time?'

'Telephone calls are not allowed,' Matron replied. 'Mothers calling their children at all hours of the day and night! As if we had nothing better to do but field such calls. But you know this. I don't know why you keep asking. Perhaps,' she said, as Mary Butler was opening the door to leave the office, 'your mother does not want to visit.'

'What?'

'You mean — *I beg your pardon, Matron?*'

The girl stood at the threshold. 'What didja say?' The old fierceness had returned, a rush of blood throbbing in her head.

'Don't you go back to your old ways, girl. Don't you talk to me with that tone.'

'You reckon me mamma don't wanna visit?'

'Don't you raise your voice to me.'

'An' don'tcha say nothin' bad 'bout me mum, alright? Don't

you never say nothin' bad 'bout her.' And then she snarled some words in a language Matron did not understand.

'You're speaking the devil's language, aren't you? That's right, isn't it? And you have the gall to come into my office and raise your voice. Leave my office immediately. I shall attend to you later. And here I was, actually believing you'd changed. You'll never change. Never. You're a wicked girl, Mary Butler. You and all your kind.'

Mary Butler, however, stayed where she was, thinking, thinking. Matron Caroline positioned the pen with great care beside the others, placed her hands on the desktop, raised a quizzical brow then said, 'You're still here.'

'Are you gunna steal me kid?'

'What?'

'You got it in your head already, ain'tcha? You ain't gunna let me keep Billy, are ya?'

'I think you should get out of my office.'

'Think you're gunna do to me boy what yer done to me an' me brother?' The girl approached Matron, leaned across the desk so that the woman, becoming afraid, pushed her swivel chair well back. 'You leave me boy alone, alright? I'm warnin' ya.' She stormed out of the room, slamming the door behind her.

Matron stared at the shut door. It didn't matter, she thought, how hard you tried. It made no difference what you did to improve this appalling race. They would always remain coarse in manner, ungrateful and, yes, undeserving of all efforts made to lift them out of the wretchedness of their miserable lives.

When Mary Butler was once again heard speaking her own language, Matron Caroline personally washed her mouth out with soap.

The girl knew she had to escape. She would alert her mother first so they could flee Sydney together with little Billy.

Mary wrote a letter to her mother and, because she suspected Matron was reading her correspondence, gave it to Sister Jenny to post.

The young woman read the name on the envelope. 'Who's Shirley Butler?'

'It's me mum.'

The smile on the sister's face was replaced by a hard considered stare.

'What?' Mary said. 'What's wrong?'

Sister Jenny stood there too long, saying nothing.

'What? Tell me, Jenny.'

And then the smile returned to the woman's face. 'Oh, sorry, just thinking of something, Mary. Sure. Of course. I'll post it right away.' And the Sister walked quickly away.

Mary Butler stormed into Matron Caroline's office.

'How dare you —'

'You sendin' me letters?' She placed both hands on the glass top. 'To me mum! Me cards and stuff. Didja?'

Matron Caroline adjusted her glasses. She reached into her pocket for the little bell to summon assistance. 'Get out. Get out you insolent girl.'

'Tell me! I wanna know! Why didn'tcha send 'em?'

'Do you want to know? Do you? Do you really want to know?'

'Tell me now!'

'Because there's no one to send them to. She's not at La Perouse, you stupid girl. She's dead. Your mother's dead. Now get out of my office.'

'Just sign it.'

'What is it?'

'It's nothing to be concerned about,' Matron said. 'It's a health form. For your baby. You want him to be able to receive medical assistance when he needs it, don't you?'

Mary Butler was in Matron Caroline's office. The older woman sat behind her desk. Sister Jennifer stood to one side.

'Hurry up, girl, I'm busy.' She was tapping the glass top with the fingers of one hand, the other holding the pen which Mary now reached across and took.

Mary Butler dipped the nib into an inkwell, passed her eyes over the form, hesitated, then looked at Matron, who threw an exasperated look out the window. Mary glanced up at Jenny Nicholls. The Sister stood unusually stiff and still, holding her hands so tightly that Mary Butler saw the whitened knuckles. Sister Jenny did not return Mary's glance but stared down at the form; and there it was, the Sister's slightly furrowed brow that was intended for Mary, and that barely perceptible shaking of the head, once to the left, once to the right.

Mary Butler threw the pen across the desk, globs of ink staining the form and Matron Caroline's tunic.

'There, you can stick that pen up yer arse.' And she turned to leave the office.

'Come back! I did not say you could go!'

'Go? You can go an' get fucked!' And she slammed the door.

Matron picked up the pen. She dismissed Sister Jenny, drew the forms closer to her then signed them herself on behalf of the girl, using Mary Butler's name. She gathered up, folded, and put the adoption papers for Billy Butler into a large envelope.

After being told by Sister Jenny what the papers were for, Mary Butler waited until well after midnight, rose from her bed and took her baby into a broom closet. She held a sharp kitchen knife over the flame of a candle, then cut deep gashes into the right arm of her baby, between the elbow and the shoulder. Billy's screaming woke every person in the orphanage.

When Matron Caroline saw what Mary Butler had done she immediately rang the doctor and the police. There must be no delay. This young mother was clearly a danger to her child. Mad, mad, she'd always had the potential to do such a thing. Why had Matron waited so long? The baby should have been adopted out the day it was born. You show a little kindness to this black girl so she can spend some time with her child and look how she repays you.

The matter was referred to the Lollipop Man who, it was well known, took a keen interest in such matters.

Mary Butler woke up suddenly. It was 3 a.m. and Billy Butler was not in his cot. She rushed to the window. In the gravel driveway she saw an idling black car, and in the back seat sat a woman, holding Billy. The Lollipop Man was in the driver's seat. He drove away. The hysterical mother had to be restrained by three nurses.

Later that week, Sister Jenny told her the news. Mary Butler was going to be sent to a mission at Mulgoa.

'I'm going back home, Mary, to the farm. Leaving tonight. Mum's a bit crook. Besides, I don't like it much here, y'know?'

The child–mother opened her arms and the two of them embraced in silence.

'It's bad, Mary, it's bad. Never knew such things went on in the world. In your own bloody country. I'm sorry.'

She got up and left hurriedly, not turning at the door, as Mary'd hoped and expected, for a final wave. On the chair beside her bed she found an envelope. Inside was a small wad of money.

She did not expect to ever see her son again. But more than thirty-two years later, after recovering in hospital from a terrible beating, she returned to her home in Redfern to find it'd been redecorated; and, some time after she'd got rid of that glass-eyed man, who'd come round, she knew, to steal her little Johnnie, she saw, standing unsteadily at the threshold of her front door, his hands trembling uncontrollably, the smell of petrol on his clothes, that impostor who claimed he was her long lost son, Billy Butler.

Mary Butler grew dependent on the grog. Sometimes, when she was really plastered, she'd cradle a flask of plonk in her arms and sing the white man's lullabies to her imaginary son, which was a great joke to anyone who might've been there to observe her. She'd go into town seeking various forms of escape, lying in the arms of any blackfella who promised some comfort. She avoided the whitefellas or those blacks who had too much white blood in their veins: you couldn't afford to have another half-caste taken away from you. A black kid, however, was another matter. One as dark as, say, Mary Butler's own mother would have those white do-gooders leaving her alone.

Mary couldn't recall how the hell she'd ended up in Townsville. It'd been such a long and aimless road that meandered back into her blotted past, connecting the shacks, park benches and barns she'd stayed at, the coastal and inland towns she'd passed through.

And then she arrived: nothing much made sense, except the fact of the wharf at Townsville where she stood at dawn; that sure was real. And the little black boy whose hand she clutched, whom she'd called Johnnie for no particular reason. He was real, too. Yeah, she'd hang on to him, alright, even long after she'd been told the days of the whitefella coming to take your kid away had passed; even when she no longer had to invent some other name when the coppers stopped her in the street to ask her this and that. Butler's me name. What of it, eh? Ya gunna take me kid again? Eh, fuckface?

The ferry arrived at Hayles Wharf at 4.30 a.m. It took her to the Palm Island Aboriginal settlement, where some of the blacks were consumed by a hatred for all whites which exceeded her own. She was spat on by one of the full-bloods and called a little white bitch.

She packed up and left the seething hatred on the settlement after one week. On hearing that the Lollipop Man was long dead she decided she'd return to Redfern. As for Billy, someone'd heard he'd fallen into bad ways, become addicted to all sorts of crap and died. Anyway, it was easier not expecting to ever see him again. A woman could get on with the business of surviving each day as it came. There was Johnnie, too. She was told he'd find in Redfern a community of blacks to grow up with, who couldn't give a shit if he was a full or half-blooded black, or which tribe or part of Australia you came from. No one interfered with his damn good intentions to screw up your whole fucken life. Yeah, Redfern was the place to go.

EIGHT

A crook time for the Bunnies

SEPTEMBER TO OCTOBER 1999

Even Tom O'Flaherty's chooks, which he'd once butchered for the Sunday roast, were dying off of old age. But Old Tom himself was still hanging in, even if he didn't have the strength, as he'd joke, to pull a greasy stick out of a dead dog's arse, surprised he'd lived so long. What was it, the daily schooner of black and tan, or Sheaf stout with a slice of lemon? Surely not those innumerable cuppas with Bob Ryan, who'd come at 9 a.m. on the dot, come rain, hail or whatever?

His days, he reckoned, were spent mostly piss-fartin' about, waitin' for the telegram from Queen Lizzie. And then came this whole business with Souths and the fame it brought him. Life, he knew, could still throw up the unexpected, slapping you across the face or biting you on your ancient wrinkled bum, like the day when he played one of his reel-to-reel tapes for Johnnie Butler, and Bob Ryan went all cold and speechless and his face turned as white as butcher's paper.

Not that long ago Tom'd been the local historical society's prize speaker, delivering an informal yarn at the town hall down the road. He loved to talk about the Rabbitohs, taking along some of those relics he'd spent an average bloke's lifetime collecting. Most of all it was those spinechilling recordings he'd made which he liked to play, of men talking about some milestone in their playing careers. And then the shit hit the fan for the Bunnies, reporters came and went from his home for the personal interest story when word got out of his recordings, and all sorts of blokes in suits started to show an interest in the tapes, offering inducements if only Old Tom'd donate his collection to this or that museum. Yeah, life was full of surprises alright.

'Well, Tom,' the Major said, 'you're famous.'

'What's that?'

'I saw you on the telly last night, Tom.'

'Pardon?'

'Have you gone deaf, Tom?'

'No. But what's this *Tom-this*, *Tom-that* business? I'm famous, as you just said. So it's Mr O'Flaherty to you, sonny.'

The great George Treweek's grandson came by one day. And Tom, knowing what was on his mind said, 'Would you like me to open the display case? Would you like me to take out the ball? Would you *like to touch*?'

And he let the young man hold the football that his grandfather had held to his chest the day he broke through the entire English pack to score a try.

'There's a step ladder over there behind the door. Bring it here. Get up. There, the photo third from the left, standin' in the middle row. That's your grandad. Now, on this wall there's a shot of him goin' in for a tackle. That was in '31. I'll tell you about that game. Sit down, son.'

Yeah, who would have thought it, Thomas O'Flaherty, the

celebrity. There sure was no end of surprises in life, alright.

But there was the expected, too.

Both Tom and Bob Ryan had lived for so long in the one suburb, getting to know those who delivered the milk and the papers, the shop owners and street cleaners, that hardly a month went by without some old codger they'd known passing on. It was a melancholy ritual they went through. Old Tom'd open the front door for his mate to enter his home, but the Major would stand there, his hat still on his head, pausing in silence at the threshold.

'Not another one, Bob?'

'I'm afraid so, Tom.'

'Well, come out with it. Who is it this time?'

'Mark'

'Mark Fitzjames?'

'Yes, Tom.'

'Ahh, dear Marcus. He put up a good fight.'

'He surely did, Tom. He's at peace, now.'

All the old-timers were going, their kids selling the terrace that had been in the family for yonks. And if the home was in the better half of Redfern, near South Dowling Street, well, it made some people's eyes go all glassy just thinking about what their place was worth.

'You're sitting on a fortune, Tom.'

'I know. I've been thinkin' of sellin'.'

'What? You're joking?'

'Sell the house, make a bundle. I always wanted to pull a good Irish stout in me own pub. *O'Flaherty's Irish Pub*. Got a good ring to it, eh mate?'

'Well, while you're still young enough, and if it means that much to you, you should go for it, Tom — I mean, Mr O'Flaherty.'

The old man takes Johnnie's breath away

Major wonders whether you've both arrived early at Tom's. He takes out his fob watch, opens the lid and stares at the large clock face, all serious and breathing hard, like he's looking at your report card (he's asked you to get an interim progress report from your teacher). He takes you up and down one block of South Dowling Street, stops once more outside Old Tom's, consults the Waltham then, satisfied, opens the gate. He takes you by the shoulders, positions you to his right, rings the doorbell.

The old man opens the wooden door but leaves the flyscreen shut. He scowls at Major Bob. 'You're ten seconds late. Dunno what the world's comin' to,' he says, winking at you, 'when even good men can't get to a place on time. Come in, son, come in. Yeah, you too, I s'pose, big fella. How's your mum, Johnnie? Comin' home soon?'

'Nah. Them bones still broken, all plastered. She's still sore.'

'And how's the Major treatin' you?'

'Good, Mista Tom.'

'If he gives you any trouble you'll tell me, okay?'

'Okay, Mista Tom.' You like him. He's a cheeky old bugger.

'Bunnies ain't doin' too well are they? Gettin' walloped each week. Didja see last week's game?'

'I ain't never seen any game. Major's gunna take me this Sat'day.'

'Yeah? First game, eh? Might bring us some luck. But good times'll come sooner or later. 'Slong as the Bunnies are still around, that is. Just hope young Bobby here's around to enjoy them with me when they do.'

But you're no longer listening. It's your first time inside his house and it takes your breath away. You stand there, mouth open, taking it in. The teachers at school'd told you of his lounge room but nothing they'd said prepared you for this. There are rows upon rows of framed photos of every first-grade Souths team, from the cornice down to the tops of the couches, mounted display cabinets, one with a weathered guernsey of a player who, the label says, *Fell in the Great War* (you recognise Major's beautiful handwriting). There are mannequins, headless torsos that stand in all four corners of the room, decapitated ghosts wearing the labelled cardinal and myrtle of different eras. There are socks and caps and boots hanging off hooks, framed players' contracts and letters and, on the piano, two silver-framed photos, one of Clive Churchill in 1955, nursing his broken wrist, another of John Sattler in 1970, his shattered jaw all awry, both men lifted on the shoulders of their jubilant team-mates.

While Major's in the kitchen fixing you all a cuppa, Mista Tom takes you to a wall in his dining room.

'Here, look at this, son,' he says, nodding at a photo gone amber with age, of some village in a country whose name means nothing to you. 'Ireland. It's where me dad comes from.'

He shuffles along the wall, raises his trembling arm to indicate a photo of men with huge moustaches dressed in their Sunday best, sitting on chairs out in the open, their wives, in their frilly dresses, standing behind them. All stare unsmiling at the camera.

There's another shot of a young couple and a boy standing on a wharf.

'That's me grandfather and grandmother,' Old Tom says. 'And that little fella there? That's me dad. Gettin' ready for the trip out to the new country.'

You follow that line of photos, organised chronologically (by Major, you're told) from left to right. You witness the ageing of that couple, follow the life of the boy as he grows to manhood. Underneath one shot, taken on the verandah of Mista Tom's terrace, this same man stands, a baby in a huge hooded wicker pram to his left, a woman to his right. The caption reads: *13th July 1900, Mr T. O'Flaherty, Born South Dowling Street, Redfern. With Father and Mother.*

Old Tom, still living in the same house after all those years! In the same suburb, by golly! And still able to recount all the major events of his parents' life, in order of their occurrence! When there are so many years of the Butlers' lives your mother can't account for, and place names lost in time, and identities of blood relatives that remain a mystery.

Major returns with the tea things. He gives you a heavily sweetened milky mug then takes over, as is his way. He points to this photo and that, taking you through Souths' history from 1908 to the present day. In your imagination you create a timeline, like your teacher's taught you at school, placing, at strategic points, those significant events the man describes. Major's going on like one of Tom's mad chooks, his memory and recollection of events and facts reaching so far back in time it makes you dizzy trying to keep up with him.

'I'm buggered, Bob. Let's leave the tape of Clive for another day. Do you mind, sonny?'

You return to your own home that day with a bag chockers with photos of the current Souths team, pennants, a lapel badge and a key ring that Mista Tom's given to you. Your terrace smells nice. It's been cleaned. Thanks, Major. The pantry's full of all sorts of goodies. Those blokes that Major's organised to do the painting still have a stack of work to do. You've kept it a secret from your mamma. When she returns from the hospital, what a surprise it's gunna be. You can hardly wait.

You go from room to room, searching methodically — under the new beds, in the old kitchen cupboards, even through those clothes of your mamma's that Major hasn't chucked out — but there aren't any photos, no letters, not one relic that might explain your past to you.

But those bare walls in your bedroom — why, you could begin

your own collection of newspaper clippings of the Rabbitohs, and photos, too, like the one they'd taken of your class recently. In years to come it might be you resting on a walking frame, gazing back onto a past as rich as Old Tom's. And once in a while some little kiddie, maybe even your own grandson or granddaughter might visit and stare in amazement at Old Johnnie's Life Story, driving you nuts asking all sorts of questions.

You put a chair on the desk in your room. Climb up, use sticky tape to hold up the laminated prints on the left hand side of the wall, as high as you can reach. You get down, cut a small rectangular piece of paper from a school exercise book and write: *Sowth Sinney Rabitos 1999.*

You stick the label under that team photo. You get down, stare at all four walls, imagine one covered with all manner of Souths memorabilia, the other three with photos and drawings of yourself, your mother and those ancestors you're gunna bring to life.

You're taking too long to get back to Major Bob's. He arrives, agitated, sees what you've done, smiles his approval. After dinner in his home he gives you a red and green cap and scarf and a Souths guernsey, which he'd intended to give you for Christmas. You sleep in all that Souths gear. When Major Bob gets you up before dawn for your walk you sit up abruptly, see all that red and green and know it hadn't been some wonderful dream you'd had.

You wear the lot to school. Your teacher smiles after you ask her whether you can do a project on rabbits, when all the other kids are doing the early explorers.

Old Tom plays his tape

'Haven't had the heart to listen to this tape since Clive was struck down. Died too young, too young.'

'Well, Tom, this is one I don't think I've ever heard.' Major Bob was pouring a cuppa for them all.

"Sthat right? Now, Johnnie, I wantcha to get the picture. It's the day after we'd won the 1970 Grand Final. Many of them players'd come to me home with their wives and girlfriends, for a barbecue. 'Cept John Sattler. He was still in the hospital, shattered jaw all wired up. This's the last time I recorded Clive.

'Twenty-nine year ago, son, in this very room, some of the players in the backyard round the barbie, others on the verandah, some in the kitchen, The Little Master sittin' right there on that couch you're on, mike in his hand. You ready, Bob?'

Mista Tom's younger faraway voice has you thinking of that lovely pork crackling that Major gives you each Sunday for lunch, crisp and hard-edged. And those boring old 78s he plays on his wind-up gramophone he thinks gives you a bit of a kick. You feel like laughing when he plays *Two Cigarettes in the Dark* (again), but he reckons music died when the wax records gave way to plastic, so you sit there all sombre, making out like it's good stuff.

The younger Mista Tom begins by specifying the time of day, date and location, his voice rising above the din heard in that very room all those years ago.

You're already in awe of the player whose voice can silence and still these two old blokes, that can have Major sit leaning forward, suspended halfway between the couch he sits on, and the coffee table on which stand the old reel-to-reel and the bowl of sugar.

You listen as Clive Churchill describes the tackle that broke John Sattler's jaw in the first five minutes of the final. In the background you can hear Old Tom hushing that crowd of men and women whose confusion of voices constantly intrudes.

And then things become a little confused as Churchill's heard insisting that some other bloke in that room has his words recorded for posterity. You see Major frown his curiosity, cock his head to one side and glance at Mista Tom.

'Who's Clive introducing?'

'Dunno, Bob, can't remember.'

Major takes advantage of the pause in the tape to reach for the sugar.

You hear Churchill introduce the black man from the bush who has, the Little Master says, a stack of promise, whose crazy exploits on the field have all of Redfern buzzing. Here's a fella, says Churchill, who'll soon be playing first-grade for the Rabbitohs and who will, one day, play for Australia.

Major's focusing on the floor, stirring your tea over and over again when you know, you'd noticed on so many occasions, that he only ever stirs three times, always clockwise, before placing the spoon on the saucer, to the right of the cup's handle. And why stir so hard so the tea spills out onto the saucer? You look now at Mista Tom, his cuppa held halfway to his open mouth, staring hard and unblinking at Major.

'And exactly where,' his younger taped voice asks, 'are you from?'

'We had dinner, then came back an' started 'nother camp.'

'In New South Wales?'

'I dunno the country. We came 'round, got water, 'long Larrimah, maybe. Then we came right back up 'long that camp, y'know.'

'Larrimah? Is that where you're from?'

'Maybe. I followed me mother, right through the long grass. We camp, like, from there. We went 'long the scrub, then we ran away, met a big mob of people.'

'These were your people?'

'Nah, they're from everywhere. An' all the old ones cryin'. Them whitefellas they came to rob me mother. Robbed me later, in Sydney, maybe me sister, eh.'

'They stole from your mother?'

'Them whitefellas. Me mother she carved our name on a big tree. Put our name with a knife, see. Then I got lost. Dunno how. I'm just a little kid, dunno whether I'm gunna live or die, then I found me name on the tree. So happy I sang out a long time, like me mother tol' me many times. I sang out me name so's me mother hears an' she comes runnin'. I sang out it's me, *Jiiiiimmeee! Buuutler!*'

The tape comes to an abrupt end. Mista Tom's switched it off. Major sits staring at the machine, still stirring your tea. He gets up to go, mumbles something you don't catch. He leaves you to make your own way to his home, something he's never done before.

Yeah, Tom sighed, life was full of surprises alright.

Jimmy Butler comes to La Pa

Who'd've bloody thought it, eh. A man looks forward to getting on in life, reckoning he'll be able to mix more comfortably with other blokes and sheilas. He thinks that when he's old he won't be afraid of the dark and stuff no more. It'd been okay for a while after Jimmy Butler'd met his Rosie-girl and they'd fartarsed dead broke out bush in that old banger of a Holden ute. Didn't matter so much then being who and what he was. Rosie was there to prop him up. But then she insisted on coming back to where she'd been born all those years ago; and, once in Sydney, all those old fears came back to him. By the time she'd passed on they had their claws in him alright. So here he was, packing shit for no reason he could put his finger on, with the return of that old sensation, of falling through life like someone'd pushed him off the edge of a cliff or something.

But Rosie'd loved the place. And he'd got knackered always being on the move. So he stayed.

But jeez, some things seemed so unfair. It's not as if he'd asked for a lot in life. Having someone to put their arms around him, to tell him he was okay and they liked him — that's all he'd ever wanted. Before he came upon Rosie, some fella going out of his way to pat him on the back after he'd rounded up the cattle, say, or for the number of dingoes he'd shot was enough to have his bottom lip go all-a-trembling and his eyes go all teary. He just didn't get it. No one else he knew was such a sad-sacked sissy.

But then he met Rosie. Crikey, she hung in. What a bonzer bird. After all, how many times did a bloke have to be shown he was loved? He drove her nuts with those constant needs to be told he was a good and worthwhile blackfella, to be led by the hand and shown that the shadows lurking in corners were only an oilskin jacket and a pair of denim daks hanging off a doorknob, or the branch of a tree in a starlit night making mischievous shapes on the side of their canvas tent.

And now that she was gone he was scared he wouldn't be able to keep her dying wish. Just one schooner and that'd be it — back on the piss and back in the gutter where she'd found him all those years ago. Who'd now give him the stern look and severe talking-to, go crook at him then hold him until the mad craving had passed? Ah, onya girl, 'cause no one knew like she did how important it was to keep him busy doing the jobs that weren't needed doing, like fetching some more fluid from the swollen stern of a baobab tree when the canvas bags were practically full, or hunting for native hens beside a swampy stream when there was enough salt-dried meat in their esky. Or walk him by the hand to great boulders in the distance, where they'd sit and blabber and watch the emergence of the evening stars.

And even after all those years of wandering, when they both knew Rosie was on her last legs and they came to La Pa for her to die, even then the demons still came. He felt like such a weak prick. Here was his seriously crook Rosie-girl comforting *him* in the sudden darkness of their bedroom when the light bulb blew. Afraid of the dark at his age? What sort of a dickbrain was he?

In those first few weeks after their arrival, when she still had the strength for it, they'd stroll down onto Congwong Bay Beach or walk across the bridge to Bare Island or, more often than not, go down to Frenchman's Bay, where they'd sit and watch the planes taking off and landing at the airport across Botany Bay. And after he'd drunk several cups of tea from the thermos he often carried with him and the mad desire for the piss'd passed, he'd have to practically carry Rosie back up the track. He'd lie her on their bed and watch her sleeping, his mind turning to the time, all those years ago, when that big bloke with the cockeyed glass eye (what was his name?) told him, in the same week as he'd got the sack from Eveleigh, that Souths'd had enough of his shenanigans, and dropped him.

Occasionally he heard stories about those great Rabbitohs of the 1970s that he could've been a part of. It was enough to have a bloke slap his forehead with the palm of his hand.

On waking, Jimmy Butler turned on the radio. He couldn't bear to listen to the voices of the great Souths players he'd once trained alongside, coming out in vocal support of their old club. Anyway, soon the decision'd be made, everyone'd calm down and find something else to get all worked up about. He switched the radio off, grabbed his book of jokes from the floor beside his bed and walked to the shops.

Along the way he saw posters on telegraph poles proclaiming Souths supporters' outrage. He bought the *Tele* at the newsagent. A couple of blokes were jabbering on about all the latest baloney to do with the Bunnies.

'Those fuckwits runnin' the game,' one was saying, 'wouldn't dare. Would not dare, I tell you.' Jimmy Butler fled their talk.

He made his way to the cemetery. Who'd've thought it, coming back to Sydney for some peace and South Sydney being the talk of the town.

He sat by Rosie's grave, poured himself a tea then took out of his back trouser pocket his tobacco pouch. He slowly and thoughtfully rolled himself a Drum, lit it then said, 'Mornin', Rosie.' He cocked his head and, looking at a gravesite a few metres away, called out, 'G'day, mum!'

He turned to the sports section of the paper. It was all Souths talk, pages and pages of all that bullshit. He tossed the paper to the ground, opened his joke book and read out aloud a couple of ripsnorters. His daddy-long-legs did a crazy dance as he sat there, beside himself with laughter.

Some ten kilometres away Kon Tsakiris was fuming. Some slant-eyed power point, probably Triad-connected, had won the Super Saturday Lottery. In the country for a few months and lands the big one. This was ridiculous. What a waste of nine hundred dollars. Money wasn't safe in his hands. Whatever he had, he had to invest quickly, or else he'd blow it on some other mad scheme. He walked out of his lawyer's office, all cashed up having sold his business to a bunch of pooftahs who, he reckoned, had fewer business brains than him (if that was possible). He took out a dollar coin he'd found on the street (surely a lucky sign) and tossed it five times. Each time it came up heads. Another sign. He took a taxi to a broker in town and invested the lot in HIH.

In the Kookaburra Café, four young men gasped with delight on finding four priceless pub posters stashed behind the bookcase used to store grocery items that the previous owner'd left behind.

Someone's dibbie-dobbed Major Bob in. Either that or your black mates've become really cheesed off with his uncompromising stand and realised there's no talking sense to the man.

Major's just had a haircut and shave at the barber. The back of his neck's all pink and prickly and covered in a thin layer of talcum powder. The skin on his face's as smooth as a baby's bum. His hair, recently coloured and too dark for someone his age, is parted in the middle, oiled down and, as Mista Tom often says, like a robber's stockinged head.

He looks like he's about to chuck a mental at any moment. Two men in suits clutching a swathe of papers stand at Major's front door, threatening to call the police if he doesn't agree to hand you over that very moment. Major's had enough of arguing. You watch him draw himself to his full height, raise his brows, stare down at them with that unblinking glare of his then, without saying a word, wave them off his verandah with the back of his hand, approaching them step by step until they back out onto the footpath.

You're looking forward to the September break. More time to spend on the murals you've begun on your bedroom walls. You're working like a mad ferret, sticking up onto one wall whatever Souths stuff you're given, on another copying pictures from a book Major's found for you in the local library on Redfern, pre-white settlement. Your mum's in rehab. She won't be out for a few weeks yet.

Zoe's kitchen was churning out an assembly-line of trays of baklava. Church music and Greek natter blared out over the suburb as her helpers came and went. There was an article on her in the September edition of *Woman's Day*. She still refused to disclose her special prayer. Here was a woman who, people said, had been married to a scumbag of a hubby, who'd given his marriage the bullet for reasons they couldn't fathom. Now look at her, this reffo made good. Whatdyaknow. Prob'ly loaded, too.

Not everyone who'd experienced some footy disappointment was trying to avoid the past. While Jimmy Butler sat at the cemetery, another bloke in another part of Sydney was planning to meet head-on his own footy regrets. Victor Batrouney was methodically cutting out from the three morning newspapers every reference he could find on the Rabbitohs, and pasting them into a large leather-bound folder he'd bought specially for the purpose (imported from Italy, soft kid hide, embossed, a real beauty). He was sitting at the barbie table setting to the rear of his gym.

He'd completed his hill runs and sprints early and'd just returned to his home, the papers under his arm, a great decision, after some deliberation, having been made. He was waiting for the hour when he'd ring a mate and tell him he was going to forego the weekly Turkish coffee and game of backgammon. He was going to get stuck into the telephone directory instead, working the phones till he'd tracked down O'Hara, his old school footy coach. He wondered whether the man was still alive. He hadn't seen him since the day he'd bumped into him at the Sydney Cricket Ground after Souths' sensational Grand Final win in 1967.

After Susan Batrouney left to do some shopping, Victor went into his three-car garage (two of his cabs were out on the road) and took down a dust-covered tightly packed cardboard box from the top shelf of an old wardrobe, used for storage. He blew away the muck, stripped off the layers of masking tape then took out his old footy boots, school socks and shorts and, finally, that mothballed red and green guernsey that O'Hara'd given him, which he'd worn but never played in. He polished the boots, opened the internal door leading into his home, glanced through the panes of mock leadlight glass on either side of the front door to ensure his wife was not returning home unexpectedly early, then went upstairs, carrying all that footy gear.

He put on the shorts, socks and boots. Not as tight a fit as he'd imagined. He took the naphthalened guernsey out of the bedsheet he'd wrapped it in over forty years previously. It was tight across the shoulders and under the armpits.

He stood in front of the full-length mirror in his bedroom, closed his eyes and saw himself running onto the SCG for that 1967 Grand Final between Souths and Canterbury. He heard the mighty roar of the crowd. And just before kick-off he scanned the faces of those sitting closest to the white picket fence, seeing the approving face of O'Hara and, of course, his whole Lebanese clan, in amongst whom he saw, there, the beaming face of his proud mother and the ghost of his father.

He felt the shudder in the ground as the sell-out crowd chanted his name.

Ba-trou-ney! Ba-trou-ney! Ba-trou-ney!

He lifted an arm in acknowledgement. He tore a great hole across the shoulder of the guernsey.

NINE

No one asks Jimmy what he thinks

The succession of orphanages and homes Jimmy Butler'd stayed in had become a blur of confused images. He could recall a large hardwood door, a brass knocker and leadlight panels with decorative birds and leaves, but was it the door of the Anglican orphanage in northern Queensland, or the sheep station in western NSW? And that train ride someone'd put him on that seemed to go on forever — was that to the home in Melbourne where a man had him sleeping in a musty damp caravan? Or to the Parker family whose kids'd run their fingers down the markings on his arm, and ask him all sorts of questions about the movements in his life, most of which he answered with made-up responses?

Several years after Terry Parker returned from the Jap prisoner-of-war camp to the family farm near Ginlambone, outside Nyngan, he and his wife began taking in young blackfellas, paying them a full white man's wage, much to some neighbouring station owners' bewilderment. They grew a variety of crops, but mostly ran cattle on that station of theirs that no man could see the end of, even after a hard day's riding. It was as flat as a damper in most parts, dry in great patches when the rain didn't fall, but Jimmy Butler liked it that way: fewer places for the bad men and spirits to hide. When the Parker kids were away, boarding at their Sydney schools, the Parkers'd have Jimmy sleeping in a room attached to the back of the house, to keep an eye on him when the nightmares came. Try as he might to push the demons away, their awful embraces and caresses found their way through his flailing arms. He woke up one night to find himself alone in a room and not a smelly caravan that'd been jacked up onto bricks; that he wasn't in Melbourne but on a farm, that there at the threshold to his room were Mr Terry and Miss Vera, and not some grizzly bearded man unhitching his trousers. He apologised over and over for waking them.

Terry Parker went back to bed. Vera stayed up, made Jimmy a cup of tea and brought him some of those scones she was famous for. She'd stay with him until he could confront the night alone.

'I'll keep the light on, 'sthat okay, Miss Vera?'

'Of course, Jimmy.'

'Tea's good, miss.'

'Jimmy, you know we'll be bringing the crop in soon.'

'Yes, miss. Mr Terry, he tol' me.'

'We're going to need you, Jimmy. Don't let us down again, will you?'

'I'll tell you straight, miss, I won't see me mob till we shift all that crop.'

Jimmy Butler disappeared two days later.

The Parkers heard he'd gone into the nearest settlement where he'd bought cheap plonk. He'd joined his own people, sat around a fire and got wasted every day for a week. He returned a month or so later.

'I left me mob, miss, an' walked over 'em low hills, camped 'lone, y'know, on this rough dry track what been a river bed an' all. I love them little ol' trees what grow 'longside them dried-up creeks, like ol' men, an' that low sky like you can touch. Oh miss, you shoulda seen it, the 'rizon an' the sky meetin' like ghosts, y'know, all hazy an' that. Dried out there, from the piss I mean, and them demons they're gone, so I come back, miss. Sorry.'

The Parkers came to expect that there'd often be times when they'd wake to find him gone. Once he returned after an absence of many months.

'This other mob, they taught me to keep off the grog, an' how to creep up on them hens, wild ones, I mean, near the water. We cooked turtles on the fire, eh, and them galahs in a pan they're real good. I chased an emu and roo, y'know, catched 'em sometimes. I love that bush life miss. Sorry I wasn't here when yer rounded up them cattle.'

Terry Parker put on a dozen extra hands when the work was full on (they'd arrive on cue, without him seeking them out).

At the end of one long day's work, he and his wife sat with all their workers on two long trestle tables pushed together under a stand of acacia trees, next to the barn where all but Jimmy slept. They ate together, watching the kites, tilted languidly in the warm afternoon light, swooping in long slow circles, waiting for scraps. After the food'd settled, Jimmy and the others played footy on the hard earth, sending up clouds of dust as they played their chaotic, light-hearted and improvised version of rugby league. In the past they'd played with a tennis and golf ball, a loaf of stale bread and once, while it held together, a small watermelon. On this afternoon they had a fair dinkum league ball that Terry Parker'd bought for them in town.

They played and played, their black ghostly figures silhouetted against a setting sun. Terry Parker watched Jimmy closely. The ball seemed to be tied to his hand with a string: he had this uncanny knack of anticipating its bounce, swooping down to gather it cleanly before scurrying off with that ridiculous loping run of his. It took your breath away just watching. The boy'd do an unexpected back or forward somersault, jackknife his stick-pencil body then roll on the ground, get up, kick a mullygrubber, collect the ball, do a mighty loop-the-loop and outrun the lot of them with his nitwitty sprint, leaving his and the opposing team bewildered and in hysterics, cacking themselves like demented hyenas.

After the game the Parkers called him aside. Jimmy stood, breathing wildly, all stuffed, his hands on his hips.

'You're a good player, son,' said Terry Parker.

'Yeah, 'sgood, y'know, them boys an' me after all that hard yakka, have some fun, eh.'

'Yes, well. But Jimmy … you're very good. I've never seen anyone do what you do.'

''T's just a game, Mister Terry.'

'No, Jimmy. I mean — I mean you're damn good. Fast over a distance, very quick off the mark. They can't lay a hand on you. Look, I've got a friend who'll come out this way to watch you, if I put in a good word. He's a scout for footy players. I'll get on to him.'

'You bin tellin' 'bout me, Mister Terry?'

'I know him through Legacy. He's involved with Souths. Do you know about South Sydney, son?'

'Oh, shit yeah, great team, them Rabbits.'

'No promises, now. But if he likes what he sees — well, who knows what can happen. I mentioned you to him a little while back. Seems he knows you.'

'Knows me?'

'Do you know anyone in Sydney?'

'Sinney? No. Don't wanna go neither. 'Sgood here.'

Bob Ryan sat on the verandah with the Parkers. Jimmy Butler noticed this city bloke sitting forward in his chair, leaning on the railing, occasionally rising to his feet whenever he did one of his crazy runs. Jimmy swerved low to the ground, and how he didn't fall flat on his face was a wonder to the man. Bob Ryan threw his head back and laughed when Jimmy Butler hurled the ball over the heads of the opposition, collecting it before it hit the ground. He pulled a swiftie when the ruck had most players on the ground in a confusion of arms and legs, stuffing the ball behind his shirt, then bolted for another try. He dazzled, he guffawed, he made an arse of himself, he played a blinder, he won his team the game.

'You've got a great future in Sydney, lad,' Bob Ryan said, after the game.

But Jimmy Butler was happy just mucking about with his new mates. He'd found some comfort, at last, on this flat earth that was in the process of becoming his home. The Parkers were good to him. Why leave? And here was this white bloke making plans for his future. It scared the shit out of Jimmy Butler that they could do that, when all he wanted was to be left alone, to make some contact with a group of blackfellas that'd last long enough for them to become family.

The big city bloke was standing there, arms folded, rocking backwards and forwards on legs spread wide apart, staring, Jimmy noticed, at the scars on his arm.

'We've won two of the last three grand finals, Jimmy. And Clive Churchill's staying on as coach. You've heard of him, I'm sure. This is no ordinary team, lad. We planned for this back in …'

Mr Terry was nodding his head, his arms folded, too, something these cocky white blokes did when they stood in a circle taking charge of your life.

'The Grand Final will be played in a few weeks, Jimmy,' Bob Ryan said. 'There'll be a break over summer, giving you time to settle in. The squad will start training in the new year. If all goes well you'll start off in third grade then work your way up. I'll find you a job at the railways and a room in a boarding house nearby. If we can get you moving this week, I'll be able to ...'

Jimmy Butler looked at his black mates who were preparing a fire they'd sit around that night, telling stories. He saw the imaginary try line between the acacia and the fence post he'd crossed so many times. He looked across the featureless earth, dry and windblown, and felt a terrible heartache.

'I'd be so proud of you, son,' said Terry Parker.

Now even he was getting in on the act. That's what they did, speak to a bloke in that soft caring voice and smile, feeling all holy and good while they fucked about with your life.

'What an honour,' said Terry Parker, 'running onto the SCG wearing the red and green.'

'An opportunity like this only comes once in a lifetime, Jimmy,' Mrs Vera was saying.

So here they all were, ganging up on him when he'd've been happy to stay on their farm forever.

'We'll be following your career closely,' she added.

'As long as you stay off the grog, lad, the sky's the limit.'

'Mr Bob?'

'Call me Major. Major Bob.'

'You know me from before?'

'No, lad. I'll pick you up at ten in the morning.'

'It's alright, Jimmy,' Mrs Vera said. 'Sooner or later you'll have to move on. And you're ready. For bigger and better things. Come on, I'll help you pack.'

It was only after the bloke from the big smoke'd left that it occurred to Jimmy Butler that no one'd asked him what he thought of their plans.

Jimmy screws up

His time in Sydney lasted seven months.

Major Bob, who was in charge of the bay Jimmy Butler'd been assigned to at Eveleigh, took and kept him under his wing. But there was so much that intimidated the young man. There was the confident banter of his fellow workers, for instance. He was never quite sure whether he was supposed to laugh at those jokes directed his way or take some offence.

'You bin okay, Jimmy-boy?'

He looked up from his work to see them grinning out of the sides of their mouth, their eyes daring him to respond.

'You bin go walkabout yes'day, jungle-boy? We bin lookin' for you, no can find.'

'Where you bin at smoko, Jimmy? You bin sittin' under coolabah tree, drinkin' the white lady?'

They baited him with comments about the grease and dirt on his face that wouldn't wash off. They looked at him with eyes that constantly challenged, with a swagger that threatened. Nah, he didn't like this place. He wanted to go home.

Bob Ryan found him crouching in a cubicle in the loo during one lunch break, sipping from a flask. The Major threw the flask away and gave him a severe warning.

But it wasn't just this garrulous lot of blokes that intimidated him. It was the pounding heavy equipment that hammered all day long, the rising billowing clouds of steam and smoke after the morning forge fires were lit, the dirt he constantly breathed in, the heat from the molten metal that was being shaped in the bay next to his, the noise, the relentless noise. Blacksmiths belted at those pieces of iron they bent at will. Carriage workers drilled and hammered into skeletal carriage bodies. Other workers, filthy in their overalls, would gather to see the liquid metal pour out of the firebox and cheer for the beauty of the work. When some fellow brought down the hammer on a job he was working on, sending sparks flying from one end of the workshop to the other, some other bloke, in playful response, would create a cloud of burning oil that'd rise spectacularly. They competed against each other with the level of noise. They played games with showers of sparks fashioned in certain directions. It made no sense to Jimmy Butler: he couldn't, for the life of him, understand why, in amongst all this activity and sound, he felt so damn lonely.

He hankered for a dawn that was bright and clear and cool. He dreamed of rocky outcrops, stony-bottomed gullies, broken ridges and vast treeless plains. This crazy city, with people living on top of each other and so noisy it drove a bloke nuts, was as shitty a place as he'd ever known.

'You missed training again yesterday, Jimmy.'

'Sorry, Major.'

'You're not back on the grog, are you?'

'Just a little.'

'Just a little?'

'I'll stop.'

'You'll tell me, won't you, if there's anything bothering you?'

'Yeah, sure, Major.'

'Clive's got high hopes for you. You know that, don't you?'

Bob Ryan sought him out when Louis the Fly was retiring after forty-three years at Eveleigh, to listen to the speeches and the farewell poem. But he was nowhere to be found.

He tried to find him when Driver Dan was about to leave on his final trip, and the men'd gathered in their hundreds for his farewell, the whistles on all the trains cock-a-doodle-doodling as he drove out of the station, his engine decorated with paper streamers and chalked messages.

'Where were you, Jimmy? I looked everywhere for you.'

Some weeks later Jimmy failed to turn up for the annual workers' picnic.

'What's going on, lad? I'm trying to help you.'

But how could he tell the Major he'd had such a bad night, running out of the boarding house so that others wouldn't hear his cries when the bogeyman returned. He'd found his way to the park where he'd heard other blackfellas met after hours.

Bob Ryan took Jimmy Butler by the elbow and drew him to one side. They stood behind a cast-iron column that supported an immense overhead crane. Jimmy Butler kept looking up at the monster above his head.

'It's not going to fall on you. Now — tell me, and no lies.'

The steam hammers and Davey Press were making a hell of a racket.

'I can smell the alcohol on your breath, Jimmy.'

One week later he failed to turn up at work two days in succession. After another missed training session, Major Bob walked much of Redfern, finding him asleep under a fig tree in the park opposite Tom O'Flaherty's terrace, empty bottles strewn about him.

'I can't cover for you much longer,' the Major said. 'You're on your last wicket.'

'Major?'

'Yes, Jimmy?'

'I wanna go home.'

'Are you joking, lad?'

'No, Mister Bob.'

'But — but Jimmy?'

'Yeah, Major?'

'You've got no other home.'

But Jimmy couldn't go knocking on the Major's door after midnight when his past would emerge from some dark hole. And he couldn't say no when he felt the lonely heartache overwhelm him and his mates came by, throwing pebbles at his window from the street below. For the little boy rocking backwards and forwards in a rank caravan, lying face down on his bed and holding onto his pillow until the horrors of the night ended, there was only one source of comfort.

Those with the authority over Bob Ryan'd had enough. The Major's pleadings came to nothing. Souths gave him the boot the same week he was sacked from Eveleigh. Two days later he disappeared.

I fair dinkum luvya, Rosie

Several weeks after his return to Sydney, in May of 1999, and the procession of his new and her old friends'd become a ritual.

On her last night they came through the darkness and stillness. Rosie wouldn't allow a drop of grog in her home, so they brought their own thermoses of tea and coffee, the women carrying their bags with the balls of cotton and embroidery needles that Rosie'd taught them to use. They'd sit with Rosie and Jimmy until she retired inside.

Nearby could be heard the voices of those men and kiddies who enjoyed the night fishing. Waves broke with a gentle rhythm on the beach.

Jimmy Butler asked his wife if there was anything she wanted, a glass of water, perhaps, but no, she would lie on the mattress he'd brought out for her, propped up on three pillows, and enjoy the quiet, the occasional snatches of conversation, watch the needles flash in the light of the two external naked light bulbs. The women were hunched over their work, staring intensely at the delicate embroidery, their flurry of hands and fingers a pleasant distraction.

'Makin' youse a rose, Rose,' one woman said, smiling.

Another suddenly cursed, her quick fingers suddenly stopping the deft work. 'Can'tcha get a stronger globe, Jimmy? Can't see what I'm doin' in this light.' The woman took out a pair of scissors then pulled out, thread by thread, the pattern that was all wrong.

Jimmy Butler looked at his wife in the dim light, the yellowness of her skin, the sunken eyes, the cracked and dry mouth. He went inside, returning with a wet cloth to moisten her lips.

And then the stories began.

'Re'mber when eight of us shared one bedroom, and that hessian curtain separatin' us from the oldies?'

'Re'mber that one tap we went to each mornin' to fill the cans with water? An' the weekly washin' of clothes what we done each week together?'

'Re'mber that abalone you could still find in them days, Rosie, when your mum and dad's house was mine, and mine was yours? Them were the sharin' days, eh.'

Everyone murmured and sighed their agreement.

'Mum'd take her pan down to the beach with your mum and make the fire. An' all them fellas sittin' on the sand, round the fire with no care in the world. An' the season for mullet. Dad'd fish with all the other dads and we'd help the mums cook 'em on the beach. Everyone'd smell the fish cookin' an' come down an' we'd share with 'em all. Everyone gettin' their fair share. Re'mber, Rosie?'

They sat in silence for some time, listening to the sounds of the water, conscious of the woman drifting in and out of her deep weariness.

Rosie stirred. She looked apologetically at each person in turn, said she was tired, would go inside. And when Jimmy Butler lifted her up in his arms, they all stood out of respect.

Jimmy Butler emerged a few minutes after he'd carried her mattress back into their home.

'We'll be off now, mate,' Jacky said. 'Some of the boys'll be goin' fishin' tomorra, if you wanna join us. 'Bout five in the mornin'. Reckon they'll be bitin', too. I'll be down the southern end, okay?'

Jimmy Butler woke up at five-thirty the next morning. He sat on the edge of the bed, contemplating the streetlights seen through the thin curtains. The moon, like the lights, was wrapped in a fine and unusual haze — nonetheless, a full moon there was and, as far as fishing off the beach was concerned, he believed this to be a good sign.

As he sat on the bed, his feet searching for his slippers, his wife stirred. He got up, knocking over a glass of water standing on a short-legged stool in which his wife had placed her false teeth. Rosie opened her eyes, turned to face him.

'Y'okay, sweetie?'

'Yeah, fine, Rosie.'

'Heard a noise.'

'Sorry. Knocked this glass over.'

She paused a moment, her gaze following the line of her husband's arm on the bed. She looked at the wedding band which he'd boasted he'd never removed from his finger since the day they'd been married.

Jimmy Butler twirled the ring around several times. 'It's stayin' on, Rosie. 'Til the day I die. It's stayin' on.'

She smiled weakly.

'Moon's out,' he said. Jimmy looked out the window for what he knew was already there, for something to do. He couldn't very well walk out of their bedroom now that his wife was awake, not at least until some more words'd been exchanged.

'Strange glow,' Rosie said.

'Bloody oath.'

Jimmy's feet found his slippers. He'd sit there, waiting until she was done, staring at the moon and its odd glow, the fog wrapped around the telegraph poles and lights, imagining the sudden flash of silver as the fish emerged, struggling desperately, from the beach. He did not want to think about the terrible struggle his wife's body was waging. It was the fish, yes, the fish he wanted to preoccupy himself with, the nerve-tingling excitement he felt as it tugged at his bait, then the shock of knowing he'd caught one, that exquisite moment when his rod suddenly bent, its taut curve that was the most beautiful and symmetrically pleasing shape he knew, as if man and fish, beach and wave had combined in some union, some wholeness he could never have expressed in words.

'Big waves down there,' she said.

Rosie was right. There were large waves breaking down on the beach. This was strange. It was normally so flat and still.

'Can't hear no wind,' Jimmy said.

'Go on. You go. I'll be okay.'

Jimmy Butler nodded and got off the bed, smiling grimly as he placed his wife's teeth in the now uprighted glass. He took it into the bathroom, filled it with water, returned it to the stool then went into the kitchen.

After a quick and light breakfast, Jimmy Butler checked his shoulder bag to ensure he'd packed, before going to bed the night before, his knife, sharpening stone, an assortment of swivels and sinkers, a range of hooks and lines and a bait holder. Picking up his fibreglass rod leaning against the door, he threw the bag over one shoulder, grabbed his lunchbox then left the house. He was immediately confronted by the haze that he and Rosie'd first detected through their bedroom window.

It was when he reached the end of his street, which was where the downward sloping trail began that led through the scrubland to the beach itself, that he was stopped in his tracks. Most of this scrub, certainly all the beach — the sand, the rocks at either end, the waves — in fact, the entire bay reaching to the horizon had disappeared beneath a vast and thick blanket of fog. From where

Jimmy stood it was only the rhythmic pounding of the waves that indicated the presence, the very existence of a beach. The man smiled. He delighted at the unexpected sight. He set off vigorously down the trail, and it was not long before he'd set foot on the beach itself, rejoicing in the indefinite shapes that loomed, perhaps in imagination, perhaps in reality, on every side. There was no defined sky or bay — apart from the sand at his feet all had become one, lost in common obscurity, and the man searched blindly for the water's edge at the southern end, where he hoped to find Jacky. It was a challenge he enjoyed, and he found himself chuckling as a section of the fog lifted suddenly, and he'd lunge at such an opening before it closed. And through the consuming cloud, mist, fog, salt spray — which one? all of them? — he could hear the relentless thumping of the waves. It was to their breaking that he directed his movements — that, and the voices of the other fishermen, unseen, their childlike banter that the wondrous dawn had given rise to, and the thin cleft of the emerging sun, seen as a fine red line far into the distance.

Jimmy Butler arrived at the water's edge, setting down his lunchbox, shoulder bag and rod. He could feel the quickening of his heart.

'That you, Jimmy-boy?'

He turned to his left to see a rod, whose line had been cast out to sea, but not the man holding it, who was immersed in the fog. The rod hung in the air, suspended, a conjurer's trick, its line taut as it stretched towards the sea only to disappear before reaching its destination.

'Jacky?' he replied. ''Sthat you, mate?'

'Yeah. Bloody unreal. Been livin' 'ere all me life an' never seen nothin' like it.'

'Other boys 'ere?'

'Yeah,' Jacky laughed. 'There's a line of us, but you wouldn't know it. Crikey, wouldn't the missus love this?'

Jimmy Butler stood, hands on hips, breathing in the wonder of it all.

'You still there, Jimmy?' Jacky laughed.

'Still here, mate.'

'Fish are bitin', too. Channels right in front of us. Sandpit to yer right. Good gutter 'longside the sandpit.'

And then Jimmy Butler saw her. One moment there was nothing to his right but fog, the next moment she was there, without having placed a towel on the sand or removed whatever she'd worn over her one-piece black costume. There was no towel. There were no clothes discarded on the sand. The young woman stood so close to him that he could've taken two large strides towards her and touched her.

Jimmy blinked at the woman. He felt a shudder go through his body as he stared unashamedly at her, the girl's beauty, her proximity to him. She stood, legs slightly apart, hands on hips, scanning the thickening and thinning fog. The lines on her face were well defined, her nose meeting her forehead in a straight line, something he'd never seen in a black girl. She stood erect at that juncture separating child from woman, moving her head slightly from side to side.

And just as suddenly as she'd appeared she ran towards the waves, dived into the fog and surf and disappeared. Jimmy Butler stared hard, hoping for a further glimpse of her. He walked into the surf, the water up to his knees.

'Oi!' Jacky cried. 'Where ya goin'?'

And then he saw her for the second and last time. The waves lifted, the newly risen sun a glowing indistinct presence on their crests, before tumbling and dispersing their music and momentum. On one wave which rose slowly, full-bodied, he saw a flash of black gold that he knew to be her. Then, out of a rolling bank of fog the wave and woman appeared. The water lifted out of the thick vapour to take a distinct shape, both the woman and the wave making their way towards Jimmy Butler. She rode the wave until it had all but spent itself, then stood, her black body glistening in the filtered light of the obscured sun. The young woman turned to look at him. She held his eyes for a moment, then another, smiled, ran into the surf, disappearing once again.

Jimmy Butler turned abruptly, making his way out of the water. He passed his rod, lunchbox and bag, brushing past Jacky, quickening his pace without seeing or hearing him. But Jacky'd seen the man's face and was afraid.

'Jimmy! What's up?'

Jimmy Butler groped through the fog, certain of his direction. He stumbled, too, the walking made difficult because of his wet trousers which clung to his legs and his soggy shoes, which he'd not discarded before entering the surf. He paused briefly, his wheezing loud and hurried, cursing all those roll-your-owns he smoked all day and half the night as he took off both shoes and threw them to one side.

'Jimmy! What's goin' on? Y'okay? Jimmy!'

He stumbled onto the trail that led him back up through the scrub, its steep incline making clumsy his every step, until he was on the street that led to his house. From there he ran until he found himself wheezing violently at his front door. Jimmy Butler remained there for some time, steadying his wild breathing, sitting on the doorstep until the riot of his blood'd been calmed.

He entered his home, stood in the doorway of the bedroom and looked at his wife, who was fast asleep. He approached slowly, knelt beside the woman. He took in every detail of her face: her thinning hair, the sagging lines around her mouth and neck, the space between the ridge of her nose and eyes where he'd once loved to surprise her with an unexpected kiss. He remembered their youthful passion, how fiercely he'd once held her. And he remembered the shuddering of her body as she first stood naked before him, and how he, overcome by her beauty and his desire for her, had wept like a child, and how she'd held and comforted him.

Still kneeling, Jimmy Butler reached across and gently stroked Rosie's hair. He placed his hand on her cheek, where he left it for some moments. He bent closer and kissed her, softly so as not to wake her, in that space between her nose and her eyes.

Jimmy Butler got up. He left his house. He returned to the beach. The fog had thinned noticeably. The black woman was nowhere to be seen. He prepared his bait under the watchful eye of Jacky.

'Y'okay?'

Jimmy smiled. 'Yeah, real good.'

'Wheredja go?'

'Home.'

'Home?'

'Yeah. Just forgot somethin' back home.'

He then cast his line into a shallow gutter near the water's edge.

TEN

Johnnie and his rabbits

Holidays! Yippeee! Your house is nearly all done and it's a ripper! How does the big bloke do it? He bullies, cons, sways and sweet-talks (but never crawls, you notice). He pulls in old favours still owed, comes a cropper when a few hesitate. You're there to see how quickly some change their minds (alright, alright, I'll be there Tuesday, bloody hell, no need to chuck a mental). Most come smiling and happy, in ones and twos: blacks, Greeks, skips, Lebs and Chinamen, from Legacy and from Souths, from the RSL and from his and Zoe's churches carrying boxes of cutlery, crockery, grocery stuff, clothes, second-hand furniture, indoor and outdoor plants and pretty things to put up on the walls and in the corners of rooms. But some come grumbling and really, really pissed off (Kon looks like he could kill someone), saying all sorts of nasty things about him behind his back, but still they arrive and, with their radios and cassette players blaring — Greek music for the painters, hip-hop for the tilers, classical for the gardener — help in getting rid of the old and carrying in and positioning the new, cleaning, scrubbing, peeling, painting, washing and hosing down walls, tiles, ceilings, the lounge and dining rooms, bedrooms, kitchen, laundry and bathroom, the sides and back and front of the house, even sweeping the footpath. And through it all he's there, supervising (if you're going to do something, lads, do it quickly and do it well), dragging you along to show you how to inspect the quality of a painter's work (It's an undercoat, fer Chrissake, Bob! Jeez, give us a break! I'm a bloody volunteer! Ya wanna do it yerself?), telling you you should never, never, never look too happy with the work any tradesman ever, *ever* does! Yaya Zoe's there most days, too, bringing around sweets and making coffee and tea for the workers, shaking her head and clicking her tongue in admiration at the transformation. Even Old Tom's wheeled around one day to see the wonder of it all, and why he doesn't look happy but opens and closes his mouth and licks his lips like he's about to say something as he's taken from room to room, and half-closes his eyes on being told your mum doesn't know of the changes but is going to be surprised, is a strange thing. The welfare people drop by one day, too, with something they call a summons. They go through your house after Major's read a letter they've handed him, overwhelmed by the racket and the activity. You watch as they step out onto the footpath, giving each other little smiles and nods. You see them speak into their mobiles. They ask you, all polite, now, if they can speak to Major. He tells you to tell them to push off.

And everyone finds time to go into your bedroom to see the work you're doing, too, those murals taking shape on the three walls, that fourth, above your bed, a tribute to the Bunnies.

'Who are these people on this wall, lad?'

'That's me granma an' grandad, me mum an' dad.'

'And what of these two?'

'That's you, Major, an' that's me when I grow up.'

'Ahhh, we'll always be friends then, is that right, Johnnie?'

'Yeah. I don't ever wanna leave Redfern. You stayin', Major?'

'Ohhh yes. I'm not going anywhere. Now, who's this man kicking the football?'

'Ernie.'

'Ernie?'

'Ernie th'Torney. He's that fella what runs up an' down them hills. That's his nickname, y'know.'

'What? The Hill Run Man? You know *him*?'

'Let me look at his car. Sat in it one day. Used to live in Redfern. Reckons he knows ya.'

'Knows me?'

'Asks 'boutcha all the time.'

Kon Tsakiris read an article in the local rag about a Portuguese bloke who'd made a packet after opening up a tiny takeaway chicken burger shop in North Bondi several years previously. And now? Franchises all over Australia ($400,000 each, paying 6 per cent royalty on every sale), floated on the Australian Stock Exchange, plans to expand in America. Annual sales of fifty million! With flame-grilled traditional chicken, of all things, despite all those other chook outlets! It had Kooka Kon making all sorts of schemes with the money he and Zoe could make with her baklava that people were going nuts over.

Yaya Zoe pouted her lips, listened in silence, frowning and half-closing her eyes as he spoke.

'We need a catchy name,' he said, his eyes shining, hands gesticulating wildly in the air. 'Something people will remember. What do you think about *Kookaburra Kon and Yaya Zoe's Traditional …*'

And then she turned on him. 'What? *Kookaburra Kon and —*'

'Alright, your name first. *Yaya Zoe's —*'

She stood, glaring. Kon saw the woman's eyes shift to the rolling pin that lay amongst the sheets of pastry. She wasn't going to whack him one, was she? The man got up off the kitchen chair.

'Alright we can drop my name. We can call it —'

'Leave. Now!'

'Come on, Zoe. Jesus Christ, we could —'

'And now you blaspheme! In my home? Get out! Get out, blasphemer!'

Major arrives the Saturday of Souths' next home game. You take him to Yaya Zoe's, who's told you to pass by on your way to the Sydney Football Stadium. She presents Major with a huge carry bag. On one side is a colourful depiction of an old Greek temple, on the other the bold words, decorated with bolts of lightning: *Greeks Rule, OK?* He looks at you out of the corner of his eye. Yaya's beaming. He's got a cranky coming on. You can tell.

Round the corner Major Bob stops, rifles through the bag. You hear him mumbling to himself, shaking his head: thermos, moussaka, nuts, drinks, oranges, apples, baklava, plastic plates, knives …

He takes out a cotton handtowel depicting ancient men in robes *Doin' the Zorba, Man!* then says: 'I hope you haven't eaten for a few years, lad.'

You hold his hand as you walk over Moore Park, cross Anzac Parade then enter the stadium. You look longingly at the little red and green flags other kids are waving in the air. He buys you one, resists your attempt to throw your arms around his large girth in appreciation. You climb the stairs, enter the stand dizzy with apprehension and wonder, and stop, pulling on his hand.

'What? What is it, Johnnie?'

You stare down from that great height onto the field. The preliminary games are over.

'What are you staring at, lad?'

You point down to the near-empty ground.

'There's nothing there, Johnnie.'

Major looks at the oval, at you, back at the field, then into your eyes.

And then Bob Ryan recalled, in a rush of remembrance, how his own head had once buzzed with excitement and the blood in his arms and the back of his neck had gone all cold when he, little Bobby Ryan, and his mate Leo Batrouney had caught their first glimpse of the ground at the beginning of each season; how the deep green oval of the SCG had sent an exhilarating shiver down his back when he saw the painted white lines giving form and order to that field of contest, its emptiness during those moments before the players ran onto the ground standing in stark contrast to the stands, and the Hill, too, filled with a swaying heaving crowd, the banners lifted high, the flags flying, and everywhere he looked men and women and kids like him and his mate pouring down the aisles to get to their seats or that patch of grass on the mound. And that shock of recollection when he attended, with Tom, his first game in three years after returning from that camp, and how he'd trembled with the joy and despair of it all becoming, he thought grimly, the most one-eyed supporter of them all.

'Remember this day, won't you, lad. It's a special day, indeed it is.'

Major fights his way to where the most raucous and passionate supporters of the Bunnies sit. You see the people you've got to know since arriving in Redfern: there's Bob the Butcher, barely recognisable now that he's out of his bloodied apron and not standing behind a counter; there's Ned the Neck, hurling abuse at the opposing team, which has yet to run onto the ground; kids who normally don't give you the time of day when passing you in the corridor at school are there in large groups, giving you the thumbs up.

You can't put your finger on it, but golly it feels good sitting amongst this crazy lot. After all, you inhabit that same patch of earth called Redfern, walk the same streets, purchase stuff from the same shops, breathe the same air.

And then comes that moment you've been waiting for, when the Rabbitohs run onto the field. You lift your flag high and wave it from side to side in great sweeping half-circles, go cold all over, overwhelmed by the spectacle of movement and colour and the acclamation of the crowd; and of memories as you recall Mista Tom's and Major's stories of the exploits of players of old: they come to life, you seeing men long dead running onto the paddock, doing short sprints here and there, running up and down on the spot in preparation for the contest that's about to begin.

One of them gestures an acknowledgement to the crowd but you, yeah, you know, don'tcha, he's singling you out in the stand.

The players take their places for the kick-off. You see the order of their positioning, as Major'd explained some nights previously, all contained within those lines marking out the field. You look again at the goalposts standing at opposite ends of the ground, like great sentinels, the man'd said. The old bloke was right. It's *a grand sight*.

Souths cop a beating, getting rissoled by a team that's steamrolling its way to the semis. You shuffle out of the stadium with some supporters who are doing their block. You pick up off the ground what others discard: a torn flag, one red and green mitten, a key ring. You've eaten very little of the food Yaya Zoe'd packed.

'Ah well, we can always dream of the good times that'll surely come,' says Major. 'That's what being a supporter is all about, seeing your team through the tough times.'

Your team, the man'd said. *My* team, you think. It gives you a warm feeling inside.

From where you walk back to Redfern you can see Mista Tom on his verandah, waiting to hear, in detail, Major's analysis of the game.

You go straight to your own home, sticking on your wall those bits and pieces you'd collected after the game.

Later that afternoon Major collects you. He's put Yaya Zoe's food in his fridge and pantry. You both return the empty bag to the woman.

'The moussaka — is good?'

'Good?' he says. 'Good?' he repeats. 'Zoe, you're the best.'

You and he exchange conspiratorial looks.

Major stands outside an unassuming terrace in Chapman Street, Surry Hills. 'It was in October of 1907, ninety-two years ago, Johnnie, when Souths' founding fathers met to discuss the formation of our club. Can you see them, lad, walking through that very same doorway? Three months later they met at the Redfern Town Hall and it was all done. Come on, I'll show you the room where they met.'

The school holidays are filled with all sorts of structured activities, thanks to Major Bob. There's your daily walk, brekkie most mornings with Yaya Zoe, preparing Major's yard for the annual Redfern Spring Garden Competition and, most time-consuming of all, working on your project on rabbits in the local library. There are the pictures to draw, the stats to record, the maps showing those parts of the world where that resilient little terror's made its home. Its hardiness is a comfort to you.

The footy season's drawing to a close. The decision to do with Souths' future is only weeks away. You had to be Blind Freddy not to feel that deep sense of foreboding that's taken hold of Redfern. Doesn't help that your team's getting belted week in, week out. You've seen the games yourself when they got done over like a lamb roast.

Bunnies in Death Throes, screams the *Tele*.

You help Major with his shopping. Bob the Butcher grumbles about the administrators of the game, bringing down his cleaver on a side of lamb with such aggression that you stand well back from the counter.

'And that,' he growls, 'is what I'd like to do to those dickheads!'

Bunnies to Be Skinned Alive.

With school starting in a week Yaya Zoe insists you get your hair cut. You sit on the high chair while Barber Nick hacks at you with an uncharacteristic recklessness, his scissors a blur of metal round your ears. You're glad to get out of there in one piece.

Rabbitohs' Imminent Death.

You sit on the library steps each morning, waiting for it to open. You're amazed to read of the Volcano Rabbit, which lives in the high tablelands of Mexico, and the Hispid Rabbit from the Himalayas. Most of all you love the story of the rabbit in Australia. By golly they're tough, thriving after a drought and a bushfire, in deserts and forests, in spite of predators and the man-made diseases heartless blokes are spreading to wipe them out. The Rabbitohs'll be just as ballsy, too. Yeah, they'll survive, alright.

You draw a rabbit in a Superman cape, another, the last, showing a bunny standing on its hind legs, arms in the air flexing its muscles, fierce eyes challenging the world, a huge blood-red heart, like that in the picture of Jesus on Major's mantelpiece, only this one's beating under a red and green footy guernsey.

You're done. Your teacher'd asked for five pages. You've completed twenty-three.

You go home, find the two rabbits in a hutch in the backyard Ernie the Attorney'd promised he'd buy for you and have delivered to your home. Thanks, Mr Hill Run Man.

It's the final few days of your school break and Major's varying your dawn walks. It's amazing how every street has a story to tell. Give the man a listener and he'll rattle on forever. He can have you sit at a bus shelter and point out for you where the boundary stones of Redfern once stood, now replaced by a set of traffic lights or the widening of Clevo. You enjoy staying this side of those imaginary stones. It's a world you've come to know well. Claim Redfern as your own, the man'd said. They're your lanes and parks, lad. And then there's its history. This is yours too, Johnnie.

The Saturday before the resumption of school Major takes you to Redfern Park.

'There used to be a cricket pitch here when I was a kid. Now, stand there, lad, a little to the right. There. That's where Victor Trumper stood at the crease when he hit a six clear out of the park, breaking a window in the shoe factory that once stood where Souths' car park's now situated. The owners of the factory never repaired that window. They placed a plaque next to it, honouring that great occasion. When Souths bought the building they had the entire broken window, frame and all, placed in a display case when the building was demolished. It's gone now. If Tom'd been able to get his hands onto it it'd still be around today. Now that's a shame.

'And this area where we're sitting now? This was part of the land owned by the Gadigal people. They lived here for thousands of years before the coming of the white man. And over here, Johnnie, there were once huge blackbutt and bloodwood trees, angaphoras and banksias. They were all cut down to make room for the white man's settlement. In fact this whole park used to be a large swamp.'

So you see the blacks making the hoop nets to catch yabbies. You see them fishing in the swamps and streams. The whole area, Major'd told you, was abundant with figs, the fruit of the lilly pilly tree, tubers from orchids, native grapes, apple berries and bolwarra. You see the Gadigal people sitting under a great blackbutt tree telling their own stories, never dreaming of the time when the stands of trees'd be cut down, the waters'd dry up and they'd be forced off their own lands.

Are their spirits still here, you wonder, in and around the bitumen roads and factories, the warehouses and terraces? If Major could resurrect that legendary cricketer, known throughout the British Empire, whom he'd never laid eyes on, and that moment when Trumper'd belted that ball high in the sky and clear out of the ground, startling the factory workers, can you not also see the gnarled tree trunks that are no longer there? Wade in the swamps long gone? Fish for yabbies in the streams that no longer flow? Can you not dream up that which once was? Use words and drawings to give life to that which is not dead, but asleep?

It's Sunday evening. Major walks you to your home. You gather some of the things you'll need for school tomorrow. The man sits in your kitchen while you draw several preliminary pictures of your grandma and grandpa on one wall of your bedroom. They're collecting yabbies and hunting for birds in the swamp.

ELEVEN

Ernie the Attorney comes home

It was in the first week of October when Old Tom rang Bob Ryan.

'You'd better come over, mate.'

'Now?'

'Now. Trust me. You wouldn't wanna miss this for the world. Hurry.'

Major Bob had Yaya Zoe come around to his house while he hurried to Tom's.

'Siddown, Bob. Take a look. Over the road.'

The Hill Run Man was running up the terraced slopes, a ball in his hands.

'It's the same as always, Tom, except that — is he wearing a Souths guernsey?'

'Yep, sure is. Got a big hole across the shoulder. Now, take a look. Over there. In the car park next to the school's gym.'

'His car? The red sports car? He always parks it there, Tom.'

'No, no, no. The tree. Look at the trunk of the tree near the bench. Can you see him?'

Major Bob stared hard at the figure of a man sitting on the

ground, his back up against the massive tree.

'D'ya recognise him?'

'Tom, I can see better out of my glass eye than you can out of your two. He's too far for us to —'

'It's O'Hara.'

'Frank O'Hara? But how can you tell from here?'

'Saw him arrive by cab 'bout 5.30 or so.'

Bob Ryan stared first at the fellow under the tree, then at the figure of the Hill Run Man, who'd sprinted to the top of the inclination. Bob Ryan frowned. Tom was smiling knowingly.

'What are you grinning at, old man?'

'O'Hara's hidin'.'

'From our bloke on the hill? How do you know?'

'Arrived half an hour or so before our mate up there,' said Old Tom. 'Crept round the side of the tree so's he couldn't be seen. Our Hill Run mate up there was lookin' for him.'

'Oh, come on, Tom. They're too far. How do you know — Tom, you called me around for this?'

'D'ya remember where O'Hara went when we sacked him from coachin' the third-grade side?'

'Yes, yes I do. He was head coach of rugby at Sydney Boys High.'

'You wanna know how I know it's him?' He produced a small set of binoculars. 'I've been watchin' him with these. Take a gander.'

'You crafty thing.' The Major took the binoculars and found the man at the tree. 'It's O'Hara alright. Rotten egg of a man.'

'Friggin' hell he was. D'you remember who he coached? At that school?'

Major Bob fell silent. Old Tom saw that his mate lowered his head to consider the ground.

'Now, take a look at the bloke comin' down the hill. You wanna know who I reckon that fella is? It's Victor. He's come back to Redfern, Bob. Victor Batrouney. It's your mate's son. It's Leo's boy.'

Bob Ryan, Old Tom thought, was shaking his head too hard. When he hadn't even had a good look at the fellow through the binoculars. And now the Major was holding the binoculars so firmly to his head that Tom could see the whitening of his skin. The Major removed the glasses, passed them to Tom and, without so much as looking at him, said, 'It's not him.'

Old Tom took the glasses and grunted. 'Well, whoever it is he keeps lookin' at his watch. Waitin' for O'Hara to turn up.'

'He doesn't know O'Hara's there?' Bob Ryan was no longer interested. He put his hat on, checked the zipper of his fly and stared at the few passing cars.

'Nope.'

'Well, so much for Frank O'Hara.' Bob Ryan stood. 'He's not a man I'd like to see again. I'm off now, Tom. The boy and I haven't done our walk yet.' He left hurriedly.

Old Tom lifted his glasses and saw the Hill Run Man gather his ball and bag then walk to his car. He moved the binoculars and was focusing on O'Hara when that man, without getting up from where he sat beneath the tree, began a slow handclap. Tom O'Flaherty shifted the glasses from one to the other, saw the look of contempt on O'Hara's face after he'd got up and approached the other bloke. The Hill Run Man rushed to his car, dropped his keys, struggled to open the door, dropped his keys again and, when he finally threw himself behind the wheel and started the motor, crunched gears, accelerated quickly then belted in a chaotic zigzag down Clevo, leaving behind him the smell of the exhaust, the lingering sound of the squealing back tyres and a thin cloud of smoke.

Tom O'Flaherty swept the glasses around in the direction Major Bob'd taken, to see if he'd witnessed the scene. The old man saw his mate's protruding gut from behind a telegraph pole, where he was hiding. Saw him biting his knuckles.

One damn thing led to another. Contacting then meeting his old coach was one thing, but spying his father's old mate over the road was too much. His mother'd been right. The past festers in some corner of your head, emerging one day to exact some bloody retribution.

And why have such a yearning for Redfern anyway? What was the big deal about that crappy suburb with its mixture of warehouses and boutiques, factories and yuppy brasseries, its congested streets, foul air and painful memories? He loved his six-acre block in the Hills district. He'd been telling himself for years that its distance from Redfern'd made it all the more appealing. Well, if that was the case, why drive all that way into the city to train? And why place orders for advanced olive and cedar trees which'd transform corners of his property into a little Lebanon? Why was he of late spending so much time going over his school annuals, rereading that letter his old man'd written from that ghastly camp, seeing in the gentle face of his father some admonition? He wasn't a kid, for Christ's sake! Where did this sudden yearning come from? Guilt? Alright, he hadn't pursued law. Well, Vic, take a look at that fleet of cabs in that monster garage. And that bookshelf of first edition Whites and Maloufs and Murrays, signed by the authors. Not to mention those walls of Drysdales and Whiteleys, worth a row of terraces in the suburb you'd stormed out of all those years ago, leaving a mother tearing at her hair. You'd done good, right? Your old man'd be proud of you, wouldn't he?

First there was all this business with Souths that was going to see them kicked in the arse. Then contacting that madman O'Hara, who'd had such a tyrannical father's hold on Victor when he was at school. And finally seeing Potatohead (it's what he'd called Bob Ryan when he was a kid), sitting on some old bloke's verandah. Did the fat bloke recognise him? Probably not. Too long ago. And that terrace he sat on every bloody day was too far away from his hill runs, right?

Victor Batrouney bought all three morning papers. He sat at an outdoor setting in the paddock furthest from the house, cut out all references to Souths then filed them in the folder he'd purchased from DJs for that purpose. He angrily reread the previous day's post-delivered Annual Report from the Chairman of News Corporation, the organisation which'd seized control of rugby league in Australia.

'Virtually every minute of the day in every time zone on the planet, people are watching, reading and interacting with our product. We're reaching people from the moment they wake up until they fall asleep. We give them their morning weather and traffic reports through our television outlets around the world. We enlighten and entertain them with such newspapers as The New York Post *and* The Times *as they have their breakfast or take the train to work. And when they get home in the evening, we're there to entertain them with compelling first-run entertainment on Fox. Before going to bed we give them the latest news. And then they can crawl into bed with one of our bestselling novels from HarperCollins.'*

Victor Batrouney instructed his broker to sell off all his News Limited shares.

Oh Susan, what have you done?

Susan Wynter's family were horrified when she announced she was going to marry this taxi-driving Lebanese Maronite whom she'd met when they were both studying law. The long and proud Anglo-Celtic line came to an abrupt end with their only child's marriage to this dark, curly-haired wiry man. Yes, this chap had done well. There was that selective high school he'd gone to, the wedding at St Marks at Darling Point rather than at St Marons in Redfern, that growing fleet of cabs at his young age. But dear oh dear, why did he have to end his studies? And he was so … well, Lebanese-looking.

Victor Batrouney learnt which knife and fork to take hold of when the entrée was served. He sat looking interested as they spoke, putting up with their long pauses, their slow and deliberate manner when searching for the right word or phrase that had him yearning to escape, alone, onto their balcony overlooking the water. It was a long way from the raucous Redfern dinner table and that community of terraces where, to be heard, he would shout from wherever he happened to be.

Susan carried her coffee to the outdoor table he was sitting at. And moments after she'd sat down he blundered out those words. He hadn't intended it. Sure, it'd been on his mind, but it was something he was going to keep to himself.

'I am a success, aren't I, Susan?' He was staring at his coffee. 'I'm not a failure, am I?'

Susan Batrouney (everybody knew Batrouney-Wynter wouldn't stand the test of time) took her husband's hand. 'Good Lord, Victor. How on earth could you —'

'Did I ever tell you about my old footy coach? Frank O'Hara?'

'Yes, you did. More than once.'

'Oh, funny that. Can't remember telling you. He always said I wasted my talents. In footy, I mean.'

'It's just a game, dear.'

'Yes. Yes. Of course. But then I didn't complete my Law Degree.'

'Victor, all those long hours over all those years driving taxis. You —'

'Susan, I'm thinking of going back to uni. And something else.

I need to go to Lebanon. I'd like to see the village my ancestors came from, you know? To see their graves, walk into their homes, speak to people who remember them. If you prefer to stay I'll go alone.'

Victor hits the blower

He worked the phones, ringing every O'Hara in the phone directory, smiling grimly as he recalled the man's military approach to training.

'Are we tired?'

'No, sir!'

'I can't *hear* you! Are — we — tired?'

'No, sir!'

'Are we enjoying ourselves?'

'Yes, sir!'

'And do we want to do another hill run?'

He took Victor Batrouney aside after training. 'How long? Listen, kiddo. I saw you this morning, doing your hill runs. Saw you scooping up a loose grubber, do a couple of nifty steps. No one in the comp can accelerate like you from a standing start. You should be tearing the opposition to shreds. But no, you play that fumbling shit-scared game week in, week out. There's nothing you can't do, y'know, 'cept tackle blokes bigger than you. You've got it all, d'ya hear? I'm tired of telling you. When you finish school, go to Souths if you want. They'd snap you up. Sky's the limit.'

O'Hara made to go, stopped, turned again to face the boy. 'Know why you're so damn tentative? Do you wanna know why?' The boy braced himself for the king-hit he knew was coming his way. 'It's 'cause you're so gutless. Keep playing like you did last Saturday and you can take a running jump into the seconds. Don't let me down, Bat-rooney.'

He wanted to make good. To please O'Hara. The man might've had the boy cowering when they approached each other in opposite directions down the corridor, O'Hara's eyes searching out his if only to stare him down. But he was a legend in the school, had played for Australia, knew personally so many of the greats — had Victor's own father been such a forbidding figure of a man?

Victor Batrouney continued doing wonderful things at every training session. But each Saturday he stuffed up. What was going wrong?

Something held him back on the field. Perhaps it was those great crowds that came from private schools to watch their boys play against Victor's own selective government school. Perhaps it was all those Anglo men in suits, some retired army blokes with clipped moustaches going off their brains as they barked their criticism from the sideline. And their wives, in hats and gloves, drinking tea under the marquee, who knew how to say sweet fuck-all but make it sound so important. He'd stand there, all teeth and fumbling hands, not knowing how to respond.

Then there was the atmosphere in the change room before and after each game and training session, the swearing and the backslapping and banter that intimidated him, the boys giving each other wedgies in their undies then wandering around in the buff after the shower together. He'd invent all sorts of reasons to bathe alone in his cossies after everyone else'd gone. Usually he'd shower at home.

Then again perhaps it was the mother who'd never remarried. Shamla Batrouney lived out her frustrated young widowed aspirations through her only son, scornfully dismissing the rugby he played. She did not attend a single game. She would not even wash his footy clothes. She reminded him constantly of the letter his dying father'd written. She'd thrust it in his face when his grades began to fall. Had it framed and dyna-bolted to the wall above his desk in his bedroom.

Victor Batrouney was dropped from the Firsts. A few weeks later he was relegated to the Thirds.

Ten years later, in 1967, and Mary Butler was standing in Caroline Smithers' office, chucking a mental and an ink-filled pen across a desk, globs of ink spraying the Matron's starched white uniform.

Theodora Ngalligill was lending the weight of her jaw-clenched stare, eloquence and rage to join those protestors who were invading pollies' offices to demand the creation of Aboriginal Medical and Legal Services. She started up a roster system of drivers who cruised the night, picking up street kids and those too pissed to find their own way home. She began visiting blacks down at Long Bay Gaol. When asked about her relationship to the prisoner, she'd say she was their Nanna. She bullied those in need of medical attention to visit those white doctors sympathetic to blacks. She barrel-chested her way into court proceedings, storming into a courtroom one day to rail against a system that'd allow a fourteen-year-old to appear without representation. She stayed behind after the ruckus was over, to talk to blokes in wigs and gowns, apologising for her actions, impressing with her prodigious knowledge of a dozen Aboriginal languages and her implacable and imperial presence. They had their photo taken with her. It made it onto the third page of *The Sun*. The reporter nicknamed her Nanna Dora. The presiding judge used his influence to have her given unrestricted access to blacks in all gaols in NSW.

Jimmy Butler was disappearing for months at a time from a farm out at Ginlambone, sitting alone on his haunches around a fire, talking and cracking jokes out aloud to keep the demons away, watching the sun dip low over far-flung hills, making all sorts of promises to himself to stay off the grog and away from that mob that'd laughingly press another bottle in his hand.

Konstantine and Maria Tsakiris were working two jobs apiece. The money was piling up in their bank account, the Greek man checking his statements like a dieting fanatic checking his scales. And the future, well, she looked a beauty, mate.

Major Bob Ryan'd long been living alone, renting a one-bedroom flat in Redfern. If he saw his old man it was purely by chance. They'd dip their hats, exchange polite words about the weather as if they were neighbours who couldn't avoid talking to each other over a fence. Bob Ryan was talent-scouting for the Rabbitohs. He worked at Eveleigh with Tom. And, he told himself, he loved the Greek woman like a sister.

Zoe was working like a demon in that furnace of a kitchen, mumbling prayers and sliding trays in and out of her old stove, every spare penny going to the bank to pay off her loan. Once, a congregation of icons in her *iconostasio* joined her in an Easter chant.

As for Tom, well, he was not yet *Old* Tom. He sat on the sideline at a tiny table, ringing his ancient wooden-handled bell for the start and finish of every Souths home game. Anyone with any memento to do with the Rabbitohs they no longer wanted knew to pass it on to him.

And Victor Batrouney stood at the halfway mark at the SCG with his new wife and saw Souths win that year's Grand Final. On their way out of the ground, in amongst the great jubilant throng of Souths supporters, he felt someone jabbing him hard in the shoulder. Victor Batrouney turned.

'You could've been out there today,' Frank O'Hara shouted, 'if you weren't such a little mummy's boy!'

It was the end of September 1999, thirty-two years since he'd last heard O'Hara speak, but Victor immediately recognised the snappy hard-edged voice, that imperial aggro manner that'd once had him grinning his silly sheepishness. All his old fears returned.

This was madness. When he'd always thought it was O'Hara who had a screw loose, here he was, at his age, holding the phone in his sweaty hand, shit-scared of a man in an old aged people's home that he hadn't seen for all those years, terrified yet respectful of this bloke's no-bullshit approach. He hadn't expected things to come this far. What chance of finding him after all that time, of him being alive, of him taking this crazy vague call?

Perhaps it was the ludicrousness of Victor's request. Or the daily boredom of O'Hara's life. Whatever the reason, the bastard hung on, his brain ticking over. Victor Batrouney heard him clear his throat of phlegm.

'Let me get this straight,' he said. 'You want to meet me some time in the future.'

'That's right,' Victor said.

'But you won't tell me when.'

'I'm not able to yet.'

'And you can't meet me now 'cause you're going overseas.'

'I'm leaving next week.'

'You want to meet me at six in the morning. Opposite Sydney Boys, right? To show me something?'

'That's right.'

'But you won't tell me what it is.'

'I'd rather not, if you don't mind.'

'You'd rather not,' he said. 'You'd rather not. And you won't tell me your name.'

'I can't. Not yet.'

There was a long pause.

'You're kidding me.'

'No, no, not at all.'

'Will I bring me whistle?'

'If you'd like you —'

'So, this has got to do with footy. I've trained you, haven't I? Did you ever play for Souths?'

Victor Batrouney felt a nerve tingling behind his right knee. There was a twitch in one of his eyes.

'You're an old boy, aren't you? Of Sydney Boys High? That's it, isn't it?'

Off to Lebanon

Victor Batrouney got out of the battered Merc he'd hired for the day to stretch his legs. The names of the Orthodox villages in the mountainous area east and south-east of Tripoli — Kousba, Btarram, Bishmizzeen and Douma — were familiar to him. He'd gone to Redfern Public School with kids whose parents'd come from these tiny villages, but he'd had little to do with them outside school, his mother (his whole clan, really) insisting he mix only with Lebanese Maronites. Victor did not enter the ruins of the Orthodox church: across the decades he could still hear his mother's harsh, shrill words and see that terrible frown that made ugly her face, warning him off too close a contact with kids not of their faith. He heard also the door of their Redfern home, the day he finally walked out of his mother's life, slamming shut behind him, the flyscreen swinging on its hinges.

But here there were no homes he could visit. There were none of those of his parents' faith buried in the local cemetery, no stories for him in the old stone homes or the snow-laden paths. This was not his world.

The cab driver took him down the narrow steep road towards the Maronite villages in the Qadisha Valley. The hamlets and tiny collections of houses they drove through, many deserted, were silent and still. Theirs was the only vehicle on the road. A cold wind blew off the ice on the road. When he entered, at last, the outskirts of the village of his grandparents, Victor Batrouney would have liked to stop the cab, get out, kneel and kiss the ground. But he was embarrassed, so he said nothing to the driver when he arrived at a clearing and stopped, for Victor to get out and see, from a distance, the village he was about to enter.

On one side he saw mountain peaks covered in snow, on the other the deep chasms and gorges of the valley, disappearing in their own shadows. He could see whitewashed stone homes with their red roofs, one of which was surely his grandfather's. He looked for the domes of the church but could see none.

He arrived at his family's village of Kasharram. Victor Batrouney got out to walk. Some of the locals watched him through shutters slightly ajar, then quickly withdrew when he looked their way. The two cafés were empty. Goats grazing in the ruins of houses retreated from the man. The church Victor the Fierce Moustache had helped restore over eighty years previously with money sent out from Australia lay in ruins, too dangerous to enter. There was no priest to show him the books in which were recorded the names of those baptised, married or buried. All the records had been destroyed in the fire that had gutted the church after the bombs had fallen decades before.

Victor Batrouney approached the baker who was about to close for lunch. The man behind the bench smiled out of a face covered with a fine layer of flour. He'd been the village baker for over fifty years, he said, waking at four every morning, spending five hours preparing the dough and baking the bread then, after sweeping down the work benches with an old straw broom, going home. This had been his life. Ahhh, well, what can you do? In a year or so he'd close down the business. Of the Batrouney family, however, he could recall very little. They'd left before he was born. Perhaps the widower Moussah Hanka could be of assistance. He was the oldest person in the village, lived alone since his wife had died, but his memory, the baker said, was now failing him.

The road out to this old man's farm was a slippery narrow track. Victor went on foot, sidestepping the potholes and slush. Moussah Hanka came out of his tiny home that was set well back off the track, leaning on a goatherd's crook, and walked slowly, on bowed legs, down the path to the road. Chickens scuttled out of his way. A donkey looked up uninterestedly. A thin dog strained on its leash, barking savagely. Smoke curtseyed from a wobbly chimney.

Moussah Hanka had startling blue eyes set against the tough leather of his face. He wore a goatskin coat, a fur-lined jacket and, on his feet, thickly soled sandals, their criss-crossed straps bound over several layers of socks. He welcomed the Australian with great warmth.

Victor Batrouney helped the old man stoke the fire, pour homemade wine into cups, set the low table with heavily salted, wrinkled olives, stale crusty bread, dry haloumi cheese, shreds of lettuce and some overripe tomatoes and cucumbers. They sat on an old thinning rug on the earthen floor and talked, Victor Batrouney trying to piece together the stories the peasant told him with what he already knew. But of the Batrouneys, Moussah Hanka could remember very little.

But surely he could recall the day when the entire Batrouney clan departed, following the steps of that man Victor the Moustache, when they'd been the first family to leave in great numbers? The Batrouneys'd all left pledging to return once they'd made their fortune, but none did.

No, no, Moussah Hanka could not. The name was familiar to him. But it was too long ago. He was now too old, too old. He'd been such a small child at the time, and, not long after, so many others had left. All those departing gestures, men carrying huge suitcases, women with babies in their arms, a blur of weepy faces.

For Victor, then, the reality of his grandfather's life would remain in Redfern. At least there he could visit the homes the elder Victor'd lived in, the stores he'd run before losing the lot in the 1920s. He could sit in the high-backed seats of the Kookaburra Café where his grandfather would go each night after dinner, to chat, argue and gossip, drink Turkish coffee, smoke his imported

Lebanese tobacco, play backgammon and sing songs of longing for the old country with men of his generation, all of whom lived in that part of Redfern called Little Syria. Victor had the photos. Men in dark suits, black Stetson hats and white collarless shirts buttoned to the neck, huge moustaches and sad eyes, staring seriously and formally into the camera. He remembered how severe they looked to him when he was a boy, and how their faces would lighten whenever he walked into the café, still dressed in the uniform of the selective school he'd gained entry into (how proud your father would have been, they'd say), to make some purchase for his mother. In the background of one photograph were the leadlight fixtures of the café, the grand silver cash register and the wind-up gramophone with one of the many 78s brought out from Lebanon on the turntable.

Victor Batrouney stood. He was about to bid his farewell to Moussah Hanka when he thought of one more question to ask. In the years before the Great Depression his grandfather had sent a small fortune to help pay for the restoration of the church. Did Moussah Hanka know about this? No? Was there no tablet commemorating his grandfather's name he could see, and touch? The whole family had gone without so that this money could go to a cause dear to his heart, and now no one even knew? How could this be?

The filter-less cigarette hung from Moussah Hanka's lips. He bowed his head then shook it sadly, the smoke curling around his head like a halo. He placed both his hands on the table, then began to beat a slow and mournful rhythm with the open palm of one hand. Moussah Hanka took the cigarette out of his mouth with his other hand, then began to sing. Victor could understand little of what he sang, but felt this old man's sorrow for those who'd left the motherland, never to return, their memories and stories lost forever. And maybe, Victor thought, he sang of the succeeding generations who returned to look for the grave that existed no more, or the fragment of a story someone might recall, only to discover a hollow and cold wind whistling through the remains of unclaimed properties.

Victor Batrouney fled Lebanon as soon as he could. He knew he'd never come back.

By the time of his return, Souths supporters were counting down the days for the NRL's announcement. Victor Batrouney resumed his training. He continued his forty-minute drive to Moore Park. He gave no answer to his wife that satisfied her curiosity. She'd watch him drive off most days through the parted velvet curtains in their bedroom, and wonder what had got into him. One day she used the street directory to approximate the distance of the round trip to Redfern and checked the speedometer before he'd left and on his return. Yes, it was okay. He wasn't having some dawn affair. He really was going silly with all this training.

His first training run was on a Sunday morning. He knew Bob Ryan'd be at early Mass. Johnnie'd told him that was his routine. As he got out of his car on Clevo, he saw the boy walking across the park with a black man. Johnnie stopped to talk. The other man continued walking. Victor Batrouney was concerned.

'We're goin' out t'Sintennial Park. Gunna kick a ball 'round, feed them ducks. He's gunna show me that tree what he lives under.'

'A tree? He lives under a tree? Johnnie, who is this man?'

''Sokay. He's me brother. Gotta go. Yer rabbits're doin' good. Called 'em after two Souths players. See youse!'

Victor Batrouney watched them for some time. The older black man walked clumsily. He's drunk, Victor thought. My God, at this time of day, he's drunk.

He trained for an hour or so then, instead of driving back home, crossed South Dowling Street and walked to the Kookaburra Café.

There it was, still there after all those years. Inside were a number of young men in singlets putting the final touches to their work of renovation. Outside, a huge banner hung from the balcony: *Opening Soon*. One man, who had the name Roberto emblazoned on his top, was polishing the old silver cash register. Another was sanding an obstinate corner of one of the high-backed seats. The leadlight lamp covers and the marble black-and-white tiles had been restored, the original crockery and cutlery cleaned. The old prints on the walls — my God, the cedars of Lebanon, the same ones he used to longingly gaze at as a child — and more recent ones of Greece had been framed. The large wind-up gramophone stood on a conspicuous table, covered in plastic. The old scales, now gleaming, still hung off a chain attached to a beam in the ceiling, the tray filled with ornamental gourds. And leaning up against one wall were three huge pub posters. In one, two men and a woman, dressed in elegant evening wear, sat around a table, drinking Pilsener. The other two portrayed Souths players scoring tries.

Victor Batrouney continued his walk. He crossed Redfern Park, where the entire Batrouney clan'd congregate under one particular fig tree after Mass most Sundays for a picnic. He walked to St Marons and, from the street, heard the Mass that was being celebrated. He'd been an altar boy himself, once, searching for the beaming face of his proud mother whenever he emerged from behind the icon screen, holding a candle for a procession. My boy, my boy, how proud your father would have been.

Opposite the church was the terrace the man'd grown up in. He touched the brick fence.

And recalled the terrible fights when he refused to give up that Australian girl he was going with for the one chosen for him from the old country. And the meetings of aunts and uncles, who sat him in the centre of the lounge room, shouting into his face their accusations of his betrayal — of his blood, his mother country, his own mother and, most importantly, the father he'd never known.

But he would marry this girl, and if they had no intention of attending the wedding then he would marry her in her Anglican church.

He moved out of his home several months before the wedding. He ignored the pleas of his aunts who begged him, on the street as he bundled his packed bags into the boot of his car, to think of the woman who was beside herself with anguish, of the husband she'd lost, of the sacrifices she'd made, of the hopes she'd invested in him, her only child, who was, at that very moment, walking out on her forever. As he was about to drive off his mother appeared at the doorway. She threw out over the fence and onto the street those gifts people'd given her on the occasion of the birth of her son.

After his wedding he tried to contact her. But his mother slammed the phone down when he rang. She closed the door angrily in his face when he called by. I am no mother. I have no child.

She refused to see him even after the birth of his (Anglican) children. And then the cancer took hold. The word got through to Victor Batrouney, who hadn't known of her long struggle. He rushed back from an overseas holiday for the reconciliation that occurred too late, too late.

The family'd bathed Shamla Batrouney's body then transferred her to the packed lounge room. A great wailing erupted the moment he entered the room. His aunts rose, wringing their hands, their anguish and grief distorting their faces. There was his Aunt Najla who used to hold him in her arms when the Mass was too long and his legs hurt; there was Aunt Samia, who'd wept with joy when he'd gained entry into Sydney Boys High School and delighted in his progress before the grades began to fall and he withdrew into himself. They stood, strangers to the man they blamed for their sister's death.

Victor Batrouney's Uncle Yousef, wearing a black marker on

his chest and a three-day stubble on his face, stepped forward, offering his hesitant hand. All waited to see whether Victor Batrouney would bend to kiss the proferred hand as a sign of his respect and as an admission of the errors of his ways. But no, all he did was shake it, as if they were equals. There was, then, no embrace or kiss for Victor Batrouney. Aunt Samia placed her limp hand in his, lifting her face to show him the eyes that still smouldered.

The night after the funeral Victor Batrouney sat alone, opening the parcel his mother had packed for him. He unwrapped the first of the many layers of material around a frame, untied the carefully knotted string then spread apart the sponge protecting the glass on which his mother had written, in black texta, *You have disgraced your father*. He saw the letter from his father, written from the prisoner-of-war camp, expressing his desire that his child should go into Law. Before he knew what he'd done, Victor Batrouney'd hurled the frame across the room, the glass shattering against a wall.

A frowning woman's face appeared at the front window of the terrace. Victor Batrouney, in shorts and T-shirt, unshaven and still sweating, must've looked a sight. He pushed off, returned to his car and drove home. His wife asked him why he'd taken so long. She did not understand his curt reply.

A fucken gutless wog
3 OCTOBER 1999

Victor Batrouney arrived at 5.45 a.m. He sat in his car, listening to Radio National as he waited for Frank O'Hara. By six o'clock he was sweating so much the Souths guernsey he was wearing stuck to his back and the leather upholstery.

And over the road an old man was watching through his front room window, the binoculars screwed to his head, a mischievous grin on his face. The old man got on the phone. He called a mate. Within five minutes Tom O'Flaherty and Bob Ryan were sitting on the verandah, and saw it all.

Victor Batrouney was disappointed and relieved that O'Hara was nowhere to be seen. Was a crazy idea, anyway. Didn't really matter, did it, what O'Hara thought? It's not like he was his dad, or anything.

He went through his routine nonetheless, running up and down the hill like it was some sort of assault, burning off his anxiety about meeting his old coach after all those years. He bounced the ball on the ground on his way down the slopes, managing, more often than not, to catch it, bending low to minimise the angle of its rebound. He kicked it high during his short sprints on the field, regathering without it once hitting the ground. He lined up for the opposition's kick-off, facing those internationals of his imagination. He picked the ball up off the ground from a running start, accelerated, the ball held tight to his chest, sinking his hips in the manner of the Ella brothers, those champion Aboriginal players he admired, his legs reaching forward in long strides, alternately changing both his speed and the angle of his run. He kicked the ball over the heads of the tacklers that'd closed in on him, focusing on the ball as it rebounded here and there, then swooped down on its erratic bounce like some bird of prey. And then he executed the goosestep that left them all floundering, exploded into open space and dived over the line for the match-winning try.

He saw the crowd in the stands rise as one as he made his way to his car, the clapping continuing long after their cries'd subsided. He opened the boot, threw in the ball; and still the clapping persisted, like the echo of some faraway tolling bell. He was about to unlock the driver's door when he realised that the clapping was not some creation of his imagination. Victor Batrouney looked over the road, saw the man who'd been with his father at that death camp standing behind a pole — Bob Ryan was looking Victor's way, but it was not him acknowledging his play. And then he saw O'Hara emerge from the shadows of a fig tree. His old coach, smirking and shaking his head.

'Must've been pretty good in your day,' he shouted. 'Never seen a bloke your age do such things!' O'Hara began walking towards him, supported by a stick.

Victor Batrouney remained standing next to his car's driver's door, the keys in his hand, his old coach's sudden presence leaving him speechless.

'What did'ya wanna show me?' he said, as he made his way closer to the younger man.

'That,' Victor Batrouney replied.

'That?' O'Hara stopped in his tracks. 'Whatd'ya mean by *that*?'

'What I just did. The running. The kicking.'

The older man narrowed his eyes. 'Who the fuck are you?'

'Does it matter? You just said you liked what you saw me do.'

'Is that it? Is that what all this's about? Jesus Christ!'

Victor Batrouney went to unlock the door of his car.

'Hang on a sec. You don't get off so easily. I wanna know who you are.'

Victor Batrouney smiled his sheepish smile. 'I've heard what I wanted to hear.'

'Oh, you've heard what you wanted to hear, have you? Well, fuck you, mate.' He advanced closer. 'Look at me! Lemme see your face! Look up, you little piker!'

Victor fumbled with the car keys, dropping them to the ground. As he was bending down to recover them he heard O'Hara say, 'Are you tired?'

Victor Batrouney struggled to get the key into the door.

'I can't *hear* you?'

He dropped the keys a second time.

'Are we having fun? Heard what you wanted to hear, my arse. Well listen to this: I remember you. What'sa matter, little mummy's boy having trouble opening his pooftah car's door? Ooooh, poor little Bat-rooney.'

Victor Batrouney threw himself into the car and tried starting up the motor, hearing O'Hara's roar through the open door and the screeching of the starter-motor.

'Could've gone all the way. But you know why you didn't? 'Cause you're a fucken gutless wog! Were then, still are!'

The following week he filled out the forms Susan'd acquired for him while he was overseas. He was hopeful that as a mature-aged student he'd be accepted into the Law course.

During that same week he went into the city to submit the forms at the uni. He came across a copy of the local rag. He saw a photo of Bob Ryan, who'd won (again) the Redfern Spring Garden Competition. The Major stood in his front garden, beside the tree he'd brought back from overseas as a seed which, he'd told the reporter, he'd planted as a memorial to an old mate who'd not returned from overseas duty. Victor Batrouney knew it was only a matter of time before he stood outside Bob Ryan's terrace, summoning up the courage to knock on the man's door.

TWELVE

Johnnie Butler meets his brother

TUESDAY, 12 OCTOBER 1999

Warm October days. Wisteria blooming and the footpaths purple underfoot. Gardens ablaze, the jacarandas getting ready to take over the whole city, the sky an endless blue, intense and taut to the horizon. A man walking through Redfern'd think the whole world was bursting with goodness. But the Major, well, he knew more than most how on such lovely spring days a man could wake up and find tiny sores on his leg that'd turn nasty in days, kill him off in weeks; how on a night gorgeous with stars and a fat friendly moon he could make his way to an outside loo for a welcome piss only to find a mate swinging off a rope tied to a tree. You could turn a corner whistling a tune, as happy and chirpy as a sparrow, telling yourself life couldn't get any better, only to be greeted by a brick falling out of the sky.

'What's on yer mind, Bob?' asked Tom.

'Ah, nothing much.'

'How's me little mate?'

'Johnnie? He's looking forward to his mother returning home.

They reckon it'll be some time this week. He wants to sleep in his own home, you know. Now, I mean. On his own.'

'On his own? At his age? Is that wise?'

Bob Ryan nodded. 'He'll be fine. You should see his drawings and paintings, Tom. He's got a real talent.'

'You've told him Souths'll be gettin' the arse?'

'Yes. You've been right all along, Tom. We can't beat the big end of town. Unless we have something over them, something they're afraid of.'

'Heard an interview this mornin'. On the wireless, just before you came round. With one of them News Limited 'xecutives. He was talkin' live from New York, 'bout the future of the game.'

'From America. Talking about our game from America.' The Major shook his head in mock disbelief. 'And what did this chap have to say?'

'Nothin' we 'aven't heard before. All that nonsense 'bout rationalisin' the game. Goin' international. Gettin' rid of dead wood.'

'Is that what we are, Tom? Dead wood?'

The old man made a grunting sound. ''Parently. Anyway, went on to crack a joke. Told a story 'bout some big meetin' he was supposed t'have last week. With all them other 'xecutives and their big boss, Murdoch. Said they all got a message sayin' they was to meet at Murdoch's home, not the office. So everyone turns up for the meetin', flyin' in from all over the place, waitin' and waitin' on the street in their limos, no one's home, see. Waitin' for Murdoch to arrive.'

'He didn't turn up?'

'Well, yes and no. Murdoch went home alright. Problem is, he's got homes all over the place, and he'd sent the message from Sydney. Everyone went to the wrong home. They all went to New York.'

'I see,' said the Major. 'That's a joke, is it, Tom?'

''Xactly what I thought. He had a good chuckle while tellin' it.'

Major Bob stood up to go.

'By the way, given any thought to our old mate? Might be able to help when Mary comes home.'

'Who, Tom?'

'Jim. Jimmy Butler. Does he know Mary's in hospital? Does he know Mary *exists*?'

'How would I know, Tom?'

'Have you told Johnnie 'bout him?'

'How do you know it's him? It could be another Jim Butler.'

The old man looked at Bob Ryan with his head cocked to one side, mouth turned down at the corners. He then rolled his eyes, exhaling theatrically.

'Oh, alright, alright, it's probably him. And the answer's no. I haven't told Johnnie.'

'Why not?'

'I don't know.'

'Jesus, Bob, it's his uncle, his bloody uncle.'

'I didn't think of it, I guess.'

'An' somethin' else.'

'What, Tom?'

'I didn't know till now Jimmy and Mary were brother an' sister — why didn'tcha tell me?'

You paint over your pencil drawing of a giant snake furrowing its way into the earth. It creates a curving depression that forms a creek bed. There are its waters feeding into a swamp. On the shallow banks of this creek are deep clefts in the rocks and boulders made from the axe of the Fighting Lizard Man. That's him, looking scary as hell standing on the bough of that great blackbutt tree. Women wade in the waters of the swamp gathering waterlilies, yabbies and freshwater mussels, or look for hairline cracks in the ground where they know the yams are buried. You know all about this stuff. Major's borrowed all these books for you to read and copy from, eh.

And while the women use their digging sticks to uproot their yams and edible roots, their men, plastered with mud to remove any trace of human smell, stalk an emu, exactly where Victor Trumper once stood at the crease. You've drawn him, too.

Your ancestors lie in wait in the tall grass to ambush a roo, where Ernie told you he once sat with his Lebo rels for a picnic. There's Major joining the hunt, and even though you've drawn him as a kid there's no mistaking the hat, tie, braces and glass eye, and that fat pumpkin head (hee-hee-hee) of his.

You know Souths are going to get done over. Major's told you. The kids at school dread the day. They wonder how they're going to fill the winter months if their team isn't on the paddock. They wonder, too, if worst comes to worst, what they're going to do with that lifelong dream of one day playing in the Rabbitohs' first-grade team. So you include two rabbits in that evolving mural. They float in and out of watercourses and, like in a dream, change into human form. The mural tells a story, turning the corner of one wall to continue onto the next. Here the Rabbit Men follow ancestral paths through scrub that leads away from the swamp, carrying firesticks dipped in resin. They continue to a clearing where they fasten bundles of leaves and grass around their ankles and arms while others, tapping sticks, beat a rhythmic song to their rabbit dance.

Redfern's a shitty suburb, some of those outsiders are saying. Bulldoze and start again. Well, the locals reply, we might just close off the streets and throw up barricades 'cause of all that crap. Those wankers who don't know what Redfern's all about're sliding into the new millennium and they're dancing to the edge of the cliff, laughing with big ugly open mouths and sounding like flocks of silly kookaburras. Sydney's going troppo, the residents reckon, colliding with its own brashness, giving the past a disdainful flick. The CBD rising like a distant monolith, wrapped in a gorgeous haze that's filling lungs and doing beautifully poisonous things to the harbour at sunset. Fat-wheeled hoon cars burning rubber up and down South Dowling Street and Clevo, dragging other like-minded motorheads, chucking wheelies in cars so hotted up the drivers fry in the early summer heat. Christmas is coming, they're told, and everyone's getting fat. The pre-Chrissie sales are on and people, getting in early before the Boxing day sales, haven't got a clue why they're constantly on the run, always looking to the future, to tomorrow, the coming weekend, the next celebratory occasion. They're knackered by mid-afternoon, feeling like the fag-end of a tired and twisted roll-your-own. They've no time to look over their shoulders to the past, and even if they did they couldn't give a shit. They're on the move, man, so jump on board or piss off outta the way.

But here, bounded by four streets minutes from each other, the residents know it's the past and present that's colliding, straining the bones of those who sit in their yards, on the verandahs or on a street corner, wiry men in hats, like retired jockeys, and women with curlers in their hair and a ciggie hanging out of the corner of their mouth, jabbering on over the fence and going over all that's gone wrong. They can hear the rumbling city traffic from a distance, but here, ignoramuses reckon it's nothing but a scumbag area of rundown factories and stuffed warehouses, sad corner shops and suspect syringed lanes. But in those rows of terraces there're people who've been living in them for yonks, residents who could be out the back of Woop Woop for all that they know (or care) of what's *out there*. It's what's *in here* that counts, mate. And I can tell you, the inhabitants proudly say, some of us stand still long enough to hear the whole damn place sigh for what was said and done, long ago. There are spaces here, in quiet narrow streets, in the back of old churches long shut down, in tiny public spaces of green with a single bench where people stand or sit alone and hear the rumours and the regrets, and see life peeled back to its raw nerves, tingling for what could've been. But try telling that to those pricks who don't know what it means when you say you wanna live out your life amongst streets you call home.

Mary Butler's strung out, and she doesn't know why. She needs Nan, but Johnnie's told her she's left Townsville for Darwin, where some poor kid's been bagged by the cops for minor theft and thrown into gaol for a month. Johnnie's keeping some secret from his mamma about what's happening to her home, but he won't say what it is. Ah mamma, wait till you see what we've done to our place.

Mary Butler hobbles around the ward on her crutch, distributing pieces of baklava from the tray Yaya'd sent with Johnnie. She's wheeled out into the courtyard where she's left for a while to sit in the sun. She sees a beetle, in a frenzy as it's attacked by an army of ants. Best to put it out of its misery. She stands over the writhing beetle, aims the end of her crutch, kills it. Mary Butler bends as low as she can to ensure the beetle's dead. Feels a sharp pang of pain when she sees dozens of ants twisting and squirming, dismembered, still alive. Jesus, Mary, can't you do anything right? Come back, Nan, I needja.

You return to school and sit anxiously in your chair, waiting to be summoned to the teacher's desk. And when your turn finally does come you know she's pleased with your project. Unlike the other kids you don't just look down at your folder as she marks your work, but occasionally up at the woman herself, to see in her face if she's as pleased and as proud of what you've done as you'd hoped. You ache for her touch and her smile. You love the distinctive soapy smell of the woman. You move your chair closer to her so that her arm brushes against your elbow.

She pauses to spend some time looking at those illustrations of the bunnies right at the end of your project.

'Why, Johnnie. These pictures. They're beautiful.' And then she has the class look up as she shows them your work.

The kids give you a hard time during recess. Yeah, you're the teacher's pet, alright, but all's forgiven when you score a couple of tries during the game of touch footy at big lunch.

When class resumes you ask the question you've rehearsed many times.

'Why, of course you can bring your bunnies to class. What are their names, Johnnie?'

'One's Churchill, miss. But I call 'im Clive.'

'Clive? You mean *Winston* Churchill?'

A great moan erupts from the class.

'And what's the name of your other rabbit?'

'Satts. Called 'im after John Sattler.'

'And who's John Sattler?'

'Ohhh, miss, don't you know nothin'?'

As you make your way down the corridor at the end of that school day, your teacher stops you. 'I've got a note from the office. Your brother was looking for you.'

You frown. 'Me brother?'

'The secretary told him he'd have to wait until school was over.'

'Me brother?'

'He didn't wait. I didn't know you had a brother, Johnnie?'

Nor do you.

You wait until you hear Major leave. You get out of your bed and walk into your mamma's bedroom. You love the bright colours and the fresh smells of her room. There's a new bed, too, that's not just a mattress on the floor but a real one with a wooden bedhead that's been recently stained. There are sheets and pillowcases which, despite being new, Yaya Zoe insisted on washing and ironing. There are blankets in pastel-coloured checks, a chest of drawers full of lovely soft embroidered things that smell of Johnson's Baby Soap (Major's favourite), new lamps on new bedside tables. Golly, they've been good to you, all those blackfellas carrying stuff into your house, grinning and laughing, and Major pissing everyone off telling them what to do. St Vinnies pitched in, The Salvos, even some of Yaya Zoe's crowy friends. And everyone agreeing not to tell your mamma when they visit her in hospital. Boy oh boy, what a day it's gunna be when she enters your home and she sees it all for the first time. Maybe she'll be so overcome with joy she'll fall to her knees and spread open her arms, and you — why, you'll run like a little terrier to her and feel the tight embrace you long for.

You carry the rabbit hutch from the backyard into your mamma's room. You fetch the torch from the kitchen, turn it on, switch off all the lights then get into your mamma's bed. You look at those illustrated books Major's given you. One tells of the baby Jesus. You play with the faces of those depicted in the illustrations. The colour of the skin of the mother of the infant Jesus darkens. It comforts you to see Jesus' black mother draped in that blue shawl, her face aglow in the light that enters the stable.

You get under the sheets to look at Major's other book. You make a cave. You feel like an Indian in a teepee. Tomorrow you might get dressed in that outfit Yaya Zoe gave you, all those frilly leather things, the bow and arrows, the tomahawk and plastic sandals, and play at hiding from the bad cowboys.

You recognise the faces in Major's book, having seen the originals on the walls in Old Tom's lounge room. At the bottom of several pages are the words: *Reproduced with the kind permission of Mr Thomas O'Flaherty*.

When it comes time to sleep you shine the torch towards the

hutch: 'G'dnight Clive. G'dnight Satts.'

A few houses away in either direction, you know Major and Yaya Zoe are asleep in their beds. You look first one way, then the other: ''Night Yaya. 'Night, Major.'

And just before switching off the torch you say, looking towards what you reckon is the hospital: 'G'dnight, mamma.'

But Johnnie Butler'd turned to face Centennial Park where his brother slept under a Moreton Bay fig tree.

And just before dawn Johnnie Butler got up to go to the loo and found that the Major'd slept on the couch. The boy went back to his room. Later, he heard the man get up, quietly put away the sheets he'd slept under, creep to the door, shut it, then knock, making out as if he'd just arrived for their walk together.

The decorating, furnishing and painting of your home, the stocking up of all sorts of grocery items are complete. Mamma's coming home in a couple of days. Major's a good bloke, but you're tired of eating the same food (in silence), of playing chequers after dinner when you'd rather be watching TV, of sitting straight-backed (as he insists) in the lounge room as he reads something out of the latest *Reader's Digest* or the Bible. That night you plead with Major to be allowed to sleep in your home alone, once more.

He checks to ensure all the windows and the back door are locked. He's purchased a mobile phone which he places on the floor next to your bed.

'Well, Johnnie, you remember my telephone number, don't you?'

'Yeah, Major.'

He takes another long look at your murals. 'Beautiful, lad. Your mother will be so pleased.' He follows again the story you've created, shakes his head and says, 'Just beautiful.' He looks down at you. 'I'm proud of you, Johnnie Butler.'

You smile. 'Rabbitohs gunna get kicked out soon?'

'We'll all know this Friday. Now, you read for a while then get some sleep.'

You hear him wandering about the house, checking each window again. He returns to your room. 'It's best to leave one of the bedside lights on, okay? I've left the loo light on in case you need to go. I'll deadlock the front door but leave your key in the lock.'

'Major? You wanna sleep here tonight?'

'Do you want me to, lad?'

'I wanna be by meself. 'Sthat okay?'

'Okay, Johnnie, okay.'

'You're like a daddy to me, Major.'

You see his face harden, go all red like those crabs he boils for you. There's a sadness in his eyes you sometimes see in your mum's face. You don't get it. You've just told him something nice and he's gone all cold on you. He stands there doing nothing, all serious, like those pictures of all the previous headmasters on a wall in a corridor of your school. Your house is quiet. The new fridge hums, the clock in your mum's bedroom ticks, the man's breathing is too loud, too loud. His fat face looks suddenly like a baby's. You open your arms. He hesitates and then embraces you, but quickly, pulls away and then, not looking at you, says, 'You'll be okay on your own, won't you?' His bottom lip's gone all wobbly.

'Yeah, Major.'

'Well, goodnight then.'

You hear him open the front door. There's a pause. He shuts it and reappears in your room.

'You do remember my telephone number, don't you?'

'Yep.'

'Good, good. Well then, goodnight again.' He pauses at the doorway of your bedroom. 'Set my mind at rest, Johnnie. Tell me my phone number.'

You get up later, expecting to find him on the couch. He's not there. You're glad. You've got your house to yourself. C'mon, mamma, I'm waitin'. We've got a new life startin', y'know? An' like Major sometimes says, it's gunna be *grand*.

Major Bob falls asleep. Dreams that a forest has shifted, gone right off the rails, overwhelming him, the tent he's in. He chokes on the steam being exhaled out of the earth and stumbles, in a frenzied attempt to find Leo Batrouney, over vines trailing the ground, through aerial and above-ground roots that've run amok. Men are walking about clapped-out like the living dead, or else they're as pissed as farts.

The next day you hear that Souths' training session that night could be the club's last. After dinner with Major (it's Thursday, so you had bangers and mash and a glass of home-delivered Crystal Cola) you tell him you want to go home to work on your mural. He walks you to the front door.

'I'll be back in a couple of hours, okay lad? Keep that mobile handy, won't you.'

You begin your work but almost immediately decide to walk up the road to Redfern Oval. It looks like rain so you put on a raincoat. You sit on your own on the Hill, in the dark, in front of a thick stand of trees. On the other side of the oval a large gathering of supporters, under umbrellas and in raincoats, stands near the players' tunnel. From where you sit at the highest point on the grassy knoll you can see over the fence and into the darkness of the park you'd walked across.

The spotlights come on abruptly. The players thunder out onto the field to the cheers of the supporters, some emerging players throwing footballs to each other, others sprinting, giving chase to the ball they'd booted ahead. Their voices and the cries of the supporters fill the void of the night.

The players begin a synchronised movement, the ball sweeping along the line, each player taking the ball, doing a short sprint then passing it to the person to his side.

You watch this line of men racing up and down the field. You see that other line, too, that Major often talks to you about, that links these blokes to those others who once trained and played on this same ground. Was it really all coming to an end? Just as you'd discovered and become attached to this — well, this tribe of warriors, you like to think — was it really all about to die?

The rain falls as a fine haze, sparkling against the floodlights and the light of a half-moon. You lift the hood of your raincoat as the players — perhaps in acknowledgement of the many mums and dads and kids who've come to watch — form two teams and begin playing a game of footy against each other. Not long after the game begins the sky opens up and the rain buckets down. The tired end-of-season ground becomes a quagmire, the celebratory game a mad sort of wake. All caution's chucked to one side. The players yelp, they shout, they laugh, and by the time they're into the second half of their game they're all caked in mud. You find it hard to tell one player from the other. They're like those blacks you painted on one of your walls. This is a crazy sort of communal dance. At one moment you can't make any sense of the jumble of bodies (it's supposed to be a game of touch), at the next, order's restored and out of the chaos the forwards regather around a ruck. They're playing fair dinkum, now. Something's taken hold of them and they're fighting for possession of the greasy ball.

You see them, and much more. In imagination you assemble the greatest of the great who've ever worn the cardinal and myrtle.

There's Tommy Anderson, who has the distinction of scoring Souths' first-ever try, way back in 1908. There's George Treweek, who dominated forward play in the 1920s and 1930s, packing down for a scrum with the captain of the Rabbitohs teams of the 1960s and 1970s, John Sattler. And directing play's the Little Master himself. The oval and the Hill are in motion, a great cry swirling around the ground as the spectators sway and the rain pours down in great sheets. You see the opposition score two tries in quick succession to create a narrow lead. The Bunnies gather into a tight knot under the goalposts for a hurried conference to discuss tactics before the resumption of play. You summon different players from different eras to fill those positions and a game plan that demands a lightning change of pace, a bulldozing run, a deft kick of the ball and a tightening of the blind-side defence. You alter positions as the run of play demands, conjuring up great sweeping movements of the ball.

And then Clive Churchill takes the ball. Outlined against the haze of floodlight and falling rain, he probes, circles for the opening that must surely come. It's a sort of dance he performs as he holds the heavy ball in the crook of his arm, falls at the feet of those who've closed in on him, rolls in the mud, leaps up, turns, fends off one then two players, swivels out of a slippery tackle, somersaults over the last line of defenders, breaks into open space, scores a try.

And you stand, too, along with all those other supporters, raising your hands over your head and clapping as the players leave the field. You know that if you look over the fence and into the darkness, to where Redfern Park is, and where the marshes once were, you might even see your own grandad performing a dance of his own. You remember that on clearer nights than this, on one of the missions you'd stayed at, the men lighted up the night with firesticks, others swung bullroarers or chanted from behind great gum trees. Some hissed, mimicking the cries of animals, others stamped their feet. And with your arms still in the air and clapping the departing players off the oval, from somewhere far into the distance of time comes the droning rhythmic sound you recognise, and can't resist.

Golly, these men could tell stories. It was a gift, alright. And you have a gift, too, 'cause you know how to listen. They showed you how a blackfella could slap his thighs to the beat of sticks struck together, the emu feathers tied to his feet, and make the sound of the wind. They told tales with elaborate steps and jerky hand movements, you seeing the hunted prey stopping in the clearing or long grass, its ears pricked in alarm. The tapping of the sticks'd grow louder as they'd stamp and thump out their story on the ground, whirling this way and that as the tapping sticks — from the stands? the trees behind you? the marshes where you might see your grandad moving his arms and legs in similar movements to your own? — sing their song, both man and child raising their knees high as the prey is stalked.

They told stories of how a blackfella could dance to the sway of the earth and sky, becoming kangaroo, emu, or the earth itself. So you crouch low, leap high, swirl and spin. Out of all those images dancing before your eyes, can you not become that which most appeals to you? Can you choose? Can you not hop and bound this way and that, becoming — what?

You fall to the ground, exhausted, breathing in time with the beating sticks. The rain's eased off. You remove the heavy raincoat.

You'd not become the Rabbit Man, as you'd hoped. Just a little kid, little Johnnie Butler, dancing like some mad thing in the rain.

The players've left the field. The supporters are all gone. But the tapping of the sticks continues, a solitary sound in the black night which is, you know, a remnant of your dreaming. You sit on the ground, breathing hard.

'Hey, little fella, I bin lookin' for ya. Went by yer house tonight. Nice place, eh. Seen ya walkin' up ahead so I followed.'

You look up, stand when you see a man emerge from the trees wearing a long and heavy overcoat. He throws to one side the sticks he'd been beating.

'You sure are one crazy kid.' The gangly man laughs out aloud. 'What'cha doin', brother?'

You stare, unable to speak.

'You got a tongue to do some talkin'?'

You nod your head.

'Siddown little fella. You wanna hear what I gotta tellya, for sure. I bin tryin' a long time ter come to Sinney, an' here I am, an' findin' you, no sweat. Come lookin' fer our Uncle Jimmy an' I find you! 'Sthat good, or what? Ha! Where's La Pa, Johnnie?'

You shake your head.

'You dunno where La Pa is? Don't you ever go to see yer uncle?'

'Uncle? What uncle?'

'You Johnnie Butler?'

You nod your head.

'An' mum never tol'ja 'bout Uncle Jimmy?'

You shake your head.

'Fucken 'ell. Where's mum?'

'In hospital. But she's alright now. She's comin' out this week.'

'Tha's good, 'cause I bin lookin' for youse a long, long time. I'm Billy.'

It means nothing to you.

'Ain'tcha glad ter see me?'

You look confused.

'Mum tellya 'bout me?'

You shake your head.

'She never tellya nothin' 'bout me?'

'No.'

'You dunno who I am, eh?' The man leaps to his feet, removes his coat and shirt and shows you the markings on his right arm, above tattooed words that say Mother Mary. 'See these? Yer mum got the same as them?'

You stare at the familiar scars and nod.

'I'm yer brother. I'm Billy, Billy Butler. We get a family now, eh? An' I'm safe, eh. Yeah, fucken right. Safe at last.'

Spending time with Billy
THURSDAY, 6 A.M.

It's two days since Billy's arrival and he's outside your bedroom. You don't let him in. You want to surprise him when you've completed your mural. You stop and make him brekkie. At times he shakes uncontrollably, laughs one moment, cries the next, but it's all joy, all joy.

You go back to your room, work in a frenzy to finish before your mamma comes home. Someone knocks on the door. It's time you went on your walk with Major but your head's filled with too much that's happened and too much that you've dreamed. Your world's gone all mute and your heartbeat's pounding like a mad thing. You grab crayons, textas and whiteboard markers, dip your brush into watercolours, get up onto chairs and the desk. They've told you your mamma'll be home in a couple of days and you so much want her to stare in disbelief and wonder at what you've done. You and her and Billy! School can wait, Major can wait, your eyes are as big as saucer plates, you're singing, you're talking to yourself and you know, by golly, don'tcha know, the world's a beautiful thing.

And now your mamma's become the centre of an intricate web of colourful lines which flow away from her in all directions, lovely flourishes and great swirls embracing that brother of yours, and that uncle, too, that Billy tells you he and your mamma and you are gunna visit together. Ah, Johnnie, we're all comin' back, mate, one'll follow th'other, no worries, all'll come aroun', you'll see, you'll see.

"Cause this is our country. Redfern's our country, 'cause we're Gadigal people, right?'

'Right!'

'What are we, little fella?'

'Gadigal people!'

'Too right, little bro. She's been singin' out for us, eh, to come back home, 'cause this is where we belong. 'Cause what are we, Johnnie-boy?'

By the time you get to the front door, whoever'd been knocking is gone. Sorry, Major.

Billy takes you to that huge Moreton Bay fig tree in Centennial Park that he sleeps under. You kick a football about until he's too buggered to continue, then sit and listen to him telling you stories, of the bridges and sheds he's taken refuge in, the number of times he's been taken in as a vagrant, the jobs he's tried to hang on to.

'It's a bad world out there, Johnnie. You're safe here in Redfern. You re'mber that, brother. Funny but our mum she never tol' you nothin' 'bout me. Not one word?'

That afternoon Billy takes you to the gym in the Block and points to those great black sportsmen and women displayed on the walls.

'You proud, boy?'

You nod your head.

'An' don't you ever forget what Billy said, eh. This here is your home. We're one big family.' His hands shake as he speaks. 'Goin' back to the park. I'll come back later, okay? Now, tell me what I toldya.'

Billy Butler walked out of Redfern, crossing South Dowling Street near Tom O'Flaherty's terrace. He made his way in a jagged line through Moore Park, pausing regularly to find his bearings. The world was becoming vague to him. The shaking of his hands worsened, his head throbbed and, in one terrible moment, he walked into the path of an oncoming car on Cleveland Street. The driver swerved to avoid the staggering man.

It should've taken half an hour or so to find that tree. It was early evening when he finally stumbled across his belongings, which he'd tucked away between its great roots. He scrambled to find his glass jar wrapped in a jumper. He unscrewed the lid.

Yeah, he'd wait until his mum was gunna return. Tomorrow, wasn't it? Isn't that what Johnnie said? What a moment that was gunna be, eh. He'd knock on the door and, after she'd opened it, he'd immediately remove his shirt, point to the scars on his arm and say, Hello, mum, it's me, Billy. I've come home. Hold me, mum. I been searchin' for you for a long, long time.

He threw the jumper over his head, held the jar to his nose and inhaled the fumes of petrol.

But how come you didn't say nothin' to Johnnie 'bout me, mum?

The Rabbitohs are a-goner, and Johnnie loses his marbles
FRIDAY, 15 OCTOBER 1999

Bob Ryan rose earlier than normal that morning. He'd slept badly, thinking about Souths. It was too early to wake the boy so he went on his walk alone. He returned home, had breakfast and sat in the kitchen, waiting for the time when he'd go by and collect Johnnie and take him to school. He'd gone through the entire previous day and not seen the boy. How could he've done that? Meetings at the club to help organise a rally, then with a local printer in the afternoon to design a pamphlet — what a lame excuse. That was bad, bad.

He knocked at the boy's door but no one answered. Perhaps he'd gone to school for the game of touch footy some of the kids played before lessons began. Bob Ryan walked to the school. No, there was no game in progress. The playground was deserted. Must be at Yaya Zoe's.

He called in to see the Greek woman. No, the child had not joined her for breakfast. Had probably eaten at home before setting off for school. Perhaps Bob'd been walking in one direction and Johnnie was going in another? This was what she'd feared. Hadn't she told Bob not to let the child sleep by himself? What was he thinking, leaving a boy of Johnnie's age alone for so long? She was surprised, disappointed, hadn't thought he'd be so irresponsible.

Bob Ryan left, admonished, speechless, guilty and flustered, and walked to Tom's. He rang the school just after nine o'clock. Yes, the secretary would ring him at home or at Tom's if there was a problem. No, she wouldn't forget. Yes, she'd speak directly to Johnnie's teacher to ensure the boy was present and okay.

'Well?' Tom asked after Bob Ryan'd hung up.

'They'll be in touch if there's a problem.'

'You goin' to the club for the announcement?'

'I need to know the boy's okay. I left him on his own, Tom. I left him on his own.'

'Yeah, well, I'm not gunna say I told you so. You still gunna see Mary Butler when she gets out next week?'

'You've already asked me, Tom — three times in two days.'

'Ahhh. And the answer?'

'The same as before. Are you going to ask me again?'

'Pro'bly.'

And then Kooka Kon arrived.

So many ways to tell a story. When the Major'd only ever thought it could be done with words. Kooka's stubbled face told a tale. Poor bugger. A bloke only had to look at those shadowy eyes and that slouched figure walking to Tom's in those old clothes, the bum of his daks shining like a mirror, the elbows of his shirt worn practically colourless, puffs of cigarette smoke signalling his forthcoming arrival. Look at him now, grown old before his time, a gorgeous Friday and him wearing that doomsday mask. Major Bob and Tom exchanged a smile and a sigh. They'd had their tea. Cheered each other up with positive talk of legal appeals and marches after that day's announcement. And then there was the arrival of old misery-guts.

'Mornin',' said Tom. 'Death in the family, Kon?'

'No, no. Why do you say?'

Tom shrugged his shoulders.

'Come on, Kon,' said the Major. 'Sit down and I'll make you a cuppa. We'll cheer you up, old son. Tom's got a few slices of Yaya's baklava. I'll get you one.'

Look at him, thought Old Tom. Sitting there hunched forward, staring with squinted eyes through the cigarette smoke at nothing, dropping ash all over my verandah. Looking like a sad lame horse knowing it's about to get a bullet in the head. The tea and sweet arrived.

Tom said, 'Two, four, six, eight, bog in, don't wait.'

Kon managed a grim smile.

Right. That was it. Enough was enough. Tom decided to let him have it.

'You know how old I am Kon?'

'Of course.'

'How long d'ya reckon I've got?'

Kon didn't like talking of death. He looked around for something in timber so he could touch wood and said, 'Don't tempt him, Tom.'

'Who?'

'Death.'

'That's all Greek bullshit superstition. You wanna know what I think? An' I'll be fair dinkum. Reckon I'll cark it any time between right now, an' I mean right now, with you sittin' there an' drinkin' tea, an' … let's see … at the outside, let's say two years. An' you know what? On a day like today I like to sit here with Bob an' talk. An' smile. Maybe crack a joke or two, know what I mean? An' maybe what we say to each other's not worth a dog's bone, but most times we come an' go with a gidday an' a smile. I've got no time for your misery, mate. So lighten up or piss off. If you know what I mean.'

Kon Tsakiris sat up, held the cup halfway to his mouth and looked at the old man. Tom was staring hard at him, nodding his head emphatically to emphasise how dead-set serious he was. The Greek glanced at the Major, who was making out like he was considering something over the road. Was seeing him that bad? That Old Tom preferred he no longer visited? He'd hit him for six, alright, but there was more to come. Kooka Kon could see Tom's mouth working away, preparing the next blast.

'An' while I'm gettin' stuck into you, I'll tell you somethin' else. I pay Zoe for them trays she brings round. As I should. But you, you come every day an' never bring nothin'. Nothin'. Not a packet of bikkies or tea or sugar. I'm a pensioner, sport. I like to save me money to send me grandkids somethin' special on their birthdays an' for Christmas, know what I mean?'

Major Bob looked at the poor Greek bugger out of the corner of his eye. He heard one, just one slight whimpering sound. He wasn't going to cry, was he? Don't, Kon, because there won't be any sympathy from Old Tom if you do. Kon Tsakiris nodded then wiped his nose with the sleeve of his shirt. The Major looked at the top of the man's head. It looked helpless and weak.

'I'm arse out of luck, Tom.'

'Bullshit, Kon. You're arse outta will.'

'Those men they bought my business. Everyone's telling me the shop looks beautiful, that it's going to do well. I couldn't bear to … you know —'

'Well, if it's a goer, good luck to them. Nothin' you can do 'bout it. Ya can't change what ya can't change. You've worked hard, mate, no one can take that away from you. But things didn't go well. For whatever reason. You've gotta get on with things. Get a job, sport. You're not too old to work. Whatya doin', sittin' 'ere every day with a couple of old fogies like me an' Bob? Getchaself a new dream, Kon.'

There was a horrible pause. Kon stared at his cup. No one spoke.

'I miss my old village,' the Greek man finally said. 'All the tiny streets, kids playing, everyone knowing everyone. You step out of my home and you take ten steps — and there's the water. When we were kids we used to catch the octopus. Fish all day and swim when we had holidays. Figs growing everywhere, wild, and prickly pears, pomegranates. And wild olive trees, thousands of them. Every year everyone going on the same day after church to collect olives. The grandfathers and grandmothers, the grandchildren, carrying their baskets. That was nice. All the women singing the old songs. Maria and I we were happy there. When there was a wedding, everyone got invited.'

'Go back, Kon,' said the Major. 'After all these years, you've never returned.'

'Can't, Bob. When I left I told them they were all stupid for staying. Maria and I came and we said we'll not stay forever. We came to work, make money, I'd go back a big man. And then Maria and I we lost money on the shares, and some of my relatives back home, I advised them, and they lost money too. I can't, Bob. You know what it is to live in a village and no one respects you? They'll laugh at me.' He sighed deeply, then said, 'I don't respect myself.'

'Oh, Kon, don't be so hard on —'

'No, Bob. I know, I know. I am a fool.' He got up to go. 'Thank you for the tea, Tom.'

'Get a job, mate,' the old man said. 'And one other thing. Next time you come — I like Scotch Finger bikkies. Arnotts, not that cheap Home Brand bullshit.'

Later that morning Tom rang Bob Ryan on his mobile. The Major was at the club, waiting for the NRL's announcement.

'The school just rang, mate.'

'Johnnie's okay?' asked the Major.

'His teacher tried to get you at home earlier. Apologised for ringin' late. Didn't get the message from the secretary until —'

'Cut to the chase, Tom.'

'Boy's not at school.'

The Major made another call to the boy's terrace, hoping he'd be there. No answer, again.

He went to Yaya Zoe's but she wasn't home. And then he glanced up the road. He saw a small group of people gathered on the street near the front of Johnnie's terrace. They looked up as one at the Major. He arrived quickly, but before he could speak they all heard the sound of falling furniture. There was the briefest of pauses and then a heavy scraping sound on what the man knew was the new lino in the kitchen. Some piece of furniture was being dragged from one end of the room to the other. There was another pause, a longer one this time, then the heavy thud of a table, or the fridge, or God-knew-what. And then a plate was thrown through the glass panel in the front door.

The door stood slightly ajar. Bob Ryan opened the front gate, approached, then hesitantly pushed the door open. He stood at the threshold, staring open-mouthed at the broken crockery, the contents of both the pantry and the refrigerator. From where he stood he could see into the kitchen where the fridge itself, the kitchen table and chairs had all been thrown onto their sides. He took one step into the house which now lay strangely quiet and glanced into the front room, which he'd had converted into a lounge room. The prints on the walls had been torn into shreds. The couch and armchairs had been slashed open, the stuffing pulled out and strewn all over the room. And on the floor of this room was Johnnie's mother, a bottle of whiskey in one hand and a serrated knife in the other. But where was the boy?

The woman slowly realised she was not alone. She tried to focus on this man who'd entered her home. She stared vaguely through heavy lids, looked away, remembered his presence then focused her eyes again, searching his blurred face with some interest.

The confusion in her face slowly dissipated as her eyes narrowed on this man, whose features were becoming clearer by the moment. Her eyes squinted their hatred. She knew this man. It was him who'd come years before for her brother, whom she'd watched from the window as he bundled Jimmy into that black car; who'd grabbed her out at La Pa, who'd driven off with Billy in the back seat outside the Glebe orphanage. The Lollipop Man. The man who'd walked past her home that night when she'd thought she'd seen a ghost.

She bared her teeth and snarled at him. She struggled to her knees, her mouth working at the saliva she was going to spit into his face. And then she was going to kill the fucker. She held onto the wall, the bottle still in one hand, the knife in the other, and raised herself up off the floor. She stood upright against the wall, unable to stand without its support.

'Yer comin' inter me home,' she said. 'Yer comin' inter me home!' She had him frazzled, scared. He backed away, one step, two. 'Who gives yer the right! Who gives ya the fucken right!' Look at him, the fat old bastard, shaking his head like the thieving bastard that he is. 'It's you, eh, what came inter me home, painted them walls, what threw out me stuff. Yer walked in without askin'.'

She saw the fear on his face. He's scared, Mary, he's shit-scared, and you're gunna twist that knife into that wacky eye of his. And then he says it. Just like that, the fucken gall of these white pricks.

'Where's Johnnie?'

'Ya want me boy, eh?' Jesus, look at him, nodding his head even though you've got him shitting his pants. But they can't help themselves. They've gotta come in and run your whole fucken life.

'Where is he?'

She struggled towards him but fell heavily back onto the floor. 'What have you done to him?'

'Done to 'im? What've *I* done to 'im?' She could feel it all, now, the years of running, the strangers holding her down, their stale beery breath in her ear and their furry tongues down her throat, the dust-ups in the parks, the stuffed life with the memories tearing at her gut, the puked mornings when she had fuck-all idea where she'd been and what'd happened the night before, the homesick throbbing in her brain for people she could barely recall, black cars driving down roads while her own mother knelt on tram tracks and her, her dreaming like a dog for a life, any life but the mongrel one these bastards'd made for her. 'What've *I* done?' She laughed, she cried, and him, coming back after all those years, coming back from the dead, for fuck's sake.

Bob Ryan rushed out of the house just before the woman lunged towards him. 'Get outta me house! Come back an' I'll fucken killya! Ya hear?' She slammed the door shut and hammered at it with her fists. There was a muffled sob. Through the broken pane of glass she was seen making her way down the corridor. Then there was silence.

The Major's mind was racing. Call the police? No, no, who could foresee the consequences if the authorities were called? What to do, then? Force his way back into the house? Fight his way down the corridor and into the boy's room, where Johnnie might be cowering in a corner, under his bed or in his wardrobe? Or go to Yaya Zoe, who was the only person he knew whom Johnnie's mother trusted?

One of the neighbours spat out his disgust. 'I'm calling the cops.

Had some peace and quiet while that bitch was in hospital. I've had enough.'

Before Bob Ryan knew what he was doing he found himself rushing at the man. He made forceful threats. He jabbed his finger into the fellow's chest. Bob Ryan's face'd turned a blotched livid red. His body and voice were trembling with rage.

He went to Yaya Zoe's, forgetting she was absent, and beat on her door. And then he remembered; and then he sat on the step leading into the Greek woman's home, his back against her door.

One woman, of a similar age to the Major who'd lived opposite him all her life, turned to her husband and said: My God, what is it with Bob and these black people?

Fifteen minutes later Yaya Zoe found the Major sitting on her doorstep. He explained what'd happened. They rushed to the Butlers'. Bob Ryan remained on the footpath. The Greek woman opened the gate, walked up the path, stood in the shattered glass on the verandah and, through the opening in the panel in the door, cried, 'Ma-reea! Maa-reeeah!'

No sound or movement came from the house.

'Is me, Ma-ree. Zoe.'

Silence.

'Tzo-neee! Open the door Tzo-nee!'

Still no response. The woman tried the door. It had not been locked from the inside. She pushed it open then took a step back. She peered down the hallway. Yaya Zoe called out several times more but there was still no response. Mary Butler, it seemed, had gone. But where was the boy?

Yaya Zoe stepped down the hallway and into the kitchen, then signalled to the Major that it was safe to enter. On the floor near the front door the man saw a bloodstained child's exercise book. He read the cover. A diary. He waited until Zoe was preoccupied then picked it up and tucked it into his trousers and under his shirt. The Greek woman went to the boy's bedroom.

The door was shut. There was blood on the handle. The woman screamed. Major Bob rushed to her side. They both heard the distant sound of police and ambulance sirens.

The Major stood beside Yaya Zoe, both of them staring hard at that handle and the streaks of blood that ran down the door and into the carpet. Major Bob pushed open the door with the toe of his shoe.

The photos of the Souths teams, the newspaper clippings, all of Johnnie's memorabilia on one of his walls, as well as the project on rabbits that had been placed open on his desk had been ripped and torn into many pieces. Blood was strewn across the mural on the other three walls. Johnnie's Souths guernsey had been torn from the collar down; a bloodied pair of scissors lay on the floor. And everywhere, on the walls, on the bed, on the child's desk, on the clothes that'd been pulled out of the wardrobe and scattered all over the room was blood and that white down which, the woman thought, was stuffing from the couch and armchairs. But where was Johnnie?

Yaya Zoe held her face in her hands. Major Bob put his arm around her shoulder and tried to explain that it was not the blood of the boy. But she was not listening. He looked about the floor until he found what he knew to be there: the boy's rabbits'd been slaughtered in a mad frenzy. He pointed with his shoe to one of the heads that'd been torn off the body, its skull crushed, lying amongst a pile of clothes. It had, the man guessed, been used to smear blood across that part of the mural depicting the Butlers' life story.

'Ohhh, Mary, Mary,' Bob cried, 'what've you done?'

The police arrived, asked their questions, took down notes. The woman, they said, would be found soon enough, in some nearby park, alley or one of the disused factories or warehouses earmarked for development. The boy, too, couldn't've gone far.

Bob Ryan escorted Yaya Zoe home then contacted Kooka Kon. The Major picked him up in his car and together they spent the rest of that day and half the night searching for the boy and his mother. They gave up well after midnight. No word from the police. Or Aboriginal welfare, which'd organised its own search.

The following morning, before dawn, the Major and Kon resumed looking. Major Bob'd divided Redfern into grids, and they drove up and down the streets in their methodical search. They stopped and asked questions of workers making their way to the factories for the early Saturday shift; later that morning they spoke to kids in the parks. Zoe joined the search. After the second day, still no trace of either Mary Butler or Johnnie.

On the third day the two men made multiple copies of a poster giving details of the missing woman and her child, which they stuck on telegraph poles.

Kooka Kon enjoyed the drama. It was a distraction from the forthcoming opening of his old café, which too many people'd told him about. The search filled his empty days.

Tuesday, 19 October 1999

The jogger approaches you. There's a great sigh everywhere, in the trees that whisper their suffering to you, in the ground that's breathing its pain. Shadows move all over the place, from the fronds of tree ferns and the heavy clouds passing over the Moreton Bay fig tree you're sitting under, from your own right arm when you extend it, dripping its misery and unspeakable hurt. You're giddy and your eyes are heavy-lidded with the whole mess the world's got itself into.

You breathe in and out deeply, in unison with the heaving, weeping earth. The jogger's shadow is on your face, now its getting into you, eating your guts, taking a grip of your brain. That's good, that's good, take me away, Mr Joggerman, where there's silence and where I don't have to see the awful things people do to each other, where I'm not reminded of the horrible things I'd said to Billy.

There are twigs and grass and dirt and spider webs in your hair and on your trousers. There are deep cuts in your right arm, between the elbow and the shoulder, which you'd inflicted on yourself with your pair of scissors. You look at a screw-top bottle lying next to you, the blood-soaked sheet you're lying under. The joggerman's talking to you but he's far, far away, on the river of that great sigh that's taking him some place else. And you, you lie face down on the ground and examine the little world of ants and things, going about their business of living while all about you there's noise, sirens, people getting off bikes and holding still their baby's stroller, gathering around you and whispering. But you've gone somewhere else where they can't see you, covered, you are, in corduroy, or velvet. Maybe it's a fog. Black faces are staring into yours, speaking, waving their hands before your eyes. Major arrives, pushes past your black mates, falls to his knees. Is it your head he's putting one arm around? Is it you he's holding tight, rocking backwards and forwards and crying Johnnie, Johnnie, Johnnie.

He looks into your eyes but you can't or don't want to look into his. Better, safer to fix your eyes on some spot to the left of the man. Speak to me, say something, the man's mouth says, to somebody, to you, to nobody. Better, safer to look at some undefined object over this man's shoulder, to the stretch of lawn, the pond, a stand of gum trees.

An almighty row breaks out. They're all shouting. Pointing at each other. Police throwing up their arms in despair. Major taking you by the hand so tightly it hurts while the mums and dads of the black kids that're your mates are telling him he's a fucken do-gooder white bastard who should mind his own business. But you love the man. You'll be safe with him. He's huge, got a stomach as big as a basket you can bury your face into, he's predictable, and you know he loves you. You throw your arms around him and close your eyes. That's it, that's it. That's shut them all up. You're going home with him, to that home where the curtains are always drawn shut, keeping out the bad stuff in the world.

You reach up to take his hand. There's Kooka Kon, looking like a big kid, all lost and confused. He's alright, Kon. Wouldn't harm a fly. You let him take your other hand and the three of you walk to the copper's car. You'll stay with Major. Yeah, with him.

Four days previously, when Major Bob'd last seen Old Tom and the boy's mother'd returned home earlier than expected, thousands of Souths supporters'd gathered in the club to hear the terrible announcement. The ninety-one-year history of the Mighty Bunnies'd come to an end.

While in the Northern Territory, Nanna Dora was joined by a couple of blacks she'd helped put through Law courses at uni, giving interviews to all those eastern state reporters who'd converged on Darwin after yet another death-in-custody. She organised stand-offs outside Don Dale Detention Centre, gave speeches, wept as she led a march to the family home of that judge who'd imprisoned that fifteen-year-old girl for twenty-eight days for stealing a bottle of glue.

THIRTEEN

Billy Butler's story

FRIDAY, 15 OCTOBER 1999 — ABOUT 5 A.M.

This is the last time i rite to you mum cos soon im gunna get up and walk and come noking on your door and the mad seerchingll be over eh and when the hugging and the crying is over and you and me and little Johnnie can sit down and reed this exesise book what ive been riting in all them yeers ever sinse i started the looking for you and i cant tellya how nervoos i am just to think of seeing you and the look on your face and you saying is it you Billy and me saying yeah mum its your Billy he come back after all them yeers wandering and finding you just in time cos now i no ill kick the bad stuff you helping me and them voyces theyll leave me lone but im gunna stop riting for a sec cos the lites not so good and the shakes theyve come on so bad

Billy Butler woke up early on Friday, 15 October, thinking it was the day when his mum was due home from the hospital. He'd wait awhile before setting off for her home. And do something about those voices. He was sitting under his tree, the voices returning, barely a whisper initially, then their accusations becoming a throbbing in his head that became so loud it was like some bloke was hammering at a hollow metal pipe right next to his ear. And then the condemnations became a chorus, chanting their awful warning, Yer mum don't love ya, yer mum don't love ya. How come, Johnnie, she didn't tellya nothin' about me? He fumbled for his small backpack, made many clumsy attempts before he succeeded in unzipping it, upended the bag, unscrewed the lid of the jar that'd fallen on his lap then held it hard to his face, covering both his mouth and his nostrils. He made a succession of brief inhalations, the fumes of petrol giving quick relief. The throbbing receded. The voices were silenced. The heavy clanging stopped.

He looked out into the still, vague morning. He heard the rangers unlocking the massive gates into the park. He made out the isolated cries of birds awakening to the new day. He saw early morning joggers and walkers on the circular path. Soon the sun'd rise over the treetops. He'd eat from the scraps that'd fallen out of the bag, rise, shake the grass clippings and dirt from his baggy sloppy joe and the jeans which hung loosely from his lanky body, make his final entry in his diary, pack away those few belongings of his then head off for Redfern.

In other parts of Sydney others were also going about their business of greeting the new day. Mary Butler stood leaning on a crutch in the shower of the hospital in Darlinghurst, turned on the water then sat on the plastic chair placed under the nozzle. She'd dress, have her breakfast and, regardless of what the doctor said after his morning rounds, would discharge herself. She'd had enough of the hospital. It was time to return home.

In Redfern itself Major Bob Ryan'd wait until it was time to collect the boy and together they'd walk to his school. It was, he knew, going to be a momentous day. Souths were going to be given the flick, no risk. There'd be all sorts of people who'd need comforting. There'd be protests to plan, calls to make, posters to be stuck up on telegraph poles. He decided to go to Redfern Oval to kill some time. Go in if the gates were unlocked and walk once around the boundary fence, as a gesture, he supposed, of solidarity with the club. His entry, however, was barred. He went back home.

Old Tom was sitting in his lounge room in his dressing-gown, feeling all flaked out. The dream'd soon be over. Souths'd be cast aside like an old dishrag, and all this stuff on his walls and hanging off doorknobs and coat hangers'd become, in time, meaningless crap to anyone but diehards like himself. Well, in the end it was just a game, wasn't it? Maybe he would give Redfern the hoo-roo and go down the coast and move in with his daughter.

Jimmy Butler was down at the beach, coughing his guts out, his long legs jackknifed on the sand, kidding himself the Rabbitohs could go to hell for all he cared. He tried skipping stones across the surface of the water, like Rosie was once able to do. No bloody luck. He'd told himself often enough he couldn't give a rat's arse about the Bunnies. They'd ditched him all those years ago, hadn't they? Serve the pricks right. He rolled another Drum, lit it and walked barefoot in the water, feeling the pits. When the sun began to rise over the waters of Botany Bay, making the thick clouds the colour of fireworks that'd once had Rosie open wide her mouth in wonder and delight, he let out one God-almighty sob, knelt in the shallow water and cried like a baby.

Victor Batrouney was sitting up in bed squirming in embarrassment at the thought of the fool he'd made of himself. What a wanker he'd been. O'Hara was right. He was gutless, a mummy's boy, after all these years still hankering for the approval of those who were dead or who had one foot in the grave. Well, he'd show them. He'd read of blokes older than himself taking up the cello, learning ancient Greek, joining mountain-climbing clubs. He'd do that law course, dammit, and have his photo taken, of him in robes and under a wig, enlarged and framed, and put up over his mock fireplace. He'd offer his services free to the club and have his name in the paper as being one of those who'd fought successfully to have Souths readmitted into the comp.

Kon Tsakiris was snoring like a foghorn. His wife reached under the pillow for her earplugs. She paused to look at her husband. He looked so calm and peaceful, like he had a bank account groaning with millions. A big innocent kid who didn't know what was good for him. She'd gone past their old café and seen what those young blokes'd done to it. Funny thing, all this business to do with making money. It's not like he would've really gone out and bought a flashy car and a big house on the water, like he'd always said. Probably wouldn't've even known what to do with a pile of money if it fell in his lap out of the sky. He just needed all those noughts on his monthly statement to feel like he'd done something worthwhile with his life. She reached across and kissed him on the cheek. Poor Kon. My husband. My baby. Even in his sleep he looked like a loser.

Nanna Dora confronted one of the prison guards outside the Don Dale Detention Centre. He told her that old black bags from Sydney looking like galahs under Akubra hats should mind their own fucking business. Saliva built up in the corners of her mouth. She spat out a lifetime's rage at what's been done to little kids like Angela Wood, who'd done herself in.

How long can this struggle go on, Nan? She's weary, spent, her whole body's taut with anger, she can't believe her people are still dying in the white man's gaols.

Her unruly walk took her to a nearby park where she sat heavily amongst the roots of a giant fig. One of her supporters brought her a mobile. She was informed that Mary Butler'd been in hospital, that Bob Ryan'd taken charge of Johnnie Butler despite black welfare's protests, that he'd been in and out of Mary's home without her knowing.

Am I black or white, Sista?

BILLY ARRIVES IN MELBOURNE, 1977

Superintendent Dodson was happy to take in the young Billy Butler, whose last name, on arrival, was changed to that of Morris. The man understood the necessity of creating some distance between those half-castes and their parents, some of whom, on discovering the whereabouts of their children, would create terrible scenes outside the gates of this Melbourne orphanage. Anyway, thought the superintendent, it wouldn't be too long before a permanent home with a sympathetic white family was found for this particular ten-year-old, who had such sweet and gentle ways, and whose unblemished skin, gentle to touch, was so light in colour he could almost be passed off as a white boy. Shame about those black eyes and the broad nostrils, though.

It was a time of great confusion for the boy. What was he to make of this new name he'd been given? And it only made matters worse when he wept. The other kids, black and white, made fun of him. He was such a sook, whose shyness and inability to respond to their jokes made him a permanent target. He'd turn a beetroot colour when they taunted him. Kids blacker than him called him a little white bastard. The white kids excluded him from their games because he was a dirty little nigger. What was he, black or white?

Mr Dodson'd take him aside and, putting his arm over his shoulder and speaking in that soothing way he had, tell him of the great future that awaited him if only he could forget he had that tiny bit of the native in him. Sister Jane, however, would tell him of the pride he should feel in being an Aborigine.

'What's wrong, Billy?' Sister Jane asked. 'You can talk to me. Do you want to? Is everything alright at school? You know you mustn't take two plates of food again. Superintendent was not happy. Why did you do that?'

'Wasn't for me, Sista.'

'Who was it for?'

'For me mum.'

'Your mum? But Billy … I don't understand. Your mum isn't —'

'Like t'ave it there. On the table. Like she's there, sittin' next to me, y'know?'

'Ohhhh, Billy …'

'Hurts, Sista.'

'What hurts? Where, Billy?'

The boy sat tightly in the chair, his knees pushed together, his arms wrapped tightly across his chest. 'Hurts everywhere, Sista.'

She reached out a hand to touch him. But the boy, for all he could do to fathom his confusion, pushed the woman's arm away in a sudden and violent movement, when it was her comfort he needed the most.

'Close the door, boy,' Superintendent Dodson said.

Billy stood before the desk looking into the face of the man who, clothed in a satin dressing-gown, sat in a large leather chair, smoking a pipe. A glass of scotch, heavily iced, stood to one side. The man eventually looked up, put aside the pen he'd been writing with, sipped noisily from the glass then stared without speaking until Billy looked away.

'Look at me, boy.'

The man's face softened. His voice became gentle as he spoke of the great authority he had which allowed him to punish the bad and reward the good. He told Billy of the weight of his responsibility, and how it grieved him to see some of those in his care going down the wrong path.

Billy squirmed as he stood there, intimidated by the man's slow and deliberate manner, the wreaths of smoke that played around his face and the light of the heavy brass lamp on his desk.

Superintendent Dodson had Billy walk around to his side of the desk. The boy glanced at the pens, notepads, books and trays of papers and letters, all neatly arranged on the glass top. He looked up at the book-lined walls, arranged in some order he could not comprehend. He smelt the aftershave lotion on the man's face and the alcohol on his breath.

Gregory Dodson took out of his dressing-gown pocket a scented handkerchief. He wiped the tears from the boy's eyes as he spoke of the notes the law required him to keep of the wrongdoings of each child in his care, and how it hurt him to see those like Billy defy those rules which were there, after all, for the children's own good. He must never ever take two plates of food again. Did he understand this? He did? Ahhh, that was good. He rubbed the boy's back in a gentle circular motion then, with the finger of one hand, straightened the locks of the boy's hair that fell down over his eyes.

'You've got hair like a white boy.'

The breathing of the man and the boy filled the room.

Gregory Dodson abruptly dismissed Billy and returned to his work. The boy opened the door and, just as he was about to leave, reached over to the bookshelf nearest the door, grabbed a meerschaum pipe from an ornamental wooden stand and quickly pocketed it.

Billy Morris' bed and wardrobe were the first to be searched later that evening. When the pipe was found under his bed he was taken to Superintendent. Billy was made to bend over a chair. He was beaten with the black leather strap Gregory Dodson kept in the top left-hand drawer of his desk, the man accusing him, with each beating across his bare buttocks, of the deceit and uselessness of the race to which he belonged.

Sister Jane, disturbed by the amount of time Superintendent Dodson held the boy back for the long talking-to, knocked hesitantly on the door, only to be told gruffly to leave.

Billy sets off for Redfern

CENTENNIAL PARK, 15 OCTOBER 1999 — ABOUT 6 A.M.

Billy Butler held fast to the ground, pushing himself hard up into a sitting position against the fig tree as that snake emerged again from under the ground. His eyes darted wildly here and there at the creature's sudden appearance, his legs twitching as the snake paused in its wild slithering to raise its head to stare and grin its malice at him. He waited, full of terror, as the snake slyly considered him before sliding off into the long grass. Billy Butler saw the grass move as it made its way into a flower bed; then he laughed out aloud. The snake, he knew, was escaping from the muffled sound of water flowing beneath the tree, and the sudden transformation of the fig into a Christmas tree. It sparkled in the dawn light and Billy, retreating into his childhood, saw himself with his head in his mother's lap; and she, listening to his stories, stroked the head of this boy who'd never given up his search for her.

It's all over, Billy. You've come home. You've come home to your mum.

He got up but there was little feeling in his feet. He couldn't control the movement in his legs. The awkward stomping in his walk forced him back down onto the ground.

'I'm comin', mum,' he said, laughing violently. The Christmas lights were flashing on and off.

Billy Butler sat, and tried to calm the trembling of his hands. He struck several matches before he was able to light a cigarette.

After he'd smoked for some time he gathered his possessions and stuffed them into his bag. He took hold of the stick he kept with him, to lean on whenever he needed support. He raised himself up off the ground, checked his balance and, when he knew he was able to walk, bent down to pick up his backpack. He threw it over one shoulder then clumsily set off for Redfern.

Billy reckons he's a bad boy
MELBOURNE, 1977–81

Billy was taken in by a succession of foster families for varying lengths of time. Some hoped that if things worked out, they might even adopt the boy. Billy endeared himself to them all at first, the way he stood there wringing his anxious hands, eyes cast to the floor, answering their questions in that soft and polite voice of his. After some time in their homes, however, his respectful gentleness in the orphanage became something else, an uncomfortable moroseness, even a brooding threatening presence. They'd return him to the home after a month, a week, one couple after a day.

Not so with an elderly Scottish couple, whom Sister Jane knew well. Francis and Margaret Connolly's own children had long grown up and gone their own ways. One of them, Sister Jane told him, was doing fine work amongst the blacks in another state.

At least once each year the Connollys took him in during one of the many school holiday breaks. Francis Connolly, Billy quickly realised, hated all things English, and would rail against the imperialistic ways of the Anglo-Saxon. He'd tell the boy how, true to their form, they'd invaded the black man's nation and did what they could to destroy the culture of the Aborigine. The Connollys took it in turns to read to the boy each night, informing him of the legends and stories of his people. They told him, in that emphatic way they had, that he had every reason to hold his head up high rather than mope, immersed in his silences. They read stories of their own forebears too, who'd fallen fighting for their freedom from the English kings. They showed him photographs of the paintings of their ancestors which still hung on the walls of great castles in Scotland. Billy longed to have a photo of himself in kilts, sitting on a rearing white stallion, brandishing the hereditary sword which, passed down from one generation to the next, Francis Connolly'd once allowed him to hold. One night the man awoke to discover the tartan clothes taken out of his display cabinet, the boy struggling to hold up the kilt that was far too big for him.

That day, the man and woman took Billy to the museum and pointed out to him the various displays of the black man's culture.

'That's your inheritance, Billy,' Francis Connolly said. 'Don't you go dreaming about being a white boy, okay? You're Billy Butler, that's who you are.'

When Billy returned to the orphanage at the end of the school break he spoke to Sister Jane.

'What's me second name, Sista?'

The woman frowned. 'Morris. But you know that. Why do you ask?'

'Mr Connolly reckons it ain't. Reckons it's Butler. Says he's seen it in me file.'

The woman raised her eyebrows. Francis' views were not ones to be easily dismissed. 'I'll look into it,' she said.

The woman rang her old friend. She investigated the boy's papers. That night she went to his dormitory and sat by the side of his bed.

'He's right, ain't he?'

Sister Jane nodded her head.

'Said I'm from Sinney. An' me mum's name's Mary. 'Sthat right?'

The woman reached across to touch the boy's hand and, seeing him flinch, withdrew. 'That's right, Billy. But there's no record of where your mother is now. She left Sydney not long after you were born. I'm sorry, son.'

'An' me dad?'

'Nothing there about your father.'

'He a black man?'

The woman paused.

'Sista?

'I don't think so. You're too fair. He was probably a white man.'

'Am I black or white, Sista?'

'I'll tell you what you are, Billy. You're a sensitive, lovely boy.'

'Don't feel lovely.'

By the time Billy Butler was in high school it seemed that no permanent home would ever be found for him. Sister Jane'd retired. Francis and Margaret Connolly'd moved out of Melbourne, joining their son to do voluntary work on a mission in Western Australia. Mr Dodson, who'd once remarked on the pimples which covered the boy's face and the disproportionate size of his nostrils, no longer gave him much attention. He'd been such a pretty boy when he'd first arrived, he'd say, shaking his head. What happened?

Most of the holiday periods were spent in the home.

One year, a childless couple who taught at the school Billy attended took him in for the entire Christmas break. When they gathered in the dining room for their first dinner together Billy placed an empty plate beside his, as the Connollys'd allowed him to do. When he saw the couple exchange a glance, he said, 'It's fer me mum. 'Sthat okay?'

The Beckers smiled. 'Of course,' the man said.

After dinner they retired to the lounge room. Mr Becker sat at his desk in his dressing-gown, a watchmaker's glass screwed into his right eye, his newly acquired stamps in a neat order under the light of a bright brass lamp. He held tiny tweezers in his left hand as he bent over the desk, a look of intense concentration on his face. The man went about his work methodically, taking down one album after another, his tweezers poised in the air as he considered, frowning, on which page to place each stamp.

His wife sat in a huge tub chair. She looked ridiculous sunk in that monster of a thing. Look at the way she turns a page of the book she's reading, so bloody cool and an aren't-I-just-so-clever look on her face. A teacher's face, the corners of the mouth turned down, eyebrows raised.

Billy sat on a three-seater couch, the book Mrs Becker'd given him in his lap. He could feel his muscles tensing but did not know why. He could feel the black mood coming on. *Oh please God, don't let me fuck things up …*

On two walls of the room were dark, heavily stained bookshelves. From where he sat the boy could see the books were arranged according to subject matter: several shelves were devoted to *English History*, which was the subject the woman taught; a whole wall was dedicated to *Fiction* (it was labelled like it was a library, what show-offs), each book placed alphabetically according to the author's surname. He breathed in the smells of stained timber, books and quiet order and thought of Mr Dodson. Billy Butler imagined himself getting up off the lounge, approaching the shelves, then, with little effort or fuss or fanfare, throwing each bookcase, in turn, to the floor. He smiled to himself at the thought of the expressions on their faces.

Mrs Becker saw his smile. 'Nice to see you smiling, Billy.'

Fucking hell, she was a deadshit alright. Look at her, smiling away like someone's grandmother, all sweet and Bob's-your-uncle.

And then Billy felt guilty. He squirmed on the lounge. He bit his lower lip. Here they were, taking him into their home, their *home*, for Christ's sake, and him imagining all sorts of wicked stuff. He was bad, bad. Superintendent Dodson was right.

'Do you want to see my stamps?' Mr Becker said.

Billy Butler smiled weakly, stared at the rug, shrugged his shoulders. His hands were a tight ball on the open book balanced on his legs.

'Would you like to go to bed?' He shrugged his shoulders again.

It was a large room with one window, draped with velvet curtains. Billy Butler was shown the wardrobe where he was to hang his clothes, not on the floor or at the end of the bed as he'd done earlier that day, and the corner where the woman insisted he place his bag and shoes. In the morning Mrs Becker'd show him how he was to make his bed.

'We'll have breakfast at eight,' she said. 'Then we'll go boating on the river. Would you like that?'

Mr Becker leaned in the doorway, smiling, after the boy'd got into bed and his wife'd adjusted the light bed cover. And when it seemed as if she was about to reach over and kiss him, Billy Butler turned his head to face the wall. The woman frowned but let the moment pass without a comment. Mr Becker's smile quickly disappeared. Things did not look good. Their first day together and — well, there was tomorrow on the Yarra. That'd lighten things between them.

When they closed the bedroom door Billy Butler sat up, reached across to the mother that wasn't there and hugged her. He kissed the air several times.

They arrived at the river late the following morning, rowed for a while then sat on the bank to have lunch. Mrs Becker smoothed out the blanket on which they were to sit, Mr Becker and Billy standing to one side as she placed the knives, forks and plates in a strict order around the containers of food positioned in the centre of the blanket. She considered her work for some time before signalling to her husband, with a slight nod of her head, that they could sit. Billy followed the man's lead and took off his shoes, which were placed on the grass, in a line next to those of the woman's.

After they'd eaten she gathered up all the crockery and cutlery, placing them in plastic bags. She returned them to the picnic basket, passed over a novel she thought Billy might like to read then took out her own book, which she'd been reading the night before. Mr Becker lit a pipe. Billy hated the rotting stink of pipe tobacco. He watched the man out of the corner of his eye. The pipe was sillier than that shitty thing Dodson smoked out of. It looked stupid, a wooden bowl with a stick thing in the corner of his mouth. The man opened his newspaper and read aloud to his wife from an article about the ongoing story of the Siamese twins, recently born in Melbourne, and the miraculous operation that'd successfully separated them.

'Amazing,' the man said.

'Is there anything what's not amazin'?' Billy said.

'*That's* not amazing,' the woman said.

'Eh?'

'You shouldn't say *what's*. It's *that's*.'

'No,' said the man to Billy. 'In fact, I think that sometimes.'

'I think it all the time.'

'Do you?' said the woman, who was pleased. 'Do you, Billy?' she repeated, putting down her book, regarding him in a new light.

'Them twins —'

'*Those* twins, Billy.'

'Those twins got stuck together 'cause they love each other. In their mum's tummy. They was lovin' each other so much they was huggin' an' huggin' as they was growin' so they got stuck together.'

'Why, Billy,' said the woman, crawling on her hands and knees towards him over the blanket. 'What a beautiful thing to say,' she said, putting an arm over his shoulder.

Billy Butler reacted sharply. He pushed the woman's face away with both his hands, one of his nails scratching her cheek.

'Billy!' the man cried.

'Don'tcha kiss me!'

'But Billy —'

And then he shocked them all — the man, the woman and himself — with what came next. 'Fuck you! You ain't me mum! 'Sthat what yer tryin' ter be?'

The woman leapt to her feet and walked quickly to the car. The man grabbed the picnic basket, the blanket, his and his wife's shoes and rushed after her. Billy Butler struggled behind. He wanted to run past the man, overtake the woman, rush ahead of her then stop, turn to face them both, let them see his tears of remorse and say *Sorry, sorry, sorry*. But all he could do was drag his bare feet on the ground, his shoes in his hands, immersed in his wretchedness. Mr Dodson was going to give him hell. I've been telling you, haven't I? For years I've been telling you what a wicked thing you are?

They sat around the dinner table that night in silence. Billy was unable to look into the woman's face or respond to the man's gentle questioning.

Halfway through dinner he got up and went to his bedroom. He closed the door, got into bed and pushed his face into the pillow, shaking his head from side to side. 'I'm not a good boy,' he said. 'I'm not a good boy,' he repeated, over and over.

The following morning the couple rose well after Billy. The woman discovered that the brooch she'd worn the previous day, left on the kitchen bench the night before, had gone missing. It was found in Billy's bedroom. He was returned immediately to the orphanage.

Superintendent Dodson had him brought to his office after he'd received the report. He took out of his desk the black leather strap.

'Why did you hit her?'

Billy stood in front of the desk, shoulders hunched, head bent low.

'And the brooch? Why, for God's sake?'

Billy Butler wrung his hands.

'It's going on your file. You know the punishment. Bend over the desk, Morris.'

'Me name ain't Morris. I toldja before, me name ain't Morris.'

'You assault a good woman, steal her jewellery then come in here and — drop your trousers, Morris.'

'Me name's Butler an' you can go an' get fucked.'

Billy Butler was caught stealing a number of times, from the orphanage, the school he attended, the local shops. When he ran away after being caught with a bottle of whiskey he'd taken from Superintendent Dodson's office, and was discovered with a group of young men known to the police, he was sent to BoysTown.

The Dreaming Butlers

MOORE PARK, SYDNEY, FRIDAY, 15 OCTOBER 1999 — ABOUT 7 A.M.

Billy Butler felt the frustration rising in him as he tried to find his bearings out of Moore Park and into Redfern. He abused a group of boys who were making their way to school and who had, he knew, crossed his path just to stare at him. He knew that some people were observing him from behind the windows of their terraces, while others hid behind the trunks of trees, watching him. He sat on the grass when the voices returned, sticking his fingers hard into his ears to silence their terrible condemnations, then held his head in both his hands to quell the throbbing headache. He shut his eyes to avoid the glare of the morning sun, threw off his backpack, fumbled with its zipper until the side pocket was opened, took out a small plastic bag then rolled himself a cigarette from a blend of tobacco and marijuana. He sat on the field until the cigarette was smoked then lay down and slept. By the time he awoke the roads were full of cars. He got up to cross South Dowling Street.

Mary Butler'd had a sleepless night. While the other patients in the ward were having breakfast, she took the sleeping pills the night nurse'd given her. She lay back, browsing through the local rag, waiting for the pills to take effect.

She glanced at an article about that year's Redfern garden

comp. Saw a photo of the man who was confident of winning. Standing next to a tree he'd brought back from overseas as a seed. Him, him, that ghost, posing for the photographer, holding her Johnnie's hand.

She discharged herself, despite the protests of the nurses. She stood on the footpath leaning on her crutch, woozy from the pills, flagging down one vacant cab after another. The drivers'd see her raised arm from a distance, drive towards her, slow down as they approached then, seeing how unsteadily she stood and the colour of her skin, speed off.

The woman felt the old anger returning. She picked up her bag and began hobbling to the nearest taxi rank. Mary Butler saw the vacant light on the roof of the last cab in line, opened the rear door before the driver had a chance to look at her, got in, gave her hostile directive.

She had the driver stop at an early-opener. She got out to buy some grog. On returning she discovered the cab was gone. Her things'd been thrown on the footpath. She stuffed the bottles in her bag then set off for home on foot and crutch, burning with fury.

You walk from room to room, breathing in the smells of all that's new in your home. Major's told you your mamma's coming home in three days. By golly, you can hardly wait. Someone knocks on the door. You don't answer. You've got all these finishing touches to put on your murals and you haven't got much time. You want to sneak over to the park to muck around with Billy. Later that morning the phone rings. You ignore it.

You have a light breakfast, take your rabbits out of their hutch and play with them on the floor of your bedroom. You wonder about Souths. Everyone reckons they're dead meat.

Billy on the move

I dunno why I was steeling mum and why i was so angry at everybody when they was being so good to me you cooldnt blame them coppers cos I was hanging out with The Black Boyz what made me feel like we was bruthers but one nite we got to drinking and anyway we was crewsing them streets but how was i to no they'd nocked off the car so when the coppers they pulled us over no won beleeved me I had nothing to do with it and I tell you mamma jail aint a pretty place and when I got out cos I was yung and they give me nother chanse but its hard when you go for a job and they look at you in that funny way and I new I had to get out of Melbourn else id be in with The Black Boyz agen doing bad stuff

It made Billy Butler feel so useless, waking up each morning feeling shit-faced and grotty with sweet fuck-all to do. It made no difference where in Melbourne he might've been, in the park on a sunny day or wandering the streets a free man, trying to convince himself he didn't have a care in the world. Because when he saw all those ponced-up blokes marching off to work in their smart-arsed clothes, a sense of purpose in their very walk, or the young mums dropping off the kids at school in their shiny four-wheel drives, the black mood invariably returned. And the bastard'd hang on, too, accompanying him like some shadow he couldn't shake off.

Billy Butler was sitting alone late at night outside the Art Gallery when he was observed by two passing policemen, his dishevelled clothing attracting their attention. It was scary, the way they'd draw their car so slowly to the kerb, like the motor wasn't even running. Two burly blokes in blue, their heads turned towards him, eyeing him up and down, just like Dodson used to do, without blinking or saying a single word. Billy could read the contempt in their eyes. He felt himself shrivelling up inside. He knew he was leaning forward on the bench, his knees going hell-for-leather, first one way then the other, like some little kid busting to go to the loo. He stared at the pavers, hoping that when he finally looked up they were no longer there.

'Name?'

How could they do that, speak with such authority, getting to the point so bluntly without so much as a how-ya-goin? Billy wrung his hands in that childlike manner he hated, looking first to the left, then to the right away from the vehicle, wondering where all this would lead to.

'Billy,' he said.

It scared the shit out of him, the way the copper on the passenger side could turn his head to look straight ahead through the windscreen and sigh in mock exasperation then, without even glancing back at him, say: 'Full name?'

'Billy Butler.'

'Wait there. Yeah, on the bench. You wait.'

And what was he to make of the authority they had over him which had him sitting on that bench utterly stuffed, when he could've made a bolt for it. When they reclined in the bucket seats of their car and listened, so quiet and still, to some other bloke on their car phone, occasionally glancing at him like he was a piece of meat in a butcher's window. When he waited while the two men cocked their heads to one side as they listened to the crackling voice that told them the story of his life. Run, Billy, into the night. These fat bastards haven't a hope in hell of catching you. Friggin' go, mate.

'Lookin' for a car to steal, Butler?' said the driver behind the wheel.

'Or a brooch, maybe?' said the cop on the passenger side.

'Like women's jewellery, do you Butler? Maybe you like women's clothing, too.' He turned to the other policeman. 'Maybe we should have a look-see. Maybe Butler's wearin' women's undies.'

Their laughter rocked the car. Until the policeman nearest to Billy assumed the features of a sympathetic adult talking to a distressed child. 'Ooooh, don't cry, Billy, don't cry. Poor cry-baby Billy.' After he'd had his fun he turned all serious and sombre. 'Look at me. I said, look at me, dicknose. I'm comin' back round here in a half hour or so. An' I don't wanna see your face. I don't want any trouble, okay? I said, okay? So why don't you be a good little boy and move along. In fact, why don't you get the fuck out of my area completely, eh? Is that a good idea? I think it's a great idea. What do you think, Butler? 'Sthat a good idea, or what?'

Billy left Melbourne that very night.

He went from town to town, finding it safer, when stopped, to say he was a Maori or an Indian. He invented names for himself. He found himself detained on several occasions when he couldn't produce the documentation proving his identity.

He crossed into New South Wales, spending a few seasons on the Darling Downs doing odd jobs on stations or just keeping on the move, sleeping under or on top of a small tarpaulin, depending on the weather. He worked as a rabbiter, a stock hand and fence-mender, avoiding, where possible, the attention of the police.

Outside Darlington he found employment on a farm which ran cattle and grew fruit. He collected cattle manure and threw it into large drums of water. After several weeks of soaking he poured the fertiliser over the roots of the trees. When the fruit ripened he assisted with its picking. His wages were banked for him as he worked out the contracted months. This was good. Kept him off the grog. And he'd have a nice sum to live on while he travelled the country, searching for his mum.

When the seasonal work came to an end he fronted up for his wages only to be told the bulk of it'd gone towards the costs of his accommodation and food. And that's when he lost it, going on a drunken rampage, smashing windows and making all sorts of threats to the station manager and his wife and daughter. The police were called. Billy Butler was taken and charged at Griffith, attending the hearing without legal representation. He was sent to the Kinchela Aboriginal Boys Home near Kempsey, 1500 kilometres away.

When some members of the group he belonged to in the home tried to burn down their dormitory, they were sent, en masse, to Tamworth Boys Home, the toughest youth prison in the state.

But when they let you out mum you aint got much munny or desent clothes they just open them gates and say there you are we dont wanna see your face agen so what do you do to eern a kwid when no won gives you a job and they no you was lokked away so you gotta move on and try starting agen but you get hungry now and then and you got nowere to stay and you stink even them caravan parks take won look at you and wont let you pich your tent so you gotta sneek in when no wons looking so you can yuse there shower

He was caught breaking into a home. The prosecutor read out in court Billy Butler's record.

'He says he only wanted to steal something to eat. That it was merely hunger which motivated him. But I ask you to consider the criminal record of this man. And when you do you'll see that this is a criminal who must be locked away. There's the matter of the assault some years back on that childless teacher in Melbourne who, out of the kindness of her heart, did not evict him from her home after he'd attacked her. And how did he repay her understanding and compassion? By stealing a family heirloom, one handed down to the woman by a great aunt.

'Then there's the violence he inflicted on the manager of the farm we've all heard about. Even worse, the terrible things he said he'd do to that man's wife and daughter. When they'd tried to give him a new start in life.

'This man is a threat to society. The leniency shown in the past in sending him to Boys Homes, when he could just as easily have been sent to adult gaols, has clearly not been appreciated.'

And i tried to tell them cos there was no won agen to speek for me about the no plase to sleep and the hunger and i dunno why but i started talking bout you mum and the words they came out all over the plase and the juj he was sitting there staring at the papers on his deskthing or looking at his woch or talking to some fella taking notes and there i was borling me eyes out like they said i was just won big crybaby and when i seen no won was lissening i started speeking reel lowd but that juj he just sez i gotta respect the cort and that was my problem i had no respect and he took of his glasses and looked at me like Dodson and those to coppers and he spoke reel slow like i was stupid or something and he sez i had a lesson to lern and he sends me to jail but can you tell me mamma why sum of them blackfellas they take the nife and cut themselves reel bad sos the doctas called its a mistery to me and can you tell me why and how i started sniffin the gloo first then i got onto the badder stuff

Mary Butler arrives home
ABOUT 7.45 A.M.

Mary Butler arrived home sore, weary and mad as hell, her head spinning from the effects of the pills. She stood on the footpath frowning at the flowering shrubs in her front garden which someone had planted, and the trees that'd been hacked back so's the branches no longer hung over the fence. Those bastards next door'd always complained about leaves and bullshit, and what do they do while she's away?

She put down her bag and opened the gate. The woman

glanced at the house next door and saw the elderly couple watching her through the slats in the blinds. She mouthed an exaggerated *fuck you* at them then thrust two fingers in the air. They quickly withdrew, frightened. Mary Butler let out a triumphant cackle.

She picked up her bag, advanced to the front door, leaned the crutch against the wall then knocked.

You're wondering why Billy's arrived early. You return the rabbits to their hutch, see the shape of someone other than your brother through the frosted glass panels in the door, open it hesitantly.

You throw your arms around your mother's waist, burying your face into her breasts. 'You're home! You're home!'

You look up at her. She's staring down the hallway at the lovely pictures on the walls, the wonderful new furniture she doesn't recognise, breathes in, too, the unfamiliar smells.

'What,' she says, and you can almost feel the blood roaring in her head, 'what the fuck's been goin' on?'

She hobbles into your bedroom, sees the picture of you and Major which you'd cut out of the paper and stuck on your wall.

You tell her he's the saint what fixed up your home.

Billy finds his Little Angel
JANUARY 1999

Billy Butler settled in the bush wherever he could find work. He'd move on when the seasonal work was done or if he'd got the sack after too much binge-drinking. Or he'd pack up and leave abruptly in pursuit of any black woman going by the name of Butler. He stayed in Mulgoa for a while, sleeping in the same shed in which, a couple of the elders told him, his mother'd slept years before. He found his way to the Aboriginal settlement on Palm Island, but on learning she'd fled a long, long time before (with a small son), left the following day. He passed through many missions, playing with half-caste kids less than half his age.

Won day sum bloke in the Top End he rekoned it was a big joke to tell me you was on Groote Eyland so i catched the ferry and it wasn't you but it was nother Mary we was both in a bad way with them voices in our heads and befor she done herself in we luved eech other like crazy sos i thort i was in hevan

Little Angel, as Billy called her, had drifted to the Northern Territory from Pukatjo, in South Australia. She'd travelled from town to town, hitching rides, stealing food and grog, siphoning petrol out of cars to sniff. But she was a hopeless thief. She got caught many times. Sympathetic cops'd let her off with a warning. She headed, on impulse, to Groote Eyland, arriving in Alyangula not long after Billy Butler's own arrival in that town.

This won was different to all the rest so long as i was there we both felt safe like nothing bad coold ever happen and she d ask me all the time if i was gunna leeve and you no i never got tired of telling her i was never gunna leeve cos her asking was telling me she was gunna always be there for me too and them voices in her head they left her for a while too

Billy Butler'd had brief encounters with many women, black and white. The relationships would last a night, some even a few weeks. Until the women'd get exasperated when he couldn't do the job on them, finally kicking him out of their beds or the back of their cars. He was, one woman said, a useless prick with a useless prick. All hands and that breathless passion of his and that embrace that almost broke them in two that promised so much but which, more often than not, came to bugger-all. It got so that he was scared shitless at responding to any offer to go out for a quickie behind a pub or in the park, terrified of another failure. To summon up the courage he'd throw down one more schooner then duck out to the loo to sniff the glue or flask of fuel he carried. He'd take a piss and say, looking at the dick in his hand, Now don't you go lettin' me down agen, old fella.

But hell, Angela was different from all the rest.

'Don't care, Buttles. Jes t'hold me's okay.'

'You don't care? You sure? It don't matter if all's I can do is holdja?'

'Nah, 'slong as ya love me. Ya love me, don'tcha Billy-boy?'

And he wrapped his arms around her, burying his face in the nape of her neck. 'You don't care,' he said, 'you really don't care.'

'Crikey, mate, ya bloody cryin'. Ah, Billy, yer such a sook. A big sook with a big nose. Never felt so safe in all me life. You've saved me, ya great big silly-Billy. Tell me agen ya won't leave, like all them others.'

Feeling safe and unthreatened, he made love to her at last.

'I'll never leave you,' he said. 'Yer Billy's here, alright girlie? An' we'll have babies, eh. Lots of 'em. We'll make us a fam'ly. Our own fam'ly. Let's make that promise agen, Angela, to kick the grog and the sniffin'.'

Every night for three weeks they fucked like a couple of blue-arsed flies. Billy Butler was delirious with joy. And then the voices in her head returned. She was caught breaking into a newsagency to steal some glue.

The magistrate read the details of her previous offences and the warnings given by sympathetic police in a string of towns between Pukatjo and Groote Eyland. He warned her that were she to steal again, he would imprison her.

Two days later she broke into a council building. Oil and paints were found in her possession by the night security guard.

'Do you,' said the magistrate, *'want* to go to prison? You really are giving yourself enough rope to hang yourself, aren't you? You are to spend twenty-eight days in Darwin's Don Dale Detention Centre. If you steal again upon your release you will be sent away for a longer period.'

Billy Butler leapt to his feet to protest. But the magistrate, sitting behind that large wooden bench in those robes that looked to Billy like some dressing-gown, paused in his deliberations to stare at him. Billy half expected the man to say, in that quiet but firm authoritarian way these blokes had, No respect, no respect, young man, that's your problem. Billy stood there, dry-tongued and weak-bladdered, his mouth opening and closing like a beached fish gasping for life.

'I'll be comin' to see ya, Angela!' he shouted as she was led out. She turned to face him, smiling weakly. 'Ev'ry day, Angela. Okay?'

He arrived the next day to visit, feeling guilty for reasons which eluded him, scared they were going to grab him, haul him in, throw him sprawling into a cell. He'd had a few schooners at an early opener to summon the strength. He found it hard to stand without support. He was sent away.

He returned sober the following day, standing for more than an hour on the other side of the road opposite the entrance to the Centre. He was intimidated by its high walls and fences and heavily barred gates and a beefy man in uniform who stood at the entrance. Recalling Billy Butler from the day before this man shook his head, wagged a finger. And Billy, unable to protest, walked meekly away. And so that he wouldn't have to face the man again, he decided to wait out the remaining twenty-six days of Angela's sentence. On her release he'd tell her they were going to travel to Sydney and start a new life together in the black community of Redfern that he'd heard about.

Angela's headaches worsened. She asked every day if Billy Butler had visited. She began to abuse the guards. She made a name for herself as being uncooperative. When she informed one of the guards of the voice in her head which told her to attack other inmates, she was put into isolation.

On the tenth day of her confinement one of the guards, bringing Angela her dinner, found a drawing on the floor of her cell. A girl was shown sitting under a tree. In one corner of the picture she'd drawn an angel, in the other, a devil. The guard threw the picture into a bin.

She began experiencing violent mood swings, was quick to anger and, on the fifteenth day of her sentence, was found by a guard hiding under her bed to avoid the light that streamed into her cell from the barred window. She claimed that people were constantly watching her, and thought herself to be going mad. She complained bitterly of some bloke called Billy who'd broken some promise he'd made to her.

Twenty-four days into her sentence she was discovered in a sitting position on the ground. A sheet was tied around her neck. The other end was tied to the metal bedhead. She'd died in the early hours of that morning.

The pathologist stood to give his account on the first day of the inquest.

'It takes little time and effort to commit suicide by strangulation. It is not necessary to hang from the ceiling or jump from a chair. The weight of your head alone is enough to cut off the blood flow through the jugular veins. Once that happens, or once your tongue is pressed up and back to block your windpipe, unconsciousness comes in about ten seconds.'

The doctor illustrated Angela Wood's death with the assistance of diagrams for the benefit of those conducting the inquest and the large number of reporters who'd flown to Darwin. The doctor then read out aloud the note the girl had written before killing herself:

I don't want to die cause I'm too young but I was so lonely and them voices was driving me mad. Now I'm grown up and soon I'll meet my people in heaven.

As Billy Butler fled the court he heard the doctor say, 'She was only fifteen years of age.'

Nanna Dora arrived in Darwin the following day.

Billy Butler laughed in his sleep. He lay in a tight ball by the side of a road leading out of Katherine in the Northern Territory. He was curled up next to a stand of stunted acacia trees, his shirt wet with sweat, his hair sticking to his glistening forehead. He laughed even louder when he was roused by a cloud of dust caused by a passing van. The copper's vehicle stopped, reversed, turned and was angled so that its headlights shone on the jerking, twitching figure of the black man who was cackling like a demented kookaburra.

A low wind mooned and whistled through the scrub. The night was still and dark. Something scuttled in the bushes. Rag-arsed skeletal trees stood in the haze of dust and headlights. The two coppers got out of their vehicle and walked to the black man. They towered over him as they considered what to do. They observed the cramping legs and stomach, heard the black man mumbling incoherently, saw that his face and coat were covered in vomit.

What to do? Leave this useless bonehead to die out here? Obvious he'd been on a bender. Such a fucken sadsack. Ugly, too, nose like a gargoyle, hooded duffle jacket all monkish and slimed with puke. Great. Just great. And all those reporters who'd descended on the Top End writing those damning accounts of Darwin's redneck authorities. As if the coppers were responsible for the suicide of that mad black sheila. You didn't want those Sydney yuppie reporters coming at you with their notepads and dictaphones and bleeding-heart attitude because you'd left some drongo by the side of the road to die.

The coppers stopped their noses and held their breath as they picked up the man and slid him into the back of their van. He was driven to the station, placed in a cell. When he awoke he saw a small barred windowless opening high up on one of the concrete-block walls. Shards of glass lay on the concrete floor. And was that a woman, a black woman lying on the single mattress pushed up against the far wall?

'Mum?'

The woman does not stir.

''Sthat you, mum?'

A hesitant moon appears. Pieces of glass on the floor of the cell glisten.

Yeah, it's his mum, alright. And him? Why, he's a little kid again, safe from all those big people who scare him. And what about all those vague shapes in the cell? One's a Christmas tree and there, next to his mother's a shape that can only be a pressie, from Santa, eh.

Billy laughs. 'Santa brang me a pressie.'

The woman lies asleep.

'Santa's good, eh? He's a saint.'

Yes, he hears her say. He is a good and kind and gentle saint.

'People 'ave to die before they can become saints. 'Sthat right?'

Of course, the woman says. The good and kind die young and they go to God's kingdom.

'But if Santa's a saint an' 'e's dead, how come he brang me a pressie?'

It's a miracle, my child.

'Nah, dead fellas can't bring no pressies. You lyin' to me, mum?'

Billy Butler crawls to the bucket in the middle of the cell and sees, yes, it's unmistakeable, a little card on which's written, *To Billy, a sweet and gentle and good boy.*

So that Billy Butler begins to weep. He isn't a good boy. He's doubted the existence of Santa. And the honesty of his mother. That Mista Dodson was right. Billy is a bad boy.

'I'm sorry. Yer still love me?'

He drifts off to sleep only to wake up with a start. A bright light illuminates the cell. There's no Christmas tree. There's no gift from Santa. The woman's gone.

'When are you gunna shut-the-fuck-up?' The ex-Sydney copper was standing on the other side of the open doorway, a lighted torch in his hand. 'Ravin' all night like some fucken loonybin. Where you from?'

'I'm a Gadigal.'

'A what?'

'I reckon I'm a Gadigal.'

'Reckon? What d'ya mean yer reckon? Don't you know where you're from? What's your name?'

'Butler. Billy Butler. You got any other Butlers round 'ere?'

'Nah, but I know where you can find 'em. I know where you can find plenty of 'em.'

'Where?'

'Buckingham Palace. Plenty of butlers there. Where the fuck is Gadigal anyway. 'Sthat a town or what?'

'Sinney.'

'Sydney? What, a suburb? Never heard of it. Say, you related to that footy player? Jimmy Butler? Played for the Rabbitohs years ago. Seen him play. So much fucken talent an' he gave it all away. Just went walkabout one day, just like that. Useless prick, like all you lot.'

'Jimmy Butler? In Sinney?'

'Now shut-up an' let me get some sleep.'

'Wait.'

'What?'

'The woman what was here.'

'What woman?'

'The one what was lyin' here. She gone?'

The man's eyes narrowed. 'Maybe,' he said. 'Then again, she might be outside. Why?'

'She Mary Butler?'

'Could be. What of it?'

'You tell her somethin' for me?'

'Sure, why not. I'll do that.'

'You tell her I bin lookin' for her? Tell her I love her?'

'Yeah, sure, righto. 'Ang on a sec.' The man left, returning moments later.

'Didja tell her?'

'Yeah, I told her.'

'What'd she say?'

The man grinned out of the corner of his mouth. 'She told me to tellya you're a useless cunt.'

He slammed shut the door of the cell, laughing loudly.

'Useless race,' he said, 'fucken useless race of no-hopers.'

The following day Billy Butler began the long journey to Sydney.

Billy meets his mum

REDFERN, ABOUT 8.30 A.M.

It took Billy Butler some time to calm his nerves and regain control over the crazy voices in his head. He got up off the grass on Moore Park and made to cross South Dowling Street. He paused in the middle of the road as the peak-hour traffic rushed past and around him as he tried, once more, to find his bearings. Drivers veered this way and that to avoid knocking him down. They pushed their heads out of windows and let rip with their abuse. Car horns blared. Tyres screeched.

Tom O'Flaherty, who'd been reading the *Tele*'s sports articles on Souths, looked up and observed the commotion outside his terrace. He watched a man, who was obviously drunk, walk past his terrace, intrigued by his peculiar gait. For some reason he found himself thinking of Jimmy Butler.

Mary Butler saw what that whitefella'd done to her home. Even worse, when she threw open the door of her son's room and saw the local rag's picture, and a mural, part of which showed that big bloke with the wonky eye and a fat head, holding Johnnie's hand, his picture labelled with the words *My new daddy*; when Johnnie told her it was that very man who'd come into her home and organised the removal of the old furniture and the delivery of the new, had supervised the painting, dusting, sweeping and hosing; when Johnnie told her how he himself'd been sleeping, until recently, in that man's house, she did her block. Struggling with the crutch under one arm, taking huge gulps from one of the bottles of grog she'd just bought, she set about destroying what that fucking white intruder'd done. Johnnie ran crying into his bedroom. He slammed the door shut, cowered in a corner as the sounds of things falling and breaking and his mother's terrible rage filled the house. He sat there, eyes shut, open-fingered hands grabbing either side of his head, back aching from the effort of pushing himself harder, harder into the corner.

Minutes after Major Bob'd fled, Billy Butler arrived, oblivious to the dispersing crowd. He knocked on the door. No reply. He knocked again. The door swung open. He entered, did not notice the chaos that the woman, kneeling in front of him, had caused. He stared at her, speechless, until he was finally able to whisper: 'Mary? You Mary Butler?'

The woman was leaning on an upturned chair, a bottle in her hand. They just don't leave you alone. Another whitefella coming into your home without even knocking.

'Who are you? Whatd'ya want?'

The man walked down the hallway, dropping his stick and backpack. His diary fell out of his bag. He stepped over the mess on the floor.

Fucking hell, will you look at this. You ask a question and they don't even answer. 'What're ya doin', comin' in 'ere? Whatd'ya want?'

'It's me,' he breathed, 'it's me. I bin lookin' for ya. I —'

'Lookin' for me? Some fat white bastard sentcha? Eh? Eh? Ya got lollies to give to me kid?'

'I've come for you, an' for Johnnie, an' —'

'Get outta me house. Now.'

The woman smashed the bottle against the wall, stood and advanced towards the man. 'Fucken think ya can come in whenever ya want. Get outta me house or I'll —'

'Mum, please. It's Bill—'

And as he stood there, the room spinning about him, the woman swung the broken end of the bottle across his face. Billy Butler reeled backwards, a deep gash on his cheek. 'Ooooh, mum, don'tcha know? I'm yer little fella. I'm Billy.'

Mary Butler dropped the bottle, closed her eyes, fell back against the wall then slid to the floor. 'Billy's dead,' she whispered. 'Billy's dead.'

'Don'tcha want me?'

'I wantcha ter get out,' the woman breathed. 'Can't fight youse no more ... let me be. Just wanna die. Let me be ...'

Billy Butler looked up to see his brother standing in the doorway of his bedroom. He saw the mural on the wall behind him and two white rabbits on the floor. The man's dark eyes rolled deep in their sockets. He began to tremble. Voices, returning in a rush, hammered their accusations at him. Large drops of sweat broke out on his forehead, face, the back of his neck. He tightened then ground his jaw. He pushed past Johnnie and staggered into the bedroom. Hearing Billy whine and growl, Johnnie backed away from the room, staring as his brother stumbled about. Neither of them noticed their mother get up, stagger out the back door then into the rear lane.

Billy Butler saw the pictures of his brother holding the hand of his new daddy. Saw his mum, grandmother and grandfather, smiling out onto the world. He heard the voice of some little angel asking him over and over again to tell her of his love for her. Tell me, Billyboy, tell me ya won't ever leave me. Ya saved me Buttles, ya saved me Billyboy.

An awful choking sound came out of the man's throat when he saw the two rabbits staring up at him. They were accusing him. Of his treachery. Eyeing him up and down. Blinking their scorn and contempt at his uselessness.

'Don'tcha stare at me,' he growled, advancing towards them. 'Look away! You fucken look away! Now!'

Johnnie watched in horror as his brother picked up first one rabbit and then the other, dismembering them with his own hands. The man held the still twitching bodies of the rabbits as he smeared their blood over the murals, covering the faces of the family he now knew would never be his.

And when he'd finished his work and the voices'd receded; when he came out of the room to see his mother gone and his little brother's face contorted in terror, the man held out his bloodied hands to the boy, whispering over and over and over, 'Ooooh, Johnnie, what've I done? What've I done?'

'Get out!' Johnnie cried. 'Get away!'

'Ohhh, Johnnie, don'tcha want me too?'

'Go to hell! Leave me 'lone! I hatecha! I hope you fucken die!'

Billy grabbed one of the bedsheets that Yaya Zoe'd washed,

ironed and folded for his mother, held it to the open wound on his face and rushed out the back of the house.

You see a pair of scissors on the floor. As you cut deep lines in your own arm, the sounds of your cries recede like the fading roar of a faraway storm. Replaced by an expanding thumping sound filling the growing silence between the rooms, the pieces of furniture, between you and the whole wretched world. Shadows lengthen. You can barely hear your own voice, calling, calling. A great churning sigh heaves in the house, gets right into your bones, finds a place in your heart where it subsides. You leave, brushing past the neighbours who've regathered on the street. You run to Major's house but he's not at home. You make for Centennial Park, for Billy.

You find him in a sitting position, one end of the bedsheet tied around his neck, the other onto a large, low branch. He's still warm. You hold onto him until he's cold.

You stand unseen from some distance when the police and ambulance finally arrive. You watch from the world you've retreated into as your brother's body is taken away.

FOURTEEN

They all come home

A few days later. Souths've been given the heave-ho, your whole world's closed in on you and your mum's pissed off. You stand in Major's lounge room pulling at the elasticised belt of your shorts, staring at your reflection in a rain-soaked window, tracing the outline of your own strange boy's face. You're living in a soft velvet dream, listening to the sighing of the whole damn world. It's dreaming of itself, Johnnie-boy, it's exhaled you into its silence. Your eyes, mate, two milky pools reflected in the water in a soup bowl positioned under a leaking ceiling. You emerge from wherever you've hidden and for reasons you can't understand, take a look at this whole awful world, and it's mad, mad, mad. Run, sport, before it sucks you out of your lovely hideaway.

All sorts of people are telling Major he has to give you up. A couple of them are out on the footpath. He chucks a huge mental. You've racked off alright, and now you're lying face up on his beautiful wet lawn out front, while feet away he's using words, bad words no one's ever heard come out of his mouth. He takes you inside.

You're holding Major by the hand when he takes a call on his mobile. You feel your own heartbeat throbbing as Nanna's voice, which you can hear, roars its fury. You can imagine her wide-eyed glare as she plunges through Major's protests. The man's lounge room is crowded with their bellowing, both of them going at it at the same time.

There's a stand-off. Silence fills the room.

'You still there, Theodora?'

Major's red-faced, he's breathing into the mobile.

'Speak to me, Nan.'

You think of that movie you saw recently on telly, *The Clash of the Titans*.

Old Tom's not letting up. He's nagging Major to go out to La Pa before it's too late and the cops have you physically removed from the big fella's house. But Major's retreated behind his crook eye, refusing to see what's so bloody obvious. Can you imagine it? Mum's bro a few suburbs away and her knowing nothing?

Zoe prays for you every day, dispenses her Chrissie gifts two, three times a week, but nothing works: you're somewhere they can't reach, and the talk is you're going to be placed in some institution.

Friggin' hell, life was a funny business, Old Tom thought. The human drama was the greatest show on earth, no worries. And a man didn't have to travel the world to see it in all its stupidity, unpredictability, mystery and grandeur. Just sit on your verandah and watch it play itself out. Over the road or right next to you. Grown men busting a gut doing hill runs for Christ-knew-what reason. Others, dog-eared faces full of failure, coming rag-arsed every second day, whimpering about lost opportunities to make a quid. A little kid who'd gone on the blink, eyes like those of an old cove who's seen too much. And Bob Ryan, as if his good eye'd clouded over, certain the boy'd come back soon. That was Tom's old mate's phrase, God bless him: He'll come back, you'll see, you'll see. When everyone else thought the kid should be hospitalised here was Bob having himself on, blasting anyone contradicting him, threatening legal action, firing off letters, being a real pain in the arse.

But there'd be no more enquiring about *that matter of some shame*. One day Bob might blurt it all out. Unresolved issues often did that. And if not, well, perhaps some stories were best left untold. In the meantime there was the boy with moronic eyes who moved like a fog on still water, whose dreamy face stared at nothing. Or everything. Was that it? Had he seen too much? The kid'd sit on Tom's verandah, pale and washed-out like an ancient sun-bleached statue, occasionally exhaling his old man's sigh. Only this time those blacks doing their block wouldn't be fobbed off. Nanna Dora rang Tom, telling him she was flying back after some funeral in Darwin. The word around the traps was she was going to give Bob hell for what he'd done to Mary Butler's home. But try talking to Bob. What to do? Get onto Jimmy Butler out at La Pa, that's what.

Major Bob reckoned that by January the boy will've returned to his former self. Yeah, well, sure, Bob, sure. Can't you see, mate, that he's lost more than his voice? There were no words from the boy, no tears, few changes of expression, little reason to think he knew where he was or who he was with. Unless you tried to take him out of Redfern. The fog, mate, ain't gunna lift soon, can't you see that? Everyone else can.

There was no sighting of the boy's mother, no rumours of her whereabouts, no hint of her very existence. There was talk of the death of some blackfella out at the park. Some people wondered whether it was the same man Johnnie'd been seen with. Old Tom mentioned this to the Major. Bob Ryan shrugged his shoulders, moved the weight from one side of his arse to the other but said nothing. No one gave this black man further thought. Except Tom, who'd seen the Major's baby skin suddenly glow like a boiled prawn. You never fooled me, sport, an' you ain't puttin' nothin' over me now, either, so what's the story?

Johnnie Butler accompanied Major Bob wherever the man went. Unless he made to venture over Clevo or South Dowling Street. Then the boy'd stiffen as the man went to cross the road. He'd back up against a shopfront or fence, pull back from the Major's hold on his hand, wrap his arms around a telegraph pole.

But how could it've been otherwise, the Major said to Old Tom one day. When he'd walked the streets of Redfern himself with the child when his mother was in hospital, warning him of the dangers of the outside world. When it was him who'd given the boy a sense of belonging to the place. Taken him through what'd once been the swamps where the Gadigal people'd lived, hunted, dreamed. Shown him where the old boundary stones of Redfern'd once stood.

And hadn't Billy also told you of the dangers *out there*? Hadn't you seen for yourself in Centennial Park one day, moments before your world'd closed in on itself, what could happen if you ventured out of Redfern?

Some of the boy's toys and books, which showed no trace of the violence done on that terrible day, had been left in a neat pile in the backyard by those who'd done the cleaning. Major Bob, Kon and

Yaya Zoe left the boy in front of the TV while they went to collect Johnnie's things.

They returned as quickly as they could. On entering, they discovered the cause of the loud racket they'd heard as they were making their way back to Bob Ryan's terrace. The boy was in his new bedroom, tears channelling down his face, bloodied and bruised fingers and hand trying to nail down to the wooden floor the legs of his bed. He was never left alone again.

Kooka Kon, Major Bob and Yaya Zoe took some food over to Tom's for lunch. They sat in the lounge room around the kitchen table they'd dragged into the room, surrounded on all sides by the ghosts of Souths' past. The front door was left open to let in a breeze. The flyscreen was shut. Halfway through their meal came that knock on the door which Old Tom'd long expected. He did not recognise the features of the man seen through the screen, but Old Tom'd seen the man's car parked outside his home.

'It's for you, Bob.'

'Me?'

'Go on, Bob. Let the man in.'

Major Bob opened the door to see Victor Batrouney, who, the younger man was to say later, had finally come home.

The welfare authorities, alerted by Nanna Dora by phone, came in force for the boy, tracking Bob Ryan down at Old Tom's. It was a good thing that Victor Batrouney was there. He examined the papers. He told the Major there was nothing he could do. Those documents they were waving in his face gave them the power to take Johnnie, and now, right now.

They'd come with the police, too, a polite man and woman who said that while everyone appreciated Bob Ryan's intentions, the boy had to go. They listened with great patience to his arguments but the answer was no, Mr Ryan (*Major* Ryan, thank you) could not have another week, another day or, for that matter, another hour with the boy. The matter had dragged on long enough. No one wanted things to get ugly. Could he please bring the child out from Mr O'Flaherty's house.

And then Victor Batrouney had his brainwave. When the coppers and the government people saw with their own eyes Johnnie Butler's reaction when Victor tried to take him over South Dowling Street; when they were walked around the corner, accompanied by the Major, Victor, Zoe, Kon and Tom, in his wheelchair, and shown the child's attempts at creating some sense of permanency and belonging by trying to nail down his bed, they paused. Bob's heartbeat quickened. These people'd gone quiet. They were actually listening to Ernie's suggestion. You little beauty, Victor!

It was an unusual situation, not at all what they had in mind. But Victor Batrouney obviously knew something of the law. And if this James Butler, whom Mr — sorry — *Major* Ryan and Mr O'Flaherty personally knew was indeed the child's uncle; if he was the only known blood relative of the boy; if he was prepared to move from La Perouse to Redfern, where Johnnie Butler had his friends, school (and a vast number of unofficial guardians, they smiled), and care for the boy for a limited trial period; and if such a trial turned out to be in the boy's best interests — well, they were prepared to reconsider, take the suggestion back to their superiors, ring Nanna Dora and see what she had to say.

Nanna Dora was driven straight to the Major's home on her return. She gave him heaps. Johnnie Butler'd never seen the big fella look so helpless.

Yaya Zoe went to Major Bob's home the following day. The Major was delighted to see that the cab that'd come to take him, Dora and Tom to La Pa was generously festooned with all manner of red and green flags and stickers. A good sign.

Yaya Zoe stood at the door of the Major's home holding Johnnie's hand, smiling her huge toothless smile at the possibilities of what that day's events might bring. She learnt something that day. As the taxi pulled out from the kerb to go and collect Tom, Major Bob wound down his window to wave at the boy. And when Johnnie raised a hand, after those many weeks of unresponsiveness, the Greek woman knew that even a glass eye could well with tears.

Jimmy Butler drew on his cigarette. He was sitting halfway between the graves of his wife and mother when he saw the taxi pull up and stop on the narrow road some distance away. He wondered why it stood idling for so long, saw the vague form of three people in the back, the shape of a wheelchair in the rear compartment.

The following year's footy comp was on everyone's lips. And if people weren't talking about the injustices of the white man's world that saw the black man's team kicked out of the comp, then they'd go over and over the details of the death of some fella who'd done himself in, out at Centennial Park, whose body no one'd come forward to claim, whose poor mother might be in some part of Sydney or, more likely, on some settlement in the bush, unaware her boy'd died a lonely death and was buried, somewhere in Botany Cemetery, in an unmarked, unmourned grave.

Souths given the bullet, another black man dead. Some bugger of a thing was always falling out of the sky to remind you of all that shit you were trying to forget.

And here was this idling Ford with stickers in a continuous line on the front bumper bar proclaiming the driver's support for the beleaguered Bunnies, a red and green flag tied to the aerial — and that fluffy thing dangling from the rear-vision mirror, was that a rabbit, or what? Well, the cab'd move on soon and he'd regain possession of that part of the cemetery. In the meantime he'd talk his way out of his bad mood. Relive with Rosie those carefree days out bush. Tell his mum that her boy'd had a good life. 'Cause that's what it was, wasn't it?

One man in the rear of the cab wound down his window. The people in the taxi were, he could see, watching him. Now they were opening doors. Jimmy Butler saw the unmistakeable figure of that man with the glass eye. Jeez, after all them years, who'd've thought. Look at him, comin' at me like he was on some mission, that melon-headed battleaxe with the give-'em-a-once-over eyes. He wants somethin'. Can'tcha tell. Christ, they never leave youse alone.

Biding time

They tell stories, the old Greek woman and those Redfern blokes. You sit there twitching like a sleeping dog, staring out at the world with those sleepy eyes. Usually you're *over there*, wherever the hell that is. But sometimes you're *here,* in which case you tune in to their tiny world for a while. You get an inkling for the untold stories. Ernie the Attorney bristling if someone mentions his mother or father. Your uncle, chortling like a hog, his child's stick-pencil figure bumping against whoever's on either side of him as he makes an arse of himself telling another joke — but look at the sadness fill his eyes if someone asks about Rosie or mentions his footy days, or when he just sits there all still and quiet with nothing to say. Look at Major suddenly glowing like a red light bulb, staring down whoever makes mention of the violence in your home that day. There's your own story regarding Billy that you wouldn't let on about even if you could talk. You, at your age, with secrets. Them, at their age, eh?

More often than not no one knows when you're back. They jabber on, continue with their game of chequers, do bugger-all but look out onto the blokes hooning it up and down South Dowling

Street on a busy late morning, or consider the mottled late-afternoon light doing beautiful things on the slopes of Moore Park. And how could they know you're back anyway? Your foggy eyes usually give little away, which is how you prefer it. Them not knowing, that is. And then you go back to that shadowy world that murmurs like the toneless hum of distant bees. Away from the heaving weight of the sighing world that'll breathe its sadness all over you if you stay. Get out, Johnnie, get out, sport, it's a shithouse place here. Go to where you're safe, mate.

The start of the 2000 footy season was a terrible time for Major Bob and Old Tom. No training sessions to attend. No discussions on the upcoming games. Knowing there'd be no in-depth analysis of the tactical errors which'd brought about a terrible loss. Or the back-line movement that'd sealed victory. When it was just the two of them sitting on the verandah it was hard to shake off the melancholy that'd settled on their lives. It didn't help when they kept reading and hearing about those young players who'd grown up in Redfern, who'd once proudly worn the red and green and were soon to don the guernsey of another club, perhaps winning games, for goodness' sakes, for those teams that were Souths' traditional enemies.

One day, Kon and Victor joined the two older men.

'The trial for reinstatement's starting in June, Bob,' said Victor. 'We won't know the judge's decision until after the Olympics. Some time in early November, I'd say.'

'Round the time of my birthday,' the Major said. 'A victory would be the sweetest gift of all.'

'It's not looking good. I'd prepare myself for the worst.'

Major Bob looked across at Johnnie Butler, who was staring at his hands gathered in a ball in his lap. The man stroked the boy's head. 'No, Victor. We'll be back. We all come back in the end. Like

Jimmy, and you. Johnnie'll come back, too. Victor, can you do something for me? Some way down the track, if Mary doesn't return, I'd like to see Johnnie legally adopted.'

'Bob — they'd never allow it. You're too old.'

'Not me, Victor. Jimmy. Things are working out well between the two of them. But the kid's in limbo at the moment. It's just something I think that's worth looking into, don't you?'

'Yes, I'll do that. I'm surprised that Jimmy didn't mention anything to me about it.'

'Well, I haven't said anything to him.'

Tom and Victor exchanged a look.

'Don't you think you ought to?' said Victor.

The fundraising to assist Souths' legal costs shifted gear.

Yaya Zoe finally relented. She'd allow Kon Tsakiris to assist in making the extra trays of baklava on condition that there was no more talk of him partnering her in the business. The extra trays he helped her make, festooned with a red and green papier-mâché border, were seen all over Redfern. When word got out that the proceeds of these trays were to go to the club, business expanded even further. Kooka Kon still harboured the desire to see the business cater for a bigger market. The Greek version of Starbucks. Why not? Greek sweets and coffee, some light food, bouzouki music in the background, him behind the till, his wife and Zoe in the kitchen. He didn't dare breathe a word of his hopes to the woman.

He did try, however, to work out the proportion of the ingredients that went into the sweets. He stood near the kitchen doorway, made out he was busy doing this and that for an opportunity to listen in on her prayer as the trays were slid into the oven. But she was too cunning for him. She'd lower her voice, quicken the prayer. Her words were a garbled mess. Damn.

Major Bob, Nan Dora and her kids organised locals to go door-to-door, asking for a gold coin. They had people on street corners every Saturday morning selling tickets for chook raffles. They helped organise a roster of people who got on the phone at the club, harassing pollies and shock jocks, fielding questions from supporters.

Victor Batrouney got busy, too, organising a luncheon. He approached every Lebanese community organisation he knew of and asked for their list of members. Some obliged. In April, the date and the venue were fixed and the invitations, bearing his name as President of *The Lebanese for the Rabbitohs Fundraising Committee* were sent out. And on those posted to all members of the Batrouney family, none of whom he'd seen for over thirty years, he wrote in a green pen, on the top right-hand corner where his words would not be missed, *Hope to see you there — Victor.*

Billy's Dreaming Tree

Victor Batrouney arrives at your terrace one Sunday morning in May. You're sitting on the floor in the lounge room watching cartoons on the telly. There's a great wall of silence between you and him as he stands over you, talking. You hear his voice, the words hanging about his face, floating in that space between the two of you like a draught. Uncle Jimmy's standing next to him. Their voices and the sounds from the TV interlock, a bumper-to-bumper confusion of sounds.

'Good morning, Johnnie.'

You don't respond. You don't understand. The room's closing in on you, your breath quickens, you're a muted presence, wherever you are.

'Are you ready for our walk, Johnnie? Johnnie? Shall we go on our walk?'

Jimmy sighs. You know the sound. It's something you often

hear. From him, from everywhere, rolling in like a great gentle bank of fog to cover you completely in its vast expanse of sadness. You look up. Yeah, it's Jimmy alright, just him and that long breath hanging about his weary sad face that's full of shadows. You want to reach out and hold the poor bugger. You love him, don'tcha sport.

'He's like this,' he says to Victor, 'most of the time.'

No, you're not, it just seems that way, Uncle Jimmy.

'I've got something for you, Johnnie. I've got a present for you.' Victor Batrouney takes you by the hand and leads you to the yard. 'Go on, open it.' He walks you to a cardboard box. You can hear your heart beating. The box seems to expand. It's full of expectations. He lifts the flaps then stands to one side, next to your uncle. Jimmy's frowning. What's going on? his face says. But you know, oh yeah, you know.

You approach the box slowly and peer in. Fall to your knees, pick up the two baby white rabbits, each with a red and green ribbon tied around its neck. Press them both against your cheeks. Dark things lift. Invisible stuff, awful feelings float away. It's a miracle. You notice how soft the long grass is. The firm ground. Your heartbeat and that of the earth, beating in time. Two men standing nearby, faces full of anticipation. You blink your gratitude to Victor, and there, there, the hint of a smile. You can feel it travelling across your lips.

Some time later Johnnie and Victor Batrouney left for their walk. Jimmy got on the phone when he knew the Major was back from Mass.

'He smiled? You say you saw him smile? And he played with the rabbits?'

'Seen it with me own eyes.'

'Thank God.' And he rang Yaya Zoe, Nan Dora and Old Tom

immediately to give them the good news.

He's coming back, I tell you. He's coming home.

Worth a prayer, Bob? Yes, he goes to the secret room, lights a wick floating in a bowl of olive oil, goes down on his knees before the wall of icons the flame illuminates and offers his gratitude. Thank you, thank you.

Victor Batrouney holds your hand as you stand in Redfern Park.

'I used to knock about here,' he says, 'when I was a kid. My family used to come here for picnics each Sunday after church. My cousins and I'd climb those trees. Grandmother'd sit on blankets, right there.'

And your own grandma once stood in the timbered swamp. And your grandad stalked a roo which sat, staring, poised for flight, erect on its hind legs spread out wide, watching warily before suddenly turning like a wheel and bounding away.

And now your grandparents are staring up at the flying foxes feeding on heavily scented blossoms. The fruit bats're quarrelling and squealing before exploding into flight, clouding the sky with their wings.

'Come on Johnnie, let's walk.'

You're standing outside a single-storey terrace, opposite Saint Marons. 'I used to serve as an altar boy in that church, Johnnie.'

But you tune out. Because you see a small tree growing out of a large crack in the brick wall of a vacant factory down from the man's former home.

'The seeds,' Victor says, 'get blown into the cracks between the bricks. Sometimes they take root, like this one.'

You walk to the tree. You touch its leaves. You love this tree. If someone doesn't rescue it, it'll die.

'It's a fig tree, Johnnie.'

You know, you know.

'It's a Moreton Bay fig tree.'

Yes, yes.

That bloke really could give everyone the shits. Carrying on again like the Sheriff of Redfern. Whoever dreamed up that title sure knew what he was talking about. It's a tree, for God's sake, just a tree. What's the problem? If you let it grow the roots'll eventually bring the whole wall down. And besides, hadn't we all gone searching for the boy on those occasions when he'd gone missing? And hadn't we found him, together, by that tree, stroking its leaves? Wasn't it clear to anyone who had eyes to see that the fig held some appeal to the kid? Crikey, Bob, put a sock in it and bloody well calm down.

Two Sundays later, Victor, Jimmy and Kon (the Major refuses to help; you'd think you were off to rob a bank), armed with all sorts of tools, take you to the factory and ease the roots out of the cracks. You carry the small fig tree to your home where it's placed in a large ceramic pot purchased for you by Victor. You help fill the container with a special potting mixture then drag it next to the rabbit hutch. And though you can't open your mouth to say, you understand that it has to have a name. It is, you know, Billy's Dreaming Tree.

The three men and the boy then went for an aimless walk. Victor Batrouney came across some elderly residents whom he could recall from his days when he lived in Redfern. They all now knew him as the boy who'd come home, the one helping Souths fight the good fight. Their talk was of the Rabbitohs and how the whole sporting world, preoccupied with the coming Olympics had, it seemed, forgotten about the poor Bunnies. They discussed Victor's

September fundraising luncheon, the November appeal. Victor, Kon, Jimmy and the boy then went on their way, turning one corner, then another.

Then they saw, from a distance, the crowd that'd gathered outside Kon's old café. There was no mistaking the people on the balcony which led out from what was once Kon's bedroom, or the many balloons tied to the wrought-iron fence. The new owners hadn't changed the name. It was still called the Kookaburra Café. Kon stopped, stood staring open-mouthed at what was, clearly, a line of people waiting to get into the new brasserie. He walked ahead of the others, looking up at the people crowding around the tiny tables squeezed onto his old balcony, reading the colour supplements of the Sunday papers, sipping their hot beverages and eating their croissants.

Kon Tsakiris crossed the road without checking for oncoming traffic. He pushed his way through the crowd and pressed his face up against the window. There was his old café. It hadn't changed all that much, really. On the walls were the framed prints. Light from specially positioned brass ceiling lamps, the type he'd seen in the windows of local art galleries, was directed onto the pub posters, which took pride of place at the front of the shop. The recently French-polished high-backed seats; the old marble tiles on the floor; the art-deco light fittings above every table — all'd been cleaned of their layers of grime and dirt, the missing pieces replaced. They'd barely changed anything, the Greek saw. Just given the place a good spit and polish.

'Incredible, isn't it?' he heard one of the men lining up to get inside say.

'It's like a museum piece. The whole shop's like a museum piece,' came a woman's reply.

'Look at those pub posters. Painted on the back of glass, you know. They weigh a tonne. You can't buy them. No one does them anymore. Worth a fortune.'

Kon Tsakiris heard the continual ringing of the bell on that old silver cash register. Saw those at the front of the queue touching the scales and the old wind-up gramophone Major Bob said might be worth a quid or two. Observed some of the clientele, who were sitting at the tables, turning over the old crockery and cutlery, reading the English manufacturer's labels.

'Like a time capsule,' somebody said.

Waiters darted here and there, struggling to keep up with the orders.

Kooka Kon stared in disbelief as the one wearing multiple earrings, who had the name *Roberto* emblazoned on his T-shirt, took out a wad of notes from the register and stuffed it into his trouser pocket.

Kon Tsakiris shrugged off the comforting arm of Victor Batrouney and the sympathetic words of Jimmy Butler. He broke into a fast walk, went home alone and, for the first and only time in his life, got well and truly drunk.

Cathy Freeman bolts in

The fundraising luncheon was held during the Sydney Olympics. As chance would have it, coinciding with the 400-metres track final. A huge screen and dozens of monitors were set up in the auditorium so everyone had a clear view of the Aboriginal woman running for gold.

Major Bob was sitting with Victor and Susan Batrouney, Old Tom and some other mates. The Major looked like a stuffed walrus in his dinner suit. His shirt was strangling him. His bow tie was a missile about to be launched. Victor was dressed to the nines in a formal suit purchased for the occasion, his wife as proud as a schoolgirl. Tom was in an open-necked shirt in a suit that smelt of old men.

'Over three hundred people, Victor,' Major Bob said. 'We're

packed to the rafters. Well done.'

Victor Batrouney sat agitated and distracted. Soon he'd have to take the mike and conduct the auction. More than that. He couldn't continue to avoid asking for the seating arrangements, to see who from the Batrouney family'd responded to his invitation. He scanned the room, looking for a familiar face. He played with his food. He glanced at his watch. His armpits were saturated.

'Jimmy's on his way, Victor,' said the Major.

'Hm?'

'Jimmy's running late. He told me he's got an announcement for us.'

'Ahhh.'

Would Victor Batrouney recognise his cousins after all those years? Had he already passed some as he played the host and wandered around the ballroom earlier that evening, his face aching from all that smiling? Were they as nervous as him? Waiting for him to make the approach? As for his uncles and aunties, were any still alive?

Jimmy Butler'd been attending the annual Aboriginal Rugby League Knockout Competition when the idea of Souths touring the bush first occurred to him. Footy teams came to Redfern from all over: there were the Redfern All Blacks and the La Perouse Panthers; the Moree Boomerangs and the Muli Muli Coraki United Team from the Northern Rivers; there were teams from up and down the coast and from the western plains. It was after the final of this comp that Jimmy Butler suggested to the club's directors that the red and green should be showcased to rural Australia. Keep the playing side of the club alive while everyone waited for Finn's decision. Let the lawyers slug it out. We should keep a team on the paddock, play games in country towns as a way of thanking our bush cousins for their moral and financial support.

And so 'The Bunnies Go Bush' took to the road. And no one could say no to Jimmy Butler, who reckoned he'd been the first to come up with the idea (he hadn't) when he asked if he could assist with the tour. Nan Dora looked after Johnnie while Jimmy was away. The Bunnies travelled to Dubbo, Orange, Wellington and Bathurst. They drew supporters everywhere they went. One of their biggest crowds was against the Maitland Pumpkin Pickers. They completed their tour with matches in Gunnedah and Umina. By the time they'd returned to Sydney, the day of the fundraiser, the idea of an Academy had taken root in Jimmy's mind.

He arrived at the ballroom just as Victor Batrouney was about to get up to begin the formalities.

'A what?' said Major Bob.

'An Academy. Jimmy Butler's Academy. To train all them young blackfellas what wanna play fer the Rabbitohs. I can show 'em things.'

'And charge?' said Old Tom.

'Nah, do it for nothin'. Keep 'em off the streets, y'know. Teach 'em not to give up, like I done. Teach 'em to kick the ball when them bastards think yer gunna run with it. Do what's unexpected, like I used to do. Got meself a job, too, by the way. Like what ya said, Tom, down at the markets. Nan found it for me.'

When Jimmy Butler got up to go to the loo Old Tom said, 'Boy oh boy, who'd've thought it. He's comin' along fine, our Jimmy boy.'

Bob Ryan turned his dodgy eye on Tom and said, 'You're kidding, Tom.'

'Pardon?'

'You're not serious, are you? You don't think he'll actually go through with this Academy and stick to his job?'

'Yeah,' said Tom. 'Yeah, I do.'

'Well, you're wrong. And you know it. He'll give up, like he always gave up.'

Old Tom gestured that Bob Ryan lean forward, so that no one at the table could hear what he was about to say. 'Sometimes, Bob, you can be a real bastard. Have I ever told you that?'

The Major raised his eyebrows. Old Tom, his face set as hard as rock, looked up at Victor, who was now on the stage.

Were his cousins looking at him from the back of the ballroom, watching him with some pride as he skilfully managed his audience? That's our boy up there. Welcome home, welcome back, Victor, we've missed you, cuz.

The stage was set, the mood created for a wild selling-off of memorabilia. And, as if on cue to assist in the strengthening of nostalgia and high expectations that swept the room, the giant screen behind Victor, its volume turned off, began showing highlights of Cathy Freeman's athletic career. The final would be run in one hour's time. No time to lose — the auction had to begin now.

Ridiculous sums were paid for autographed photos, the right to be present in the dressing room on the occasion of Souths' expected return to the comp, the privilege of shaking hands with the legends who were present at that function. The highlight, however, was the auctioning of those items donated by Mr Thomas O'Flaherty, who received a standing ovation. Victor Batrouney, carried away by all sorts of conflicting emotions, bid against himself for a football, signed by many of Souths' greats way back in the 1920s. He promptly donated it back to the club to be auctioned a second time.

By the time Victor Batrouney sat down, the auction over, the 400-metres final was about to be run. Victor asked for, and was given, the seating arrangements for the function.

A great silence descended on the ballroom as the Aboriginal woman crouched for the start of the race. Outside the city hotel, in every suburb of Sydney, in every city, town, and hamlet across the nation, the streets were empty. One of the largest telly audiences in

Australia's history gathered to watch Cathy Freeman run, urging her on with its collective will.

Before the race was over Victor Batrouney'd scanned all the names on the lists three times. Not one member of his family had responded to his invitation.

When the black woman stood on the podium to collect her gold medal everyone in the auditorium stood as one with her, belting out the loudest, most raucous, awful and enthusiastic rendition of the national anthem anyone'd ever heard. There was hardly a dry eye in the crowd. And no one, it seemed, was more overcome than Victor Batrouney.

As the evening was drawing to a close, Bob Ryan took over Victor Batrouney's role to announce that the target of raising fifty thousand dollars had been reached.

And the Greeks, not to be outdone, had a function of their own. They raised one dollar more than those Lebs.

Finn's decision

The Olympics were over. The day of judgement quickly drew near. In Redfern people became snappy. The whole suburb was all but buggered-out with the waiting and was ready to spit the dummy. You could sense the tension. It was ripe for a real barney. Someone swore his mongrel bitch cocked her leg to take a piss — a shocker of a sign. And when successive trays of Zoe's baklava came out flat and tired-looking and smelling like dog's breath, and Major Bob Ryan left home one day without his hat, and Kooka Kon found and hung onto a good mood — well, things really looked crook. People needed a lift, something to grin about, to celebrate while they waited, strung out, for that Paul Finn to bring down his judgement. *Bring down* — there was even something ominous about those words people'd latched on to.

It was Yaya Zoe who suggested a surprise eightieth birthday party for Major Bob. And what better place to celebrate than in the club.

On Friday, 3 November, hundreds of Souths' supporters gained admittance into the courtrooms. A few kilometres from the CBD thousands clogged the clubhouse itself.

Johnnie Butler was found standing on South Dowling Street minutes before Finn's brief delivery. Yaya Zoe got all dolled-up and went for her walk, was led home, where she fell asleep.

The judgement was given. Major Bob led the supporters in that rousing rendition of Souths' anthem. Time to rally, boys and girls! The fight for reinstatement has just begun!

And when the boardroom doors were flung open and Major Bob collapsed, he knew he could no longer avoid confronting the past. Bob Ryan lay on the floor, attended by a doctor, seeing the smiling face of his old mate Leo floating face up in a river. And then there was the boy who'd cried out his name: *Major, Major, Major*. Bob Ryan knew where the kid'd gone when his world'd shut down. And it was time everyone else knew, too.

He instructed Kon Tsakiris to go and collect Yaya Zoe, and Jimmy to ring Nan. The rest were told to go on to Old Tom's where they were to wait for him.

Kooka Kon knocked several times on Yaya Zoe's door. When she did not answer he entered, finding her curled up asleep on top of the blankets on her bed, holding an icon to her breast, her hair out of its bun. He shook her several times before she awoke. She opened her eyes, expecting to see an angel, a saint, perhaps even God Himself. Instead, there was the worried, unshaven, little-boy's face of Konstantine Tsakiris breathing the stench of cigarettes into her face. Had he died, too?

Kon was proud of himself. When the old woman began to wail, mourning the fact that God'd decided against accepting her, Kon knew what to say. A great miracle had occurred that day! God had spared her so that she could witness what they'd all seen: the boy, the boy'd found his voice! He'd emerged at last from that world he'd retreated into more than a year ago. He'd come back, glory to God!

So, this was the miracle Saint George had promised. It was for Tzonnie that the saint'd nodded his head. It was not her time after all. She changed into a plain black smock. The Greek man and woman walked as quickly as they could to Old Tom's. Zoe's arms were outstretched as soon as they turned into South Dowling Street. Johnnie ran to her. She covered his face with kisses.

And while they wait for Major to arrive, the four men and two women ply you with questions for no other reason than to hear your voice. They're all loopy and ga-ga with joy. Jimmy throws in a couple of double-knee smackers. Their guffawing willy-nillies up and down the street.

Major Bob Ryan went home from the club. He sat in his lounge room for some time, gathering the strength and courage to do what had to be done. He drank a glass of port, followed by another, then he went into his third bedroom and knelt before his icons and prayed. What to pray for? The truth, Bob, just the truth, dammit. He collected two books, one a child's exercise book, the other a large hard-backed folder, then walked slowly to South Dowling Street, feeling like eyes were watching him from every window.

He approached Tom's ominously, like an undertaker, a raw and naked mournfulness on his face, his black leather shoes scraping the ground. He was sweating something awful, his hair shining like it'd been done over with a black texta. He did not shake Tom's hand. He did not doff his hat. He shook his head at the suggestion of a cuppa.

But he sure knew how to tell a tale

As the story unfolded, Yaya Zoe's expression alternated between that of a detached Greek saint and a suffering Christ. Nan Dora smouldered. Victor Batrouney looked into a world of inexplicable sadness and thought of his mother. Old Tom's only movements were to lick his lips and shift his ug boots. He rested heavily against his walking frame, blinking over at Moore Park like he'd drifted off somewhere. And Kon Tsakiris, his face lined like an old weather map. Cigarette ash lay at his feet. He thought of reaching out and touching the sad old man that Bob'd become, then thought better of it.

And what about Jimmy Butler and Johnnie, whose life stories were slowly becoming clearer? Jimmy was looking straight ahead, chain-smoking one cigarette after another. Johnnie leaned forward in the sombre quiet, fists against his cheeks. The two heard the details of that day Jimmy'd been plucked from the streets of Redfern. Of the day their mother and sister pummelled the rear window of a car as Shirley Butler knelt on the tramlines. Jimmy heard the details of the life and death of the nephew he did not know existed, Johnnie of the brother he'd only briefly known. All stolen, Jimmy, Mary, Billy, by the same man.

And you know how to listen. The day'll come when you'll tell your tale, too: of you shouting out your hatred of your brother, of the bloodstained sheet you'd removed from his neck and how you'd sat under that tree holding onto him as the warmth ebbed from his body; of watching from a distance as the police and ambulance arrived to take his limp and sad body away. Of the pain of waiting for your mamma to return.

Go on, thought Old Tom. It's been a long time comin'. Now finish it, Bob. Bring it, for God's sake, to a close.

Bob Ryan stood and presented to Jimmy and Johnnie the diary of their nephew and brother. 'This belongs to you.' He paused. 'There's another diary,' he said, still standing. 'It's the journal of the man who took you, Jimmy, from your mother. Of the man who stole your mother, and your brother, Johnnie.'

'The Lollipop Man,' breathed Tom.

'Yes,' said the Major. 'My Father.'

He extended his hand as a token of friendship and remorse to Jimmy, but the man refused to take it.

Jimmy Butler was staring over at Moore Park.

'Your father,' he said.

'Yes, Jimmy. My father.' Bob Ryan looked ancient and weary.

Jimmy Butler ground out his cigarette, placed his elbows on his knees. His face in his hands. 'Didja know?'

'You mean, at the time?'

'Yeah. Didja know?'

'Yes, Jimmy. I knew. I'm sorry.'

The boy opened the gate and began to walk in the direction of his home.

'Johnnie,' said the Major.

'You leave 'im be,' said Jimmy Butler.

'Johnnie! Johnnie!'

'I said, you leave 'im be.'

Jimmy Butler then walked out onto the footpath but, instead of following Johnnie, walked the other way, in the direction of The Bat and Ball Hotel.

When he arrived at the pub he stood outside, fighting the urge to go in and drink himself into a stupor. He recalled his deathbed promise to Rosie. And then he left taking the long way home.

The old man cleared his throat. 'Not your fault, Bob.'

'But I knew, Tom! For the love of God, I knew. And what did I do? Fuck all!'

Yaya Zoe and Nan went inside to make a pot of tea. Victor went in to help, for something to do. Kon joined them, unable to cope with the tension on the verandah.

They drank their tea with hardly a word being spoken.

Some fifteen minutes or so after Johnnie'd left, they saw him crossing South Dowling Street some distance from Tom's terrace. There was no mistaking the decisiveness in his walk. Or, for that matter, the rabbit hutch he held by the handle, his other hand holding the Moreton Bay fig which he'd removed from its pot.

'Bob!' Nan said. 'Leave him be! Come back!'

Johnnie Butler plants a tree

In the end, crossing the road and leaving the security of Redfern is all too easy. You stand on the footpath, look both ways, wait until there's a break in the traffic then cross the street. With your mind fixed on that other much larger fig tree in Centennial Park, where all those unresolved issues of your life are gathering, you make your way across Moore Park.

You kneel on the ground not far from where they'd found you over a year ago. You dig for seeds from the long grass as shown to you by your uncle. Jimmy'd be so proud of you. You get up, wander here and there gathering the new growth of leaves from the weeds which grow in abundance. You're talking out aloud, surprised at the sound of your own voice. A kid could lose himself in this section of the park set aside for native vegetation, as distinct from the carefully ordered stands of European trees, shrubs and flower beds preferred by the picnickers and walkers. Especially if you kneel, and you're little. Beyond this world of wild tussocks and native grasses, there are those who come to run, or ride their horses or their bicycles on the circular path and road. Beyond these and outside the park are the busy roads. But here it's a world of dreams and imagination.

You return to the hutch, open the lid and hand-feed the seeds and leaves to your rabbits. You carry them in your arms towards the lake. The grass parts as you make your way to the swamp.

You watch your bunnies exploring the world into which they've been released. You see yourself standing in that moist earth as your grandma and grandad might have once stood, alert for any sign of life. You return to where you'd laid the sapling, kneel then dig, pausing now and then to listen to the noises and observe the movements of the abundant life around you: birds, alarmed by your presence, flitter from tree to tree; other rabbits, long used to the isolation of this section of the park, observe from a safe distance; a turtle makes its way laboriously to the lake in which swans and ducks forage for food. And beneath your hands and in the fists of rich earth you throw to one side is the myriad of insect and worm life, struggling in their own way to survive. The noises and movements of all these creatures going about their daily lives groan and creak in the still spring afternoon. You reaching further and further into the ground as you dig, with each handful seeking forgiveness from the brother whom you'd last seen, there, several metres away, propped up against that tree, whom you'd failed to save.

The boy'd walked too fast for Bob Ryan. Johnnie didn't see him struggling to keep up with him. The distance between the two grew with each passing moment. But it didn't matter. The man knew where the boy was headed. The Major saw, from a distance, the boy standing where he'd found him a year ago, hungry and silent. Major Bob sat on a park bench, not only to catch his breath but also because, for one of the few occasions in his life, he wasn't sure what to do. Nanna Dora joined him a few minutes later.

You sit up, kneeling by the hole you've dug, your hands on your knees. *Sorry, Billy, sorry, sorry.* You brush the soil from your knees and hands then walk to where the sapling lies.

This tree, you know, will form part of the story of your own life as it struggles to survive. Like the earthworms you found under a rotting log you cast aside. And the insect life you saw fighting to emerge from its chrysalis. Everything merging and separating, all life forms singing their own song, humming and circulating, agitating and rattling in that joyous afternoon. This sapling you're now planting, that huge tree under which Billy died, that other fig at La Pa, which your uncle's told you about, called King Billy's Tree, all sing the same song, tell the same tale. This is my tree. This is my park. You claim them all as your own as you position the sapling then fill the hole with soil, pressing down hard with your hands to secure it. There's a continuity here which comforts you. You understand that you can create your own story. You sense that there's no straight line in time, as your teacher'd once told you, marking a neat beginning, middle and unfolding future. You see the past returning repeatedly in great undulating circles, never-ending swirls expanding constantly to encompass the story of your life and of those who've come before you, and of those not yet born. This tree you've just planted, its canopy one day reaching out to merge with that of the tree which'd once been your brother's home, and King Billy's Tree. They're all the same tree.

And many years into the future, scaling the trunk of this sapling, you can see your own grandchildren sitting on one of its branches high up off the ground, telling stories to each other of their ancestor who, as a boy, had one day paid homage to his own kin one sunny spring day after he'd returned from a silent world into which he'd retreated.

Major Bob and Nan Dora saw the boy stand, his work now done, and begin his slow dance.

You lift your knees, stamp the earth lightly with your feet, as Billy and Jimmy'd shown you. You hear some echo as you jerk your head this way and that, slap your hands onto your thighs as a clapping of another sort resounds in the grass and branches. You move to the music of clap sticks which, you know, your brother beats in time with the rhythm of all those stories told to you by your mother, uncle and brother, Old Tom, Yaya Zoe and the Major, a tapestry of music that sings of life and death, of the struggles which you sense are to come. And with the clap sticks comes the sound of metal studs beating a path on the hard earth. The breeze ruffling the leaves in the trees whistles with the sound of a soaring ball. You see it kicked high in the sky, hear the thud of boots and there, his wrist broken, is that man Churchill urging his men on, one of whom is Jimmy Butler wearing the red and green. Your uncle takes the ball, bends low, fends off one player before passing it to John Sattler who, with his free hand holding his shattered jaw, makes a break. It's 1908. And on the sideline is Tom, laughing as he rings his old brass bell.

Long after Johnnie'd left, Major Bob Ryan and Nanna Dora got up from the bench and looked at the boy's work. At her suggestion, they then scoured the park until they found one of its gardeners.

Nan's request was most unusual — certainly against regulations. Bob Ryan gave the man more details than he would've preferred. They showed the gardener the tree the boy'd planted which was, as it turned out, not a bad position for a fig. Could he?

Major Bob and Nanna Dora returned later that week to ensure the man was as good as his word. They saw, to their delight, the three large wooden stakes that'd been driven into the ground to support the sapling, several strips of hessian securing it to each stake and a large pile of mulch around its trunk.

A funeral and a rally

In the days leading up to the rally on Sunday, the twelfth of November, Bob Ryan did not go on his morning walks. He stayed away from Tom's, too, lest he bump into Jimmy and the boy. He kept in touch with the old man by phone, however, keeping him informed of the promotional activities to do with the protest, which filled the Major's days. On the Thursday Tom told him he would be attending a service which was to be held the following day.

'What service, Tom?'

The old man hesitated. 'Didn't think Jimmy was gunna tellya. Thought you should know.'

'Know what, Tom?'

'Jimmy'd asked Victor to locate it. Billy Butler's grave. He's gunna have some sort of memorial service. On the site.'

Silence.

'He's asked us all to be there. 'Cept you, that is.'

'I see.'

'Sorry, mate.'

The phone rang at two in the morning on the day of the service. Bob Ryan sat up in bed, hesitating to answer. A call at that hour of the night made an ominous sound. Its obstinate summons could only mean one thing. He got out of bed slowly, considering who might've had an accident or, worse still, who might've passed on. Is this how it would happen? If he were to outlive Yaya Zoe, Nan or Old Tom, would it be a call in the middle of the night informing him of their death?

He spoke into the phone with a formality that sounded strange to himself. 'Bob Ryan.'

'G'day, Bob.'

'Jimmy? Is that you?'

'Yeah, it's me.'

'Is Johnnie okay?'

'Oh yeah, Johnnie's real good.'

'And you? Are you alright?'

'Yeah, I'm real good, too.'

'What's up, Jimmy?'

'You wanna come over?'

'I'm on my way.'

He found Jimmy Butler waiting for him outside his home under the nearest streetlight. The Major saw the door of the man's terrace open. Jimmy held a finger to his lips.

'Don't wanna wake Johnnie,' he said. 'I couldn't sleep. Somethin' I gotta know.'

'What is it, Jimmy?'

'When you come all them years ago out bush, to the Parkers', an' seen me play, an' you brang me to Sinney. Was it 'cause of yer ol' man? 'Cause I was a Butler? Or 'cause I was a good footy player?'

Major Bob looked down at a loose rock on the footpath near his shoe. 'Initially,' he said, ' because you're a Butler. But then I saw you play.'

'I was good, eh?'

'One of the best, Jimmy.'

'Fair dinkum?'

'Oh yes, fair dinkum.'

'Could've played with John Sattler an' all them others, eh?'

'Yes, Jimmy, you could have.'

'I blew it, eh?'

Pause.

'Bob? 'T's true, ain't it?'

'Yes Jimmy, you did.'

'Somethin' else. 'Bout Johnnie. You helpin' him 'cause he's a Butler?'

Major Bob was scraping the loose rock with the toe of his shoe. 'Yes. But I'm also very fond of him.'

'You love 'im?'

'Yes Jimmy, I do.'

Jimmy Butler led the man into his home. Major Bob followed his example, taking off his shoes at the door and walking on tip-toe down the hallway. Bob Ryan was led to the boy's bedroom. At Jimmy Butler's invitation he peered through the door that was slightly ajar. A lamp on a bedside table was switched on.

Ahhhh, the man sighed. He trembled to see a set of crayons and watercolours on the floor. On the wall were the outlines of a new mural. He saw a small sapling labelled *Billy's Tree*. Next to it he saw the unmistakable figures of Jimmy, the boy and himself standing arm in arm.

The two men crept out of the house and stood on the footpath.

'I read Billy's diary,' Jimmy said. 'Over an' over.'

Bob Ryan nodded but gave no reply.

'Read it to Johnnie, eh.'

The Major pursed his lips and nodded again.

''Aven't read yer ol' man's yet, but. Bin too much pain, Bob.'

'Yes, there has been.'

'Too much pain an' sufferin'. An' death, too. Too much death.'

Bob Ryan would've liked to extend his hand but was afraid of another rejection. He wondered where all this was going.

'We're meetin' later terday, at Bot'ny Cemet'ry. Ya wanna come?'

You stand in a semicircle while your Nanna Dora chants her mournful prayer in a language no one but she understands. As she sings you place balls of paper, dry leaves and twigs on the unmarked grave. Major, responding to Nanna's nod, lights the fire. As she continues her chanting you take out a wooden stake and push it into the grave. On it are the words *Billy Butler, Loved and Mourned*. You then place a child's exercise book on the fire.

Everyone watches in silence as your brother's bloodstained diary goes up in flames.

Nanna reminds you she'll never rest until she finds your mamma.

On the way home you give the other diary to Major. 'Me an' me uncle, we don't wanna read this, Major.'

They'd hoped for a big turnout but no one, not even Major Bob and Old Tom, expected this.

It was, the papers were to say the following morning, the largest rally seen in Australia since the days of the protests against Australia's involvement in the Vietnam War. They wrote of the girl who, with her father and mother, drove down from the farm after the milking'd been done; of a bloke called Ned the Neck who said that if Souths weren't going to be readmitted into the comp, he'd never watch another game of rugby league again. They wrote of the woman in a wheelchair who'd been a Souths supporter for seventy years, who said that the moneymen, as she called them, should give up running the game. 'You tell 'em,' she said. 'It's our game, not theirs.' They wrote of the family who came pushing a pram, a large placard held aloft by dad which read: 'They've closed down our banks, police stations and post offices, now they want to take away our game. Maintain the rage.'

People came from all over Sydney and beyond, waving streamers, carrying red and green balloons and great banners as long as the road was wide. They came on foot, on motorbikes and in golf buggies, from the towns and villages up and down the coast, from the rural areas of central and far-west New South Wales and Queensland, from Toowoomba in the far north and Ballarat in the far south. They came in chartered buses that clogged the arterial roads leading into Sydney, the dispossessed and the voiceless, chanting: 'The game began with Souths. The game'll end with Souths.'

Most were there because they were, simply, Souths supporters, responding to the club's cry that the fight was not over until the people walked away. Others came because they hated big business, some because, on the day Souths lost their appeal, they'd seen grown men and women weeping on the telly. Then there were those who couldn't care less about the game but had an uneasy feeling that a great injustice'd been done. Some came on a wave of nostalgia and others came to say they were there.

The march began outside the clubhouse. Latecomers, joining that throng from the many side roads and lanes, swelled the protest until, by the time the marchers'd reached Central Station, the southern end of the city'd been brought to a standstill. They marched down Chalmers Street, turned into Eddy Avenue and, when that great tide poured into George Street, saw an even larger gathering assembled outside the Sydney Town Hall.

And somewhere in this vast crowd, numbering up to one hundred thousand people, was a group of men, an old black woman in an Akubra hat and a boy. They marched for the Rabbitohs, of course. But there were so many other reasons they'd linked arms. Some for that aching sense of loss for a way of life, a person, an ideal, a dream they could never hope to achieve, or simply for the fellowship of those whose arms they held. The boy, who marched between his uncle on one side, and a big, tall old man on the other, could already see himself beginning a new mural. It'd depict a line of blokes and a woman walking arm-in-arm and there, in the corner of the wall, he could see his mother, a suitcase in her hand, coming home.

Some time during that celebratory march, Major Bob glanced at Kooka Kon. The Major'd read of some scandal involving the gross mismanagement of HIH, but decided to reveal nothing of what he knew. He looked to Victor Batrouney. The younger man, seeing the considered expression on Bob Ryan's face, smiled. The Major neither averted his eyes nor returned the man's smile. It's a tad late, Victor, thought Major Bob. Not too late, however. One day soon I must tell you about your father and the manner of his death. But not yet.

You tug at Major's arm then point to a bloke walking ahead of you.

'Yes, lad, that's him.'

He takes hold of you by the elbow and pushes his way through to the great man.

'There's someone here,' Major says, 'who'd like to meet you.'

The man looks down at you. 'What's your name, son?'

'Johnnie.'

'Same as me,' he replies.

He takes your hand and shakes it. 'Pleased to meet you, Johnnie.'

'Your jaw's okay now, Mista Sattler?'

'Oh, yeah, jaw's fine, son.'

Old Tom's been driven to the Town Hall. After the last of the many speeches his wheelchair, with him in it, is carried up onto the steps. A microphone's taken from its stand and held near his waist so that, when he rings that bell, swinging it clumsily backwards and forwards across his thigh, it's heard by all. And as for its ringing, well, you know that it echoes down George and Park Streets, thundering up and down the eastern coast then westwards into the largest towns and smallest villages in the bush, returning to the city to hammer its challenge at the doors of the National Rugby League until, at last, it's joined by the sound of one hundred thousand voices chanting their defiance and outrage: Never Give In. Never Give Up. Never Say Die.

You meet Yaya Zoe at Mista Tom's later that afternoon, where you and Victor are welcomed, as full members, into The Committee. Yaya and Nan are offered the same honour. They say they've never heard anything more ridiculous in their life.

You celebrate your induction with a cup of tea and a handful of Scotch Finger biscuits from the Home Brand packets Kon's brought around.

On 6 July 2001, Justice Finn's ruling was overturned by a majority of one. The Mighty Rabbitohs were readmitted back into the comp.

On Friday, 15 March 2002, a sell-out crowd watched South Sydney play their first game after their reinstatement. Old Tom rang his bell from the centre of the field as the players ran out of the tunnel. The Mighty Rabbitohs played their old foes, Eastern Suburbs. They got done like a dinner but, by crikey, it was good to have them back.

Acknowledgements

Billy's Tree was initially written as a creative component for the Doctorate of Creative Arts award at the University of Wollongong. I am grateful for the Australian Postgraduate Award (APA) given to me in 1999 by that university's Faculty of Creative Arts.

There are many people to thank for their encouragement and support during the time it took to complete my book. I thank Dr Clem Gorman, my university supervisor, Lyn Tranter, of Australian Literary Management, Henry Rosenbloom, the publisher at Scribe, and Aviva Tuffield for her editorial assistance.

I thank my mother, Maria, and my friends Dr M. G. Michael and Dr Katina Michael for their unflagging enthusiasm, interest, and practical and moral support.

I thank my children, who have become young adults in the time it has taken me to complete this novel. They have gone for long periods of time without their father. I have much making-up to do.

Finally I thank my wife, Krystall. This book could not and would not have been written without her.

A section of an earlier version of Chapter 9 appeared in *Literature and Aesthetics* (October 1997).